THE ZAMANI REGION

Lake Msitu

THE SISTERS' BIGHT

Kidogo River

The Greater Jungle

Heart
of the
Jungle

LKOSSA

The Lesser Jungle

THE KUSONGA PLAINS

BANDARI

THE
AMAKOYAN
SEA

Ndefu River

THORNKEEP

Eastern
Ndefu River

THE KUSINI REGION

THE MACHUNGU SEA

North

Sandli

BEASTS
OF WAR

BEASTS
OF WAR

AYANA GRAY

putnam

G. P. PUTNAM'S SONS

G. P. PUTNAM'S SONS
An imprint of Penguin Random House LLC, New York

First published in the United States of America by G. P. Putnam's Sons,
an imprint of Penguin Random House LLC, 2024

Visit us online at PenguinRandomHouse.com.

Library of Congress Cataloging-in-Publication Data is available.

ISBN 9780593405741

1st Printing

Printed in the United States of America

LSCC

Design by Marikka Tamura
Text set in Arno Pro

To Mom and Dad—this one's for you.

ATUNO—god of skies, heavens, and stars;
symbol: heron

AMAKOYA—goddess of seas, rivers, lakes, and streams;
symbol: crocodile

TYEMBU—god of deserts, in the west;
symbol: jackal

BADWA—goddess of jungles and forests;
symbol: serpent

ITAASHE—goddess of valleys, mountains, and plains;
symbol: dove

FEDU—god of death;
symbol: hippopotamus

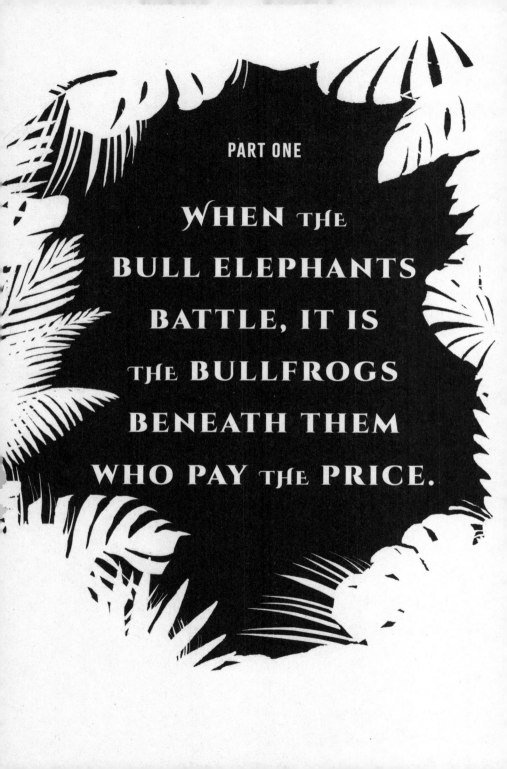

PART ONE

WHEN THE BULL ELEPHANTS BATTLE, IT IS THE BULLFROGS BENEATH THEM WHO PAY THE PRICE.

Tͪᴇ BOY ᴀɴᴅ Tͪᴇ BULL

AKANDE
Year 894

I smell the river before I see it.

Its water is fresh, but even at a distance, I sense a wrongness, the stink of blood and looming violence. Knots bunch between my shoulder blades, a pounding in my ears loudens with every step I take. A prickling coolness threads down my spine, underlining a fear that's dogged me since I snuck out of my parents' house a few minutes ago.

That fear? I'm probably going to die tonight.

In Kugawanya, it's mid–harvest season, which means the evening air is temperate and mild. This late, the sky is starling black, and the city's streets are deserted save for a few vacant stalls left by the wayside. I pass one usually occupied by a farmer who sells the freshest apples I've ever tasted, and flinch against the memories of walking along this same road with Babu not so long ago. Just like that, my dead grandfather's voice slips past my mind's armor. I expect to hear anger, but the old man's disappointment is worse.

I expected more from you, Akande.

I push away that voice as I reach the city's edge, marked by the Ndefu River. Seventeen years has given me plenty of time to memorize the way it carves through my homeland like an engorged serpent. Tonight, it snatches tiny slivers of starlight from above, giving the illusion of a thousand shimmering scales dancing wild upon its surface. I can't help but wonder if this is the last time I'll ever really look at this river, and I swallow hard as the reality of what I'm about to do sinks in. I survey the banks, which are empty but for a few fishermen's longboats moored among the reeds. A sudden movement behind one of them startles me.

"Akande?"

Well, I'd *thought* these banks were empty.

Even in the dark, moonlight traces Izachar's outline as he emerges, tentative. Most people mistake my best friend and me for brothers—we share the same height, build, and oak-brown skin. We're not real kin, but we're still two sides of the same leaf, which is how I know that Izachar is scared. Our gazes meet.

"How are you feeling?" he asks.

"Fine." It's a lie, but saying it makes me feel better. "I'm ready."

"Akande." The pretense of calm drops from Izachar's voice. "Please. You don't have to do this."

"I do, Iz."

"There has to be another way to get the money." Izachar rakes a hand through his curly black hair. "There has to be something we haven't thought of."

I give him a meaningful look. "You know there isn't."

Izachar faces the river, his mouth set in a tight line. "The Bull has never lost a fight," he murmurs. "He's a champion, a seasoned prizefighter." He doesn't have to say the rest of what he's thinking. I have a guess.

He's a seasoned prizefighter, and you're just a scrawny boy. A kid.

"It's not too late," he says. "You can still call this off."

For a moment, I actually consider doing just that. I imagine turning around and going home, slipping back into my bed with my family none the wiser. I could do that, and I almost do, but then . . .

Then I remember Danya's eyes.

They're a deep golden-brown color, like nutmeg. I feel a sensation like fluttering butterflies between my ribs at the thought of them, at the thought of *her*. Just like that, I remember why I'm doing this and shake my head.

"My mind's made up, Iz. Don't try to stop me."

Izachar sighs. "Then there's nothing else to say. Let's go."

Downriver, a tight huddle of men stand half illumed in the Ndefu's reflection. Some of them are young, around Izachar's and my age; others look old enough to be my grandfather. I know why they're here. Secrets in Kugawanya hold like water in a cracked pot; word of the prizefight has gotten around and clearly attracted bettors. As we approach the men, I pick out the two I'm looking for.

Jumo the Bull, my soon-to-be opponent, is already smirking at me. He's shorter than I am, but several years older, and holds himself with the confidence of a natural-born fighter. Beside him stands Yakow, a wizened old man with chestnut skin and thinning gray hair.

"Akande." I smell the chewing tobacco on the bookmaker's breath as Izachar and I stop before him. He spits. "Now that you've joined us, we can go over the rules before we begin." He rattles them off, even though I already know them. No one will be allowed to intervene once the fight has started, and it will last until someone yields, or dies. A familiar fear grazes me at that reminder, but just as quickly I sneak a glance at the satchel of winnings slung on Yakow's shoulder. I imagine everything I could buy with the earnings from this fight if I win it. A renewed hunger rises in me, smothering my fear.

I need that money.

"As a final reminder"—Yakow gives me a cautioning look—"the use of splendor in this fight is prohibited."

"Daraja freak," Jumo mutters.

I lunge, but Izachar has the sense to drag me back. Around us, the men begin to jostle one another, excited. This is what they're here for: a fight, a showdown between the boy and the Bull. From a distant place in my memory, I hear my babu's voice again. This time, he doesn't sound disappointed, but stern. That's the version of my grandfather I remember best.

Focus and control, he reminds me. *Keep focused, and stay in control. That is how you win.*

"Do you both agree to abide by the established rules?" Yakow asks, glancing between us.

"I do," says Jumo.

"Akande?"

"I do."

The bookmaker purses his lips. "I'd like you to shake hands."

Jumo steps forward and squeezes my hand hard, trying to crush my fingers. I squeeze back, refusing to wince even as my hand throbs in pain. When we both let go, Yakow nods.

"If we're ready—"

"Wait!"

I turn to see Izachar brandishing a small coin purse.

"I want to place a bet on Akande," he says, tossing it. "I'm betting he lasts at least two rounds."

Yakow snatches the purse from midair, then gives Izachar a considering look as he weighs it. "How much?"

Izachar doesn't miss a beat. "All of it."

The others mutter as Yakow denotes the bet on a small square of parchment before stowing the coin purse in his satchel. Izachar starts to turn away, but I catch his arm.

"Iz, where'd you get that kind of coin?"

"I saved up," he says mildly, "from my apprenticeship."

I shake my head. "You can't afford to lose that money."

A shadow of a smile touches my friend's lips. "Then I guess you'd better last at least two rounds."

"It's time!" Yakow's voice cuts through the air before I can respond. "Fighters, approach. Everyone else, out of the way."

Izachar claps me on the back before he and the other bettors hike farther up the riverbank. Now only Jumo, Yakow, and I remain at the water's edge.

"I want a clean fight," Yakow warns. "Round one will begin on the count of three, when you hear my bell." He produces a tiny silver one from his pocket. "One, two—"

Jumo and I both move before the word *three* ever leaves the bookmaker's lips. He backs away quickly as Jumo lowers his head and charges me like the bull he's been named for. Instinct kicks in, and I duck just in time to hear the whoosh of air as his fist sails inches above my head. A rush of adrenaline courses through me, and I try to stay calm as I dance out of his reach. Jumo may be stronger than me, but I've got faster reflexes. Babu would tell me to take advantage of that, so I do. The next time Jumo swings, I pivot, then shove him in the small of his back. The move throws him off-balance, and he falls flat on his face, earning laughter from the spectators. Jumo springs to his feet, pawing mud from his mouth and snarling.

Good, says Babu's imaginary voice. *If he's angry, he's not in control. And if he's not in control, you have the upper hand. Use that.*

I'm ready when Jumo rushes me again. He's more aggressive this time, using his bulk and a series of punches to drive me toward the river. I'm careful to stay just out of his reach.

"Is this how you fight?" Jumo jeers. "You won't even *try* to hit me?"

The third time he advances, I flinch, pretending to be afraid, but I don't move back. He's so intent on landing a punch now that he lowers his guard, and that's the opening I need. With everything I have, I swing my fist upward. There's a satisfying click when my knuckles meet Jumo's jaw, followed by a splintering pain in my right hand. Jumo reels back, and there are cries of surprise from several of the bettors. When I glance at the banks, I see Izachar whooping, and hope swells within me.

Then my world explodes in a shower of stars.

My body flies backward, slamming down hard in the mud. Distantly, I understand what's happened; I shouldn't have looked away from Jumo, even for a second. The river laps at me, soaking through my clothes as I lie there, but that barely registers over the ringing in my ears. It takes a moment for the sharp ache between my eyes to find me. Something warm gushes over my lips and dribbles down my chin. When I look down, I see huge blots of red staining the front of my tunic.

My nose is broken.

Yield. The new voice in my head sounds suspiciously like Izachar's as I rise, unsteady. *Yield before you get killed.*

I can't, I argue back, *I need the money.*

The ringing in my head has faded enough for me to hear the bettors' cheers and boos. I blink hard, willing Jumo's blurred outline to sharpen as he leers.

"You want some more, kid?" He cracks his knuckles, and I fight a wave of nausea as I spit blood. "Yield, if you know what's good for you."

"No." My words come out thick, but audible. "I'm not done."

Jumo's brows rise in momentary surprise, but then he starts toward me, his hands curled into fists. There's a new look of resolve on his face, and I understand that the next time he hits me I won't be getting up. He means to kill me. I try to muster the strength to raise my guard, to *move*, but everything hurts now. I don't have anything left.

Time slows to a crawl in those last few seconds. In the space between them, I let myself think about Danya one last time. I think of her smile, and the beads she wears in her hair sometimes. My throat tightens when I think about her smile.

I failed you, Danya. It's an apology she'll never hear. *I'm sorry.*

Jumo is nearly upon me, and I brace myself for death. I

anticipate pain, and the quiet that'll come in the after. What I don't anticipate is the tiny rock that hurtles through the air and hits him on the shoulder.

"HEY, DUNGHEAD!"

My head snaps right at the same time Jumo looks up, confused. In the darkness, it takes a beat, but then I see: Someone else is making their way down the river's sloping bank. I have a sudden, sinking feeling. Seconds later, my worst fears are confirmed.

"*Namina?*"

The tufts of kinky black hair poking out of my sister's night bonnet would normally be funny, but any humor to be found in this situation is canceled out immediately by the force of Namina's glare as she tucks a small slingshot back into her dress's belt loop. Jumo looks between us, scowling.

"Who are *you?*" he asks. She soundly ignores him and keeps staring at me.

"Namina." I gape at her. "What are you doing here?"

"I could ask you the same," my sister says coolly. "Trying to get yourself killed in an illegal prizefight, really? Have you lost your mind?"

She's scolding me the way our mother would. Involuntarily, my face grows warm. "Stay out of it, Nam."

I expect another glare, but instead my sister's shoulders slump. "We've already buried Babu," she murmurs. "And you would have us bury you too."

Guilt slams into me like a sack of stones.

"Hey!" One of the bettors steps forward. "I placed a wager. Is there going to be a fight or not?"

Namina throws the man a withering look before marching

down the rest of the slope. She comes to a stop in the small space between Jumo and me, then crosses her arms.

"What's this?" Yakow suddenly steps forward, looking bewildered. "What are you doing, girl?"

My sister scowls at the bookmaker. "Last time I checked, prizefights were illegal in Kugawanya," she says, "especially fights involving minors like my brother. I'd bet that there are quite a few people in this city who'd be very interested in finding out who's organizing them." She gives Yakow a meaningful look, and the old man's brows knit. Their silent standoff lasts less than a minute.

"Everyone, clear out!" the bookmaker says tersely. "This fight's canceled. You'll all be refunded in full, minus my convenience fee."

"What convenience fee?" asks one of the men.

"The convenience of holding all your coins, fool!" snaps Yakow. "This bag's heavy, and I have sciatica!"

Jumo makes a disgusted sound, then stalks away. There are groans of disappointment among the bettors, but no one seems eager to test my sister's threat. While Yakow issues refunds, I face her.

"Do they know?" I ask. "Mother and Father?"

"Nope," says Namina. "I snuck out about ten minutes after you." She frowns. "Is your nose broken?"

"Probably."

"Then you're a dunghead too."

I chuckle, wince at the very real pain in my nose, then note the sky overhead. Already, the first hints of pale morning light are bleeding into the dark, and the stars are winking out one by one. "We should get home."

Namina nods. We're only two years apart, but in that moment, she looks so much older than her fifteen years. I watch as she goes ahead of me, hiking up the bank and stopping halfway to let Izachar offer her a hand. I sigh as I catch the unmistakable look that passes between them. The idea of my best friend courting my sister isn't exactly exciting, but I suppose I could learn to be okay with it, eventually. Izachar and I would definitely need to have a talk, but—

"You got lucky, kid."

I didn't hear Jumo return. Now he's standing right behind me with mud on his face.

"You know if your sister hadn't saved you, I'd have won," he says.

I smile despite my broken nose. Jumo wants a reaction, and I know it'll only frustrate him more if I don't give him one. I also don't want to dwell on the fact that he's probably right. Somewhere in the back of my mind, I know I'll have to deal with the other consequence of this fight being canceled—I didn't get the money I needed—but that's a problem for later. I start up the riverbank, but Jumo's voice carries.

"Your sister's pretty," he calls after me. "Not as nice as the one you wanted the prize money for, though. I've heard they call *her* the Rose of Kugawanya. What's her real name, again? Danya?"

The words snag on something in me, but I keep walking. Up ahead, Izachar and Namina have slowed. They're waiting for me, and still holding hands.

"She likes when her pups do tricks for her," Jumo continues. "You must be her third prizefighter this month."

I stop short and turn. "What?"

Jumo grins. "Ah, you didn't know." He actually sounds sorry. "Let me guess: She told you that her father would only allow her to marry you if you could come up with the money for a bride price." His eyes glitter with malice. "She told you that she loved you, maybe even let you kiss her a few times so you'd really believe it."

"You don't know what you're talking about," I snap, but my voice trembles.

Jumo shakes his head. "You got *fleeced*, kid. You're all the same to girls like her, just a bunch of foolish, lovesick—"

I lunge.

Someone shouts my name, but it's too late. Jumo and I collide, and the world upends as the two of us roll back down the riverbank in a mess of limbs and dirt. Fresh, nauseating pain lances through my broken nose, but I blink it away and pick myself up at the same time Jumo gets to his feet. I hear people running toward us, and there's more shouting, but I don't care anymore. Jumo's words run on a sickening loop in my head.

She likes when her pups do tricks for her.

I don't remember making the decision to summon the splendor, I only notice when the hairs on the backs of my arms and neck stand on end as I do it. The energy courses through me, hot and frantic. I'm supposed to let it move through me; instead, I allow the energy to build up inside me until a shape forms in my right hand: a glittering dagger. Jumo draws in a sharp breath at the sight of it, and I savor his fear as I advance.

He called you a daraja freak, says a savage voice in my head. *He lied about Danya. Now we make him pay.*

"Akande!"

Someone tugs at my right arm, trying to pull me back. A rush of the splendor swells within me and my hand cuts through the air, shaking them off. There's a distant thud, but my gaze is on Jumo. He looks from me to something over my shoulder, then his jaw drops.

That's when I hear the scream.

"NO!"

The sound tears through me, snapping me out of a daze I didn't even realize I was in. The dagger vanishes from my hand as the splendor dissipates, and slowly I turn toward that wretched sound. It takes a moment for me to understand what I'm looking at—*who* I'm looking at.

There's a body on the ground behind me. I recognize the curly black hair, the oak-brown skin that's just like mine. What I don't understand is why Izachar's not moving, why my friend's hands are limp at his neck. I don't understand why there's so much blood gushing between his fingers. A dull buzzing fills my ears as Namina falls to her knees beside him and begins to wail.

"What?" My own voice sounds distorted in my head. "What's wrong with him?"

"He's dead." Jumo's still standing a few feet from me. He looks nauseated. "You killed him, with that . . . thing."

I shake my head as my mouth gets sticky. In my periphery, I see people—the bettors—gathering at the top of the slope and staring down at us. There's a second scream, followed by a third. Someone calls for help. My legs go numb.

"I didn't . . ." I stumble away from Jumo, from Namina, from Izachar's lifeless body. "I didn't mean to— I didn't . . ."

No one's listening to me anymore. Namina screams again,

and my lungs constrict. It's impossible to breathe, and I can't stop staring at Izachar's slashed throat. I can't stop thinking about the fact that there was a dagger in my hand, and now there's not.

He's dead. You killed him, with that . . . thing.

No one's looking at me anymore. No one notices when I turn and run.

CHAPTER 1

DIVINE WORK

KOFFI

What Koffi remembered most vividly about her dreams was the boy.

She'd never met him in real life—of that, she was certain—and yet in her sleep their paths seemed determined to keep tangling. He was umber-skinned and tall, with curly black hair and dark eyes that hinted at mischief. They stood, facing each other, until she spoke.

"What do you want?" she asked.

No answer, but this wasn't new. The boy in her dreams never actually spoke to her, or answered the questions she posed to him. He just watched her with that same knowing half smile. Eventually, he turned from her. Then, without warning, he broke into a run.

"Hey!" Koffi ran after him. "Stop!"

The boy's steps quickened. He was leading her through a land she'd seen only in these dreams, an expanse of flat golden savanna offset by a cloudless blue sky.

"Wait!" she called after the boy. He was heading toward a lone baobab tree. One impish look over his shoulder was all he offered before disappearing behind it. Koffi slowed.

"Who are you?" she asked as she approached the tree. "I keep seeing you, and I—"

There was no boy on the other side of the tree. Instead, she found an entirely different person: a grown man. He had clay-red eyes, smooth mahogany skin, and an all-too-familiar smile as he leaned against the tree's trunk and took her in.

"Hello, Little Knife," said the god of death.

Koffi backed away, but Fedu mirrored the motion, pushing off from the tree and moving closer. She noticed he was limping.

"Don't bother to run," he said lightly, "there's no escaping, at least not here."

"How are you in my dreams?" Koffi tried to steady her voice, but it trembled.

Fedu smiled. "You and I are connected, Koffi." He stared out at the grasslands around them. "We are connected by your power, and by a shared vision for this world."

"We don't have the same vision for this world," said Koffi coldly.

"No?" Fedu arched a brow. "You *don't* wish for a world where darajas like you could live freely?"

"Not when it's made from genocide, mass destruction, and the deaths of all non-darajas," said Koffi.

The god shrugged. "I believe we've already spoken about the

17

costs of progress." He took another step forward, then winced, and Koffi didn't miss the way he touched his stomach, his thigh. The question escaped her before she could stop it.

"What's wrong with you?"

Fedu massaged his closed eyelids and took a deep breath. "I am still recovering from the blows you dealt me when we battled outside the Mistwood."

It wasn't the answer Koffi had expected. "You're a god," she said. "I shouldn't have been able to hurt you at all."

Fedu's eyes opened slowly. "No," he agreed, "you *shouldn't* have. And yet . . ." He gestured at his own body. "You have further proven what I'd begun to suspect from the moment you took the splendor from Adiah's body with such ease. I always knew that you were powerful, Koffi. But what you did to me? *That* was divine work, exquisitely destructive. We are alike, even more so than I could have imagined."

"I'm not anything like you," Koffi bit back. She wanted to run, but fear rooted her to the ground. "I would never hurt people the way you have."

Fedu's smile was now pitying. "So said the lioness to the hunter," he mused. "You do remember that lesson, I take it?"

Koffi stiffened. She didn't want to remember the story the god had once told her. But in her mind's eye, she saw the lioness and the hunter from that tale clearly, both fighting to the death, and both believing until the end that the other was the true villain. She swallowed, then deflected the question. "We'll stop you," she said in a fiercer voice. "And we'll make sure your plan never comes to fruition."

"We?" Fedu looked amused now. "Do you mean your so-called friends?" He moved to stand before her with inhuman speed despite his limp. "Tell me," he whispered in her ear, "are you so sure those friends would stand by you if they knew how dangerous you really are?"

I'm not dangerous. Koffi tried to speak, but the words wouldn't come. Fedu put a hand on her shoulder, ice-cold to the touch.

"Make no mistake, Little Knife," he said, "you may be out of my physical grasp, but I still hold you. You *will* do my bidding in the end because I know your weaknesses. Know that I will exploit *every single one.*"

"No." Koffi tried to pull away, but Fedu's grip on her tightened. In the grasslands around them, gray bodies began rising from the dirt.

"No!" Koffi was thrashing now, but it was to no avail. Fedu held her anchored as the Untethered drew closer. "No, no, no—"

"Koffi!"

Koffi opened her eyes. A new voice had pulled her from the nightmare. For a moment, she thought of her mother, but the woman now staring down at her was unfamiliar. She wore her hair in tight silver Bantu knots, and faint lines wrinkled her coppery skin. Her expression was full of concern.

"It's all right," she said gently. "Drink this."

Koffi made herself breathe, but her body didn't relax. She sat up and drank when the woman offered her a large gourd of water. Only once she'd lowered it did she look around.

She wasn't in the grasslands from her dream anymore, but she didn't know this place either. It looked to be some sort of tent.

Its air held a stiff chill, and instinctively she drew the thin blanket covering her body up to her chin. The unfamiliar woman sat back, as if waiting.

"Where am I?" Koffi croaked. A more urgent question came to her. "What have you done to my friends?"

"Everyone's fine," said the woman patiently. "You can join them after you've—"

Koffi jumped to her feet and instantly regretted it. She wasn't wearing much besides her tunic, a fact that became pronounced when a frigid gust of air blew into the tent without warning. Goose bumps rose on her arms, and her stomach growled.

"As I was saying." The woman—Koffi still had no idea who she was—got to her feet more slowly and crossed her arms. "You can join them after you've had something to eat."

Koffi stared at her. "I don't know you. You could have—"

"My dear, if I had any intention of harming you, I've had ample time to do so," said the woman wryly. "Which means, either I am the world's worst assassin, or . . . I don't mean you any harm."

Koffi had no immediate response to this.

"Now," the woman went on, "I have dried and salted meats and dried apricot here." She raised a brow. "You won't be leaving this tent to see the others until you eat, young lady. And don't get any cute ideas—I may be short, but I'm as sturdy and stubborn as an old hippo when I want to be."

Koffi eyed the tent's exit, and as if reading her mind, the woman shifted to place herself in front of it. She certainly looked like she meant business. Koffi recognized a battle lost.

"Fine," she grumbled.

Mollified, the woman gestured for Koffi to sit back down and shut the tent's door flap more firmly before dropping a sack of wrapped food into her lap. Koffi had planned to eat the minimum amount required, but as soon as she pulled out the first strip of salted beef, her mouth watered in earnest. She ate until she was full, then took another long swig of water before addressing the woman again.

"Who are you?"

"My name's Abeke," said the woman. "I work for a group called the Enterprise."

That answer inspired a whole host of new questions, but Koffi focused on the most pressing.

"You said if you had any intention of harming me, you've had ample time to do so." She paused. "How long have I been out?"

"A few days," Abeke murmured.

Days. Koffi's breath caught. Her last recollection was from the edge of the Mistwood; now she had no idea where she was or how she'd gotten here. It left her feeling unmoored. Her pulse quickened.

"There's not much in the way of extra clothes." Abeke interrupted Koffi's thoughts. "But I'll see if I can find you something. In the meantime..." She tossed over a cloak, then set about riffling through the other sacks. Koffi panned the rest of the tent, trying to combat her disorientation by gathering clues about where she was. She saw that only a small corner of the tent had been allotted for her tiny bed pallet; the rest was filled with stacks of wrapped food, stoppered water gourds, and—strangely enough—entire crates full of tiny pouches. She leaned forward to examine them more closely and realized she recognized them. They were spice and herb pouches, the very same kind she'd occasionally seen

21

Baaz use at the Night Zoo to season his food. Again, she reflected on what Abeke had said before.

I work for a group called the Enterprise.

Who *was* the Enterprise, and what did they do? Koffi found no answers as she scoured the room, but she noted a glint of light protruding from one of the open sacks. Upon closer inspection, she saw that it was a looking glass. She looked over her shoulder at Abeke, then on hands and knees she crawled forward and plucked it from the bag. At once, she went very still.

It was a small trinket, barely the size of her palm, but the looking glass revealed enough. In its smudged reflection, Koffi saw a girl with a gaunter version of her own face, but that wasn't the worst of it. Gingerly, she pulled back the neckline of her tunic, confused. There was a series of small silver-white pocks on her shoulder, strangely luminous against her skin. Something about them reminded her of stars in a night sky, but there was a wrongness about them too. Without thinking, she touched one of the pocks with a forefinger and gasped as heat arrowed through her entire body. Unease settled over her. These pocks certainly hadn't been there before she'd passed out, and they were in the exact place Fedu had touched her in the dream. Was that a coincidence, or did it mean something? Her mind began to race.

"Koffi?"

Koffi dropped the looking glass at the sound of Abeke's voice. The woman was watching her again, and now looked even more concerned. "Are you all right?"

The tent had felt small before; now it was unbearably cramped. Koffi's breath shallowed as she tried to quell a rising panic. There were too many uncertainties, too many unanswered questions.

She still didn't know exactly where she was, but she was sure of one thing. She didn't want to stay in here anymore. She needed to get out. She needed air. She looked to Abeke again, and every muscle in her body tensed.

"Now, Koffi." Abeke raised both hands in a placating gesture. "Just hold on for one—"

Koffi launched herself toward the tent's door flap. In her periphery she saw the woman move, but she was quicker. A rush of crisp air met her as she crashed through the opening, and she vaguely noted the pale gray sky overhead, but she didn't stop running. Around her, she registered other tents, and determined that she was in some sort of encampment. She passed a few people too, but kept going. Abeke had said her friends were here; if that was true, she needed to find them. She needed to find *something* familiar. The smell of burnt wood filled her lungs suddenly, and some yards away she made out a wispy line of black smoke rising from amid the tents. She beelined toward it, hopeful.

Up ahead, a trio of wagons marked the edge of the camp, and Koffi saw that five people were seated before them. Her steps slowed in relief. She knew three of the five people, though they were sitting in two distinct groups on opposite sides of a small fire. At one end sat a young man with deep brown skin, and a top-fade haircut badly in need of a touch-up. Koffi started.

Ekon.

Something in her unknotted at the sight of him. Ekon was sitting between a middle-aged man and woman, and as far as she could see, he was uninjured. She exhaled in relief, then looked left.

Across the fire sat two more people she knew. The other man,

Zain, had a long nose, cropped black hair, and coppery skin several shades lighter than Ekon's. He wasn't injured either. Koffi felt another wave of relief at the sight of him and the girl next to him—Njeri. She was the first to look up and notice her.

"Koffi!"

There was a rush of movement as Ekon and Zain both jumped to their feet. It was hard to determine which one of them looked more shocked.

Ekon broke the silence first. "Koffi, how are you—?"

"HONESTLY!"

Everyone turned as Abeke came to a stop before them. Her heavy panting told Koffi she'd been running after her with not a small amount of effort. The woman doubled over, held her knees, then gave Koffi a reproachful look. "Was that really necessary?" she said between wheezes. "I *told* you they were here!"

"Apologies, Abeke," said the woman sitting next to Ekon, nodding. "We'll take it from here."

Abeke shook her head and ambled away, muttering something that Koffi thought sounded a lot like "bad knees." In her absence, a silence held. Koffi realized everyone was looking at her.

"How are you, Koffi?" asked Njeri as she stood.

Koffi paused, unsure at first how to answer that question. "I've . . . been better," she said after a beat. A thought occurred to her. Could they see the marks on her shoulder? Did they already know about them? She tugged her tunic's neckline up and decided to change the topic. "Where are we?"

"As important as this conversation is," said the woman who'd spoken before, "it will need to be tabled for the time being. I smell a storm coming, fast."

"A storm?" Zain looked dubious. "But the sky's perfectly clear."

The middle-aged man who was sitting on Ekon's other side rose at the same time the woman did. Standing, Koffi noted that the former was considerably tall, muscular, and did not look amused by Zain. For her part, the woman grimaced.

"And yet, a storm is coming." Her tone was humorless. "Have *you* ever driven loaded wagons on these marshes? If so, by all means, please share your expertise with the group and feel free to take full responsibility for the welfare of this caravan and its passengers."

Zain dropped his gaze, looking properly chastened.

"As I was saying." The woman turned to address the rest of the group, and for the first time her eyes found Koffi's. They were dark brown, narrow, and struck Koffi as vaguely familiar. "When—not if—it rains, the ground around here will become muddy, which means no traction for the wagons, which means several days' delay." She pursed her lips. "From what I've gathered in recent discussions, time is not on our side. So, everyone grab a bag and start packing up." When no one immediately moved, she raised a brow. "That means *now*."

At once, everyone moved in a different direction, looking for items to pack, stow, or begin dismantling. Koffi found that she was suddenly the only one left standing there. The woman nodded at her.

"You're Koffi." It wasn't a question. "I was wondering when we'd meet."

Koffi hesitated. "Do you work for the Enterprise too?" she asked.

The woman chuckled. "My dear, I *am* the Enterprise. It's my brainchild." Her eyes twinkled, and Koffi started. *Why did they seem so familiar?*

"Then I owe you thanks," said Koffi after a pause, "for taking me and my friends in."

The woman's smile turned wry. "Don't thank me yet." She turned her attention to the fire and began stomping it out. "There's a long journey ahead, and this is just the beginning. So you'd better get moving."

Koffi started to turn away, then stopped. "Sorry, I didn't ask. You are . . . ?"

"Tired, sore, and in *desperate* need of a thorough foot rub by a man with good hands," the woman said pertly. "That said, most people just call me Ano."

CHAPTER 2

A TINY SECRET

KOFFI

While the rest of the camp packed, Koffi searched for a place to make herself look busy. She had just ducked into one of the tents when she heard a squeal of joy.

"*Koffi!*"

There was a yellow blur as someone hurled themselves forward and threw their arms around her with so much force she was nearly knocked over. For a split second, Koffi panicked, and then she realized she was being hugged. When the culprit pulled back, Koffi found herself staring at a girl with a halo of dark springy hair. The bright yellow kaftan she wore somehow made her look even cheerier.

"Makena," she said softly. "You're okay."

"I'm okay!"

"It's so good to see you."

Her friend smiled. "You too, sleepyhead. When did you wake up?"

"Not that long ago," said Koffi.

"And you found my tent!" Makena clapped, looking positively merry.

"Actually . . ." Koffi looked over her shoulder. "I kind of came in here to hide." In a lower voice, she added, "That lady in charge is making everyone pack up. She seems a little intense."

"Oh, you mean Ano?" Makena's smile didn't falter. "She's really not that bad. And you know she's— Oh!" Her gaze fixed on Koffi's shoulder. "Sorry, I think my hug was a little too enthusiastic. I ripped your tunic." In a flash, she'd brandished the needle and thread she always carried with her. Like Koffi, Makena was a daraja, and her affinity was in the craft of apparel. "Don't worry, I can fix it."

"Makena," Koffi started. "You don't have to—"

Makena pulled back the neckline of Koffi's tunic, then froze. Her eyes went from the silver pocks to Koffi's face. At once her smile vanished, and she withdrew her hand.

"Where did those come from?"

Koffi hesitated. "I don't know," she admitted. It was hard to look directly down at her shoulder and see them without the looking glass, but she tried. "I only noticed them this morning when I woke up. Have you ever seen anything like them?"

Makena shook her head. "Never. Can I have another look?"

Koffi nodded, and Makena inched the tunic's neckline back a second time. She pursed her lips, thoughtful. "You know . . . they kind of look like splendor?"

Koffi swallowed. In truth, a similar thought had occurred to her from the moment she'd seen the marks, but hearing that theory spoken aloud gave her a fresh wave of anxiety. She shuddered, and Makena noticed.

"There's a simple way to find out," said Makena carefully. She left the rest of the words unspoken, but Koffi inferred them. She took a deep breath, closed her eyes, and reached for the splendor in her body. It came to her immediately as it always did, and her blood seemed to warm as the foreign energy coursed through her veins.

"Koffi!"

She opened her eyes. Makena was staring at her shoulder. When Koffi looked down too, she saw the marks had turned a bright white and were glowing eerily against her skin. As soon as she stopped summoning the splendor, they dulled again.

"More of them appeared on your skin when you did that." Makena pointed. "See?"

She was right. There were definitely more pocks along her shoulder. She thought some of them looked bigger too. She met Makena's gaze.

"I don't know what this means," said Koffi. "But I'm not ready to talk about it with anyone else. Not yet."

"Then we won't," said Makena fiercely. "Not until you're ready."

Koffi was surprised to feel a wave of relief, accompanied by a surge of gratitude toward her friend. "Thank you," she whispered.

"Here." Makena reached into a sack filled with scraps of fabric. "I'll sew you a new collar to make sure no one sees them. Sit with me."

"So about the Enterprise," Koffi began while Makena worked. "Do you have any idea who they are or what they do?"

"From what I've gathered, they're spice traders," said Makena. "I don't know much more, but . . . they're good people, Koffi. We can trust them." She gave her a meaningful look. "You know, Ekon is with them."

Koffi nodded. "I'm still getting reoriented," she said. "So much happened while I was out."

Makena's expression changed. "Of course. I'm so sorry. I didn't even think to ask you how you were actually feeling after everything you went through leaving the Mistwood." She finished sewing up the collar of Koffi's tunic and sat back. "I can't imagine how scary it must've been, going up against Fedu like that. And those *spears* you made." She shuddered. "I've never seen anything like them. I barely recognized you when you were using them."

Koffi shifted on the tent's floor but didn't answer. Up until now, she hadn't given herself a moment to truly reflect on all that had happened before she'd blacked out. Now it all returned in vivid, overbright recollection, and she struggled to tell Makena that, in truth, using the splendor spears hadn't felt scary. It had felt *good*. An unwelcome voice entered her mind.

Are you so sure your friends would stand by you if they knew how dangerous you really are?

"Makena." Koffi stared at her hands. "There's something else I need to tell you. Before I woke up, I had this dream and—"

They were interrupted as a man's head popped into the tent. He was bald and wore a single golden hoop earring. Koffi didn't recognize him, so she deduced that he was yet another member of the Enterprise. He looked between her and Makena, sheepish.

"Apologies." To Makena, he said, "They're looking for you. Something about the stitching on one of the wagon's covers."

"I'll be there in a second," said Makena. When the man's head had disappeared again, she focused on Koffi. "We'll pick this up later, once we're on the move," she said. "In the meantime, promise me something, Koffi?"

"Sure."

"Promise you'll tell me if anything changes with those marks," said Makena.

"I will."

With a nod, Makena ducked out of the tent, and for the first time since she'd woken up, Koffi found herself completely alone. She'd expected to feel a much-anticipated sense of relief; instead, her nerves felt frayed. With no one to distract her, her mind went back to the dream she'd woken from that morning. She remembered the open grasslands, Fedu's face, and the boy she'd encountered at the beginning of it. He was, by far, the biggest enigma. Who was he?

Outside the tent, someone shouted, and it snapped Koffi out of her musings. She refocused. For better or for worse, Ano was right. Whatever journey lay ahead of them was only just beginning; there was no time to waste pondering dreams. She stood, preparing to leave the tent, then abruptly paused. It had been brief—so brief she almost could have ignored it—but then she felt it a second time. A throb of pain lanced through her body, starting at the point where the pocks were. Then it was gone, and she was left standing in the middle of the tent, confused.

Tell Makena, a voice in her head instructed. *This is exactly what she asked you to tell her.*

Even still, Koffi hesitated. The pain she'd felt had only been fleeting. It hardly merited raising alarm. They had so much to worry about; the last thing she wanted was to add this to their list of problems. Koffi made a decision then: The change with her marks would remain a secret, a tiny secret. For now.

By the time Koffi emerged from Makena's tent, the encampment was nearly unrecognizable. The tents that'd been staked all around were gone, giving her for the first time an unobstructed view of their surroundings. They were in open marshlands; green grass stretched for miles around, and a wispy, lingering fog hung low over it. She turned, then ducked, barely missing the giant rolled-up canvas that went over her head as two young darajas who'd escaped Fedu's realm with her carried it past on their shoulders. They offered her smiles as they headed toward Ano, who was standing in the middle of the three wagons and pointing left and right as if directing traffic.

"Put that food in wagon two, it should have been sealed already!" she snapped. "Linens and bedrolls go in wagon three. Let's move, people! Though I may look it, I am certainly *not* getting any younger standing around!"

Koffi looked around the rest of the campsite, trying to find something to do before Ano spotted her. Her heart did an impressive arrangement of cartwheels as she noticed Ekon making his way across the campsite with a basket held against his torso.

Talk to him, she told herself. *You've barely spoken since you woke up. And before that . . .* Koffi gnawed at her bottom lip. She and Ekon hadn't discussed the fact that he'd come all the way from Lkossa to find her. When she'd seen him in the Temple of Lkossa's sky garden, he'd been bloodied and broken, and she hadn't been able to give him any clues about where she'd gone. He'd still found her. That had to mean *something*, she just didn't know where that *something* left the two of them, and thinking about it made her palms sweaty.

Just talk to him.

The decision was made for her when, a second later, Ekon looked up, noticed her, and changed direction so that he was heading straight toward her. Koffi tried to keep her breath even as he approached. And then he was just *there*, standing right before her.

"Hey," he said warmly.

"Uh . . . hi."

"It's good to see you up and about."

Do not say something ridiculous, say something normal. Koffi cleared her throat. "That's a nice basket you've got there. What's in it?"

"Um . . . dirty clothes."

"Oh. Great." *Ridiculous.*

Ekon shifted the basket in question to one arm, and it took Koffi a considerable amount of effort not to look at his biceps as they flexed. She wanted to kick herself. Baskets? *Baskets?*

"Ten minutes!" Ano shouted to their left. "We are leaving in exactly ten minutes, people! I give you all fair warning: Relieve yourselves before we depart. There will be no unscheduled breaks on my caravan!"

"But what if there's an emergency?" asked Zain innocently as he passed Ano with an armful of crates. Koffi thought she heard an undertone of mischief in the question.

The woman frowned. "The same thing that happened the

33

last time, you impertinent boy. You will use a disaster bucket!"

Koffi met Ekon's eye. They lasted for about a second before they both burst into a fit of laughter. Koffi relaxed fractionally, relieved that it was that easy to go back to some semblance of the way they'd once been. "Disaster buckets?" she repeated.

Ekon pretended to look solemn. "The less you know, the better." He cracked a smile.

"I'll give that Ano lady one thing," she said as they watched her continue to yell at Zain. "She sure knows how to take charge."

"She does," Ekon agreed. His mood suddenly changed, and Koffi noted his fingers began to tap against the basket, a sign that he was anxious. He seemed to be grappling with something. Then: "She's my mother."

"What?" Koffi gaped at him, all other thoughts temporarily vacated. Slowly the pieces of a puzzle clicked into place. She thought back to the first time she'd really seen Ano, by the fire, sitting beside Ekon. She'd noticed something familiar about the woman's eyes, but she hadn't been able to figure out what. Now it seemed painfully obvious. "But I thought your mother was—"

"So did I." It was hard to identify the new emotion in Ekon's voice, though Koffi thought he was trying a little too hard to sound offhand. "Sometimes life doesn't go as planned." He pursed his lips and gave her a sidelong glance. "You know how much I *love* unplanned things."

Koffi chuckled. "I do." Something empowered her then, and she took a step closer to him. It was only a tiny difference in space, but she felt the change instantly. She tried to ignore the heat rising in her face as she put a hand on Ekon's arm. "Thank you, Ekon," she said quietly, "for finding me."

Ekon's expression shifted. There was an intensity in it that made her warm all over. He opened his mouth, started to say something—

"Ekon!"

They both looked up, stepped apart, and every muscle in Koffi's body seized.

A beautiful young woman was heading straight toward them. She had an angular face, a dancer's gait, and long black hair tied into a single neat braid. At once Koffi became uncomfortably aware of the state of her own uncombed hair. She said nothing as the girl stopped before them.

"I think we might have a problem," she said to Ekon. She turned. "You must be Koffi." She said it the same way Ano had—as a fact, not a question—then extended a hand. "I'm Safiyah."

"Nice to meet you." They both let their hands drop after a quick shake, and an awkwardness lingered. Koffi looked to Ekon and noticed that his lips had formed a tight line. He was still tapping his fingers against the basket, but at a much faster cadence. Was it in her head, or did he now look uncomfortable? Was it because of her, or Safiyah, or both of them?

"Uh, you said there was a problem?" he asked Safiyah.

She nodded, looking focused again. "It's the group's roster. We're supposed to have twenty-one people. Ano asked me to account for everyone here, but we're one person short."

Ekon frowned. "Who's missing?"

"One of the darajas," said Safiyah. She faced Koffi again. "Maybe you know him? His name's Amun."

Koffi started. "I do know him." In all the morning's activity, she suddenly realized that Amun was the only one of her friends she hadn't run into yet. "No one's seen him?"

35

Safiyah shook her head, worrying at her braid. "Not since he went on patrol duty earlier. I've counted twice."

Ekon stopped tapping. "That's odd." To both of them, he said, "Let the others know, and have everyone spread out to look for him. He's got to be around here somewhere."

All three of them went in different directions, and Koffi fought a growing sense of unease. *He's fine,* she told herself as she started looking around. *Safiyah probably just miscounted. He's fine.*

It didn't take long for the news of Amun's absence to spread; soon, everyone was looking for him. The problem was, with most of the camp already packed and loaded into the three wagons, there were few places the daraja could have hidden. A knot in Koffi's stomach tightened.

"Ano told everyone to relieve themselves before we left." Zain jumped down from the back of one of the wagons to join the rest of the group congregating at the camp's center. "Maybe he went a little farther out into the marsh to . . . ah, take care of business?"

"I was clear about our departure time," said Ano. Her arms were crossed. "He should be back."

It was undeniable now; a new, palpable nervousness hung in the air. Koffi fidgeted.

"Some of us can go into the marsh and conduct a search," said Ekon. His expression was stoic and composed, the way it always was when he made a plan. Koffi found herself reminded of the way he'd looked the first time he'd made a plan with her, back before they'd even left Lkossa and gone into the Greater Jungle. It calmed her a little.

"The rest of us should stay here," Ekon continued, "just in case he—"

"Wait!" The bald man with the golden earring, the one Koffi had seen while she and Makena had been talking before, was staring out into the marshlands and pointing. "I think I see him. He's headed this way!"

There was a collective sigh, and several shoulders relaxed as the words carried. Relief flooded Koffi as she looked in the direction the man had pointed and saw Amun's familiar silhouette racing toward them through the marshlands' fog.

"Unbelievable," Njeri muttered. "So he *was* relieving—" The rest of the words died on her lips. When Koffi peered closer, she saw why.

Amun had come to a stop at the edge of the campsite, standing perfectly still. From a distance, the fog had allowed Koffi only to make out his silhouette; closer, what she saw cooled her blood. The daraja's clothes were in tatters, ripped and torn from head to toe. His face was frozen in horror.

"They're coming," he rasped in a voice that wasn't his. "They're coming for us all."

"Amun?" Njeri stepped forward, her wooden staff already gripped tight in her fist. "Where have you been?"

"They're coming," Amun repeated. His body began to tremble, a line of urine dribbling down his leg. Koffi's stomach turned.

"*Who*, boy?" asked Ano. "*Who* is coming?"

Amun's expression grew blank as he stared beyond them. "Coming," he whispered. "They're coming, they're—"

37

Koffi noticed the metal glint a half second too late. A warning rose in her throat, but she could do nothing to stop the arrow as it flew through the air and lodged itself in the back of Amun's neck. She could do nothing to help the daraja as he fell to the ground, and moved no more.

CHAPTER 3

BODY COUNT

EKON

Amun's body hit the ground, and Ekon began to count.

He didn't want to, but the familiar tug of impulse prevailed, as involuntary as breathing. His fingers tapped a steady rhythm against his leg as time slowed to a crawl, then seemed to stop entirely. With mounting horror, he stared at the dead daraja's body, at the dark pool of blood forming around his head. Ekon had seen blood before; the sight of it then shouldn't have petrified him. Still, the nausea came in waves. His mouth grew sticky, a sheen of sweat that defied the marshlands' chill sent a shiver deep into his bones. He swallowed hard and kept counting.

One-two-three. One-two-three. One-two-three.

Another arrow streaked across the sky, landing with a quivering thud in a spot of grass only feet from where Ekon stood. He searched for its origin point, then tensed.

The man approaching was tall, emaciated, and held a bow. His ashen skin was unsettling, but what truly frightened Ekon was that where the man should have had eyes there were only two gaping black holes. Ekon drew in a sharp breath.

A gust of wind passed over the marshlands then, briefly lifting the surrounding fog for miles around. When Ekon saw what had been hidden in it, his mouth went dry.

It was an army.

He could think of no other word to describe the gray people heading directly toward their camp, numbering in the hundreds. It wasn't the first time he'd seen people like this—he and Themba had come across them when they'd entered the Mistwood—but back then the gray people had been unarmed. Now he noted that more than half of them brandished weapons—cudgels, quivers of arrows, stones sharpened to crude points. Ekon watched as several of them nocked arrows at the same time. He heard a sound like a hundred kora strings being plucked at once and knew what was about to happen. Their group was about to be decimated. He tripped over his own feet as he watched a shower of arrows rise high in the sky, then arch in perfect unison. He looked around for anything—*anything*—he could use to shield himself, but it was too late, and a part of him understood that. He fell to the ground and threw his arms over his head, waiting for the arrows to fall.

They never did.

Seconds passed before Ekon lowered his arms, confused. Around him, others who'd hunched down to cover themselves were doing the same and looking around. Ekon's gaze lifted, and what he saw in the sky above rendered him motionless.

A dome of shimmering light had expanded across the storm-ridden sky, just large enough to cover the wagons and those huddled near them. Ekon stared. From without, the gray people continued shooting their arrows as they approached, but it was to no avail. Ekon's lips parted in wonder. He'd never seen anything like this dome before, but the shimmering lights that comprised it looked familiar. His gaze dropped, and he started.

Koffi and several of the other darajas were standing in the middle of the clearing, their feet spread apart and their arms raised high over their heads. Each of them was looking skyward, and their bodies were taut with focus as that same curious light radiated from their hands and up toward the dome.

They're using the splendor, Ekon realized. *They're using the splendor to protect us.*

For several seconds, no one dared move or speak. Everyone seemed to be held under the same stupor, transfixed by the glittering dome and the darajas keeping it suspended. Ekon studied Koffi more closely. Her breath was growing labored, and he noted a tremor in one of her legs was becoming increasingly pronounced as the seconds passed. He realized that however she and the other darajas were sustaining the dome, they wouldn't be able to do it for much longer, and when it came down, their whole group would be vulnerable. The darajas were giving everyone else a moment's respite, a chance to rally.

That chance couldn't be wasted.

Ekon jumped to his feet and addressed the people crouched nearest to him. "Onto the wagons, now!"

People around him began to run. Ekon let his fingers tap a new rhythm against his thigh as he counted.

Ninety seconds.

He didn't know if that was how much time they actually had, but it was the number he used as an anchor. He began ushering

41

along people who weren't moving fast enough, and breathed out in relief when he saw others opening the wagons' rear hatches and throwing things from them quickly to lighten their loads.

Sixty seconds.

He raced toward one of the wagons to help Kontar—a member of the Enterprise—as he attempted to pull a young daraja girl up and onto its backboard.

"Hurry," he urged as he lifted her in. "We have about fifty seconds to—"

An ominous crack stole the rest of his words, and the hairs on Ekon's arms stood on end. He prayed that it was thunder, but the truth stared back at him when he looked up at the gray clouds in the sky. The dome was gone, and with it, their protection.

"Cover!" Ekon shouted frantically. "Everyone needs to find—"

He was too late. In one second, Ekon looked over his shoulder and saw the third barrage of arrows coming their way. His reflexes took over as he snatched a long wooden washboard from the back of the wagon to use as a shield and knelt. There was a hairsbreadth pause, and then the arrows began to fall. Ekon braced himself, listening as each one landed. He heard the sounds of splintering wood, tearing canvas, cries of pain as bodies fell. He yelped as one arrow struck the washboard, precisely over the place where his heart was still thudding hard. *That* was the kind of fortune he knew better than to expect twice. He couldn't stay there.

Carefully, he inched back. The wagon's canvas covering was still ripping, turning holey as more arrows pierced the fabric and likely their supplies along with it. He thought detachedly of Kontar, of the girl he'd just helped into that very wagon, and a lump formed in his throat, but he made himself keep moving, mindful to keep holding the washboard up as he crawled around the wagon's massive wheels. On the other side of it, he found Koffi, Safiyah, Makena, Njeri, and Zain huddled together. Ano was on her feet wrestling with a mule she'd clearly saved just in time. Fleeting relief passed over his mother's face as their eyes met.

"Was anyone with you?" she asked.

Ekon shook his head, hating the answer. "Just me."

Ano's lips pressed into a tight line as she peeked around the wagon. In the distance, someone screamed. "We need to get out of here," she said, "quickly."

"How?" asked Zain, flinching as another arrow thudded into the other side of the wagon.

"A lighter wagon will make us faster," said Ano. "If we can unload this one and get the mule hitched to it, we've got a shot at an escape, but we need time, and a distraction." She looked at the darajas. "They seem to be averse to your power. Can any of you give us cover?"

Njeri, Zain, and Makena shook their heads.

"I'm wiped out," said Zain.

"I am too." Njeri was breathing hard as she slumped against the wagon. "Summoning that dome took everything out of me."

"Send me."

They all looked up as Koffi half rose from her crouch to address Ano. "I can do it, I still have some energy. I'll keep them back while you get the wagon ready."

"Koffi." Makena's expression was pained. "Are you sure?"

She nodded. "I can do this."

"Wait." Ekon found himself speaking before he could stop himself. "You can't go out there alone."

Koffi frowned. "Can't?"

"What I mean is . . ." Ekon fumbled for words. He didn't know how to say what he was thinking, that in his mind the image of Koffi at the edge of the Mistwood was still fresh. He didn't know how to say that he was worried about her, and worried about the way she'd been the last time she'd used splendor. At his silence, Koffi looked from him to Ano.

"How much time do you need?" she asked.

"Five minutes," Ano replied.

Koffi nodded again, and Ekon began to tap his knees in earnest. The threat of an anxiety attack was looming the way it always did, smudging the edges of his vision black as panic set in. *No*, he thought fiercely. *Not here. Not now. I can control this.* His anxiety was a part of him and always would be, but that didn't mean it had to rule him. It could be managed. He knew that. His nostrils flared as he forced himself to take deep breaths in through his nose, letting them out through his mouth. He stole a glance at Koffi and saw a glint in her eye, the one she got when she was rallying herself. A second that felt like a century passed before she coiled and sprang forward, disappearing around the side of the wagon. Ekon's stomach knotted.

Go after her, a voice in his head commanded. *Help her.*

I can't, a second voice argued. *I'm not a daraja, I wouldn't be able to help her.*

You may not be a daraja, said the first voice, *but you're still a warrior by trade and training. Help her!*

Ekon clenched his teeth. Weeks ago, he'd all but renounced the Sons of the Six when he'd broken his vows and fled Lkossa with the Enterprise. He'd abandoned everything he'd dedicated his life to, and he'd done it largely without looking back. He didn't miss being a warrior. But that didn't mean the years he'd spent with the Sons of the Six had been erased; it didn't mean he'd forgotten his training. Try as he might to ignore it, he found that the impulse to fight, to defend, was still there, dormant but not dead. A familiar beast within him sniffed the air, hopeful.

You have to help Koffi. She needs you. She needs the old you.

Ekon made his decision.

He charged out from behind the wagon before anyone could stop him, still brandishing his makeshift shield. His vision tunneled as he surveyed the land around him, taking in the totality of the destruction. The bloodied bodies of those who hadn't been able to find cover from the arrows in time were strewn everywhere. Ekon tried not to look too closely, to register any of their faces, but some came into focus anyway. He recognized the body of an older daraja boy who'd helped him inventory their food that morning; Obioma and Abeke, members of the Enterprise, were both crumpled on the ground. His breath caught when he turned and saw that Kontar's body was slumped beside the wagon's torn cover, his limp arm thrown over the little girl Ekon had tried to help. Neither had made it. New rage boiled within him. Fewer arrows were flying through the sky, but the gray figures were almost at the encampment. He made out Koffi, up ahead, directing splendor in as many directions as she could to keep the gray people at bay, but she was woefully outnumbered. She needed help. Ekon's mind began to race.

Deflect. Disarm. Dismantle.

Years of training with the Sons of the Six returned to him as he found his footing in the marshlands' soaked earth. Rain began to fall, and he blinked the drops away as he braced himself. *Three.*

Three of the Untethered were at the front of the line. Two were holding crude cudgels, the last held a sharpened rock, but they were all moving clumsily.

He'd make short work of them.

Ekon rushed forward before he could second-guess himself, snatching a rock from the muddied grass and hurling it with all his might. His aim was true; one of the gray men who'd been holding a cudgel was hit squarely on the forehead. Ekon waited for him to recoil in pain, to fall to the ground.

The gray man did neither.

A chill stippled Ekon's skin as the gray man continued advancing, his head swiveling from side to side. Ekon swallowed and tried to find logic for what had just happened.

It didn't affect him at all.

That dormant beast within him—the same one that had come alive when he'd fought the street hyenas back in Lkossa—roared to life as he tried again. He pivoted, twisting the knife from another gray man's hand and using its hilt to knock him in the head. Like the first, there was no reaction at all. Ekon gritted his teeth. Muscle memory took over as he pivoted again, and the blade he was holding cut before him in a long arc, right across another one of the gray men's chests. The flesh tore, and the gray man stumbled back, but there was no blood. That internal beast roared in fury.

Die. Why won't you die?

He began moving faster, trying to cut down more and more of the gray people. At first, he took note of their faces—which ones were male or female, what weapons they held—then he stopped caring at all. None of them fell, but gradually they began moving away from him, their horrid mouths slackened. They weren't dying, but Ekon still racked up a body count in his mind each time he hit one.

Six. Nine. Twelve.

Deflect. Disarm. Dismantle.

Something fell away from him as the number rose, as the faces blurred. From the corners of his mind, he heard a familiar voice.

Young and athletic, smart and meticulous, whispered Brother Ugo. *You were the perfect combination . . . easy to mold into what I needed.*

Ekon pushed that voice away and kept counting.

Eighteen. Twenty-one. Twenty-four.

Deflect. Disarm. Dis—

"Ekon!"

Ekon whirled around with his fist raised as someone touched his shoulder, then he faltered. Koffi was standing in the grass behind him, covered in mud. One of her hands was raised, sending a small wall of splendor to her right to keep the gray people back, but her gaze was locked on him. She looked wary.

"Sorry!" A nasty feeling curdled in Ekon's gut. His own voice came back to him, ashamed.

You could have hurt her.

He thought of the prophecy his mother had told him about only days before, the one that said he'd kill the one he loved most. Just now, without even meaning to, he'd almost attacked Koffi. It had almost been that easy. He shuddered.

"I—I'm sorry, I didn't mean—"

"Never mind!" Koffi looked over her shoulder. "I can see the wagon. Ano's got the mule hitched, we need to go!"

The gray people had briefly moved away, but now more were

emerging from the fog. Ekon's gaze swept over all those empty eye sockets, over the sea of gray skin that reminded him of so many corpses. As quickly as it'd been freed, fear muzzled that imaginary beast.

"I'm going to bring the wall of splendor down so we can run," said Koffi. "Stay right behind me."

Ekon barely had time to process the words before Koffi let her arm fall and started to run toward the wagon. It was only a few yards away, but as the rain fell harder it seemed to grow farther. Ekon tried not to think about the bodies in the mud, or the gray people likely trudging behind them. He exhaled as they came within a few feet of the wagon, and Ano threw open its rear hatch.

"Ekon!" She wasn't looking at him but over his shoulder. "Help her!"

Ekon turned, and his stomach swooped as he saw that Koffi had slowed. Her eyes were unfocused, and she seemed to be struggling to keep upright. Her hand extended, grasping at nothing, and then she collapsed.

"I've got her." Ekon was already moving. He threw Koffi's arm over his shoulder, lifted her to her feet, and half dragged her to the back of the wagon. Hands—he wasn't sure whose—pulled him up, and as soon as they were in, Njeri dashed to the wagon's front. There was a violent lurch, and then the wagon picked up speed, rolling across the marshlands, splashing mud in its wake. Ekon stared out the back, watching the storm as the gray faces grew distant, until they were once again lost in a swirl of rain and fog.

CHAPTER 4

The EMPEROR
of the MARSHLANDS

KOFFI

In Koffi's dreams, the strange boy still smiled at her.

She was beginning to wonder if maybe she'd misread him initially. When she gave him a sidelong glance, she thought she still detected a certain roguishness, but there was an earnestness in his expression too, even something that resembled curiosity as he looked at her.

They were standing together on the plains—as they always did in her dreams—surrounded for miles by a sea of waist-high grass that glinted golden brown. Though she saw no sunlight in the cloudless sky, its warmth on her skin relaxed her. Seconds passed before she broke their silence.

"You won't talk to me," she accused. "And you won't tell me who you are. You won't even tell me what you *want*." She turned to face him, scowling. "Exactly how much longer is this going to go on?"

In answer, the boy cocked his head, but he did not speak.

"Oh, come *on*!" Koffi threw up her hands. "You keep showing up in my dreams, you owe me *something*." She paused, and suddenly an idea came to her. Not so long ago, she'd learned the value of a good barter, *if* one knew what to trade. Perhaps it was a lesson that could be put to use now. She tried a different approach.

"I'll make you a deal," she proposed. "Information in exchange for information. I'll ask you a question, and if you answer, you get to ask me one." She threw him a sidelong glance. "You keep finding me in my dreams, so I *know* you've got to have at least one question for me."

Interest flashed across the boy's face.

"Do we have a deal?"

He nodded, and Koffi breathed relief.

"Right, I'll go first." She steepled her fingers, considering. There were several questions she wanted to ask, but it was important that she pick the right one. "Okay. Why do you keep appearing in my dreams?"

The boy's lips pressed into a tight line and he looked away. For a moment, Koffi wondered if he might renege on their deal and refuse to answer. Instead, after a pause, he touched two fingers to his neck and cleared his throat. She was surprised to find that, when he finally did speak, he sounded hoarse.

"I want you to follow me."

"*Follow* you?" Koffi repeated. Whatever answer she'd been expecting from him, it wasn't that one. "Why?"

At this, the strange boy's telltale smile returned. She knew from that look that his first answer was all she would be getting.

"*Fine.*" Koffi crossed her arms, annoyed, and when the boy arched one of his brows, her frown deepened. She knew what he expected of her now. "Yes, all right. You can ask your question." She tried to avoid looking too curious. The boy cleared his throat a second time, then:

"What is your name?"

"My . . . ," Koffi started. "My *name*?"

The boy nodded.

"It's Koffi." She answered without thinking about it.

The boy grinned, and this time it was a genuine gesture, as warm and radiant as the surrounding plains. He looked at her now as if, for the first time, he was properly seeing her, and Koffi shifted her weight under his gaze. He opened his mouth as if to say something else, then abruptly turned and began to walk away.

"Wait!" she called after him. "Where are you going?"

The boy didn't stop walking, even as Koffi noticed the fields around them growing blurred. At the last minute, he looked over his shoulder and uttered a single word.

"*Home.*"

Koffi sat up as the wagon she was in jolted to a stop. The force of it knocked her against one of its inner walls, and she groaned aloud as a soreness spread from her shoulder and down her arm.

"Koffi!"

Her eyes had been screwed shut in pain, but she recognized that voice. When they opened, she found Ekon kneeling before her, his face inches from hers. She drew in a sharp breath as he studied her face. She'd forgotten the way he looked when he did that, like a trained scholar trying to memorize her very essence. A warmth flooded her cheeks at precisely the same moment Ekon's gaze dropped from her face, and he tensed.

"What are those?"

Koffi looked down, then stiffened. It was difficult to know the extent from her angle, but she could see at once what had caught Ekon's eye. The silver pocks that'd been clustered near her collarbone this morning had clearly spread; now they extended up the side of her neck and down past her shoulder to her upper biceps. They twinkled wickedly in the wagon's dim light.

"I'm fine," said Koffi quickly, though she felt anything but. The wagon was already small, and was made even more so by the number of people now crammed into it. Once again, Koffi felt the need to get out, to get air. Without looking at Ekon, she half crouched, half walked past a blur of other faces. She tried not think about the marks, or the stagnant air inside the wagon, but she felt like she would only really be able to breathe again once she'd ducked out of it completely. She jumped down from its backboard, wincing as the damp earth soaked through her sandals. Her gaze lifted in time to note the drab gray expanse of the surrounding marshlands just as Njeri came around the other side of the wagon.

"We had to stop," she was saying, "the mule needed—" Like Ekon, her eyes fell on the marks. Her mouth fell open. "Koffi, are you okay? Your arm—"

"I'm *fine*," said Koffi quickly. "Really."

Njeri shook her head. "Those marks don't look good, Kof. I really think you should—"

"I said I'm *fine*!" Koffi snapped. The words felt good for a half second, but at the expression on Njeri's face, she instantly regretted it. There was a long pause before the daraja did something Koffi had never seen her do before: She hung her head.

"I'm sorry," Njeri whispered. "I tried. Ano didn't tell me where to go, and I was just trying to get us as far away from the Untethered as I could, but . . . I failed."

A stab of guilt twisted in Koffi's side. Njeri was a daraja from the Order of Kupambana, a combat order. She was the toughest daraja Koffi knew, and most of the time, she presented as utterly infallible. Seeing her like this revealed a new, unsettling truth. The situation was dire.

"No. *I'm* sorry," Koffi whispered. "I didn't mean to blame you, Njeri. I just . . ." She tried to string the right words together to explain, but they fell apart on her tongue. The truth was, she didn't know how to tell her friend that she was exhausted, sore, terrified. The faces of the Untethered claimed a stake in her mind, haunting her with the memory of those empty black eye sockets and the rotting gray skin. Even now, one particular face seared itself into her mind. She saw Fedu's lurid red eyes, the white of his teeth as he smiled.

We are alike.

"No!"

Njeri looked up. "What?"

"I—" Koffi faltered. "What I mean is . . . you can't blame yourself for anything that happened this morning, Njeri." In a firmer voice, she added, "You got us out of there. You saved us."

Njeri shook her head. "What *you* did back there saved us, Koffi."

"I wasn't the only one to summon that dome," Koffi pointed out. "There were other darajas who helped."

Njeri shook her head. "I'm not talking about that. I'm talking about after, when the rest of us were spent and out of energy. I'm strong, but . . ." Njeri hesitated. "But you were stronger. You're the reason we got out of there."

Koffi was saved from responding as the others began to disembark from the wagon. Ano, Ekon, and Safiyah emerged first, followed by Zain and Makena. Koffi hesitated.

"The others?" she asked quietly. "Were there any . . . ?"

Makena shook her head. "We're all that's left."

Koffi had expected that answer, but that didn't make it any easier to hear it confirmed aloud. She remembered earlier, when Safiyah had said they had twenty-one people in their group. At least fourteen of those had been darajas, people who'd left Thornkeep with her because they'd wanted freedom and a new life. With the exception of Njeri, Zain, and Makena, they were all gone. She thought of Abeke, the woman who'd fed her and cared for her when she'd woken up this morning, even when she'd been difficult. Koffi hadn't been able to protect her, or the bald man with the golden earring, or the two darajas who'd smiled at her this morning. All those people had been alive this morning, and now they just . . . weren't. She wanted to cry, but the tears wouldn't come.

"May they rest eternal," she whispered.

"Listen up!"

Koffi's thoughts were interrupted as Ano clapped her hands and looked around the group. Aside from her slightly askew headwrap, the woman looked entirely calm and measured. "We've had a hard morning," she said steadily, "but I'm afraid we can't stay here either. Our rations are depleted, and we'll need to find food sooner than later. For now, *you two*"—she pointed at Zain and Njeri—"see if you can find any kindling for a fire. We may have difficulty starting one in these marshlands, but we have to try. Ekon?" She stared at her son, and Koffi thought she saw a hint of emotion. "Abeke's gone, so you'll have to manage our inventory. Determine how much food we have, then approximate how many days we have until we run out. *That* will help us set our new travel pace. And you, girl." She regarded Makena. "You're good with sewing, no? The wagon's canvas needs mending . . ."

It went like that for the next hour. Koffi didn't know whether to be relieved or insulted that, as Ano directed everyone else to build their new makeshift camp, the woman seemed to be very purposefully ignoring her. In fact, Ano didn't so much as look at her until they were seated around a small fire with sacks of rationed fruit and meat. Abruptly, she looked up from the flames.

"I want to understand something." She addressed the group without preamble. "Those gray *things*. What were they?"

"They're called the Untethered." It was Zain who answered, though his gaze stayed trained on the fire. He looked haunted. "They're inhabitants of Fedu's realm, beings he hasn't allowed to move on to the godlands. They're neither dead nor alive."

"What do you *mean*, neither dead nor—" Safiyah started to ask. Ano cut her off with a look.

"You said they're inhabitants of Fedu's realm," she pressed. "Yet they came to our camp, even though we left the Mistwood days ago. That doesn't make sense."

"I don't understand it either," said Zain. "To my knowledge, the Untethered have never left the Mistwood before. I don't know why they would now."

"Could Fedu have lost control of them?" Across the fire, Njeri still looked shaken, but her brows were now knitted in thought. "When he and Koffi fought, she injured him. What if the Untethered were able to overpower him and escape?"

"I don't think that's what's going on," said Koffi.

The entire group looked directly at her for the first time, as if her interjection finally gave them the permission to do so. It was Makena who spoke first.

"Koffi," she said cautiously, "what do you know?"

Koffi met the gaze of each person at the fire in turn. All of them wore the same expectant look, and the more intently they stared, waiting, the more distinctly Koffi had the feeling she was being cornered, trapped. *No.* The logical part of her brain quelled that idea. She *wasn't* trapped or cornered. These were people who cared about her, people who deserved the truth. She took a deep breath before speaking.

"I need to tell you all something," she started. "When I was still unconscious this morning, I had a strange dream." She stopped, considering. "Only, it wasn't really a dream. It felt like a nightmare, but it was real. In it, Fedu was able to speak to me."

"*Speak* to you?" Zain repeated. He looked disturbed.

"He was still injured from our fight," Koffi went on before she could be interrupted again. "And he told me that he still wants to move forward with his plan. But he said something else too." She squinted, trying to recall his exact words. "He said . . . that I was out of his physical grasp, but that he still had a hold on me. He said I'd do his bidding because he knew my weaknesses." She hesitated. "He also said that he would exploit those weaknesses."

Makena's expression was drawn. "What exactly do you think he meant by that?"

Koffi shook her head. "At first, I wasn't sure," she said. "At the end of the dream, I saw the Untethered and I thought that it was just part of the nightmare." She paused. "But now I think there was more to it. The Untethered are supposed to be in the Mistwood, under Fedu's control . . ."

"But now they're not," said Zain.

"Right." Koffi addressed the group. "And I don't think that's a coincidence. I think the Untethered weren't just let out of the Mistwood. I think they were *sent* out, by Fedu himself."

Ekon leaned forward. "He can do that?"

"He's desperate," said Koffi. "The Bonding is only a few weeks away, and he needs my power for his plan to work." Bitterly, she added, "He already knows that I hate when people are hurt because of me, and that's exactly what the Untethered are doing. They're killing indiscriminately. He's given them weapons. I think he believes that he can use them as a way to force my hand, to force me to return to him."

"We were able to get away from these so-called Untethered," said Ano, "but that doesn't mean they're not still chasing us, even as we speak."

No one had an answer for that.

"There's something else." It took every fiber of Koffi's being to make herself move, to pull up her sleeve and expose the marks on her shoulder and upper arm. She watched the varied expressions as she did—some looked intrigued at the sight of them while others seemed outright alarmed.

"What are those?" Zain asked.

"I'm not entirely sure," said Koffi. "They were on my body when I woke up this morning."

"Do they hurt?" asked Njeri. "They look . . ." She let the rest of her words trail off.

Koffi shook her head. "They don't hurt, but they've spread even since this morning. I think they might have something to do with the splendor in my body. It's been almost a month since I took it from Adiah, and it's been within me this entire time. I'm wondering if . . . if maybe these marks are a side effect of that."

There was a long pause in which no one said anything. Then Ekon stood. "That settles it," he said. There wasn't a trace of doubt or hesitation in his voice, and Koffi found herself yet again reminded of the way he'd been when she'd met him, when he'd been an inscrutable warrior. "As far as I'm concerned, there are now two very good reasons we need to get you to the Kusonga Plains so you can get rid of that stuff. We should go."

The reaction to his words was instant. Makena and Njeri stiffened. Zain stood too.

"I'm sorry," said Zain in a tone that suggested the very opposite, "but who exactly died and made *you* the emperor of the marshlands?"

A muscle in Ekon's jaw twitched. "*Excuse* me?"

"You're so eager to get Koffi to the Kusonga Plains," said Zain. "It's all you've talked about for the last few days. Tell me, what exactly happens when she gets there and deposits all that *stuff*, as you call it? Have you stopped even once to think about what'll happen to her afterward? What could happen to her ability as a daraja?"

Ekon glowered. "I don't care about her ability—"

"Of course you don't," Zain snapped. "*You're* not a daraja. *You* don't get it.*" He turned to address the rest of the group. "I am daraja-born, and so are Makena and Njeri. We were all raised to understand that our power is a *gift*, a fundamental part of our heritage—*who we are.*" He turned to face Koffi. "You've been denied your heritage all your life, and you've only just begun to learn about it. But in these last few weeks, I've seen what you can do with the power you have, Koffi. You might be the most power-ful daraja in generations." His expression softened. "Look, I know you and Ekon made a plan, but can you honestly tell me—after everything you've been through to try to understand and control your power—that you want to potentially just give it all up?"

"It's the only choice she has," said Ekon through gritted teeth. "Were you listening to what she said? Not only has Fedu released an undead army out into the world *because* of Koffi's power, but there are now physical marks on her body that are likely caused by it. It's clear, the splendor is dangerous for her to hold on to."

"I was listening," said Zain. There was a testiness in his voice. "But what *I* heard Koffi say was that Fedu is still injured because of her. She was powerful enough to take on a god, that means something."

Koffi found herself unwittingly recalling something else Fedu had said in her dream.

That *was divine work, exquisitely destructive.*

Ekon jutted his chin. "What are you saying?"

"I'm saying, with power like that, Koffi could potentially take Fedu on again," Zain concluded. "And I believe she could win. She just needs a little more time to hone her power."

"We don't *have* time," said Ekon. "The Bonding is in exactly three weeks."

"Koffi was only in Thornkeep for a few weeks, and that was more than enough time for her to make huge strides," Zain argued. He turned to Koffi then. "Tell him."

Koffi tried to speak but found she couldn't. The words she wanted to say were there. She knew Fedu's plan hinged on *her*, on using the very power resting in her body at this moment. The pragmatic thing to do to make sure he could never use it would be to take that option off the table as soon as possible by going through with her and Ekon's original plan. It meant she would lose the power that came with having so much splendor in her, but it would also keep the world safe. *That* was the right thing to do, but she couldn't make herself say that aloud. Something stopped her. She could remember, so vividly, making those plans with Ekon in the Greater Jungle all those weeks ago, but just as clearly, her mind cast back to the horrible things Fedu had done. She thought of the little girl he'd dangled by her hair just because he could; she thought of what he'd done to Zola in Thornkeep. She thought of all the people who'd died this morning simply because they were in Fedu's way. A part of her did want him to pay for that, even if she didn't want to admit it. Ekon and Zain were both watching her, waiting. She hesitated.

"I—"

"If Fedu gets to Koffi before she can get to the Kusonga Plains and dispose of the splendor in her body, it will jeopardize not only her life, but the life of every *non*-daraja on this continent." Ekon's eyes cut to Zain, blade-sharp. "I can see why that might not bother *you*, but some of us actually stand to lose something if

60

Fedu has his way and remakes this world." Koffi didn't miss the way he glanced at Ano and Safiyah.

Zain's drew in a sharp breath. "You know what I think?" he said in a new, lower voice. "I think you're jealous, of Koffi's power and what she can do with it—what you can't do."

At once Ekon's expression turned stony. "You're a fool," he said coldly.

"Maybe." Zain didn't miss a beat. "But I'd rather be a fool than a coward like *you*."

Koffi knew what was going to happen, but she still wasn't prepared for the speed at which Ekon launched himself at Zain, sending them both crashing into the mud.

"Ekon!" Safiyah jumped to her feet first. "Don't!"

If Ekon heard her, he gave no indication of it. He clenched his teeth and sank a fist into Zain's gut as they rolled, then reeled back as the daraja answered him with a punch of his own. In seconds, they were lost in a twisted mess of limbs and mud flying everywhere.

"Boys!" Ano shouted. "Stop this *at once!*"

Neither boy listened, and the fighting got uglier. Koffi winced as Zain landed another punch, this one right to Ekon's jaw. In response Ekon roared, then flipped Zain over so that he was held in a tight headlock.

They're going to kill each other, Koffi thought. *Or at least seriously* maim *each other.* She realized there was nothing she could do to stop it. In that moment, she felt the way she'd felt most of her life: utterly helpless.

No. A new, defiant voice in her mind pushed back against that resignation. *You're not helpless. Not anymore.* She reminded herself that she had *real* power now, power she could use.

Power she *would* use.

The splendor came to Koffi easily when she summoned it, and she relished the way her blood ran warm as it moved through her veins. In her periphery, she felt more than saw the rest of them turn to gape at her, but in that moment, she didn't care. All her focus was on Zain and Ekon. Slowly she raised her right hand, and the speckles of splendor near her palm grew dense, clustering together to form the silver-white shaft of a spear. It grew longer, until she saw a blade at its end. She raised it higher.

You can stop them, that defiant voice in her head instructed. *You're strong enough. You can stop them all on your own.*

Zain was still scrabbling in Ekon's headlock, but when his eyes fell on Koffi, he went limp.

"Koffi?" He choked in disbelief.

Ekon looked up too, and Koffi saw his expression change as his gaze went from her face to the splendor spear in her raised hand. He looked panicked.

"Koffi, *wait—*"

It was too late. Koffi barely flicked her wrist, and the spear went soaring through the air. It felt good, a natural sort of release. Ekon and Zain both scuttled out of the way just in time. The spear passed mere inches between them before striking the grass. There was a tremendous crack, a shudder in the earth violent enough to send everyone else toppling to the ground. The movement jolted something within Koffi, and she blinked, feeling very much like she'd woken from a dream. The strange voice that had occupied her mind left her as abruptly as it had come, and now the world felt clear again. Seconds passed as she stared at the scorched grass

62

a few yards away, and then a kind of comprehension set in. She'd thrown a *spear* at Ekon and Zain—a spear made of *splendor*. The same kind of spear she'd battled Fedu with.

The emotion that crawled up Koffi's back felt something like remorse, but uglier. Her stomach knotted itself over and over as the realization of what she'd done sank in, alongside the realization of what *could* have happened. She felt sick thinking about it.

"I . . ."

Everyone else was still on the ground and staring up at her, but no one was speaking. Koffi searched among their faces, waiting for someone to say something—*anything*—to break the horrible silence. No one did, and the blood in her veins began to pound like a goatskin drum. She saw the common sentiment: They were all staring at her, and they *all* looked afraid.

"Koffi?"

She was relieved when Ekon finally spoke, but his tone was distinctly subdued. "Your . . . your arm."

A coil of anxiety wound around Koffi's rib cage as she looked down at herself. It constricted tighter when she saw that the silvery marks that had previously been limited to the top of her arm had now spread nearly to her elbow. They were brighter too, eerier.

Fedu's intrusive voice crept into her mind without warning. He sounded amused.

Are you so sure those friends *would stand by you if they knew how dangerous you really are?*

No. There was pounding sensation near Koffi's temple; it was getting harder and harder to breathe. She swallowed.

No. No. No.

"Koffi." Njeri picked herself up, but her voice sounded too distant. She extended a hand. "Koffi, it's okay. Take a deep breath. It was an accident, we know that."

The words were kind, so Koffi didn't know why they set her on edge. She finally decided that it was because, despite their kindness, there was a guarded quality in Njeri's voice. She was still looking at Koffi with a visible wariness.

Like she *was* dangerous.

"It's okay, Koffi," Njeri repeated.

This time Koffi found herself backing away—from Njeri, from the rest of them, from the horrible disquiet thickening the air. She cast a glance over her shoulder, trying and failing to keep her breath even. It was to no avail.

"Koffi." It was Makena's turn to rise. "Please. Don't—"

Koffi never heard the rest of her friend's words. Without a second glance, she turned on her heel and ran as hard and fast as her legs would carry her into the marshlands.

The MAIDENS of KUSONGA

AKANDE
Year 890

This time of year, the Ndefu River is perfect for a swim.

From its banks, I watch with no small amount of envy as two girls who look to be about my age hike their tunics up to their knees and wade into its shallows a few yards downriver. In no time, they're splashing each other. Their white tunics grow wet, leaving less and less to the imagination . . .

"Akande!"

My head snaps up, and I find Babu already standing in the center of our tiny raft with an oar in hand. He looks impossibly old in this morning light, less like a real man and more like a leathery scarecrow with a patch of fluffy white hair on top. His looks from me to the girls downriver, exasperated. I have the deeply distressing feeling he knows *exactly* where my mind just was. My cheeks warm.

"Uh, I was—"

"Let's go," he says gruffly, "we don't have all day."

I suppress a groan. *This* wasn't the way my day off was supposed to go. When I'd woken up this morning, my plans had included a trip to the market with Izachar and maybe a dip in the river. My grandfather had wrecked those plans like an ox in a crowded pottery shop. When his frown deepens, I jump from the banks and onto the raft to join him. He pushes off into deeper water, and I glance over my shoulder one last woeful time as we drift away from the pretty girls.

"Stay sharp, boy." Again, my babu yanks me back to the present. "You're going to need your wits about you today."

Admittedly, the words inspire a sense of intrigue. Most of my days spent with Babu involve a lecture, lessons on regional history or government, or whatever else the old man deems important. We've spent plenty of time alongside the Ndefu, but never before have we crossed it.

"Babu," I ask as we near the river's opposite side, "where are we going?"

"You'll see when we get there." My grandfather's oar is ready. He banks our raft, and together we disembark. My gaze casts back across the river, to my home in Kugawanya. It's a bustling port city, a place buzzing with near-constant noise and life. Not so on this side of the river. Here the only thing that occupies the land is long golden savanna grass. It's quiet, and even the air smells different.

"Come!" Babu wastes no time parting the grass and stepping into it. "Follow me and stay close."

We walk together for one hour, then another, well into the glaring heat of midday. The sky above—blue and cloudless—

66

offers little in the way of protection as the sun rises. Sweat begins to slick my satchel's leather shoulder strap, making it slippery and uncomfortable as we press on. The air dries the farther we move from the river, and after a while, I find my lips feel cracked no matter how many times I run my tongue over them or sip from my gourd.

"Babu, how much farther?"

"We're almost there," he says without looking back. "It's just up ahead."

I remain doubtful. Around us, the grasslands are endless, save for the odd cluster of acacia trees. Abruptly, Babu stops short.

"Ah," he says. "Here we are."

I search, then have to work to hide my disappointment. There's nothing that sets this particular spot in the grasslands apart from what we've been trekking through for hours. I'm just about to sit down and take a swig from my gourd, and then—

Then I *see* them.

At first, I don't understand how I could have missed the four lionesses sitting beneath the acacia trees some yards from us; they're easily the biggest I've ever seen. Slowly, though, I do understand. I missed them initially because their tawny hides are almost the exact same color as the grasslands, a perfect camouflage. I swallow.

"Babu!" I keep my voice low. "There are four *lionesses* just up ahead!"

My grandfather smiles. "I see them just as well as you can, Akande."

"You—?" I open my mouth, then freeze as one of the lionesses turns to look at us. Even at a distance, I can tell that her eyes are as big as my balled fists, the same color as liquid amber, and piercing. I only exhale when she looks away.

"There is an old tale," Babu whispers, "of a cruel and greedy farmer who mistreated his four daughters. One night, in desperation, they fled to the Kusonga Plains and sought refuge here, praying each day that the goddess Itaashe would grant them her protection." He sighed. "For their courage and their piety, the goddess answered their prayers, but not in the way they expected. She turned the four young women into immortal beings, lionesses, and charged them with protecting these lands from those who would harm them. She named them the Maidens of Kusonga." He pauses, giving me a significant look. "*Some* say those lionesses still serve her to this day."

I look from the lionesses to my grandfather. "You mean . . . those are the *same* lionesses, from all those years ago?"

Babu winks. "Who can say? It's just a story I heard."

I stare at the lionesses, awestruck.

"We're going to move closer now."

"What?" I look up at Babu. "Is that safe?"

"It'll be fine, boy." My babu's gaze fixes ahead. "Just follow my lead."

We approach the lionesses together, albeit slowly. They don't move as we draw nearer. My whole body trembles with each step; I'm close enough now to see *exactly* how big these lionesses are, how easily they could tear me apart. One of them licks her black lips, and I catch a glimpse of several white teeth, each the length of my longest finger. I wince. Finally, we stop several feet from them, and my grandfather extends his arms. For a moment, I don't understand what he's doing. Then he inclines his head, and gestures for me to do the same.

"*Bow*, Akande." My grandfather's voice is uncharacteristically soft, near reverent.

I hesitate, less than enthused about looking away from the lionesses, even for a second. But when my babu nods in encouragement, I extend my own arms and bow too. When I raise my head, I find that all four of the lionesses are watching me.

"Good." Babu straightens and nods in approval. "Now we may ride them."

"We may *what*?" I don't quite manage to keep the hysteria from my voice as it cracks.

Babu's smile turns rueful. "What? You thought I brought you here just to *look* at them?"

"But—"

He doesn't wait for my response, and instead approaches the lioness nearest to him and gives her a small second bow. "May I?" he asks.

Lionesses don't speak, I know that. Still, I'm almost certain I catch a glint of recognition in the lioness's eyes as she rises and stretches like a common house cat. Then she lowers her body enough for Babu to hoist himself onto her back and kick his leg over. From his new vantage point, he looks down at me.

"Well? Are you coming, boy?"

Babu may be the old man here, but I'm the one who inches toward the remaining lionesses like a tortoise stuck in the mud. All three of them are still watching me with an intensity that makes me squirm. It occurs to me, as I stop before them, that I have no idea which to pick.

"Sorry." My voice is a squeak. "I don't know how to—" I go quiet as one of the lionesses abruptly rises. Up close, she seems larger than the other two, but it's impossible to tell if that's real or just in my head. The earth shudders with each step she takes toward me, and involuntarily I start to pray to the gods.

Please. Please don't eat me.

When I open my eyes, the lioness is inches from me. Her honey-gold gaze evaluates me. Then she turns and unmistakably lowers her haunches. I stare at her, shocked.

"Go on, Akande," says Babu from his own mount.

Carefully, I press my palms into the lioness's back. Her fur is coarse, but also strangely soft. I wait a beat before kicking my leg over the way Babu did, and at once she rises to her full height. I must be at *least* three feet off the ground.

Then, without warning, she leaps.

Instinctively, I lean forward and wrap my arms around the lioness's neck as she begins to canter across the grasslands, accelerating with unnatural speed. My eyes water and sting, the wind tears through my hair and my satchel, but I'm too scared to do anything but keep holding on. Everything around us blurs as she runs faster.

"Akande!"

I turn my head at the sound of my name and start as Babu draws level with me, riding the other lioness with an ease I recognize as practiced. There's an unmistakably impish quality in his expression.

"I admit," he shouts over the wind, "I thought you'd be faster!"

"What?"

In answer, he leans forward with new focus, and then he and

70

his lioness take off, gliding as though the wind itself is carrying them.

"Hey!"

I imitate that movement, pressing forward until my torso is nearly flat against the lioness's neck, and together we bolt forward. In no time, we've caught up to Babu, but we don't stop when we reach him. Instead, we shoot past, and a whoop escapes me. Above, the sun is still blistering; I feel its rays on my back, on the lioness's flanks as her muscles flex and tense beneath me. The thing is, I don't mind anymore. By the time she finally slows, I'm breathless. I slide off her back, and when I bow a second time, I do so unafraid.

"Thank you!"

I don't know if she understands, but the lioness *seems* to nod before padding over to a nearby water hole to drink. A few minutes later, Babu and his lioness catch up. My grandfather looks highly amused as he dismounts.

"I take it you enjoyed yourself?"

"That was . . ." My mind is racing, trying to memorize all the tiny details of the ride. "That was *incredible!*"

"I'm glad you think so," Babu says with a chuckle. "I felt the same way the first time I came to the plains."

That's enough to catch my attention. "You knew what to do," I say slowly. "You've ridden a lioness before."

"The first time it was with my grandmother, *your* great-great-grandmother," says Babu. "She brought me to these plains when I was about your age."

"But . . ." I pause, confused. "How did *she* know how?"

"Come." Babu gestures, and together we walk over to the water hole and settle at its edge. Our reflections ripple on its blue-green surface. Minutes pass before he speaks again. "My grandmother knew about the lionesses on this plain because she was taught by her father, who was taught by his grandfather, and so on," he explained. "In truth, our family has been coming to these plains for generations. Our ancestors formed a connection to them, a connection of blood, bone, and soul."

I lean forward. "How?"

"By taking the energy from these plains and letting it move through them," said Babu, "they made this land a part of them, a part of their very essence."

I sit back, frowning. "I'm sorry, Babu. I still don't understand."

My grandfather's lips press together in thought. I recognize that look. It's the same one I've seen during our lessons, when he's trying to explain something difficult. He steeples his fingers, then rests his chin on them. "You know what darajas are, don't you, Akande?"

I hesitate. This wasn't the question I was expecting. "Sure," I say tentatively. "They do magic."

I'm almost relieved to see Babu's expression turn wry. He looks more like himself.

"Not quite," he says. "Darajas are special, living conduits between the earth and the divine. They are a part of my heritage." He gives me a meaningful look. "And they're a part of yours."

It takes a half second for the words to register. "You mean, I'm . . . ?"

"A daraja, yes."

"But . . ." I look down at my own body. Nothing's changed, but I feel suddenly strange. "But I don't *have* any powers or abilities."

72

"A daraja's power can lie dormant for years," says Babu. "In our family, manifestation often happens near or around puberty." One corner of his mouth quirks. "Judging by your keen interest in those young ladies by the river this morning, I think it's safe for us to deduce that you have now passed that particular threshold. I expect your power will make itself known quite soon."

The words are like seeds, and from them a thousand new questions sprout in my mind. I stare into the water hole's reflection again, half expecting to look different already. "My parents," I say after a moment. "Do they know?"

When I look up, Babu's nodding. "They were the ones who thought it best I speak to you." My grandfather's expression softens. "I know it's a lot to digest," he says, "but you don't have to figure it all out on your own. I'll be here to help you."

"You won't." The words escape me before I can stop them.

Babu frowns. "Sorry?"

I stare down at my hands, flexing my fingers so that I don't have to look at him. "You *won't* always be here," I say quietly. "One day, you'll . . ." I can't make myself finish that sentence. I'm still looking at the ground, but I feel Babu staring at me. For a long time, he doesn't speak.

"I will die one day," he admits, "that is a certainty. But that doesn't mean I will *leave* you, Akande, not in the ways that really matter. There's another reason I brought you here. You, me, our ancestors, we're all connected to this place. When you come here, you'll always be able to find me, if you know how to look."

I don't realize I'm biting down on the inside of my cheek until it starts to hurt. "I still don't want you to go, Babu."

My grandfather rolls his eyes. "Well, I'm not dead yet, am I?"

I'm relieved to hear that his voice has returned to its usual gruffness. "And I'm not going anywhere until I've at least taught you the fundamentals about what it means to *be* a daraja, and how to use your power when it does come."

I sit up straighter. "You mean, you're going to teach me?"

Babu juts his chin. "Of course I am. I won't have *you* fouling up generations of respectable legacy with knuckleheaded tendencies."

"When?" I'm so excited I stand. "When can I start training?"

"Now." Babu's still frowning at me, but I catch the smallest shadow of a smile. "We start *right now*."

CHAPTER 5

BIGGER FISH

KOFFI

The marshlands grew darker as Koffi ran.

Behind her, she heard several voices calling, begging her to stop, but in her mind, all she saw were her friends' faces, and the same fear etched into every single one. It occurred to her as she sprinted away that they hadn't simply been afraid of what she'd *done*, they'd been afraid of *her*. She'd even managed to scare herself. Every time she thought about what could have happened if she'd thrown that splendor spear just a few inches closer to either Zain or Ekon, her lungs grew tight.

Her gaze dropped to her arm again, to the marks now covering half of it. If what had just happened wasn't reason enough to feel panicked, these marks certainly were. They were getting worse, there was no doubt about it now, and whatever they were, they seemed to be directly connected to her use of the splendor. Yet again, Fedu's voice touched her conscience, relentless.

There are few in this world who can stand in the face of real, absolute power.

Koffi ran harder, but she couldn't outrun those words, or the onslaught of intrusive thoughts trailing behind them. The worst part of this wasn't that the god of death's voice had now become a semi-permanent fixture in her mind; it was the fact that some tiny part of her was beginning to wonder if he was right, if she *was* a danger, to herself and to others. It was a question she wasn't ready to face.

She ignored the aching in her calves as she picked up her pace, running until she found herself deep in the marshlands. Around her, the fog that seemed to characterize the region churned cool and thick, drawing a shiver from her skin as she peered into it. From here, she no longer saw any trace of the rest of the group or the wagon. A sudden chill that had nothing to do with the temperature shuddered through her body. She whirled as a blade of grass tickled the back of her leg, and jumped again when she felt a brush against her arm. Her pulse quickened. She'd been so intent on running that she hadn't stopped to think about how dangerous a place like this was. It occurred to her that it hadn't been wise to run so far from the others, and yet try as she might, she couldn't temper the unsettling feeling that she wasn't entirely alone. They'd ridden in the wagon for hours, long enough, she reasoned, to outpace the Untethered if they were still being pursued, but she was still uneasy. Slowly she turned in a circle, looking from the iron-gray sky above to the muddy ground at her feet. That was when she saw it: a startle of bright yellow, vivid against the otherwise dull brown marshland grass all around her. She took a step forward, puzzled, then just as quickly froze again. Her hands grew clammy as understanding dawned on her.

She was looking down at a massive snake.

The exact size of it was difficult to discern in the grass, but she could see enough to tell that the creature's body was thicker than her own leg. Its scales were the color of an afternoon sun, interrupted only by thick bands of black. Koffi's skin prickled as she stared at it, torn between curiosity and wariness. Her knowledge of snakes was, admittedly, limited, but she knew a snake of that size was likely quite fast and would fear very little. Every instinct honed from her years at the Night Zoo came back to her in an instant. Carefully, she took a step away from it, moving as slowly and quietly as she could in the opposite direction. Snakes weren't *typically* aggressive animals; they'd only attack if they were provoked. *Or hungry.* She tried not to think about the latter possibility. In real danger, she could try to use the splendor, but . . . something in her hesitated. She felt less and less sure of her control over her own power, and less sure that she knew what would happen if she used it.

She retreated farther, fast enough to continue putting distance between herself and the snake, but not so fast that she'd trigger its predatory response. Seconds passed, and she dared glance over her shoulder. A few more steps to the left, and she'd be far enough away to make a run for it; she just had to—

The grass suddenly rustled, and Koffi went very still.

With horror, she watched as the snake's body coiled and its head slowly rose above the grass to stare directly at her. It was even bigger than she'd guessed, but that wasn't what transfixed her. No, what held her in place, rendering her immobile, was the creature's eyes. They were coin-sized, glassy, and colored the deep, verdant green of an emerald, or . . . of leaves.

Leaves in a jungle.

No. Koffi shook her head as a thought entered her mind. She'd seen a snake like this one before, but . . . but it wasn't possible, it *couldn't* be. Unless . . .

"Hello, Koffi."

Koffi started. She knew that voice and who it belonged to. She turned.

Badwa, the goddess of the jungle, was standing before her while her emblematic snake coiled near her feet. She no longer wore a modest black tunic, as she had the first time she and Koffi had met in the depths of the Greater Jungle. Instead, the goddess had donned leather armor trimmed in gold from head to toe. Her braided hair was tied in an elaborate bun atop her head, and her brown eyes shone with a fierceness that hadn't been there before. She was truly formidable, frightening.

"Badwa?" Koffi only dared whisper the goddess's true name. "Is that . . . It's really you?"

Some of Badwa's fierceness faded as she looked down at Koffi. "It is."

"How?" Koffi looked around, confused. "I thought gods and goddesses couldn't enter each other's realms?" They were certainly nowhere near any jungle or forest the goddess could claim.

"I cannot enter without *consent.*" Badwa's smile became more familiar as it warmed. "Fortunately, my older sister granted me permission to enter these lands many ages ago. I have been waiting for you."

Koffi found herself overcome with an entirely new wave of emotions as those words sank in. Her gaze dropped, and for several seconds she found she couldn't quite look at the goddess. Certainly, she was glad to see her, relieved even, but a part of her was also angry that Badwa had availed herself now instead of earlier, when they *really* could have used her help.

"Something is troubling you," said Badwa.

"I'm fine." Koffi made herself look up. "It's just . . . you've changed."

Badwa paused, and Koffi didn't miss the moment the goddess's gaze moved to her arm. "As have you," she said after a beat.

Koffi looked down at her own arm again, at the silver marks shining bright against her skin. Her chin started to tremble and she found that she couldn't make it stop. Finally, something in her gave way.

"I'm so sorry, Badwa," she whispered.

Badwa looked confused. "Sorry?"

"Everything's gone wrong," said Koffi, hanging her head. "I failed you."

"*Koffi.*" Badwa's voice was firm, but not unkind. "Sit with me."

Koffi looked down at the ground around them. There was mud everywhere and, in truth, the last thing she wanted to do was sit in it, but when Badwa sat and gestured for her to do the same, she obeyed. She was surprised to find that the earth beneath her had become dry and warm.

"I want you to take a deep breath," said Badwa, "just as we used to practice, and try to acknowledge your emotions. Then I want you to tell me how you *think* you've failed me."

Koffi hesitated. Back when she'd been in the Greater Jungle

with Badwa, they'd done this exercise any number of times. A daraja's power was based on emotional intelligence, on acknowledging one's truest self. It had been hard before, it always was, but that was nothing in comparison to how it felt now. When she closed her eyes, she saw Fedu. She saw his smile, heard his voice.

We are alike.

She shuddered.

"Koffi?"

When she opened her eyes again, Badwa was studying her.

"Just *try*."

Koffi took a deep breath and closed her eyes again, this time making an effort to focus. Fedu's face was still there in her mind, and she could still hear the lingering echo of his voice, but she pushed both away, and imagined building a wall to keep them out.

"Open your heart," Badwa murmured, "and acknowledge how you really feel. If you find you cannot be honest with anyone else, be honest at least with yourself."

Koffi screwed her eyes tighter, trying to concentrate. At once she was in darkness again, alone as different tides of emotion lapped against her. She recognized some of them—old grief, new fear, the ever-present anxiety—but there were new emotions too. She thought about the way she'd felt as she'd battled Fedu, and forced herself to name that feeling. *Powerful.* She'd felt truly *powerful* for the first time in her life. Then she thought back to the way she'd felt just a short while ago when she'd thrown the splendor spear at Zain and Ekon, the way she'd felt when all the people she'd thought were her friends had looked at her in horror. She'd felt isolated, alone, and misunderstood. She breathed in through her nose and out through her mouth before she spoke aloud.

"I feel . . . overwhelmed," she said quietly.

"Why?" Badwa pressed.

Koffi opened her eyes. "Because there was a *plan*. Ekon and I were supposed to get Adiah to the Kusonga Plains, but she didn't make it. Then I tried to get Fedu to take me in her place, but that just ended up failing, and now people have died, and the Untethered are free, and I have these marks on my arm and—" She caught herself. "And I feel like it's *all my fault*." She was embarrassed to feel tears slicking down her cheeks and pawed them away quickly. The goddess paused, looking distinctly sad.

"You are strong, Koffi," she said, "but even *you* aren't strong enough to bear the world's weight alone. Eventually you will break."

"I already *feel* broken," Koffi admitted. Her voice cracked. "I'm tired all the time, I look different, and my arm . . ." She glanced at it again, and when she looked up, she noticed Badwa's expression had changed. The goddess now looked solemn.

"I warned you that holding splendor in your body had consequences."

"They're getting *worse*," Koffi lamented. "Every time I channel the splendor, they spread."

"I have no doubt that they will continue to," said Badwa. "Keeping the splendor within your body goes against its nature. The longer it stays within you, the more it will become a *part* of you, just as it did with Adiah."

Koffi hesitated. "Will it turn *me* into a Shetani?"

Badwa shook her head. "Splendor is unique to each daraja it comes into contact with. You and Adiah, though similar in some ways, are not the same person, nor do you have the same affinity. I doubt that it would manifest in you exactly the same way it manifested in her." Her expression grew more stern. "But there *will* be consequences the longer you keep it within you, Koffi, and they will be dire. You must be more careful and avoid channeling any more of the splendor."

Koffi looked up at the goddess. "I battled him," she said quietly. "I battled Fedu, and I *won*."

Badwa tensed. "Then you are even more powerful than he thought."

"Ekon wants me to get to get rid of the splendor as soon as I can," she went on. "But Zain thinks I should keep it and try to beat Fedu once and for all." She looked up, letting the unspoken question linger in the air between them.

"It is possible that the splendor in your body will make you strong enough to take on my brother a second time," said Badwa. "It is just as likely that another ordeal like that could destroy you."

Koffi's gaze dropped back to her hands. "I don't know what to do," she said. "None of these paths forward seem like good ones at all."

Badwa sat back, thoughtful. "There once was a dragonfly who lived by a pond and feared being eaten by a catfish. One day, he decided to do something about it."

"What?" asked Koffi.

Badwa's eyes twinkled. "He appealed to a bigger fish, who swallowed the first one whole."

Koffi frowned. "What does that have to do with anything?"

Badwa gave her a patient look. "Imagine *you* are the dragon-fly," she said. "And my brother is the fish in the pond. You fear him, so what do you do?"

Koffi gnawed at her lip. "You're saying . . . I should appeal to a bigger fish, but what's bigger than Fedu?"

"Not what," said Badwa. *"Who."*

It took a moment for the words to dawn on Koffi. "The others," she repeated. "You're talking about the other gods."

Badwa nodded. "For years, my brothers and sisters have removed themselves from the affairs of mortals, but now, in his desperation, Fedu has violated his sacred duty to his realm. He has freed the Untethered and, in doing so, disrupted a natural order as ancient as we are." She leaned forward. "I believe that, like me, my brothers and sisters already sense this and understand that something momentous is coming." She gave Koffi a look. "You know that something is coming too."

"The next Bonding," said Koffi. "It's only three weeks away."

Badwa nodded. "On his own, Fedu is powerful, maybe more powerful than you. But against the combined power of my siblings and me . . ."

"The five of you could do it," said Koffi. *"You* could destroy him."

"We can do more than that," said Badwa slowly. "It is possible that the five of us could help you remove the splendor from your body too."

Koffi's pulse quickened. "You could?"

"We could," said Badwa. Her expression shifted again, and she looked more serious. "I must warn you, Koffi: Convincing my siblings to help you commit what some of them will see as fratricide will not be easy, no matter how noble your justification."

"What about you?" Koffi asked. "Could you help us convince them?"

"I can help with my brother Tyembu. He is in the west, and farthest away from here," said Badwa. She looked sad. "I'm afraid that's all I can offer. I have a duty to protect my realm, particularly in times of great peril. Even now, it is unguarded in my absence and at great risk. You will have to find and persuade the rest of them on your own."

"How?" asked Koffi. "I don't even know where to start."

One of Badwa's brows rose. "I believe your affinity uniquely equips you for finding the things you seek, does it not?"

Koffi steepled her fingers. "It does, but . . . I've never even tried to find a person before. You're saying I could use it to find a god?"

Badwa smiled. "Try."

Koffi bowed her head and tried to focus. She had practiced using the splendor to find things plenty of times with Zain while they'd been imprisoned in Thornkeep, but in that environment, Zain had always showed her what she was looking for first. He'd present an apple or a book, then hide it. She'd always had a clear image to focalize. She didn't have any images of the other gods. She swallowed.

"I can't see them," she said. "I don't know how to find what I've never seen."

Her eyes were still closed, but she heard Badwa's voice.

"You've never seen my other siblings," she said, "but you've seen parts of them, the things they cherish, their symbols."

Koffi screwed her eyes tighter and tried to find reason in Badwa's words. "I don't know what you mean."

"You do, Koffi," said the goddess. "Trust yourself, trust what you know."

Koffi sighed. What *did* she know? Growing up, she'd known about the six gods, she'd prayed to them, but she and her mother had never been allowed to visit them at the temple. It had been her mother who, over the years, had painstakingly carved a crude statuette of each god's patron animal—a heron, a crocodile, a jackal, a serpent, a dove, and a hippo. They weren't themselves gods, but they were symbols of them, the closest things her people had. Koffi started.

The symbols.

"Badwa," she said. "Can I use the symbols of the gods to find them?"

Badwa nodded.

Excitement surged through Koffi as she tried to picture those statuettes. The first one that came to mind was the crocodile, the symbol of the water goddess Amakoya. She homed in on that, letting the splendor do the rest. She was surprised to feel a familiar pull in her core, small but undeniable.

North, something inside her goaded. *Head north.*

"I figured it out, Badwa!" said Koffi. She opened her eyes. "I have to head north!"

The goddess's smile grew. "Well done."

"I can do this!" Koffi jumped to her feet. "I can use my power to find them, one by one, and I can do it before the Bonding."

She expected to see approval in the goddess's face, but

something in her had shifted slightly. In a quieter voice, Badwa said, "You understand that by using the splendor to find my siblings, there may be adverse consequences?"

"I understand," Koffi said quickly. She knew Badwa's warning was sincere, but already her mind was racing with new possibilities. She'd thought there were only three paths forward, all of them bleak. Now there was a chance to find bigger fish, to get help. There was a chance to beat Fedu once and for all. Badwa's expression was impassive as she stood.

"Then I wish you good fortune," she said, "and hope that destiny favors you."

Koffi's heart was pounding again, but this time it wasn't with fear, but some new emotion. It took her a moment to name it. It was *hope*. She hesitated. "Will I see you again?"

A small smile touched Badwa's lips. "You will. Take care of yourself, Koffi." She looked over Koffi's shoulder at the marshlands that surrounded them. Koffi followed her gaze. When she looked back, she found that the goddess was already gone.

CHAPTER 6

WOUNDS

EKON

Few monsters had lived in Ekon's mind for as long as his anxiety had.

It had made a home there when he was a small boy, gathering up his insecurities and doubts and fears like a bird collecting twigs and leaves for a nest. Over time, it had settled there, feeding and sharpening its beak with each passing year. Time had taught Ekon his anxiety's patterns; he knew its movements and habits almost as well as he knew himself. He recognized the telltale moments when anxiety was poised to attack him.

That made it no easier when it did.

From the ground, he watched as Koffi ran, disappearing fast into the fog as others called after her. A sense of helplessness burgeoned within him, and the surrounding world began to fuzz at its edges. In his periphery, he saw Zain rise, but something stopped him from doing the same. He felt a strange sensation akin to a person sitting on his chest, and couldn't ignore the fear of suffocation, though a distant logic *told* him that it was impossible. He opened his mouth, trying and failing to utter words. Instead, he made a choking sound. The fuzziness around him was worsening by the second, and through his tunneled vision, his gaze met Ano's.

"Ekon?" Her voice sounded muffled. He saw an understanding register in her expression. *"Ekon!"*

His name was the last thing Ekon heard before he slumped over in the grass and detached entirely. In the new bleary darkness, he thought he heard someone shouting; then he felt more than one person trying to lift him from the mud. In the back of his mind, he cringed with embarrassment.

Don't touch me, he wanted to say. *I'm sweaty. I'm covered in mud.* The words still wouldn't come.

A buried memory resurfaced then, and at once Ekon found himself back at the Temple of Lkossa. He'd been so small the first time he'd had a real panic attack. In contrast, the boys who'd found him in one of the temple's corridors had seemed so *big.* Ekon still remembered the way they'd doubled over and laughed, mimicking him as he'd scrabbled at his neck and gasped for air.

"Weirdo!" one of them had shouted.

"Freak!" another taunted.

It had been Brother Ugo's auspicious arrival that had saved him. Ekon still remembered the old man's anger as he'd rounded the corner and taken in the scene before him.

"Disgraceful!" His voice had trembled with righteous fury as he'd berated the older boys. "You would treat another with such cruelty here, in this hallowed place? Your forefathers would be ashamed!" He'd waited until the humiliated boys had slunk off before turning to Ekon. "*Breathe*, boy. You're going to be all right."

It had taken some time, but Ekon had eventually found his breath again. With not a small amount of effort, the old man had lowered to his knees and taken Ekon by both shoulders.

"There will always be those who can only feel strong by trying to make others feel weak," he said softly, "but you are not weak, Ekon Okojo. Your strength is in your bones and in your blood, and no one can take that from you. Promise me you'll always remember that."

Ekon's fingernails dug into the meat of his palm as the darkness abated, and he came back to the present with a jolt. He didn't want to keep thinking about Brother Ugo, but it was easier said than done. After his father had died, Brother Ugo had been the closest thing he and Kamau had had to a father. It was hard to reconcile that man, the one who'd been so kind, with who he actually was: a ruthless god. He wondered now how much of what the real Brother Ugo had said to him as a boy had been sincere, and how much had merely been part of molding him into something he could use.

His eyes slowly opened, and he found himself propped against several sacks from the wagon; he was only a few feet from a small fire. The rest of the group had busied themselves perhaps a little too deliberately with organizing things in and around the wagon, but Ano was standing across from him, staring.

"What?" asked Ekon.

Ano's lips thinned. "Don't 'what' me, boy."

"I'm fine."

"You're *not*." The words were firm but not unkind. "Listen to me carefully," she said. "I want you to move three parts of your body. Don't overthink it, just move the first three that come to mind."

Ekon paused. Three parts of his body. *Three.* He could do that. He flexed his fingers, his toes, then he scrunched his nose.

"Very good," said Ano. "Now tell me three things you *hear.*"

Ekon closed his eyes, and the world distilled. He listened to the light crackle of the fire, a gentle breeze blowing across the marshlands, and the snort of the mule. He opened his eyes again. "I hear the fire, the breeze, and the mule."

Ano nodded. "Last, tell me three things you *see.*"

Ekon was ready this time. "I see the wagon, the fire, and you."

Ano bent to squeeze his shoulder. "You did well. Feel better?"

"I . . ." Ekon frowned. "Actually, I . . . do?" He started. Only now did he realize she'd asked him to identify *three* things *three* times. "How did you know to do that?"

The corner of Ano's lips quirked. "I've had plenty of time to practice on myself."

It took a moment for Ekon to process the meaning behind her words. "You get panic attacks?" he asked incredulously.

"Don't look so surprised," she said wryly. "I've learned to manage them, but when I was a little girl . . ." She looked off into the marshlands. "I suspect it's one of many things we share."

A silence fell between them that Ekon didn't know what to do with. He made himself stare at the wagon, but still felt it when Ano's gaze returned to him.

"Do you mind if I sit?" she asked after a moment.

His panic attack had abated, but in its place there was a new type of unease as he made himself look back at Ano, at his *mother.*

The term still felt strange. Too late, he realized he was taking too long to answer her question.

"Sure."

Ano settled beside him, though Ekon appreciated that she seemed to take care not to sit too close.

"How are you feeling, *really*?" Her voice was uncharacteristically soft.

"I'm okay," said Ekon.

"Good." Ano nodded slowly. "That's . . . good."

They both stared into the fire, long enough for Ekon to realize that the polite thing to do would have been for him to ask Ano how *she* was doing. It didn't matter. She spoke again.

"I still can't believe they're gone," she murmured. "Thabo, Obioma, Abeke, Kontar. It doesn't feel real."

At this, Ekon softened just slightly. He may not have known the members of the Enterprise for as long as Ano had, but he'd traveled with them long enough to care about them. A stab of pain twisted in his gut as he remembered Thabo's hearty laugh; Kontar and his love of especially pungent spices; Abeke and their mutual love of numbers. His dealings with the Enterprise had begun as a matter of convenience, but along the way it'd become more than that. They'd been the first group of people to accept him not only as he was, but as he *could* be. They'd even gone as far as inviting him to join their crew officially, to help with operations. It had been the first chance he'd ever had to spend his time doing what made him truly happy.

"I'm sorry for your loss," said Ekon in earnest. The words were harder to say aloud than he'd anticipated.

"As am I." Ano bowed her head. "They were like family to me."

Ekon didn't want to bristle at those words, but he couldn't help it. He said what he was thinking before he could stop himself. "Guess your first one wasn't good enough."

The look on Ano's face almost made him regret what he'd said. He saw a flash of pain before her expression hardened. When she spoke again, her voice was brusque.

"You may never understand it," she said quietly, "but I did what I did because I truly believed it was best for you and for your brother at the time. I thought it was the best way to keep you *safe*."

"By abandoning us."

"Asafa was still alive!" she said fiercely. "Little boys need their fathers much more than they need their mothers. I figured—"

"That's not true."

"I'm sorry?"

"That's *not true*." Ekon said the words so quietly, he wasn't sure she would hear them. "Kamau and I needed you. We needed *both* of our parents."

"I know that now." Ano's voice trembled. "And if you think I don't face a punishment for what I did, Ekon, know that I do. I will spend the rest of my life regretting that I wasn't there for you and Kamau. I will always wonder what our lives could have been, and I'll always crave the memories I robbed myself of, the years I didn't see. The wounds from that loss will never really heal."

Ekon was furious to feel tears stinging his eyes and threatening to fall. He didn't want to feel bad, but that didn't seem to matter to his heart. He blinked hard and let his fingers tap faster against his kneecap.

One-two-three. One-two-three. One-two-three.

He would not cry, he would not show emotion—not in front of

her. Ano might be his mother, but in so many ways, she was still a stranger to him. He turned to blink the tears away. When he faced her again, he made sure to keep his voice firm.

"I'm sorry you're in pain," he said through gritted teeth. "But that doesn't change what you did. *Or* how I feel about it."

Ano sighed, and the gesture seemed to take another toll. For several seconds, there was silence between them. "No," she said with some resignation. "I don't expect it does. We can remove the arrow from the tree, but we can never completely remove the hole it leaves behind." She pressed her fingertips to her lips, thoughtful. "I know it may take time—it may take the rest of my life—but I want you to know, Ekon, that I'm here for you *now*. And I hope someday to be there for your brother too."

Ekon didn't know what to say to that either. The words ruffled him and drew out even more complicated emotions. He was angry, upset, frustrated, and . . . though he didn't want to admit it, a small part of him was hopeful. The family he'd had as a boy, the blurry one he only faintly remembered now, was long gone. He knew that, and he'd accepted it. But if what Ano—his mother—had said was true, it meant that maybe there was hope for a *different* kind of family someday, if they all made it out of this. He was afraid to let himself hope for that, but he still did. Hope was stubborn that way.

"Okay," he said noncommittally.

"Now, as your mother, I want to ask you about something *else*." Ano threw him a sidelong glance, looking much more like herself. "*Why* did you put your hands on that boy earlier?"

Ekon hadn't been expecting the abrupt shift in the conversation. "Huh?"

"*That* one." Ano nodded toward the place where Zain was sitting with Njeri and Makena, then looked back at Ekon. "I think you may have a permanent crease in your forehead. You scowl every time you look at him."

"I do *not*." When Ekon realized he was, in fact, scowling at that moment, he purposefully smoothed his face, muttering under his breath.

"What was that?"

He glowered. "I said, he called me a coward."

Ano looked supremely unimpressed. "So *that's* what you do when someone says something you don't like? You put your hands on them?"

Ekon frowned. "It wasn't just that, he . . . he said it in front of everyone!"

Ano pursed her lips. "In front of *Koffi and Safiyah*, you mean."

When Ekon didn't respond, her frown deepened.

"A word of advice, son? Impressing women isn't about what you do with your fists. In fact, it has a whole lot more to do with how you actually treat them." When Ekon didn't answer, her expression shifted. "You really care for them, for both of them."

The words Ekon wanted to say stuck in his throat.

"Do you love—?"

"We have now officially crossed the boundary of things I want to talk about with my mother."

"Oh?" Ano looked genuinely surprised. "I suppose that's fair. Sorry." She made a face. "Cut me a break? I'm about thirteen years out of practice."

Ekon realized, with a sad pang, that his mother's dry humor

was just like Kamau's. A knot of guilt formed as he thought about the fact that *he* was here, getting to enjoy this moment with their mother, while his older brother was not. He thought of what his mother had said about him and Kamau, the words from the prophecy.

One son rises in the east. One son rises in the west. Even now, he still didn't know which son he was.

"Can I ask you about something else?" he said in a low voice. "That prophecy you told me about. Do you still believe in it, even now?"

Ano's expression softened. "You want to talk more about it?"

"I want to *understand* it," Ekon clarified. "I mean, how do we even know if it's real? If everything in it will really happen?"

"What part do you mean, exactly?" asked Ano.

Ekon hesitated. "The part that said I'll kill the one I love most."

Ano leaned back a little. "There's never perfect certainty when it comes to prophecies, of course, but . . . I do believe this one, Ekon. It was told to me by a daraja with the ability to see into the future. You know by now the power some darajas hold. I don't doubt the one who spoke those words to me."

For a long time, Ekon said nothing. He didn't want to, but he could still remember the look on the face of the daraja he'd seen back in Lkossa, the one who'd visited Themba. His name has been Sigidi.

"You're asking about it for a reason," Ano prompted.

"I am," said Ekon. "I want to know if I can stop it—that is, stop myself from hurting someone I care about."

Ano's look was sympathetic. "In my experience," she said, "the more purposefully we try to run from our destiny, the faster we play right into its hands." She looked sad. "There's no avoiding destiny, Ekon."

Ekon had just opened his mouth to respond, when—

"Hey!"

He looked up, alert, at the same time Ano did. They were both on their feet at once. Njeri was pointing at something.

"Koffi's coming back. I think something's wrong!"

Ekon peered over Njeri's shoulder and started. There was no fog in this part of the marshlands, which meant that he could see Koffi perfectly even from here. She was sprinting toward them, and the look on her face was inscrutable. He recalled the way Amun had run at them before, and a fresh wave of panic overtook him. He stood, but Koffi was already slowing down, and up close he saw that she looked exhausted but determined. Thankfully, she also looked unharmed.

"Koffi?" Njeri looked cautious as she, Makena, and Zain approached. "What happened? Are you okay?"

"I'm okay." Now that Koffi was standing before all of them, Ekon thought she almost looked sheepish. "First, I want to—*need* to—apologize," she said. "For running off, and . . ." She looked between Ekon and Zain. "And for what I did before. I lost control for a second, but it *won't* happen again. I promise."

Makena was the first one to answer. "We're your friends, Koffi. It'll take more than that to get rid of us."

"I'm glad you said so," said Koffi. Ekon watched as she looked around at each of them, then took a deep breath. "Because I need to tell you all something. *I have a plan.*"

CHAPTER 7

NORTH

EKON

"A plan?" Ekon repeated. He could barely believe what he'd just heard. "Since when do *you* make plans?"

Koffi gave him a withering look as she settled before the fire and rubbed her hands together. Ano had already returned to her spot, and when she offered water, Koffi took it gladly. By now, the rest of the group had gathered around too. Only after Koffi finished drinking did she speak again.

"I have a plan," she repeated, "because I've just spoken with Badwa."

"You—?" Ekon stopped. "Badwa? You saw her again?"

"The goddess?" Ano asked with no small amount of incredulity. Her head swiveled to Ekon. "And what do you mean, *again*?"

"She saved Koffi and me," said Ekon, "while we were in the Greater Jungle." He still vividly remembered their encounter with the goddess, the power that had exuded from her. He shuddered

97

as he also remembered her extremely large and unsettling golden snake companion.

"And now she's *here*?" Makena turned around, as though expecting the deity to appear before them.

"Not anymore," said Koffi quickly. Her expression was tentative as she looked around at them. "I think everyone should sit down."

Ekon hesitated, then found his spot next to Ano again. Njeri, Zain, Safiyah, and Makena sat down too.

"As far as I'm concerned, Fedu has made his intentions clear," Koffi started. "He's going to try to use the Untethered as a means to force me to come to him. That would leave us with three paths forward. One, I surrender myself to Fedu and—"

"Absolutely not," Ekon snapped.

"Not happening," Zain added.

Koffi raised her hands. "I'm not excited about that idea either. So then there's our second option: I spend the next three weeks traveling to the Kusonga Plains like Ekon and I planned, and I get rid of the splendor before the Bonding so that Fedu can't use it. Then we hope that that's enough to get him to call off the Untethered."

"Sounds like a good plan to me," Ekon muttered.

"Except that there's no guarantee that Fedu will call off the Untethered after the splendor is removed from my body." Koffi held up three fingers. "That leaves us with a third option, Zain's plan. I could try to hone my power over these next few weeks and—before or during the Bonding—try to take on Fedu like I did outside the Mistwood. The problem is . . ." She looked at her shoulder. "I don't know what'll happen to me if I use that much power again. The first time, I was knocked unconscious for days, and Badwa warned me that the side effects of the splendor are only going to become worse the longer I keep it in my body. To be clear, this could kill me."

There was a stricken silence after that. Ekon found himself thinking about the prophecy again.

You will kill the one you love most . . . What Koffi was saying didn't sound like it was tied to him, and yet his mind spiraled into all the possibilities anyway. It left him feeling on edge, uneasy.

"I don't like the sound of any of those options, Koffi," said Zain, pulling Ekon from his thoughts.

"That's because none of them are good," said Koffi. "The truth is, we're in over our heads." She glanced at her hands. "*I* am in over my head. And I think the only way we're going to be able to stop Fedu and the Untethered is if we get help. Which is why . . ." She took a deep breath. "I think we need the help of the other gods."

Whatever Ekon had expected her to say, it hadn't been that. "The other *gods*?" he repeated.

"Atuno, Amakoya, Tyembu, and Itaashe," said Koffi. "Badwa believes that, now that Fedu has released the Untethered from the Mistwood, we have probable cause to ask for their help. My affinity has allowed me to find things in the past. In three weeks, I think I could find them."

Ekon looked among the others and was almost surprised to find the expression most similar to his own was on *Zain's* face. When it was clear no one else was going to speak, he did.

"Koffi," he said slowly, "don't get me wrong, I understand the

rationale to that plan, I think. But finding four other gods and per-
suading each of them to join our cause in three weeks seems . . .
ambitious."

"Not to mention, we don't even know how the other gods feel
about mortals," said Makena.

"Tuh," Safiyah muttered under her breath. "Speak for yourself."

"Badwa's with us," said Koffi. "That's already one out of the
five. And she's agreed to appeal to Tyembu herself. That only
leaves us with three more to find."

Ekon spoke up again. "There's something else, Kof." He didn't
like being in agreement with Zain when they'd fought only a short
while ago, but the point had to be made. "Even if we can convince
the other gods to fight for us, that doesn't fix the fact that the
splendor is still in your body, and it's clearly affecting you."

"That's just it," said Koffi. She looked excited again. "Badwa
also believes that, together, the other gods could take the splendor out of my body safely."

There was a pause in which no one, including Ekon, said
anything. Koffi was still sitting up straight, her eyes blazing
with a determination he'd seen countless times before, but this
time he thought he saw a shadow of something else behind that
look. There was a keenness there too, a hope that bordered on
wild desperation. He could almost feel it radiating off her. He
sighed because he recognized it in himself. Hope really *could* be
stubborn.

"Do we have any idea where we might find any of these gods
and goddesses?" Makena asked.

"I'm going to try to use my affinity for that," said Koffi. "I've tried once, and I think I have a lead. I thought about the symbol of the crocodile, Amakoya's symbol. We've already been moving north, and when I use my affinity she feels like the closest of the remaining gods."

Ekon continued tapping his fingers. "I still don't know about this, Koffi."

"Neither do I." It was Safiyah who cut in now. She'd said very little thus far, but when she turned to Koffi, she had a look of resolve. "What I *do* know, though, is that we'll definitely fail if we don't try." She nodded. "So I'm with you."

Ekon saw something pass between the two girls, a kind of understanding he wasn't privy to. When Koffi smiled, it was warm.

"Thank you," she said. She turned to the rest of the group. "I know what we're up against—we've got three weeks to do something that sounds impossible. But I really think this plan could work, and I'm willing to see it through if it means protecting the world as we know it, for darajas *and* non-darajas."

Barely a second passed before Njeri stood. "I'm with you, Koffi."

Makena stood next. "So am I."

"You know *I* am, Koffi." Zain stood and gave her a warm smile. Ekon didn't miss the brief moment Zain looked to him in silent challenge. He needed no more prompt as he got to his feet too.

"I'm with you too, Koffi." He looked straight at her as he said it. "Wherever you go, I'm with you."

"As am I, girl." Ano did not stand, but her gaze locked with Koffi's and she inclined her head. Ekon thought he saw something in his mother's expression that looked like respect. Koffi returned the gesture before addressing everyone again.

"We rest tonight," she said, "then tomorrow, we head *north*."

They reached Bandari in three days.

It wasn't a moment too soon. Ekon had estimated that their rations would last about that long, and he'd been proven right, but there were other reasons he was glad to see the port city. Bandari was also far enough north that the heavy white fogs of the southern marshlands he'd spent the last week in were held at bay.

To both his left and his right, the Ndefu River extended like a blue-green leviathan. This late in the afternoon, it was packed with boats big and small—from tiny fishermen's boats to long slow-drifting barges. They came and went from Bandari's bustling harbor in a kind of constant disorganized frenzy that both fascinated him and also made him itchy. He looked up from it just in time to see Ano making her way toward him with purpose. She was holding a sizable coin purse.

"I have some updates," she announced without preamble. "First, this is for you." She pushed the purse into his hands and folded his fingers over it.

Ekon blinked. "I—"

"Don't bother refusing it," she said warily. "You're three kinds of broke."

Ekon closed his mouth and stowed the purse in his satchel without another word.

"As for your transportation." She looked over his shoulder and pointed. "You see that midsize ferry down there, the yellow one?"

Ekon nodded.

"That's the *Nzinga*," said Ano. "Her captain is named Bwanbale, and he's an old friend who owes me several favors, so consider river passage for all of you bought and paid for, for as long as you need it."

"Wait," said Ekon. He paused, focusing on what she hadn't said. "Are you not coming with us?"

There was no mistaking it now; Ano looked apologetic. "No," she said gently. "I think it's best that I stay here and do what I can to salvage the business of the Enterprise."

Ekon didn't want to feel disappointment, but it found him. He forced a shrug. "Yeah, that makes sense," he said casually. "I understand."

Ano's expression turned rueful. "You lie about as well as Asafa did, which is to say, you're terrible at it." She put a hand on Ekon's face, a surprisingly maternal gesture. "I'm not leaving you for good, son. I'm just staying out of your way for a while."

"You're not . . ." Ekon's words tangled in his mouth. "You're not in the way."

"That's gracious of you," she said. "But truth be told, I think the kind of adventure you and your friends are about to go on is one for the young. I doubt I'd do much but slow you down if I came along."

Ekon felt a pressure behind his eyes, a stinging.

"Don't worry," she said with a half smile. "You may not see me, but know that I'll be keeping tabs on you, in my own way."

One of Ekon's brows rose. "You will?"

"Sure." She winked. "You think all I've gleaned from years of illegal spice trafficking is *money*? I'll have you know I've got quite the network around this continent, so I'll know what you're up to." She looked over her shoulder, thoughtful. "Speaking of things you're *up* to, I forgot to ask Bwanbale about the sleeping arrangements on that ferry." She gave Ekon a skeptical look. "You know, I really would prefer you don't sleep in any coed bunks, but—"

Ekon made a choking sound.

"But I know you'll ultimately do what you want," she said lightly. "As long as you're responsible if you decide to—"

"And I am walking away *now*."

The teasing left Ano's expression, and she grew serious again. "Safe travels, son." She hesitated again. "I love you."

Ekon swallowed. "Love you too . . . Mama." It was the first time he'd called her that. He hadn't planned to, but the word left him of its own accord. He found he wasn't sorry it had. Ano looked away quickly, but not quickly enough for him to miss the way her eyes shone overbright in the late-morning sun.

"I'll be going," she said quickly. "Good luck."

Ekon counted her steps as she strode away, watching until she disappeared into the crowds milling about the docks, and then she was gone.

By midday, all six of them were aboard the *Nzinga*.

It was, to Ekon's immense relief, a well-kept vessel. Its deck was polished to a shine, its sails bleached white, and the crew was an amiable bunch. Most of all, he found that he respected the

Nzinga's captain. Bwanbale Ilunga was not only an old friend of his mother's—the man had been quick to tell Ekon that his and Ano's friendship was based on her ability to always find him his favorite rare Asalian pepper spice blend—but he was also a man with a penchant for order and routine. Everyone, he explained, had a job on this vessel, and his schedules and stops along the Ndefu were, in his words, "as routine as the sun and moon." It meant, as far as Ekon was concerned, that for the first time in a long time, he'd be operating with a sense of real order and a semblance of predictability. Even the thought of that did wonders for his nerves as the ferry glided onto the open river and he watched Bandari grow distant.

"Hey, Ekon!"

He tensed when he saw Zain heading toward him, but to his surprise the daraja was smiling. He clapped Ekon on the back, hard.

"I've got to hand it you." He gestured around at the *Nzinga*. "This is stylish."

"Well," said Ekon carefully, "I *am* known for my style."

"Seriously," said Zain. "It's great."

Ekon's brows shot up. "You know, that sounds *suspiciously* like a compliment."

Zain rolled his eyes. "Don't go getting a big head," he said quickly. "You still fight like an Easterner."

Ekon chuckled. "Yeah, and *you* whine like a Westerner."

Zain considered. "Hm. Probably true." He walked off to stand with Makena and Njeri, and Ekon found himself smiling in spite of himself. He doubted he and Zain would ever be the *best* of friends, but maybe there was a future where they could be civil.

Safiyah had wasted no time starting what looked to be an

aggressive game of cards with some of the *Nzinga*'s deckhands, so while the rest of the group toured the ferry's bunks, Ekon headed for the front to get a better view of the river ahead. Of course, he'd now seen the Ndefu River plenty of times from afar, but there was no comparison for what it was like to be actually sailing down it.

Beneath the ferry, the water was a transparent blue-green, and every so often he saw schools of fish darting among each other just beneath the surface. He let his hand run along the boat's aged gunwale, relishing the fresh air, and tapped his fingertip against it, not because he was anxious, but because it made him happy to count the clouds overhead, the gulls twirling and diving across the sky.

Sixteen-seventeen-eighteen . . .

"Hi there."

Ekon started. He'd been so lost in his thoughts and his counting that he hadn't noticed Koffi until she was standing beside him. It took him a moment to realize she looked different.

"Uh . . ." He scratched the back of his head. "Did you get a haircut?"

Koffi pursed her lips. "I washed and rebraided my hair, if that's what you mean." It wasn't the only difference. She was wearing a crisp white tunic. "Ano helped the girls find some new clothes while we were in Bandari," she explained.

"That checks out," said Ekon.

"I misjudged her," said Koffi. She leaned over the boat's railing. "She's really nice."

Ekon couldn't quite explain why, but hearing Koffi say that made him inexplicably happy. "She is."

106

A breeze blew past them, lifting the braids off the back of Koffi's neck at precisely the moment the clouds above parted, letting rays of fresh sunlight through to shine golden on her brown skin. Ekon stared. She was radiant in that light, and he remembered that Koffi always looked most beautiful when she was hopeful. Abruptly, she turned to him.

"I've been using the splendor every so often to see if we're getting closer to Amakoya," she said. "I definitely feel like we are, but I still can't pinpoint where she is."

Ekon hesitated. "You're sure it's not Fedu you're sensing, right?"

Koffi gave him a half smile. "No. I've been using Amakoya's symbol, the crocodile, to try to find her." She paused, considering. "But I guess there's more to it. When I think of Fedu, I feel afraid. That's not how I feel now." She paused, considering, then: "If I ask you something, will you promise to tell me the truth?"

"Sure." Ekon nodded, praying the question wasn't some iteration of *What were you thinking about a minute ago?*

Koffi faced the water again. "You're the best planner I know, so I want to hear this from you." She looked at him. "Do you think this plan could work, honestly?"

Ekon paused, partially relieved and partially not. That hadn't been the question he'd expected, but it wasn't any easier to answer. He felt Koffi's gaze on him, waiting, and took a deep breath.

Don't mess this up, he told himself. *Say something positive. Something insightful. Not something foolish.*

"I think . . . it will work," he said carefully. "Because . . . because it has to."

Foolish.

He knew it had been the wrong thing to say as soon as the words left his mouth. Koffi's face fell slightly. "Wait," Ekon said quickly. "That's . . . That didn't come out right. I do think it's a good plan, it's just that—"

Whatever else he'd planned to say was interrupted by a huge crash and a spray of cool river water several yards ahead of the boat. He heard Koffi gasp as it hit her and braced himself. Still, he could do nothing as they were both knocked back, landing hard on the ferry's deck. Somewhere distant, he thought he heard someone else yell. It took a moment for his vision to resharpen. Beside him, Koffi looked equally confused.

"What was—?"

A long, keening shriek split the air around them, raising the hair on Ekon's arms and legs. Instinct pulled him to his feet, sopping wet, as a terrible shudder passed through the entire length of the ferry, and he jolted when he felt a sharp scrape along the hull.

Then he turned and met the eye of a monster.

CHAPTER 8

RIVER TURTLES, of COURSE

KOFFI

In her sixteen years, Koffi had had her fair share of encounters with mythical beasts.

This was largely because she'd spent the majority of her adolescent life as a beastkeeper at Baaz's Night Zoo in Lkossa, helping her mother and the other beastkeepers put on dangerous shows for visiting patrons as a way to pay back a hefty indentured servitude debt. In the last few weeks, she'd encountered even more creatures outside the Night Zoo—a grootslang, an eloko, and an ichisonga, just to name a few. And yet she was almost certain she'd rather have faced one of those creatures again in lieu of the one before her now.

The beast that had emerged from the middle of the Ndefu River was gargantuan, nearly twice the size of the ferryboat. At first glance, its serpentine body and bronze scales made her think of a snake. When she cast her eyes at the creature's head, however, her opinion changed. This creature had one large, gaping yellow eye, and a huge open mouth full of rows upon rows of tiny pointed brown teeth. Koffi met its gaze for only a second before it dived back into the water, thrashing as it went. She went cold as she watched its body moving just beneath the surface of the river, circling them.

"What *is* that thing?"

"I think I know." Ekon stared at the place in the water where the monster had disappeared. "I read about them once."

Koffi sighed. "Of *course* you have."

"It was in a book on southern culture and folklore, but—"

His words were interrupted by another loud splash, this time to their left. A scream rose in Koffi's throat as she saw a shape breach the water, and suddenly it occurred to her that there was something *worse* than this creature's one-eyed head to worry about: A long, spiked tail whipped between the river's waves.

"Hold on!" she shouted.

They barely had time to brace themselves before the tail made contact with the boat. Koffi shut her eyes, but she still tensed as the entire boat shuddered, as she heard the sound of wood splitting. When she opened them, she saw the tail disappearing back into the water and a huge crater on the boat's gunwale left in its wake. The rest of the group ran toward them, soaked. Koffi looked to Ekon.

"What is it?"

"I'm pretty sure it's called an ilomba," said Ekon. "I don't remember much else."

"Well, I haven't read any books about it," said Zain, looking at the hole, "but I'm thinking it probably isn't known for its friendliness."

"And here I was hoping it was just having a bad day," Koffi muttered.

They were interrupted as Captain Bwanbale raced across the deck. His clothes were sopping wet and he looked panicked.

"What's going on?" he asked. "What is that thing? I haven't seen it in these waters before."

"That's what we're trying to figure out," said Koffi.

The older man shook his head. "The *Nzinga* can't take many more hits like that or she'll go down, with us on it."

"For what it's worth," said Zain, "my vote is that we leave this vessel immediately!"

Makena's lips pressed into a thin line. "And how, exactly, do you propose we do *that*?"

Zain's expression remained solemn. "River turtles, of course."

"This river's wide enough," Safiyah cut in. "If we can find something to distract the ilomba long enough, we could go around it."

"The three of us can use splendor to drive it back." Zain nodded to Koffi and Njeri. "That is, if you're comfortable, Koffi?"

Koffi hesitated. Badwa had just warned her days ago about the adverse effects of using the splendor. She was already going to have to use it to find the other gods, and didn't want to use it much more than that, but . . .

But this is an emergency, she reasoned with herself. *Just this once, you'll be fine.*

"Okay," she said with a nod. "Let's do it."

"We'll wait for it to show its head again, then attack," Zain said to Bwanbale. "Everyone else should take cover belowdecks."

"I'm *not* hiding," said Ekon. He was looking at Koffi, but the words didn't seem to be for her. "I can keep lookout and intercept if it gets too close to any vulnerable parts of the boat."

"Fine," said Zain. To Bwanbale, he said, "Get ready to steer us forward, the rest of us will take up our positions."

Koffi needed no further prompt as she followed Njeri and Zain to the bow while Bwanbale ran to the stern. She searched the water, but its surface was eerily smooth, as though nothing had ever been there at all. The ferry glided forward, and beside her, she watched as Zain and Njeri took their stances, bracing themselves. Koffi clenched her teeth.

Wait for it. Wait for—

This time, when a crash sounded to her left, she was ready. Koffi swiveled as a massive explosion of water erupted feet away from the boat, and at once she summoned the splendor. Pain and pleasure filled her body as the energy crackled through her muscles and nerves. Her vision tunneled as she watched tiny speckles of light begin to gather around her hands. She didn't wait for a signal; instinct took over as she directed those particles of energy directly at the ilomba as it rose from the water and screeched. She watched as it hit the beast squarely in what she presumed was its chest, but it was to no avail. She tried a second time and a third, but the ilomba only seemed to grow more irritated. If the splendor she was directing at it had made any difference at all, it wasn't obvious. She turned.

"Njeri! Zain!"

The other two darajas were already in motion. As though moving in a coordinated dance, they streaked past Koffi, then split off in different directions as they reached the ferry's bow. From the left, Njeri withdrew a long wooden staff from her hip and swung it, sending a giant wave of the splendor toward the ilomba. At the same time, Zain pulled an arrow from his own sack and shot toward the creature's lone eye. The two attacks hit the ilomba at once. Koffi stilled, waiting for the inevitable moment of impact, the change in the battle as the creature succumbed to the blows. But to her horror, nothing happened. The ilomba roared, thrashing about in the water with aggravation, but now it was undeniable; none of their blows had made any difference. The ilomba didn't have so much as a scratch on its body.

"Keep going!" Njeri called out as she moved to a new spot and shot more splendor at the sky. Sweat had begun to collect on her forehead. "We just have to find a vulnerable spot!"

Zain swung his quiver away and planted his feet more firmly now. He raised both hands, paused, then directed another long bolt of splendor that lit the sky like lightning. It whipped out and struck the ilomba's neck, and it shrieked again, splashing the water. Its yellow eye fixed on him, and Koffi understood a second too late what was about to happen.

"Look out!" Njeri was closer to him, and she barely had time to grab Zain's upper arm and yank him back before the ilomba's spiked brown tail came crashing onto the ferry's deck with a bang. There were screams from those belowdecks as the spikes raked across the wood. When it reached the gunwale, it tore several feet from the boat's side before it sank into the sea again.

"Back!" Zain called, signaling wildly to the captain. "Pull back!"

Chaos broke out across the deck. Koffi heard shouting, the patter of feet all around her. There was a low groan and a flap as the ferry's deckhands moved to adjust the sails so that the boat was no longer gliding forward, but turning. She looked to the water again. The ilomba had gone beneath the surface, but any minute now it would reemerge.

"Hurry!" she shouted.

It seemed to take years, but gradually the eastern winds took hold of the ferryboat's sails. The massive boat began to drift back the way they had come. They were several yards away when Koffi finally caught sight of the huge brown mass of the ilomba's body again. It continued to crest and flash a hint of the bronze scales upon its back, but to her surprise, it did not pursue them. She frowned, now thoughtful, before turning back to the rest of the people on deck. The first person she made eye contact with was Ekon. He ran to her.

"What happened?" He followed her gaze to where the ilomba was still idling. "I thought you, Njeri, and Zain were going to create a distraction?"

"We *tried*." Njeri moved to join the two of them. She was soaked and looked furious. "It didn't work."

Ekon's expression changed. He now looked as though he was trying to figure out a particularly complex math equation. "What do you mean, 'It didn't work'?"

"I *mean* nothing affected it. No matter how hard we hit it or where, that *thing* was unfazed." She grimaced. "It was completely impervious to the splendor. We might as well have been fighting a brick wall."

At this, Ekon's face went slack. "What does that mean?"

"Bad news for us," said Zain. "That thing's not moving."

"Hang on." Safiyah was leaning over the gunwale. "Do you guys see that?" She pointed, and Koffi followed her gaze. For several seconds, she saw nothing as the ilomba twisted in the water, its scales occasionally cresting above the surface, but then she noticed something: Interrupting the beast's bronze scales was something silver and red.

"That looks like a harpoon," she said slowly.

Njeri, Zain, Koffi, and Ekon looked in the same direction. "I see it." said Ekon. "It's stuck in its side!"

The epiphany came to Koffi at once. "That explains the behavior," she said. "Some fisherman probably tried to take it down. It's not aggressive, it's in pain."

Zain's brows. "You so sure about that?"

Koffi nodded. "I learned a long time ago that sometimes dangerous things are just misunderstood things."

"I mean, don't get me wrong," Zain went on, "I certainly feel for the poor beast's plight, but . . . I don't see how knowing it's injured helps us."

"Because if it's not in pain, maybe it'll let us pass," said Koffi. She looked to the river again, watching the ilomba still spiraling and twirling just beneath the surface. She felt foolish now for not interpreting—even after all her years of training—the creature's movements for what they were: throes of pain. Like that, an idea came to her. As soon as she met Ekon's eye, he started shaking his head.

"Nope." He frowned. "Koffi, don't even *think* about it."

"Think about what?" Zain was still standing between them, confused.

"I think there's a way I can help it," said Koffi.

"How?" asked Safiyah. She'd moved to join their group.

Koffi swallowed. "I'm going to remove the harpoon."

115

"Koffi, *no!*" Ekon stared at her, a mixture of anger and fear playing across his face. "You can't be serious! It's too dangerous."

Koffi arched a brow. "Are you forgetting what I grew up doing for a living?"

"No, but . . ." Ekon looked flustered, nervous. "This is different. That . . . that *thing* isn't some caged animal at a zoo. It's wild and in the open and, last I checked, the Night Zoo didn't have an aquatic section. Besides . . ." In a lower voice, he added, "You only just recovered, you need more time to regain your strength."

That was the one point he made that Koffi didn't have a true rebuttal for. She gnawed her lip and chose not to dwell on the fact that he was right, that even though she'd had a few days' rest, her body still ached in places, and a fatigue clung to her that she hadn't been able to shake. She glanced at the silver marks on her shoulder and arm. They were still there too, a constant reminder that she wasn't all right. She pushed those thoughts away and looked up at Ekon again. "We need to get through," she pressed. "There isn't another way down this river."

No one answered immediately. Koffi watched the parade of emotions pass over Ekon's and Zain's faces in turn. Zain still looked to be in a state of disbelief, while Ekon looked perturbed. He was the one who broke the silence.

"Right," he said. "I'm going with you."

"Not a chance!" Zain stepped forward. "*I'm* going."

"Let Koffi choose, then," Ekon bit back. "*She* can decide who she'd rather take."

Panic flitted through Koffi as both boys stared her. She looked between them and tried to speak, but her mouth was getting dry as the seconds went by.

"I . . ."

"I'll settle this." Safiyah had watched their exchange in silence; now she stepped forward. *"Neither* of you are going. *I* will."

Koffi nodded, feeling more than a little relieved. "Thank you."

"No problem." She jutted out her chin and surveyed the deck before addressing both boys. "Ready a small boat for us, quickly. There's no time like the present."

CHAPTER 9

Tне RIVER GUARDIAN

KOFFI

By the time the ferry's crew was lowering their small boat off its side, Koffi's teeth were clenched so hard that her jaw had begun to ache.

More than once, the small boat scraped against the side of the ferry, jarring her and Safiyah as they drew nearer to the water. Koffi held on to its side as it swung, and Safiyah took hold of the oars. There was a grim but determined look on her face.

"Ready?" she asked.

Koffi nodded. She didn't trust herself to answer. She knew that she had to be the one to do this—she was the one with direct experience in animal handling—but that didn't mean she wasn't afraid. It didn't mean she could stop herself from thinking about all the ways this could go wrong. Her stomach swooped when the boat fell the last few feet, and they hit the water with a loud splash. She half expected that, as soon as they did, the ilomba would come their way, but to her partial relief, from this vantage point she could see that the beast was still circling the same place in the water. She took a deep breath and nodded, and Safiyah began to row. They watched together as the ferry grew smaller and smaller in their wake. From there, she could make out most of the people on it watching, Ekon, Njeri, Zain, and Makena among them.

"How close do you want to get?" Safiyah asked as she rowed.

"Pretty close," said Koffi. "Depending on how deeply the harpoon is lodged in, I'll need a good grip to get it out." She paused. "There's also a mild to good chance that I'll end up in the water."

Safiyah gave her a half smile. "If you go in, I'll fish you right back out. Promise."

The water seemed to still as they neared the ilomba's spot. Koffi drew in a sharp breath when she felt the bottom of their boat bump against something, and Safiyah picked up the oar at once. They both looked around, but there was no sign of the creature. Koffi swallowed a curdling dread.

"It's going to try to surprise us," said Safiyah. Her teeth were gritted. "Brace your—"

Koffi jumped as water surged around them. It had been terrifying enough from the ferry, but that was nothing compared to now. She closed her eyes as river water rushed at her, dousing her face and hair. When she opened them, Safiyah had been knocked over and was holding on to the boat's sides, but she was focused on something over Koffi's shoulder. Koffi turned.

The ilomba was bearing down on them, blotting out the sun itself.

Do it, a voice in her instructed sharply. *Now.*

Her mind went all the way back to her time at the Night Zoo, to everything Mama had taught her about how to deal with animals who were critically wounded or in pain. They were, her mother had taught her, by far the most dangerous animals to deal with, but they were also often the most desperate. Koffi braced herself. She'd have to be quick.

"Get me around its other side!" said Koffi, not taking her eyes off the ilomba. As Safiyah guided their boat, Koffi tried to remember the way her mother had moved in the Night Zoo when dealing with dangerous animals—she was deliberate, fearless. Koffi prayed all those years of watching her had paid off.

Please, she prayed to whatever gods were listening. *Please don't turn me into river-snake food.*

The ilomba's head turned, following Koffi as Safiyah positioned the boat behind it, and finally Koffi saw what she was looking for. From the *Nzinga*'s deck, the harpoon in the ilomba's back had looked small, but Koffi now realized it was longer than her entire body. Its curved blade was coated in rust, and at the point where it met the ilomba's scaly flesh, Koffi saw a nasty layer of greenish brown around the scales. It was rotted and looked infected.

No wonder you're miserable, thought Koffi. She looked to Safiyah, only for a second. "I'm going to try to grab it on the count of three."

"Ready."

Carefully, Koffi stood. The ilomba hissed.

Let me help you. Koffi tried her best to communicate her intention as Safiyah moved them closer. *Please, I just want to help.* She took a deep breath.

"One, two—"

Without warning, the ilomba turned away, diving headfirst

into the water. Koffi watched as its tail disappeared into the river's depths like a bronze whip, and then they were alone again. For several seconds, neither she nor Safiyah spoke.

"Well, *that* went well."

Koffi was still standing in the middle of the boat, staring into the place in the water where the ilomba had disappeared. Seconds later she saw the creature crest again, this time several yards away.

"I don't understand," she said as she sat back in the boat. "I thought I could help it. I thought it wanted me to."

Safiyah looked thoughtful. "It might be afraid of us," she posited. "I'm sure it's not exactly used to people swimming up to it with *good* intentions."

It was a valid enough point. Koffi looked where she'd last seen the ilomba and pointed. "Take me to it again?" she asked. "I want to try one more—"

Koffi had not made a sound the first, second, or third time the ilomba had appeared. This time, she yelped.

Beneath the river's surface, a mere few feet from their boat, the ilomba's large yellow eye was now staring up at them. This close, it was larger than a dinner plate. It circled them with a kind of quiet menace, occasionally opening its mouth to expose row after row of serrated teeth. Then, without warning, it rose, not in an eruption of waves like it had before, but slowly. A low hiss escaped it as its head breached, and once again its body swayed. Safiyah raised one of the oars.

"Koffi," she said in a low voice. "Stand back. If it lunges, swim toward the ferry. I'll try to hold it off for as long as I can."

"No!"

Safiyah was still regarding the ilomba. *"What?"*

"Just wait." Koffi stood again. "Lower the oar." She wasn't looking at Safiyah anymore, but she still felt the girl's gaze boring into her.

"Are you sure?" she asked.

"Yes," said Koffi calmly, glancing at her. "I need you to trust me. Please, just *stay seated*."

Safiyah hesitated, then obeyed. The ilomba was still idling by their boat, watching them. When Koffi turned to face it again, she raised her voice and tried to sound as confident as possible.

"I know that you're hurt," she called out to the beast, letting her words echo across the water. "And I know you have no real reason to trust humans, especially after the terrible thing that's been done to you. But we want to help you. I can take away the thing that's causing you pain. You just have to let me."

In answer, the ilomba hissed again.

"That doesn't sound promising, Koffi," said Safiyah under her breath.

Koffi ignored her and continued addressing the ilomba. "I'll be quick, I promise."

The creature went completely still then. Koffi watched the droplets of water slick down its body and turn golden in the sunlight. She couldn't say why, but something—an instinct— prompted her to stand just as still, to hold the ilomba's gaze as it surveilled her.

Please let me help you.

She exhaled when the beast finally lowered its head, moving closer and closer until it was within an arm's length of her. This close, its scent caught in her lungs, a smell of algae and river water.

A low hiss escaped the ilomba now; it was waiting. Koffi turned to Safiyah.

"I don't know what will happen after I do this," she admitted.

Safiyah nodded. "I trust you."

This time, as Safiyah rowed the boat around the ilomba's body, Koffi readied herself. She leaned out as far as she could, and tensed as the harpoon came into view. Once again, she counted.

One, two—

Safiyah steered her by it just as Koffi said *three* in her head. She grabbed hold of the harpoon's shaft and tugged with all her might. There was a moment of brief resistance, a second in which she worried it wouldn't come out, and then there was give, and the weapon came free. At once, the ilomba's shrieks wrenched the air.

"I've got it!" Koffi held up the harpoon, triumphant. "I got it out, I—"

A wave knocked her from the boat and sent her tumbling into the water with a crash. Somewhere in the back of her mind, Koffi realized she'd been hit by the ilomba. The harpoon slipped from her grasp as she sank, and she started. Beneath its surface, the Ndefu was clearer than she'd thought it would be, and to her surprise she saw that she wasn't alone now. Another body was a few feet from her, sinking. Panic flitted through her as she thought of Safiyah, but . . . no. It wasn't her. It was a boy, skinny in frame. Had one of the *Nzinga*'s crew members fallen overboard? There wasn't time to question it. She swam forward, looped an arm around the boy's, and kicked, bringing them both up. She gasped as they broke the surface.

"Koffi!" A few feet away, Safiyah was still in the boat, soaked but okay. "Are you all right?"

"I'm fine," said Koffi. "Someone else fell in the water."

Safiyah was already rowing toward them. "Hang on."

It seemed to take forever for her to reach them, and every muscle in Koffi's body ached with the effort of treading water and keeping the boy afloat. His eyes were closed, but he was breathing. Finally Safiyah pulled them both into the boat. Now out of the water, Koffi had a different concern. She looked around. "Where did the ilomba go?"

"I don't know," said Safiyah. "It disappeared right after you pulled out the harpoon."

Koffi frowned. That didn't make sense. The river water had been clear enough that she would have seen the ilomba if it had swum away, but she hadn't.

"Who is that?" asked Safiyah. She was staring at the boy, who was now sprawled on the other side of the boat. Koffi took a moment to really look at him. She'd thought, at first, that he was a member of the *Nzinga*'s crew, but now she had her doubts. His clothes weren't that of a sailor, and in any case, they were tattered and too dirty. She noted that he had dark umber-brown skin and long reddish dreadlocks. He looked roughly their age.

"Safiyah," she said, "do you see that?"

"See—" Safiyah gasped as she saw the same thing that Koffi had. There was a wound on the boy's side, and it was bleeding.

"That wound," Safiyah whispered. "It's in the same spot you pulled the harpoon out of the ilomba."

Koffi had had the same thought but didn't get to linger on it as the *Nzinga* drew level with them. It took some maneuvering to tie the boat up properly, but then they were being hoisted up its side far more quickly than they'd been lowered. When they reached the deck, Koffi found Ekon and Zain waiting along with Makena, Njeri, and the rest of the crew.

"Koffi!" It was Makena who got to her first. "You're okay!"

Koffi let her friend squeeze her for a moment before pulling away and turning back to the boat. Safiyah had gotten onto the deck, and now Ekon, Zain, and several of the other men on the ship had daggers and spears pointed at the young man still in the small boat.

"A stowaway," said Captain Bwanbale, coming forward and looking harried. "Check him for weapons, then cast him overboard."

"Oh, for gods' sake!" snapped Safiyah. "Do *not* throw him overboard. He's clearly not a threat, he's unconscious. What is the matter with you people?"

Captain Bwanbale frowned but didn't press the point. Gradually, those holding weapons lowered them. For several minutes, no one moved; everyone just stared at the young man, unsure of what to do as his wound continued to bleed. It was Makena who finally blew out a breath in exasperation. She crossed the deck and stepped into the smaller boat to check his pulse, then glared angrily at everyone else still gawking.

"Well, don't just stand there, get some fresh water and bandages. He's hurt!"

The commands snapped everyone out of whatever stupor they'd been, and at once they jumped into action. Makena wasn't strong enough to lift the boy, so in the end it was Ekon and Zain who had to work together to lift him out of the boat and prop him up on the deck. Someone came forward with towels, and Makena took one and began to dry the boy's face. Eventually, his eyes opened. Koffi was surprised to find they were a startling golden-brown color. The same color as the ilomba's.

"Where am I?" When the boy spoke, his voice was hoarse and scratched. Makena, still kneeling beside him, offered him some water. He drank eagerly, but when he was done, he looked more uneasy. Something about him reminded Koffi of a hare just freed from a trap.

"It's okay," she said calmly. His eyes found hers, and he started.

"*You,*" he whispered. "You're the one who helped me. You removed the harpoon."

"I am."

He looked down at the wound Makena had bandaged for him, then back up at Koffi again in visible confusion. "No one's ever tried to help me," he said. "Why did you?"

"Because you needed it," said Koffi, "and because it was the right thing to do."

The boy shook his head.

"I could have . . . You could have been killed."

Koffi shrugged. "It was still the right thing to do." In a different voice, she asked, "What's your name, anyway?"

The entire deck quieted as everyone waited for an answer. The boy looked around at each face watching him, hesitant, but when he met Koffi's gaze again, something in that golden-brown gaze yielded.

"My name is Zuberi."

"Zuberi," Koffi repeated. "How did you get turned into an ilomba? Was it a curse?"

"A curse? No, no." Zuberi shook his head. "My second body is no *curse*." He held up his head. "It's a blessing."

"Oh great, a zealot," Zain muttered under his breath. Koffi shot him warning look before nodding for Zuberi to continue.

"A blessing," she repeated. "What do you mean?"

Zuberi shook his head, and droplets of water flicked from his dreadlocks. "Years ago, more than I can remember now, I was a just a deckhand on a vessel like this one," he said. "Except my captain's voyages weren't up and down the Ndefu, they were on wilder waters to the west, in the Moto Sea. One night, on a voyage home, we encountered a terrible storm." He shuddered. "I was thrown from the ship and called for help, but none of my crew dared risk their lives to save me." Zuberi closed his eyes as if in prayer. "I was sure I would die that night. But then . . ." His expression changed abruptly to one of pure joy. "Then I saw her."

"Her?" asked Ekon.

"She came in the form of a giant crocodile," Zuberi went on, bowing his head. "I thought she was going to eat me, but she didn't. She brought me to the surface, and saved my life."

"Who?" Koffi asked. She suspected she already knew the answer, but had to ask.

"I dare not speak her true name," said Zuberi, bowing his head. "But my great mistress is known by many monikers—she is called the Water Witch, the Sovereign of the Seas, and the Ruler of the Rivers."

"Amakoya," Koffi finished. "That's who you're talking about."

Zuberi bowed his head. "The water goddess saved my life and gave me my second body so that I could live forever in the water without fear," he said. "For that kindness, I humbly serve her and protect these waters from those who might harm them. When evil came to the river some months ago, I tried to uphold that duty, but the sailors struck me with a poisoned harpoon, and in doing so they rendered me unable to change forms." He bowed his head to Koffi. "I owe you a debt I cannot possibly hope to repay."

"*Actually,*" Ekon cut in again. He had a shrewd look in his face. "You just might." His gaze flitted to Koffi before he went on. "You say you serve Amakoya? That means you know where she is."

At once, Zuberi tensed. "I would not betray my mistress's whereabouts so easily."

"We don't mean any harm," said Koffi quickly. "We're trying to find her because we need her help. And right now, we have very little guidance on where she might be. My . . ." She hesitated, unsure how much she should say about her affinity to a stranger. "We have some reason to believe she's not far from here."

Zuberi studied her a moment before he seemed to decide she was telling the truth. He relaxed again. "My mistress calls many places home," he said, "but I know her to often reside in one place—the House of Wise Waters." He cast his gaze upriver. "It is a few days' journey from here by boat. You'll pass it if you stay on the Ndefu."

"I'm familiar with that place," said Captain Bwanbale stoutly. He'd said little during their exchange, but now he stepped forward with arms crossed. "It's not one of my scheduled stops."

"Forget the schedule," said Safiyah. Before the captain could reply, Makena stepped forward, drawing level with the captain.

"Now you listen here, *Captain*," she said, pointing. "My friend just saved you, your boat, and your entire crew from inevitable death at the hands of an injured river monster when you were too cowardly to do it yourself. The absolute least you can do is make an adjustment to your schedule to take us by this House of Wise Waters."

Bwanbale looked flustered. "I—"

"We'll be quick," Koffi cut in. "Just give us the day, and we can keep going on your normal route."

"And after all, you wouldn't want to cut off your supply of Asalian pepper spice blend," said Ekon quietly.

Koffi was surprised when the captain's eyes cut to him. "You're lucky I have a penchant for it, and that your mother is a good woman." He sighed. "I'll dock at the temple to assess the damage to the *Nzinga*, but I'll only stay for a day. No more than that." He stalked off before anyone else could butt in, and Koffi relaxed.

"To the House of Wise Waters," she said. "Let's hope the Water Witch is up for visitors."

PART TWO

The HUNTER WHO CHASES TWO HARES WILL CATCH NEITHER.

The ROSE of KUGAWANYA

AKANDE

Year 891

There's something sweet in the air in Kugawanya.

The scent is distinct from the usual market odors as Izachar and I walk together down a road filled with street vendors. I inhale.

"Hm. Do you smell that?"

Izachar doesn't look at me; instead, he regards a nearby stall where a man is selling roasted guinea fowl. "Smell what?"

"*That.*" I sniff the air again. "It's like . . . flowers, or sugar. Something."

"Nah." My friend shakes his head. "All I smell at the moment is food. Gods, I'm starving."

"You're always starving."

At this, Izachar actually stops walking and frowns. "I'm a growing boy," he says indignantly. "Besides, you said we'd stop for food thirty minutes ago."

He's not wrong; we have been walking a long time. This late in the day, the sun has already begun to descend beyond the city's skyline, and the dark creeping fingers of dusk stretch long across the sky. By dawn, I know I'll have to be up and ready for more training with my grandfather. It would make sense to grab some food and call it a day. But I'm not ready to yet. In truth, it's at moments like this when my home feels most alive, and I want to savor it.

I also want to figure out what the sweet smell is.

"Akande," Izachar whines.

"Fine," I relent, and we head toward the man selling guinea fowl. Once we have our bowls, we find an empty place on the curb and settle down.

"So," Izachar asks between chews, "how's the daraja training with your grandfather?"

I shift a bit. "It's been . . . all right."

Izachar finishes chewing, then licks his fingers. He gives me a look. "When are you going to tell me how training's *actually* going?"

I hesitate, but a raised brow from Izachar pulls the truth from me, and I sigh. "It's . . . not really going at all."

"What do you mean?" he asks. "What's your grandfather having you do?"

"That's just it." I shrug and cast my gaze across the road. There's more, but I just don't know how to say it without being embarrassed. The truth? I've been trying to summon splendor for weeks with Babu without any luck. My grandfather tells me that it's all right, that my splendor will come when I'm ready, but it's hard not to feel like it's a personal failure. Instead of that, I say, "He's not really having me *do* anything. It's been boring, just a bunch of drills, and—" I stop short as I notice something.

The vendors' carts lining the street are packed together tightly, but not so tightly that I miss the small boy running behind them, fast. Seconds later, I see why. He's being tailed by three older boys considerably bigger than him. Instinctively, I stand.

"What is it?" Izachar rises at the same time I do, looking around.

"I'll be right back." Without waiting, I cross the busy road, navigate between the carts, and head in the same direction the boys are going. Abruptly, the small boy veers right, heading directly into what I know from years of experience on these roads is a dead end. The three older boys follow him into the same alley, and I pick up my own pace. It doesn't take me long to catch up to them, to turn the same corner. When I do, my heart plummets.

The largest of the three older boys has the small one by his upper arm and has lifted his entire body off the ground while he kicks frantically at the air. The other two are jeering.

"Well, well," says the large boy with a leer, "what have we got here?"

"Let me go!" The little boy's voice is a squeak in comparison, and the longer he kicks and squirms, the more he resembles a trapped meerkat. "Let me go, please!"

The large boy raises him higher still. "Not so fast, kid," he says in a more menacing voice. "You just made a grave mistake. You passed through Ox Club territory without paying our protection tax. And it's time for you to pay up, with *interest*."

The boy stops wriggling long enough to stare at his captor as the words sink in. "I—I don't have any money," he stammers. "I swear!"

"So you say," says the large boy, "but just to be sure, how about we turn you upside down and—"

"*Hey.*"

All four boys turn my way as I step into view. "Leave him alone." I hope my voice sounds stronger than I feel. I'm not the smallest boy in this alley, but I'm also nowhere near the biggest. The one holding up the little boy turns to face me. I notice he's got a blockish head and a torso that's comically big compared to the rest of his body. He looks me over, amused.

"Who are *you*?"

"Leave him alone," I repeat.

Blockhead smirks, putting the small boy back on the ground. With attention diverted off him, he immediately runs for it. Blockhead doesn't even bother trying to stop him. He's turned his full attention to me now. His eyes cut to the two boys standing on either side of him.

"It sounds like we need to be doing more to make sure people around here know our name," he says to them. "This twerp doesn't even know who he's messing with. We're—"

"The Ox Club," I say dryly. "I've heard. Tell me, did you pick that name out because all three of you *look* like oxen, or smell like them?"

That gets a reaction. The smile slips from Blockhead's face as the other two boys scowl and crack their knuckles.

"You talk tough for a guy standing alone," says Blockhead with new menace.

"Who says he's alone?"

I turn and find Izachar rounding the corner, his chin jutting out in challenge. Only I'm close enough to notice he's trembling as he stops to stand beside me.

"Ah," says Blockhead with a slow smile. "*Now* it's interesting."

"Is this what you do?" I ask, trying to stall. "Pick on little kids? That doesn't sound very *impressive*."

Blockhead sneers. "It's a dog-eat-dog city," he snaps. "Runts don't last long, I'm doing them a favor. Just like I'm about to do one for you and your friend."

One of the boys moves left, and the other moves right faster than I expect, strategically surrounding us so that there's no way out of the alley. The reality of the situation becomes clear: We're outnumbered, and we're trapped.

"What do we go?" Izachar whispers.

The truth is, I don't have an answer for him. A growing panic skitters just above the surface of my skin, like ants crawling all over my body. The three boys draw closer and I brace myself for what I'm about to do. There's a strange tingling sensation in my feet, a warmth in my legs. One of the boys rushes at Izachar. I raise my hand instinctively to block him and—

A ball of glittering light erupts from my hands.

It's luminescent, so bright my eyes water as it grows from the size of an apple to a cantaloupe in a matter of seconds. At once, the other three boys back away, all shielding their faces as the ball of strange light grows bigger and bigger. I glance at Izachar and find he's gaping at me.

"How are you *doing* that?" he asks in a hushed voice.

"I don't know." It's hard to explain the sensation moving through my body, the low hum vibrating in my bones. It's a strange feeling, but also . . . nice.

"He's one of them!" Blockhead shouts as he backs away. "He's a daraja."

I shouldn't relish the shared fear on the boys' faces, the way they're now looking at me with new wariness. I do, though. For the first time in my life, I feel powerful, like someone to be reckoned with, to be *respected*. My arm is beginning to ache, but I raise it higher. The ball of light, of *splendor*, grows bigger and brighter still; all three boys flinch away from its glow. A bead of sweat slicks down my temple, but I raise my voice as I address them.

"Don't let me catch the three of you here again," I say ominously. "Or the next time, you'll answer to—"

Without warning, the ball of splendor extinguishes.

I raise my arm higher, splay my fingers exactly the way they were before, but it's no use. However I managed to summon the splendor before, it's clear I won't be doing it again.

"Akande?" Izachar whispers.

Blockhead and his cronies have lowered their arms and are now watching me with visible anticipation, waiting. Seconds pass, and their expressions harden.

"Run," I mutter to Izachar as they start to advance a second time.

"Get him!"

I turn to Izachar. "Run!"

We barrel out the alley and dash onto the road. The sky has gotten much darker now, and most of the vendors have packed up for the day, but there are still enough for Izachar and me to use to our advantage as we weave between them.

"Get back here!" Blockhead yells after us. "I'll bash your heads in, you little twerps!"

"Go right!" Izachar's panting as he runs beside me, but I catch the words. "Take the fishermen's shortcut!"

It's the only prompt I need. We know Kugawanya's streets and pathways like we know the back of our hands. As we approach a busy intersection, we veer sharply to the right, then immediately make another tight right and duck into a side street so small and shaded it's nearly impossible to see unless you know exactly where to look. Izachar grabs my arm and yanks me to the ground, and we crouch, holding perfectly still, until Blockhead and the other two boys pass. Even after they're long gone, neither of us speaks or moves for several minutes. Finally, it's Izachar who breaks the silence.

"Are you okay?" he whispers.

I nod, even though I'm not sure if it's true. My entire body feels clammy and sweat-slicked, and I get the feeling it's not because we were running. My left arm is strangely sore, and I'm suddenly so tired that I could pass out and go to sleep right there in the alley. I let my head rest against the alley's wall and close my eyes. "I'm fine."

When I open them, Izachar is studying me with new focus. Something seems to be dawning on him gradually. "That was the first time you'd ever done that, wasn't it?"

I want to lie to him, but I can't. Beats pass before I nod.

"Well, it was impressive," Izachar admits, "but, Kan, what were you thinking, going after those guys like that? They were twice your size."

"I had to." The words leave me before I can stop them or even really make sense of them. "Someone had to."

Izachar considers, and then it's his turn to nod. "You know that's why you're my best friend?" he says after a moment. "Because you look out for people."

I face him. "Thanks, Izachar—for looking after me."

"What?" Izachar cracks a small smile. "You thought I was going to let you get your butt kicked by yourself?"

Like that, we're back to normal again, and I exhale, relieved. My body is still sore, but I force myself to stand and poke my head out of the alleyway, looking left and right.

"We're clear."

It takes me longer to walk Kugawanya's streets now, but Izachar doesn't seem to mind as he walks beside me. Most of the shops around us have dimmed their lights, and the new darkness allows for the first smattering of stars to shine through the wispy clouds overhead and wink at us. I take that sight in, trying to memorize it. Up ahead, the window to one of the bakers' shops is open, and I inhale the smell of fresh bread. And something else.

"What's your babu going to say?" Izachar asks. "When you tell him what happened?"

I blow out a breath. "Pft, who knows? If I had to guess, it'll involve a lecture about *focus* and—" I stop abruptly as we near the bakery. It's a two-story building, clearly the type with living quarters directly above the shop, and it's aglow in the evening light. On its stoop sits a girl, the prettiest I've ever seen, weaving a raffia basket she holds between her knees. I'm exhausted, but sweat slicks my palms as I watch her work. Quickly, I grab Izachar and steer him toward the other side of the road.

"Hey! What are you—?"

"*Don't* look." I turn my back and move us into the alcove of a seamstress's shop before even daring to glance over my shoulder. "You see that girl?"

"Huh?" Izachar stands on his toes and peeks over my head a moment before he spots her too. "Oh. That must be her."

140

"Her?"

"Yeah, I heard some guys talking the other day," says Izachar. "That's the daughter of the new baker. They're already calling her the Rose of Kugawanya."

We're still obscured in shadow, which is the only reason I dare to look over my shoulder again at the girl. She's still seated on the bakery's stoop, focused, and from here I can see a tiny yellow rose tucked into her wavy braids, right behind her ear. Even staring at her too long makes my face hot. When I turn to Izachar again, he has a smile that's all too knowing.

"You *like* her."

I frown. "I do not. I don't even know her."

"You'd like to, though." The smirk hasn't left Izachar's face, and on the contrary it's growing wider. "I'll bet you'd like to know her *very* well—"

I elbow him in the rib, but it's an empty gesture. When he waggles his eyebrows, I throw my hands up in defeat. "Fine! I want to talk to her. I *have* to talk to her." I look back to where she's sitting and try to keep the plea from my voice. "Help me."

"Help you?"

"I don't know what to say to her."

"Your name might be a good place to start." Izachar now sounds amused. "Just be yourself, Kan." Something in his expression shifts. "You got this, brother."

I open my mouth to protest, but Izachar isn't having it. He gives me a not-so-gentle shove into the street and, before I can turn away, makes a loud cawing sound. My ears burn as the girl looks up, then spots me across the road. She waves, and I offer the tiniest wave back.

"*Go,*" Izachar hisses from the shadows. "Or the next time, I'll moo like a cow."

It's not a threat I'm willing to test. I force one foot in front of the other and make my way over to the bakery. When its golden light falls on me, it takes everything I have to keep from scampering back into the dark, but then the girl sees me and I'm rooted to the ground.

"Well," she says calmly, "I did wonder if you were going to come say hello."

My senses are acute, trying to memorize every detail about the girl—the beads in her hair, her brown eyes, the tiny mole above her lip . . .

"So." She smiles. "You are?"

"M-my Akande," I stutter. "I mean my name is Akande."

"Akande. That's a nice name." A shiver of pleasure rolls down my back at the sound of my name on her lips. It sounds like honey when she says it, and I know at once that I could listen to the sound of her voice all day.

"Thank you." I pause. "What's your name?"

"Danya." She looks over her shoulder, and some of her hair slips back to expose her neck. "My family just moved here from Asali," she says when she turns back to me. "We're bakers, with a specialty in eastern flatbreads."

"I like bread."

She laughs and it sounds like music. "So, Akande, what do you *do*?"

"My friend Izachar is an apprentice." *Why did I just say that?* "But I'm not in any apprenticeships. I'm a daraja. I'm in training."

Danya raises a brow. "That's very impressive." She seems to consider something. "Are you from Kugawanya?"

"I am."

"Good." She hugs her raffia basket against her body. "This city's so much bigger than what I'm used to. I could use a friend to help me get a lay of the land." She inclines her head and looks up at me through long black lashes. "Would you . . . be interested in helping me with that?"

Heat floods my cheeks, and I stand straighter. "Of course. It would be my honor."

She shoots me another dazzling smile, and the stars above me look dimmer in comparison. "Good!" she says warmly. From inside the bakery, there's a noise, and she suddenly looks up. "I should probably go help," she says apologetically. "But hopefully I'll see you tomorrow?"

"Definitely."

She rises with her basket in hand and gives me one last smile before opening the bakery's front door and disappearing behind it. In her wake, the sweet smell of roses lingers, and I inhale slowly, trying to savor it like a feast. A few minutes later, Izachar comes to stand beside me.

"Well?" He slaps me on the back. "How'd it go?"

I blink several times before the words come to me. "I think . . . I think I have a date."

CHAPTER 10

The House of Wise Waters, Part 1

EKON

As a boy, Ekon had thought it would be impossible for any structure to rival the Temple of Lkossa.

With its beautiful alabaster stone and its great library, he'd thought it was the most magnificent structure in all Eshōza, second to none. But as the *Nzinga* glided toward the House of Wise Waters, Ekon realized his boyhood evaluations might now need adjusting.

Bwanbale had allowed Zuberi to disembark at a small port town the previous day, but before he'd left, the boy had told their group that the water temple was wondrous, easily one of Eshōza's most spectacular sites. Ekon had initially decided that a lot of the young man's fervor for the place was likely influenced by his loyalty to Amakoya. As they drew closer, however, he began to concede that, in honesty, Zuberi *had* had a point.

The temple was not situated on the banks of the Ndefu, as Ekon had expected it would be; rather, it was positioned right in

144

the middle of the river like its own island, impossible to miss or ignore. With its deep, weathered gray stone and the water moss and vines covering most of its outer walls, it reminded him of mystical ancient ruins. Thousands of lily pads sprouting vibrant pink flowers were clustered at its base, and though Ekon tried to count the number of boats moored around it with rope, even *he* found the task difficult.

"This is as close as I can get you," Captain Bwanbale announced when they were still a mile from the temple's shore. "You'll have to take one of the small boats and row the rest of the way. I will be leaving tomorrow at dawn, with or without you."

They poured into one of the rowboats and set out for the temple. The closer they got to it, the grander the place seemed. No one spoke as they approached. They'd barely disembarked and hitched their boat to one of the posts before they found themselves face-to-face with a tall, reedy man dressed in fine black robes. Ekon noted that they were similar robes to those of the Brothers of the Temple of Lkossa, except that these were embroidered with tiny silver waves.

"Greetings," said the clergyman. His voice was surprisingly deep. "My name is Father Kanai. On behalf of the Order of the Sovereign, I welcome you to the House of Wise Waters, the largest water temple in all Eshōza."

"Thank you, Father." On principle, Ekon bowed at once, and the others took his cue and followed suit. The clergyman smiled.

"Please note that shoes are not permitted inside the temple," he said. "Further, per the customs of this sacred place, all visitors are required to wash their hands, face, and feet before entry is permitted."

Ekon frowned. "Where are we supposed to do that?"

Father Kanai gestured to several large wooden basins of water a few feet away. Ekon looked over his shoulder and involuntarily winced.

"Uh . . . Father, is that water sanitary? It looks . . . *dubious* to me."

"Ekon!" He winced as Koffi elbowed him hard in the rib. Safiyah glared.

"What? We don't know the last time that was changed. It's a completely valid health concern!"

"Of course I cannot compel you to do anything against your wishes." Father Kanai offered them a slightly smaller, slightly tighter smile. "But be warned that if you attempt to enter the House of Wise Waters without proper cleaning, I will be obliged to use *other* means of enforcement to protect it from defilement." Deftly, he reached for his hip, and for the first time Ekon noticed a smooth blackwood rod.

"No need for that, Father," Koffi said quickly. "We're more than happy to comply." She gave Ekon a sharp look. "Right, Ekon?"

"Fine."

"Excellent!" Father Kanai's transition back to cheerfulness was so quick, it was almost unnerving. "Please follow me."

In a line, they followed the clergyman to the basin, where he very dutifully supervised while they washed, one by one. Ekon grimaced as he eyed the water, and tried to do his washing as quickly as possible. He thought the clergyman's expression was slightly antagonistic when he smiled even wider.

Jerk.

"All water in the House of Wise Waters is blessed and divine, young man," he said airily. "You could drink from that basin and enjoy great health benefits."

Ekon scowled as Zain plunged his dirty feet into the water. "I'll pass."

Once they were clean to Father Kanai's satisfaction, he rather cheerily led them up to the water temple's entrance. For the first time, Ekon saw other patrons and worshippers. He'd certainly seen his share of them at the Temple of Lkossa, but never so many gathered all at once. A long queue began at the temple's front door and extended around the corner. It didn't appear to be moving very fast either.

"What is this?" he asked.

"We're experiencing longer wait times than usual today," said Father Kanai, "an unfortunate but unavoidable part of visiting the House of Wise Waters—unless you have purchased a prayer pass in advance?"

Ekon sputtered. "A *what*?"

"Patrons who make a more . . . *generous* donation to the House of Wise Waters may wait in a slightly shorter line." Father Kanai indicated a second door with only a few people standing before it. "The pass also allows patrons to pray in a quieter, more private room and consult with a member of our Order."

Ekon was beside himself. "You can pay to skip the line at a *temple*? That's . . . that's blasphemous!"

Father Kanai tucked his hands into the sleeves of his robes and inclined his head as he smiled. "If you change your mind, please come and find me." Without another word, he headed back toward the boats to greet more new visitors. Ekon turned to face the group and was surprised to find no one else looked outraged.

When he stared pointedly at Koffi, her brows rose.

"What?"

"Aren't you . . .? Can you believe that?"

Koffi frowned. "Can I believe that certain groups of people enjoy privileges that others cannot based on status and wealth gaps and that that injustice extends even to places of faith? Do you *really* want me to answer that question honestly, Ekon?"

Ekon's cheeks warmed. "Ah, no." He changed the subject. "Have you tried using your splendor again? Do you feel like we might be close to Amakoya?"

Koffi frowned. "I feel like we are, but it's not focused. We'll need to get inside, then I'll know more."

To Ekon's relief—and partial chagrin—the line to get inside the House of Wise Waters didn't take as long as he'd expected. The air inside the temple itself was at least cool, and as he took in its interior, he found himself once again humbled. Whoever had designed this place had been very mindful of its purpose; most of the atrium was taken up by a massive pool with tiles of various blues at its bottom so that it constantly looked to be shimmering. A fountain had been constructed at its center, and on a throne of carved stone waves sat the goddess herself. He almost, *almost* had to laugh. The rendering of Amakoya here was nothing at all like the goddess he'd met once before. This statue portrayed the image of a stoic, peaceful-looking woman; the deity he and Safiyah had met had been far fiercer. The group moved to the side as more visiting patrons came in behind them.

"Any luck, Koffi?" Zain asked.

Koffi shook her head. "I don't feel pulled in any specific direction, I just have a feeling she's here, somewhere."

"This place is huge," said Zain. "If we're going to have any chance of finding Amakoya, we'll need to split up so we can cover as much ground as possible, as quickly as possible. I doubt Amakoya will be walking around where anyone can see, so we'll have to look for clues."

"There are six of us," Ekon pointed out. "So we can go in pairs."

"I'll go with Ekon," Safiyah volunteered. An inscrutable look passed over Koffi's face, but she nodded.

"Then I'll go with Koffi," said Zain. Ekon ignored a faint sense of irritation as Zain moved closer to her.

"Njeri and I can go together," said Makena. "We can each cover a separate part of the temple and see if we notice any clues. Then we can meet back here. Let's give it, say . . . forty minutes?"

"Forty-*five*," Koffi amended. She glanced at Ekon. "Forty-five's a better number."

Ekon started.

"Right," said Makena. "Let's find a goddess."

While Makena and Njeri opted to stay on the main floor, Koffi and Zain visited the prayer rooms to see if they offered any clues. When Safiyah spotted a set of winding stairs to the side of the atrium, she decided she and Ekon would cover the second floor. Careful not to attract the attention of any other members of the temple's order, they slipped up the stairs. Ekon stopped when he reached the top.

He had thought he'd seen all the beauty the House of Wise Waters had to offer, but it appeared there was one more feature left to behold. Here on the second floor, there was little in the way of walls because most of the area was made up of massive open archways that offered a full circular view of the Ndefu River. At this hour, the sun had already begun to descend below the skyline, which meant a deep golden light was cast against the river as it churned. It was a breathtaking sight.

Until Ekon noticed the statues positioned by each window.

"AHH!"

"What?" Safiyah spun around at once, alarmed.

"I . . . They . . ." Ekon held a hand over his eyes and turned away quickly. "Those!"

He glanced at Safiyah in time to see her look in the direction he'd pointed and then smirk. "Oh, those? Come on, Ekon. They're just *statues*."

For a moment Ekon was so beside himself that he actually dropped his hand. "There are plenty of statues back home where the women do not look like . . . like *that!*"

Safiyah offered a saccharine smile. "Do you mean *naked*? In fairness, they're not entirely women, Ekon."

Ekon tried to look away quickly, but it was no use. He caught a glimpse of another one of the statues and his cheeks warmed. There was no getting around it now. He'd certainly read about the creatures depicted in the statues in books; they were called *mermaids*, water beings with the torso of a human but a long tail instead of legs. He'd seen plenty of illustrations of them. But in those childhood stories—curated by the brothers of the temple—the mermaids had long hair and . . . clothes.

"Shouldn't they cover up their . . . their . . . ?"

"Breasts?" Safiyah raised a brow.

"You don't have to say it aloud!"

"There's no need to be embarrassed, Ekon, it's a body part," said Safiyah. "And anyway, cover them with *what* exactly? I don't think mermaids can just go to the market for new clothes whenever they please."

This was getting worse by the second. Ekon forced himself to look at the ground. "I don't know! Seashells?" He thought he'd seen seashells in at least one of his childhood storybooks.

"That's extremely impractical, Ekon," said Safiyah. "Seashells would be hard, uncomfortable, and exceedingly difficult to properly size. You'd know that if *you* had breasts."

Ekon made a very small, pitiful sound and continued to stare pointedly at the floor.

"All right, all right. We don't have to stay." Safiyah looked around a final time and sighed. "I think this floor is just for decoration anyway. There's nothing here but these statues and this wishing pool. Come on, we can go back downstairs and help Njeri and Makena scout out the main atrium."

Ekon was more than relieved when she went down the stairs. He took one more glance at the second floor's beautiful view before starting down the stairs, though unfortunately his eyes did land on one of the mermaid statues before he could look away. The creature's back was arched, and she looked to be in the midst of braiding her hair. For a half second, Ekon thought he saw a movement, a wink, but he shook his head.

Nope. He headed down the stairs more quickly. *Definitely, definitely in your head.*

Ekon and Safiyah's perusal of the second floor had taken up only a few minutes, which meant that for the rest of the forty-five they'd been designated, they circled the giant statue of Amakoya and helped Njeri and Makena look for anything that might clue them in on how to get in touch with the goddess. Even in that relatively short time frame, Ekon noticed the number of people actually within the temple was thinning, and when he chanced a look out one of its windows, there were far fewer boats moored to the posts around the structure. By the time Koffi and Zain rejoined them, there were only a few clusters of people left.

"Let's go to the main altar"—Koffi indicated—"to . . . uh, pray."

All of them knelt before the giant statue of the goddess and bent their heads.

"We checked all of the prayer rooms," Koffi whispered with her head bowed. "Didn't find anything."

"There's nothing on this floor either," said Makena.

Njeri glanced at Ekon. "You grew up in a temple," she noted. "Shouldn't this be your area of expertise?"

Ekon threw up his hands. "Not in *this* temple."

"Aren't they all basically the same?"

Ekon frowned. "That's extremely—"

"Excuse me."

The six of them looked up to find another clergyman standing over them. "Please be advised that the House of Wise Waters will close to visitors shortly." He glided away, and Koffi swore.

"Koffi!"

"Bwanbale only gave us until dawn!" said Koffi in earnest. "If we can't find Amakoya by tomorrow morning . . . we have to leave."

"Let's review," said Zain. He looked to Safiyah and Ekon. "You two have met Amakoya. How did you find her the first time?"

"We didn't," said Safiyah. "She found us. She was disguised as an old peasant woman called Auntie Matope."

Zain nodded. "That checks out. Along with being the goddess of water, Amakoya's legendary for her tricks and illusions." His gaze lifted. "My guess? If there's an entry to her realm here, it's well hidden. She wouldn't want just anyone finding it."

Njeri frowned. "So how are *we* supposed to?"

Zain paused, thoughtful. "What are her symbols?"

"Crocodiles," said Koffi. "They're her patron animal."

"I saw some crocodile statues near the temple's front entrance," Makena said.

Zain frowned. "That's too obvious."

"In a lot of stories, she has an affinity for pearls," said Makena, "but I haven't seen any pearls here. Not even one."

"She's called the Sovereign of the Seas and the Ruler of the Rivers," Njeri offered. "Could it be something related to that moniker?"

"There are fish in seas and rivers," said Koffi. "And there are fish in all of the pools here. Maybe you have to catch one?"

"That's still too easy." Zain shook his head. "It'd be something more subtle . . ."

Ekon and Safiyah made eye contact. They seemed to arrive at the same thought simultaneously.

"I have an idea," Ekon said. "It was right in front of me, but . . .

153

I missed it." He jerked his head. "Up those stairs, where Safiyah and I went, there are some mermaid statues. In the stories, mermaids are beings of the water, immortal like Amakoya—"

"Ahem."

This time when they looked up, there were several clergymen gathered around. Their smiles didn't quite reach their eyes. Father Kanai stepped forward with one brow raised.

"The sun has set," he noted politely. "The House of Wise Waters is now closed."

Ekon scrambled. "But . . . but we were in the middle of a prayer!"

Father Kanai's lips tightened. "Of course, and I'm sure it was an entirely wholesome prayer, but the rest of it will have to wait until tomorrow at sunrise, when the House of Wise Waters reopens to visitors. Father Uhoro will see you all out."

One by one, they reluctantly stood, and Father Uhoro—a short, portly man—herded them out of the main atrium. They'd barely stepped outside when the temple's doors closed firmly behind them. For the second time, Koffi said a choice word.

"*Still* swearing in places of worship," Ekon muttered.

"Ugh!" Koffi kicked at the door. "Of course! Of *course* we get a lead right when this place is shutting down. Now what do we do?"

Makena looked up. "How sure are you that there's something on that second floor that could help us?"

Ekon erred on the side of honesty. "Not that sure, but I have a hunch."

Makena nodded. "Then I have an idea."

CHAPTER 11

THE HOUSE OF WISE WATERS, PART 2

EKON

"For the record, this is probably sacrilegious."

Ekon shivered as a cool evening breeze chilled his skin, and he hugged the black robe he was wearing tighter around himself. The material was smooth and fine, almost as nice as what he'd been permitted to wear for those brief few days he'd been an anointed Son of the Six.

That didn't make him feel better.

He looked up. Five other people dressed in identical black cloaks stood around him. Up close, it was easier to tell that they were not exactly a match to the ones this temple's order wore, but from a distance they passed, which was what mattered. Ekon shifted his own, uncomfortable.

"Stop fidgeting!"

One of the robed figures turned, and Ekon found Koffi glaring back at him. In different circumstances, the expression on her face combined with the robes absolutely swallowing her small frame would be funny. Now, though, she looked slightly terrifying.

"I can't help it," Ekon whispered. "These aren't my size."

Another one of the robed figures turned to him. Makena. She looked slightly offended. "I did the best I could with what they had in the temple's donation box," she said mildly. "It's not my fault you're in a height competition with . . . with trees!"

"Was that supposed to be an insult?"

"Shh!"

Njeri, Zain, and Safiyah turned around together. Their faces were severe. "Shut it," said Njeri. "It's time."

All six of them stiffened, but it was ultimately Zain who made his way to the temple's front door first. He raised a fist and knocked as hard as he could on the weathered wood. In the night's quiet, the sound seemed to reverberate. Ekon counted as they waited. Fifteen seconds turned to twenty-one . . . thirty . . . thirty-three.

It was almost exactly one minute before he heard the soft pad of footsteps on the other side of the door. He held his breath as a lock clicked, followed by a low groan as one of the doors opened slightly. It was Father Kanai.

"What is going on here?"

To Zain's credit, he was fast. Father Kanai had barely opened the door, but that was all the daraja needed. He stuck out his hand and grabbed the clergyman by his wrist. As soon as they made contact, the man's expression turned blank. Carefully, Zain shouldered open the door so that the rest of them could slip past. Adrenaline coursed through Ekon's blood as he ducked inside, and once they were all in, Zain carefully shut the door behind him and let go of Father Kanai's wrist. The man looked unsteady

156

on his feet now, but Zain guided him to a bench to sit down before he could fall and injure himself.

"He'll be enjoying a nice if not very confusing dream about mermaids for a while," said Zain smugly.

"Bless him," said Njeri.

"It won't last forever," he warned. "Come on, we need to move."

This time, it was Zain who led the way as they quietly ascended the stairs. Perhaps it was because it was darker now, but as Ekon climbed, he sensed a new foreboding in the temple. When they reached the top, the beautiful sunset from before was gone, but in its place the Ndefu River was bathed in moonlight, and stars winked and sparkled across the endless night sky. It took only a few seconds for the stone mermaids to catch his attention again. Ekon tried to look away before anyone noticed, but unfortunately, Zain saw him. He waggled his eyebrows suggestively.

"Nice, Ekon. You conveniently failed to mention that these mermaids were liberated of their clothes."

Ekon tried, but he couldn't help it; his cheeks warmed again. "Yeah, well . . ." He tried to find a new place to look that *wasn't* any of the mermaids, and found Koffi. She was surveying the room, frowning.

"What are these?"

"They're called mermaids," Ekon offered. "I've—"

"Read about them?"

"Well, yes," said Ekon sheepishly. "But unlike the ilomba, there's plenty of information about merfolk. They're creatures of lore, some stories claim that they're even the children of Amakoya. Of course . . ." He paused, brow furrowed. "That *does* lead to some rather troubling questions about their paternity—"

"Focus, Ekon."

"Right, anyway . . . Zain mentioned downstairs that we needed to think of symbols related to Amakoya, and merfolk are just that—beautiful beings that resemble humans but live in the water."

"Beautiful?" Safiyah raised a brow.

Ekon raised both hands. "Objectively speaking!"

Safiyah walked around the wading pool in the middle of the room with her hands behind her back, stopping before each one of the mermaids. She studied each of them as though she could will the truth out of one if she waited long enough. When she'd made a full lap around the room, she sighed.

"I don't know, these merfolk look pretty . . ."

"*Stone*-faced?" Zain offered.

"I have another idea," said Makena. She addressed Koffi and Njeri with a sad expression. "Before Zola died, she once told me about a certain type of craftwork some darajas from our order could do. It's rare, and immensely difficult, but essentially, there are some darajas who can put splendor into harder elements like stone and manipulate it. So if splendor touched it again . . ."

"Maybe that would make a difference!" Njeri straightened and reached out to the mermaid statue nearest to her. "Should we try to use the splendor on it?"

Makena looked thoughtful for a moment. "I think it's going to have to be me. I'm the only daraja from the Order of Ufundi. This isn't my specific craft, but it's closest in relation."

"Can we do anything to help?" asked Koffi.

"No." Makena was already rolling up her sleeves. "Just stand back."

158

Ekon moved to stand next to Zain and Safiyah while Koffi and Njeri also acquiesced, retreating several feet to give Makena space. She was, by far, the shortest in their group, but just then, with her hair tied away from her face and her sleeves rolled up, Ekon thought that she looked like the fiercest too.

"Zain." She didn't look back as she held out a hand. "Take my needle-and-thread kit, please."

It was a testament to the seriousness of the moment that Zain obeyed without making a single wisecrack, and took the tiny kit from her with extreme care. Ekon counted the seconds as Makena stared down the stone statue of the mermaid nearest her. She circled it once, twice, and then stopped halfway through her third round and abruptly touched the mermaid's arm. The effect was instantaneous for both statue and girl. At once, the place where Makena was touching the statue began to glow and turn a butter-yellow color; at the same time, a groan escaped Makena.

"Makena!" Njeri stepped forward, looking alarmed. "Are you okay?"

"Stay . . . back . . . ," she said between her teeth. Her forehead was slick with sweat, and she was breathing hard, but she hadn't let go. "I think . . . it's . . . working."

"Look!" Zain was pointing, but Ekon had already noticed. The buttery light that had started at Makena's hands was now spreading across the mermaid statue and darkening from yellow, to gold, to a warm brown color. Skin, Ekon realized. He watched in awe as the light reached the mermaid's hair, and it too began to darken, changing to a deep blue black. He understood then.

It's coming alive—she's coming alive.

Makena was still straining as she poured the splendor into the stone when it happened. The mermaid's eyes suddenly opened, and Ekon was shocked to find they were a strange shade of purple, like amethyst. She sprang from the pedestal she'd been perched on without warning and dived in one long, beautiful arc into the wading pool in the middle of the room. A wave of water hit them all.

"Did that on purpose," Zain muttered.

Ekon began to count again, not the seconds this time, but the ripples of water that showed where the mermaid had disappeared. *One-two-three-four-five*... He was on eight when her head popped out of the water and she looked around at them. No one spoke immediately, but eventually Zain broke the silence.

"Ahem, *hello*." His voice was deeper than usual, and Ekon noted—with some amusement—that the daraja's chest seemed to be more puffed out than necessary. He deflated when the mermaid only stared at him flatly in response, but he pressed on. "My name is Zain, and these are my friends. We're sorry for disturbing you, but we wondered if you might be able to help us. We're looking for Amakoya, and it's urgent. We wondered if you might know how to get to her, or if you'd be willing to get a message to her?"

The mermaid rose slightly from the water, and Ekon was grateful her long hair, curtained around her face, also covered most of her torso. She cocked her head, and Ekon thought she looked smug.

"Of—of course," Zain stammered, "if you're busy, we could ask one of your ... other friends? We wouldn't presume to know your schedule—"

The mermaid didn't give him any more time to speak. She

turned from the group and dived back into the water. A flash of her bright green tail was the last thing they saw. Ekon exhaled.

"Well, that went well."

"I did my best," said Zain definitively. "Strange, most girls don't respond to me that way."

"Funnily enough," said Njeri wryly, "I get the feeling that's *exactly* how most girls respond to you."

"Shh!" Koffi raised a finger to her lips, looking wary. "Zain, how long did you say we had before Father Kanai's dream wore off?"

"Not long," he said ominously. "We've been here—"

"For twelve minutes," said Ekon automatically.

"Right."

Together, the six of them looked at the pool the mermaid had disappeared into. Njeri leaned forward, brow furrowed.

"That doesn't make sense."

"What?" Zain asked.

"We're on the second floor," she noted, "which means that pool should only be so deep, but looking at it . . ." She took a step closer. "I can't even see the bottom of it."

"It could be an optical illusion," said Makena. "Maybe—"

Her words were cut off as the pool began to ripple, and without warning there was another splash. For a split second, Ekon was reminded of the ilomba, but when he blinked, he saw it was the mermaid again, bobbing in the middle of the pool and looking coy.

"My mistress will see you," she said in a musical voice. "Follow."

"Uh . . ." Zain cocked his head, giving voice to what the rest of them were more than likely thinking. "Follow?"

The mermaid began to swim in circles without another word. They began as small movements, but gradually expanded until she was swimming round and round the length of the pool. At first, Ekon didn't understand, but gradually he saw the water change; a whirlpool was forming and churning faster and faster. Abruptly, the mermaid dived, and with a flash of her tail, she was gone again. The water, however, continued to churn.

"What are we supposed to do?" he asked.

"I think I know," said Koffi. She watched the whirlpool with a wary but determined expression before meeting Ekon's gaze. "But you're not going to like it."

It took Ekon about six seconds to catch up with her train of thought. He felt his mouth pull into a tight line.

"Please say it's not what I'm thinking."

Koffi braced herself. "I think so."

"We're going to look really silly if you're wrong."

"Only one way to find out."

"Hold on." Zain was looking between Koffi and Ekon now, confused. "What's going on?"

But Koffi had already started walking toward the pool. She stepped onto its ledge and looked down at the whirlpool with apprehension; then, before Ekon could even think to stop her, she jumped toward its center feetfirst. Ekon braced himself for the inevitable splash, for the moment her feet hit the pool's bottom, but that wasn't what happened at all. It seemed to take years for Koffi's body to hit the water, but then she kept going. With a small splash, she disappeared entirely. Makena screamed.

"Where did she go?"

"I think . . . I think she's gone to Amakoya's realm," said Ekon. "I think *this* is how we get to it."

Makena stared at him in horror.

"The mermaid said something about her 'mistress,'" Ekon said quickly. "Who else could she have been talking about?"

Makena didn't look assuaged, but now Safiyah, Zain, and Njeri had moved closer to the pool's edge. Zain put one foot on the ledge.

"Koffi's already gone," he said resolutely. "I'm going after her."

"Me too," Njeri agreed. She took Makena's hand with surprising gentleness. "We can all go together."

Makena nodded, and Njeri helped her step onto the ledge. Then she followed suit. Safiyah and Zain stepped up next, and the four of them looked at Ekon.

"You coming?"

Ekon's feet seemed to move of their own accord as he too stepped up to stand on the pool's raised ledge. From this vantage point, the whirlpool seemed much larger, and somehow fiercer. He swallowed.

"On the count of three," he said, staring into its depths. "One, two . . ."

They jumped together as he said *three*. Ekon's stomach swooped as he catapulted himself up with the others, then instantly dropped. The water came up at him in a rush, and then he was submerged in its icy cool. The sensation jarred him, but he had little time to react; the moment he had submerged, he'd felt a strange tug at his core. An invisible force seemed to be pulling him down, and when he looked up, he saw the tiny circle of light above them growing smaller. He opened his mouth without thinking and took in a mouthful of water. At once, panic set in as he thought about drowning and began to flail. The pull grew more intense, and around him, everything darkened. He thought he saw the blurry shapes of the others, but he couldn't be sure anymore; they were falling fast and he couldn't breathe. His head began to pound as he thought about how many seconds had passed without him taking a breath, he tried to tap his fingers, but in the water he found he couldn't. His lungs were straining.

I'm going to drown, he thought. *I'm going to die.*

As quickly as it had started, the pulling sensation stopped. Instead, Ekon felt a nudge in the small of his back, pushing him forward toward a new pale blue circle of light. It came at him too fast, and he braced himself, but when he reached it, there was no impact. There was only a sudden onslaught of light. Ekon choked as he flew through the air, then landed on his knees, gasping. On either side of him, he heard soft thuds and more gasps from the others. He blinked several times before he sat up, then went still.

"Ah," said a rich female voice, "and what have we here?"

And then, for the second time in his life, Ekon met the gaze of the Sovereign of the Seas.

CHAPTER 12

BEASTS of WAR

KOFFI

When Koffi opened her eyes, she was alarmed to discover two things.

The first was that, despite the fact that her last memory was of her jumping into a pool in the House of Wise Waters, she was completely dry. The second was that, despite the fact that her last memory was of jumping into a pool, she could feel *sand* beneath her.

And she'd seen no *sand* in the House of Wise Waters.

Slowly, she pushed herself up, confused. Above, where the sky should have been, she found only swirling shades of dark blue in a concave shape as if . . . as if she was inside some kind of bubble. She was still staring at it in confusion when she heard several yells followed by thumps.

"Ow!"

She jumped, then relaxed again as Ekon landed beside her,

followed by Njeri, Makena, Safiyah, and Zain. One by one, they looked up at her, equally confused.

Where are we?

"Ah, and what have we here?"

Koffi was still on her knees, but she turned in the direction of the voice that had spoken and started at once.

She wasn't sure how she'd missed the woman standing several yards away from them; it was as though she'd suddenly appeared there. Her skin was a reddish-brown hue, and her black hair fell all the way to her knees in braids that ended in white cowrie shells. When none of them spoke, she flashed a small smile, and Koffi saw a row of flat white teeth. A chill shuddered through her as understanding hit her.

"Amakoya," she whispered.

The Water Witch arched a perfect black brow; her face held both amusement and annoyance.

"You dare to speak my true name, mortal?"

Next to her, Koffi felt Ekon staring at her. No one else had moved, but slowly, Koffi stood. She was all too aware that sand still clung to her legs and tunic, but she didn't look at them. The goddess's question lingered in the silent air, but Koffi found herself unable to speak. Like Badwa, Amakoya was larger than life; even Ekon was short by comparison. Her beautiful braids moved of their own accord, swaying in an invisible breeze.

"One of my maidens tells me some of you are darajas," Amakoya went on, gesturing, "and that you have a message for me."

For the first time, Koffi dared look away from the goddess to gaze around them. They must have been in Amakoya's realm, but it was hard to describe the place itself. It looked as though they were on an island of sand, surrounded by weathered gray rocks. When Koffi looked closer at them, she saw that merfolk were perched on some of those rocks in various states of recline, all watching her curiously. Every so often, something glided along the water's surface, and she noticed more than one massive crocodile eyeing her too. She swallowed, then made herself speak.

"Goddess," she started. "My name is Koffi. I come bearing a message from the goddess Badwa."

Visible surprise registered on the goddess's face. "My younger sister?" Her gaze narrowed. "You are the second mortal of late to claim you know one of my siblings."

Finally Ekon stepped in. "Goddess." His own voice was shaking. "I was the mortal you spoke to before."

Amakoya's gaze cut from Ekon to Koffi with razor-sharp focus. Koffi watched as recognition touched the deity's features. "Ah, the boy from the marshes." Her smile turned cool as she assessed him. "You denied my water dragons a fine meal."

Koffi didn't know what Amakoya was referencing, but it didn't sound good. When she looked at Ekon, she noticed visible worry in his expression. Already he'd begun to tap his fingers at his side, but he kept on speaking.

"I found the girl I told you I was looking for." He gestured. "It's her. Koffi."

Amakoya did not look at Koffi again, but instead turned her gaze to the rest of their group. Her thoughts were unreadable as she took them in.

"What is the message you bring from my sister?"

"It's Fedu," said Koffi. "He . . . he's planning something."

Amakoya looked supremely unimpressed, and Koffi went on quickly.

"Nearly a century ago, Fedu tried to use a daraja to help him take a huge amount of the splendor during the last Bonding. It didn't work, but the next one's coming and he's planning to do it again. He tried to use me. If he succeeds, he'll have the power to level Eshōza and kill everyone in it who isn't a daraja."

A furrow appeared between Amakoya's brows. "That is not possible," she said in a clipped voice. "My brother is ambitious and vain, but he would not—"

"He's after us," said Ekon, "and he released the Untethered from his realm to try to stop us. They're still in the south, but they're making their way north. I imagine they'll be here soon."

This seemed to have some effect on Amakoya. Koffi caught the barest hint of genuine surprise on Amakoya's face, but it was gone just as quickly. Around them, she noticed the water, which had moments before been cool, calm, and flat as blue glass, had now begun to stir.

"You are certain?" she asked. "You are certain that this is his ambition?"

"We are," said Koffi.

"If this is the truth, then it upsets the very balance of this world." Amakoya seemed to be speaking more to herself now. She stared off into the distance, thoughtful.

"Badwa sent us to you because she believes there may be a way to stop Fedu," said Koffi. "If the other five gods band together, you can stop him."

Amakoya frowned. "By what means?"

Koffi hesitated. "By killing him."

The goddess's expression turned cool. "You speak of *fratricide*, the murder of another god?"

"Yes." Koffi knew there was no softer way to deliver the message. "It's the only option."

"You would have my own brothers and sisters and I turn against one of our own," she said with audible disgust. "You would render us, for your own devices, mere beasts of war?"

"If Fedu is not stopped, everyone will suffer," said Koffi. "Not just those who aren't darajas, but beings in the other realms too." She gestured at the merfolk around them. "He won't spare them once he has the splendor he needs."

Amakoya jutted her chin. "And why should I believe you?" she asked. "You are mortals, all of you."

Ekon's mouth fell open. "We . . . we just told you that we spoke with Badwa. She's the one who told us about this in the first place."

Amakoya remained unmoved. "You speak of my sister, and yet I have received no message from her directly. She did not speak to me of our brother's plan, nor did she warn me that she was sending *mortal* emissaries to speak for her." She crossed her arms. "You expect me to trust you?" The waters around them turned to waves, tossing and splashing at the sand. Her braids swayed more violently as her temper worsened. "You come into my realm with only this? Unproven messages and requests for slaughter, as though I serve *you*?"

"No!" Koffi said quickly. "That's not it—"

But it was too late. Koffi watched, with cold terror, as Amakoya began to change. The mermaids on their rocks dived into the water, disappearing below its depths as Amakoya grew even taller, even less human. Like Badwa, golden light emanated from her, but it was not a warm light; there was something righteously terrifying about it. Suddenly, Koffi understood why Ekon and Safiyah has been less than excited to see Amakoya again. The water goddess lifted her hands, and fifty-foot waves rose on either side. A terrible wind began to howl.

"You will be punished for your insolence, mortals," she said. Her voice had changed too, now raw and sonorous. "I will see to that. Let my sister think twice before presuming to send mortals to me instead of visiting me herself."

"Wait!"

Koffi and Ekon started, both turning to look behind them. For the first time, Safiyah stepped forward. For a moment, Koffi was relieved—perhaps a different person might assuage the goddess—but when she turned and saw Amakoya's face, the goddess looked enraged.

"YOU!" she seethed. "The faithless heathen, the irreverent blasphemer. You dare to show your face to me again? I will smite you first."

Any new hope Koffi had had wilted at once, but to her surprise, Safiyah nudged past her and Ekon so that she was standing closest to the goddess. The wind whipped her braid around, but she held her ground, staring up at Amakoya with a resolve Koffi almost admired. She didn't know Safiyah well enough to know what she was thinking or planning, but even if she had, she was sure she still would have been surprised by what she did then. She dropped to her knees.

"Goddess Amakoya, I humble myself before you."

The winds tossed Amakoya's braids as she looked down her nose at Safiyah with all the regard one might have for an ant before they squashed it. "You only humble yourself now, in the face of death?"

"No." In the throes of the storm, Safiyah's words should have been barely audible if at all, but Koffi heard them clearly. "I humble myself before greatness."

For the first time, Amakoya paused.

"You are right, goddess," Safiyah went on, "everything you've called me is true. For most of my life, I have been faithless, a heathen, a blasphemer."

The waves around them began to settle.

"I was all of those things because for most of my life I've had little use or need for gods or a higher power," said Safiyah. "I thought, for better or for worse, that I was responsible for my own life's path. I didn't think it had anything to do with anything bigger than myself." She steeled herself. "But in the last few days, I've seen things, things I could never have fathomed in my wildest dreams or nightmares. I've seen the untethered souls of the dead leaving a path of destruction in their wake. I've seen death." She shuddered. "And now I'm here, in the court of the greatest of the six gods, gods who I didn't believe in, and my mind is changed. I realize now how small and insignificant I truly am in the grander scheme of it all. I realize how small and insignificant I am in comparison to the radiance of *true* higher power—power like yours."

Koffi guessed Amakoya would respond to those words any number of ways; what she did not expect was for the goddess to draw herself up to her full height, looking distinctly haughty. She reminded Koffi now of the male peacocks at the Night Zoo, the ones that paraded around the zoo's lawns and preened when they were complimented.

"We did not call upon you from a place of disrespect, goddess," said Safiyah. "We called upon you because we know—*I* know—that a battle is coming, one whose outcome will alter the world we know evermore. We cannot hope to win it if the most powerful of the Six is not on our side, which is why we have come to you before all others."

At this, Amakoya's brow rose with visible interest. "You have not solicited any other god or goddess?"

"Badwa came to me," said Koffi, "but you are the first of the Six that we have sought out. We have not spoken to Atuno, Itaashe, or Tyembu." She tactfully chose not to mention that this was largely because Amakoya was geographically closest, and it seemed to do the trick.

"Atuno is the eldest of the Six gods," Amakoya mused. "According to the rules of deference, you should have called upon him first, and yet you chose to visit me . . ."

"Goddess, it is more than evident that you are by far the most loved of the Six," Safiyah went on. "Even today, your temple over-flows with so many patrons that they cannot all worship you at once."

"Do not be impertinent, mortal," said Amakoya, though there was softness in the chiding now. She looked around at the group of them, considering. "Your humility is acknowledged, but it does not change the nature of what you are asking. I have no qualms with murder itself, but the murder of a god sets a precedent I do not care for."

Koffi tried to ignore the fact that Amakoya had just admitted that she didn't oppose murder. "I understand," she said, taking care to bow the same way Safiyah had. "But it truly is the only way. Once he has the power he wants, Fedu will leave nothing in his wake that doesn't serve him." Some of the mermaids had begun to resurface, their heads and torsos emerging from the waves again. Koffi gestured around at them pointedly. "It won't just be those on land who will suffer."

Amakoya followed Koffi's gaze and stopped on one particular mermaid floating closer to the shore than the others. She was, Koffi noted, an exceedingly beautiful mermaid, with red-brown hair and curious hazel eyes. The other merfolk looked to Amakoya with deference, but this one did not; Koffi saw an informality, a familiarity in that mermaid's expression as she looked up at Amakoya, and Koffi was surprised to see an entirely different look on the goddess's face. It took her a moment to name it: affection, tenderness. She watched the redheaded mermaid a few seconds longer before turning back to address them.

"Very well, mortals," she said. "I will aid the cause my sister has sent you to campaign for."

"You'll help us?" Ekon had kept quiet, but now he stepped forward, looking awed. Amusement touched Amakoya's face.

"I will," she said. "But I have a question first." She regarded Koffi. "You found me. How do you intend to find my siblings?"

Koffi paused. "I have an affinity with the splendor," she said. "I can use it to find things." She was sure, as soon as the words left her mouth, that it was the wrong thing to say. Amakoya smiled, revealing a mouth full of sharp white teeth.

"How fascinating," she said. "In that case, I think I'll add a stipulation to our arrangement."

"A stipulation?" Ekon repeated. He looked as uneasy as Koffi felt.

"Indeed," said Amakoya. "I will help defeat my brother, but in exchange, you must retrieve something for me."

"What is it?" asked Koffi.

"A bracelet," said Amakoya, "stolen from this temple decades ago. I have sent countless champions on quests to find it; *all* have failed me."

"The bracelet," Ekon said carefully, "what does it look like?"

"It is fashioned from black pearls, taken from my own black-lipped oysters at the heart of the Machungu Sea," said Amakoya. "There are many replicas, but only one that is authentic."

"How can we tell a real one from a fake?" Koffi asked.

"True pearls, whether black or white, are never identical," said the goddess. "Each one is unique, and when the sun touches them, their coloring turns iridescent and will show hues of green and blue."

Ekon paused, thoughtful. "Can you tell us anything about the thief who took your bracelet? Were they seen by anyone?"

Amakoya grimaced. "The thief presented as male. That is all I know."

"Thank you, goddess," said Ekon. "We're truly humbled."

The goddess sighed. "A word of advice? My older brother prefers places where the earth touches the sky. I cannot speak to Tyembu's or Itaashe's whereabouts." She nodded to Zain,

Makena, and Njeri, who hadn't spoken. "And what of you three?" she asked imperiously. "Do you also bring tidings of war?"

Makena seemed incapable of speaking and merely shook her head quickly. Njeri froze. Zain offered an uneasy smile.

"No additional tidings here, goddess, and no further requests, unless . . ." He looked around. "Unless you might be willing to help us get out of here? I didn't see any stairs on the way in."

Amakoya offered another one of her toothy smiles, and Koffi found it no less chilling than she had the first time she'd seen it. Amakoya raised both hands, and as they'd done before, tidal waves rose. This time, they surrounded the entire island.

"You will see me on the battlefield, mortals," said the goddess as the waves began to swirl around them. "Pray that you have what I've asked for when you do."

CHAPTER 13

FATE

EKON

There were few words exchanged as the group made their way from the House of Wise Waters back to the *Nzinga*.

For that, at least, Ekon was grateful. His mind had been racing from the moment Amakoya had returned them to the mortal world, but now he felt it finally slowing. A bleary-eyed Captain Bwanbale had been waiting for them when they'd finally rowed back and boarded the ship, but no one had offered much information about the night's activities, and he seemed too tired to press the subject. They all retreated to their quarters, except for Ekon. He opted to move to the ship's bow and take in the world around him. Most of the temple's patrons were gone, but a few larger ferries and ships were still moored nearby. This late in the night, the Ndefu itself was calm, its surface interrupted only by the occasional frog or fish leaping up to catch an insect. He inhaled deeply and took in the river's smell, letting it wash over him. Only when he stared up at the pearlescent moon did the first wave of anxiety finally reach him.

A bracelet, now they had to find a missing *bracelet*.

Koffi had her affinity, and surely they could use that to help, but he was growing more and more concerned about the time. A week had gone by since they'd made their initial plan, which meant they had exactly two weeks left until the Bonding. They also still had two other gods to find. He thought back to Amakoya's words. *My older brother prefers places where the earth touches the sky.* That could be anywhere. Ekon tapped his fingers against the gunwale, trying to organize his own thoughts in a way that didn't immediately send him into a spiral. After a moment, he took in a deep breath. His head began to pound. Not so long ago, in the Greater Jungle, he and Koffi had made a challenging but straightforward plan. When Fedu had taken her, he'd had to adjust the plan to add in rescuing her, but the main mission to get Koffi to the Kusonga Plains had always stayed at the forefront. Now, though . . . he massaged the bridge of his nose. Now he barely recognized the original plan for all its changes and deviations, and he certainly didn't know if it was possible anymore. The Bonding would be happening soon, and now they had *another* task. He shook his head and sighed.

"Hey. You okay?"

Ekon started and turned. Safiyah was standing behind him. The evening had chilled, and she'd wrapped one of the robes they'd stolen around her bare arms. Moonlight lit half of her face and cast the other into sharp relief, but he could still make out her tentative expression. He relaxed.

"Yeah, I'm all right."

Soundlessly she moved to stand beside him, and for several minutes neither of them said anything as the ferry rocked from side to side and a western breeze passed through.

"You're a bad liar."

Ekon looked up. "Huh?"

"Your fingers have been tapping ever since we got back." Safiyah continued to stare out into the water. "And not the easygoing kind of tapping you do when you're thinking."

For a moment Ekon was distracted by the words themselves. Plenty of people noticed his tapping fingers, but he didn't think anyone had ever paid enough attention to notice the different cadences and realize that they might signify different things. When Safiyah turned to him, he relented.

"I don't know how we're going to do this."

"Do what?" Safiyah said with a half smile. "Convince two more gods to fight with us, get Koffi to the Kusonga Plains in time, or find Amakoya's bracelet?"

"All of the above."

"It won't be easy," Safiyah admitted. "But then again, nothing in life truly worth anything ever is." Without warning, she ran across the masts and climbed until she was nestled within its tiny lookout point with the breeze whipping around her hair. Horrified, Ekon glared up at her.

"Safiyah!" He said her name as loudly as he dared, given the time of night. "What are you doing?"

"Having a little fun." Safiyah swung one of her legs over the edge and then the other, so that both were kicking air. "You should try it sometime."

Ekon looked around. Except for one of the deckhands sweeping the deck below, no one was awake at this hour.

"Join me," she taunted. "Unless you're—"

"All right." Ekon frowned, then followed after. To Safiyah's credit, she'd made the climb look easier than it was. By the time Ekon reached the lookout point, he'd almost broken into a sweat, but the breeze from this high cooled him back down almost instantly. Carefully, he settled beside Safiyah. She smirked.

"The sun will be coming up soon," she noted. "We'll get a nice view of the sunrise if we turn slightly."

"We could break our necks up here," Ekon muttered.

"Or we could see something beautiful," Safiyah replied. "Who can say? Fate will decide."

Fate. Ekon had a stronger reaction to that word than he'd expected. He tensed.

"What?"

"Can I ask you something?"

"Sure."

"What you said to Amakoya," he asked. "Do you really believe it?"

He thought at first that Safiyah might laugh, or perhaps her smirk would deepen. Instead, her expression turned thoughtful, and for a long time she said nothing. She was quiet for so long that, as she'd predicted, the faintest hints of lavender began to color the night sky, signaling dawn.

"I didn't use to believe in things like fate and destiny," she finally whispered. "I kind of thought it was a type of wish fulfillment, a thing people used for cons and stuff."

Ekon swallowed. "And now?"

"Now I'm not sure," she said. "Sometimes it seems like fate is real and isn't real at the same time."

"What do you mean?"

Safiyah cocked her head and pursed her lips. "Maybe most of the time, it does feel like our lives are in our control. We make our own decisions and forge our own paths, and then there are consequences for those actions, and we keep choosing." She paused. "But then, other times, it does seem like things just sort of happen, and there isn't a way to explain it except for this idea that maybe it's bigger than us, bigger than a single moment, or a single choice. Maybe some things are always meant to be, and the choices we *think* we're making independently are just leading us toward it."

Ekon gnawed his lip and did his best to keep his tapping fingers out of Safiyah's line of vision. It was, he had to admit, an astute observation, it just hadn't been the one he'd wanted to hear. He was still plagued by one specific line from the prophecy.

You will kill the one you love most.

"Why do you ask?" she said after a beat.

Ekon rocked his head from side to side, trying to work out the kinks in his neck. "It's just something I've been thinking about more lately," he said. "Someone once told me that destiny was a path, and our job wasn't to question it, but to follow it. I thought it was good advice at first, but . . . now I'm not so sure."

"I think about the night I met you," she said. "That seemed like fate, in a way."

Ekon raised a brow involuntarily. "I saw you in the market, I followed you."

She nodded. "Because you came at just the right moment,

because those street hyenas picked *me* to follow in the first place. And later on, you and Themba chose to hide in a certain alleyway, but you had no way of knowing it was the Enterprise's alley, or that Thabo would see you and think you were thieves. Some of it just happened, and I get the feeling that no matter what you or I did, we would have found our way to each other eventually." She paused. "Tonight felt like fate," she added. "I had no way of knowing that Amakoya would listen to me, the least likely person in our group to have any effect on her. I just did it and hoped for the best." She stared directly at Ekon. "Sometimes, I think that's all we can do—hope for the best."

"*Hope* doesn't seem very logically sound," Ekon grumbled. Then he stopped. Something Safiyah had said before came back to him. "You . . . you still think about the night we met?"

Safiyah dropped her gaze. "Of course I do."

An entirely different set of emotions overcame Ekon. The anxiety around their plans was chased away by a new sense of self-consciousness, a swoop low in his stomach. The sun was now rising from the east in earnest, casting red-orange rays of light across the Ndefu and onto Safiyah's face. Radiant. There was no other word for it; she looked *radiant* in that light. Ekon found it hard to breathe.

"Safiyah . . ." His breath caught as she suddenly pressed their foreheads together but hesitated, letting her lips hover inches from his.

"Do you want me to?" she whispered. "Do you *want* me to kiss you, Ekon?"

Ekon tried to speak, but he'd almost entirely lost his voice. "I—"

"Ask," she said softly. "All you have to do is ask, and I will."

Ekon's fingers were frantic now. One hand was inches from Safiyah, but on his other side, he was counting faster and faster, trying to make his brain work in this new heady rush.

One-two-three. One-two-three. One-two-three.

Ask. The simple word reverberated in Ekon's mind. *Just ask.*

He wanted to, at least a part of him did. Safiyah's forehead was still pressed against his; this close, he could smell the grapeseed oil in her hair, he could hear each breath she took, as shallow as his own. He wanted her to kiss him, but . . . then Koffi's face flooded his mind. He was remembering the way he'd felt when *she'd* kissed him in the jungle. She hadn't asked, but . . . he hadn't minded either. He pulled back before he could stop himself and almost instantly regretted it. Safiyah's face fell, but only for a moment.

"Sun's up," she said, nodding a bit too casually. "We should head down, we'll be leaving soon."

"Right." Ekon cleared his throat. "You want to go down first?"

"That's okay," said Safiyah. She wasn't looking at him. "I'll follow you."

Ekon kicked his leg over and headed down the mast as quickly as he could reasonably manage without falling. Just as she'd said, Safiyah came right behind him, and when she was nearly down, he automatically reached out to catch her hand and help her.

"Thank you," she said with a small smile. Just as quickly, it slid from her face as she looked over Ekon's shoulder. "Oh. Good morning."

Ekon swiveled, but not fast enough. Koffi was standing on the deck with an expression he couldn't read. Her eyes dropped from

Ekon to Safiyah to their hands, which Ekon realized a beat too late were still clasped.

"Good morning," she said politely. "I just wanted to let you know that breakfast is ready. We'll eat, then head out."

Safiyah shifted her weight from foot to foot. "Thanks."

"You're welcome." Without another word, Koffi turned on her heel and headed down the deck.

"Koffi!"

She didn't stop, and Safiyah gave him a cool look before heading in the opposite direction, leaving Ekon alone on the deck, feeling more and more like he'd just managed to make a bad situation much worse.

THE WEIGHT

AKANDE

Year 892

"Babu, when can I put this thing down?"

The only answer I get is a soft, metallic chime. I cough, trying to cover up the sound, but it's too late. From his spot seated on the riverbank, my grandfather looks up and shakes his head.

"You *moved*. Restart your count."

I glare at the bronze wind chimes I'm still holding in my left hand, annoyed. Initially, I'd thought them cool-looking; in the time since, I've grown to hate them.

"Start again," says Babu.

I raise the chimes and start counting again. "One . . . two . . . three . . . four . . ." Abruptly, a breeze blows across the banks. I reorient myself, trying to block the wind and stop the chimes from hitting each other, but it's no good. The air around me fills with their gong-like sound. Babu rubs the bridge of his nose, looking tired.

"And . . . start again."

184

"But that wasn't my fault!" I protest. "The wind—"

"Focus and control, boy," says my grandfather. "Keep focus, and maintain control. *That's* what we're testing here. Now, start from the top."

"Babu, how much longer do I have to do this?" I look up at the darkening sky. "It's getting late!"

Sitting on the Ndefu's sloping bank, my grandfather looks at ease despite the slight chill in the air. He polishes his apple on his tunic before taking a loud, crunchy bite.

"You'll do it until you can count to one hundred without the chimes making a sound. Now, less talking, more stillness."

"This is *ridiculous*." The words leave me before I can stop myself. "What's the point?"

Babu looks up at me again, frowning. *"Tradition,"* he says curtly. "These daraja-training techniques have been passed down in our family for generations—"

"I think you're making them up."

My grandfather's brows rise. "What did you say?"

"None of these 'techniques' have anything to do with being a daraja! They're just random tasks. What does chasing wild chickens have to do with being a daraja?"

Babu's expression did not change. "It improves your stamina."

"Or picking rice off the ground?"

"Attention to detail," says Babu nonchalantly, "another highly important quality in any young daraja."

I huff. "You haven't let me drink anything but prune juice and water for a week."

Babu threw his arms up. "For your well-being! The *best* daraja is a healthy one."

"I'm sick of this!" I drop my arm, and the chimes hit my leg with a loud clang. "We've been training for almost two years, and you've barely taught me anything. When do I get to do something *fun*? When do I get to actually summon the splendor again?"

My grandfather's lips purse. "As I recall, I *have* let you summon the splendor, Akande. Do you remember how *that* went? The results were disastrous."

"They were not!"

"No?" Babu's tone is wry. "Izachar nearly lost a finger!"

"He's fine!" I point out quickly. "C'mon, Babu. That was one time."

My grandfather juts out his chin, assessing.

"Please, Babu," I press. "I've done everything you asked. Just give me a chance to prove myself."

Babu cocks his head to the side. I know that look; he's thinking.

"All right," he finally says. "I'm going to teach you something new. But be warned, boy." He holds up a cautionary finger. "You must do exactly as I instruct, or the lesson is over. Do you understand?"

I stand up straighter. "I understand."

Babu nods. "Put the chimes down."

I drop them with a little more enthusiasm than necessary, and my grandfather shakes his head. He beckons for me to join him by the river's edge. This close to the water, it laps at my toes. For several moments neither of us speaks as we look out onto the river.

"You understand that the splendor is a type of cosmic energy," says my grandfather. "Which means it works differently than the energy of this earth."

I nod. We've gone over this a hundred times.

"What that means," Babu goes on, "is that, with practice, the splendor can be manipulated to some extent. I want you to watch what I'm going to do. Stand back, please."

Excitement courses through me as I do what he says and move several feet back. My grandfather is an old man, but in this moment, I can believe that he was once a powerful daraja. His face is set with a kind of concentration I've never seen before.

"Watch carefully," he murmurs.

I don't take my eyes off him, but he still moves faster than I expect. With one hand, he makes a fist, pulling back as though he might punch the air. With the other, his arm extends out, pinching at the air like he's trying to catch something small. He arches his back slightly. It looks strange until I realize what's he's doing; he's taking the exact position an archer might take to nock an arrow. The seconds pass, and then I see it. Silvery-white speckles of light are forming around my grandfather's hand, but he doesn't move until there are enough of them to make a clear shape. He's now holding a sparkling bow and arrow, both entirely made of splendor.

"Whoa."

My grandfather doesn't look at me, but pulls the splendor arrow back tighter. I can practically see the splendor bow's string growing taut, and I relish the moment he releases it. The arrow makes a perfect arc, flying directly over the river and landing on the opposite bank in an explosion of light. Only then does Babu turn back to me. At the look on my face, his expression turns smug.

"That..." I look between him and the place where the splendor arrow landed. "That was amazing, Babu."

"Yes." Babu smirks. "Yes it was."

"How did you do it?" I ask.

"Splendor is a near-sentient energy," says Babu. "When summoned, it wants to do as its summoner intends. If you're thinking is clear and intentional enough, it can be rendered into a tool or, as you've just seen, a weapon. But you know what that requires?"

I nod, already knowing the answer. "Focus and control."

"Exactly," says Babu. "Without both of those things, summoning the splendor that way can be *extremely* dangerous."

"Can you show me?"

Babu hesitates, then nods. "We'll go over the movement first."

I join him at the bank's edge again and adjust my feet so that I'm standing the way he is. He moves around me, nudging and positioning me just so.

"This is uncomfortable," I complain.

"Good," he says, "that means it's right." He looks me over, then nods. "Move as though you are shooting an arrow. Nock the arrow, and hold."

I do as he says, and try to ignore a tiny pinch of embarrassment. I imagine how I'd look to passersby. As if he can read my thoughts, my grandfather snaps his fingers in front of my nose.

"Focus!" he says sternly. "Now, I want to see you nock your arrow and hold that position. Do it ten times."

It seems like a pointless exercise, but I do it anyway, tempering my annoyance as my babu continues a steady list of critiques.

"Your elbow is too low!"

"Shoulders back!"

"Keep your arm straight!"

In the end, I repeat the exercise thirty times before he's appeased. The muscles in my arms are sore when he finally lets me relax. I grumble under my breath as I massage them.

"Don't tell me you're already tired?" he asks. "We're only just getting started. Take your position."

My arms ache as I raise them again, but admittedly the movement feels familiar now. After a moment, my grandfather nods.

"Now, I want you to *carefully* summon the splendor, envisioning a bow and arrow as you do. Remember: Intent is key here, so you must remain entirely focused on the task at hand."

This is the moment I've been looking forward to, and I do my best to keep my expression composed as I close my eyes and summon the splendor. I know the moment it answers my call. A warmth starts in my feet, pleasant against the evening's slight chill, and a hum moves through my body as that energy travels up my legs, filling up my rib cage.

"Focus," says Babu.

With my eyes still closed, I picture an arrow in my mind; I think about its feel between my fingers. The splendor moves down my arms, but I hold steady, remembering what my grandfather said.

Focus and control.

I open my eyes, prepared to see a silver bow and arrow poised in my hands. I'm disappointed to see only a few speckles of the splendor floating around me.

"It's all right," says Babu. "This is your first time. Just keep focusing and really try to think about what you want it to do."

I try to do as he says, willing the speckles around me to come together, but the harder I try, the less it seems to work. The speckles begin to fizzle and disappear. A sheen of sweat forms on my brow as I try to make them to stay.

"Akande," says my grandfather in a sharper voice. "Let go of it, now."

I don't want to, but a few seconds later my body's limitations supersede my ambition. Every muscle in my body relaxes as I let the splendor go.

"Don't be discouraged," says Babu. "We will keep practicing."

The words are not unkind, but in my mind, they're warped. *He's only being nice,* says an insidious voice. *You've let him down. You're supposed to be the descendant of great darajas.*

"Let's take a break," says Babu, resettling on the banks. "We'll try again another time."

Reluctantly, I sit on the banks beside him while he pulls his half-eaten apple from his pocket. His face betrays nothing, but I can practically feel the disappointment rolling off him as we sit in silence.

He gave you a chance to prove yourself, says that same voice, *and you failed him.*

"My grandmother, your great-great-grandmother Miremba, was exceptionally good at making splendor weapons," says Babu wistfully. "She could make arrows, spears. I once even saw her summon a war hammer. It took her many years to learn to do it."

I know the words are meant to be a comfort, but they make me feel worse.

"It *will* come, boy," says Babu. "You just have to be patient." He looks to the sky. "Now, I'd better get you home before I hear from your mother. Let's go."

A new wave of disappointment hits me as I realize he means our training tonight is over. I won't get the chance to try again for gods know how long. With not a small amount of effort, my grandfather gets to his feet and begins the ascent up the riverbank. He doesn't look over his shoulder to make sure I'm following. Without warning, an idea pops into my mind. I face the river one last time, taking up the proper stance, and focus hard on forming the splendor arrow. This time, I curl my toes into the mud so hard they hurt. A buzzing fills my ears.

"Akande?"

I hear my grandfather's distant voice but ignore it as I summon more splendor than before, relishing the feeling as it floods into me in a rush. This time it isn't just the place in my rib cage that fills with the splendor's warmth, it's my entire body. I open my eyes and gasp.

There isn't an arrow in my hands, but something resembling it. The speckles of splendor have come together around my hands to form a glittering mass of energy. The sight of it almost takes my breath away. For the first time, I truly understand what my babu means when he says it's a near-sentient energy. It has a heartbeat of its own, one that matches mine beat for beat, and it's growing bigger.

"AKANDE!"

There's a new edge in my grandfather's voice. I try to turn my head toward him, but the splendor in my hands trembles, sending waves of pain through my bones. It grows bigger, too big for me to do anything with at all. Fear lances through me as it grows brighter, more powerful.

"Let it go!" my grandfather yells. "Let it go right now!"

I'm scared to, but I do it. The reaction is almost instant. My arms drop and the splendor explodes around me in a great ball of light, sending me flying several feet back. My vision is showered in stars for a moment, but after a few seconds I'm able to sit up. When I do, I find my grandfather is glaring at me.

"What—were—you—*thinking*?" His voice is dangerously, scarily low. "If I've told you once, I've told you a thousand times: The splendor is to move *through* you. You are never, ever to hold it within your body. You could have killed yourself, or worse!"

"I . . ." My voice sounds small in my own ears. "I just wanted to try one more time. I thought I could—"

"I TOLD YOU TO WAIT!" my grandfather shouts. He looks apoplectic now, and his eyes are wide with rage. "I told you to wait, and you deliberately disobeyed me. Do you know what could have just happened not only to you, but to me, to anyone nearby?"

Guilt washes over me. "I'm sorry, Babu."

"Sorry isn't good enough."

"It was an *accident*," I whisper. "It won't happen again."

Babu scowls. "Oh, you can be sure of that. It's clear I completely misjudged your maturity. I should have listened to my better instincts and waited until you were—" The rest of his words are cut off as he clutches at his stomach.

"Babu?" I get to my feet, on edge. "Babu, what's wrong?"

My grandfather doesn't answer, nor is he looking at me anymore. His mouth has gone horribly slack, and he's swaying in a way that unsettles me. A soft moan is all the warning I get before he collapses facedown in the mud.

"No!" I close the distance between us in three strides and fall to my knees. "Babu! *Babu!*" Carefully, I flip him over and hold the back of my hand over his mouth. His breath is shallow, but my grandfather isn't moving. Panic sinks its claws into me.

"Help!" I scream, praying someone can hear me. "Please, someone help!"

It takes three hundred and two steps to walk the entire perimeter of my house.

I know that because it's all I've done in the hours since my babu was brought home. It's all I *can* do.

Forty-five, forty-six . . .

If I focus on my footsteps, I don't have to think about the things I've seen. The image of Babu's limp body stays seared in my mind, as does the thought of the healers who've come in and out of our house. If I focus on my footsteps, I don't have to remember the grave look on the face of the one who just left.

Fifty-two, fifty-three . . .

"Akande?"

I'm pulled from my count as I round the corner of my house and find my mother standing at our front door, waiting for me. This late, her hair is tied up in a headwrap, and she looks like she should be going to bed, but her eyes are alert as they find me in the darkness.

"Come inside," she murmurs. "I . . . Your father and I need to speak with you."

For a moment I think of refusing, of staying out here where I can keep counting and waiting. If I don't go inside, I don't have to hear any bad news. But seconds later, I force my feet to move as I follow my mother inside. She ushers me into our living room, where my father is already sitting with Namina on the floor. She settles beside them and gestures for me to as well. I want to, but my knees are locked and refuse to bend. A knot in my stomach grows impossibly tight as my mother opens her mouth to speak, and then the words spill out of me before I can stop them.

"I'm sorry!"

"Sorry?" My father looks up at me, confused. "What for?"

"It's my fault." I look between my parents. "Babu was showing me some daraja-training techniques tonight by the river, and he told me to be careful, but . . . but I didn't listen, and then he got angry at me, and it caused him to—"

"Akande." My mother's voice is gentle but firm. "Please, sit down."

I don't want to, but I make myself take a seat on the rug across from them. My mother sighs.

"What happened to your grandfather tonight was *not* your fault," she said. "He collapsed because . . . because he's sick."

"Sick?" I look up, surprised. This isn't what I was expecting. "But—but he was fine just before . . ."

It's my father who shakes his head now. "We've spoken with several healers," he says. In a lower voice, he adds, "You know that your grandfather is a proud man, Akande. He didn't want us to know, but . . ." He blinks tears away. "He's likely been sick for a long time. His illness is . . . advanced."

"What does that mean?" asks Namina. She's braver than me, but I hear the fear in her voice.

"It means," says my mother, "that we may not have much more time with him."

The words touch me like a candle's flame: hot and stinging. I flinch away from them. "No." I shake my head. "No, that's not right. That *can't* be right."

"Akande." My mother looks pained now. I want to be more thoughtful. I want to be mindful of the fact that Babu is *her* father, that this is hard for her too. I can't. "What's coming is going to be difficult for all of us, but . . ."

I'm already on my feet, backing away from her and my father. "You're wrong!" I realize I sound childish, but I can't stop myself. "You and the healers are wrong. He's not sick, he just . . . he just needs rest."

"Akande," says my father heavily. "We're going to get through this as a family, and fortunately we still have some time to—"

I don't want to hear any more. I turn on my heel and bolt out of the house, not stopping as my parents call after me. This late at night, Kugawanya's air is frigid, but I let it wash over me as my run becomes a flat-out sprint, a race against something I want to leave behind. I don't even realize my feet have led me back to the Ndefu River until I'm at the water's edge. Only then do I fall to the ground. Only then do my parents' words catch up with me. The weight of them latches on to me, anchoring me in place and forcing me to finally face them directly.

He's likely been sick for a long time.

His illness is . . . advanced.

I blink hard as tears come, as my anger splinters in a thousand directions. I'm angry at my parents, at the healers who got it wrong. I'm angry at myself, and I'm angry at Babu, and then I feel bad for being angry at him. More tears come and I paw them away.

It's not true. It *can't* be true.

"Thought I might find you here."

I whirl around at the sound of the familiar voice and find my grandfather standing there on the bank.

"Babu, what are you—?"

"All that fuss." He rolls his eyes. "Just because I tripped and fell."

He sounds so utterly normal, so much like himself. When I continue to stare at him in silence, he frowns.

"Stop looking at me like that."

The truth is, I don't know *how* to stop. Babu isn't wearing his usual cloak, and in the moonlight with just a normal tunic on, I see for the first time things I hadn't noticed before. He's frailer. The hair on his head—the hair that's been white my whole life— is noticeably thinner. Even his breath is more labored. I'm angry at myself all over again as the truth stares back at me plainly. How could I have missed so many signs for so long?

"I'm serious, Akande," Babu threatens. "You keep looking at me like I'm a kicked puppy, and I will bite you like one. See if I won't!"

At last, I find words. "Babu," I whisper. "Why didn't you tell us?"

My grandfather shifts his weight from foot to foot, looking uncharacteristically uncomfortable. "Wasn't your business," he says gruffly.

"Why didn't you let us get you a healer sooner?" I can't keep the whine from my voice now. "Why didn't you let us help you?"

He sighs, and in a gentler voice says, "Because I don't *like* healers. I'm too old to be poked and prodded."

"But now . . ." I can't bring myself to finish the sentence. *Now you're dying.*

My grandfather gives me a considering look. "Scoot over," he says. "You're in my spot."

I do as he says, shifting so that he can sit beside me at the water's edge. When I try to help him, he glares until I retract my hand. We sit together, shoulder to shoulder, for what feels like an eternity before he says more.

"The best healers in the world can't cure what I've got, boy," Babu says eventually. "Trust me."

I tense. "You don't know that," I say defensively. "You haven't even tried—"

"Akande, there's *nothing wrong with me*." Babu's voice is blunt, unemotional. "I'm not sick, I'm just old. My failing body is merely a symptom of that. If it wasn't one thing that got me, then it'd be something else. Either way, there's no avoiding the inevitable. We all expire eventually."

I hate him for being so practical about it, so detached. There are a thousand things I want to say to him in that moment, but one in particular pushes past the others.

"I'm sorry I didn't listen to you earlier," I say. "I screwed up."

When I look up at my grandfather, his smile is wry. "You're a kid," he says. "You're *supposed* to screw up. How else will you learn?" He pauses. "I'm sorry for what I said to you. I didn't misjudge you, or your maturity."

"I'm not ready," I say quietly.

Babu's brows rise. "Ready?"

"I'm not ready for you to go. There's so much more for me to learn about being a daraja. Who will teach me?"

My grandfather sighs. "Death rarely comes at a time that conveniences us, Akande, but it is not the end." He puts a hand on my shoulder. "You still remember the time I took you to the Kusonga Plains, the first time you saw the Maidens?"

I nod.

"Then you should remember that even when my body is gone, I'll never *really* leave you," he says. "I am going to join my forebears, our ancestors, just as you will one day when you're an old man and you've lived a life that's full. If you ask me, that is a reason for joy, *not* sadness."

I swallow hard. "Then why does it still hurt?"

"Because that is the cost of love," Babu says. "It is the price we pay to truly feel, to truly *live*."

"It's a high price," I whisper.

Babu squeezes my shoulder. "And it is one always worth paying. I for one am not sorry I paid it. My life has been rich in all the ways that matter. I pray, Akande, that one day you can say the same."

The rest of the words I want to say refuse to come, but my grandfather doesn't seem to mind. Together, the two of us sit by the Ndefu's edge, content in our silence until the sun rises.

CHAPTER 14

ON THE SUBJECT OF SUGAR APPLES

KOFFI

Koffi found herself both grateful and perturbed that the next few days of travel along the Ndefu River were uneventful.

On the one hand, she was grateful that—after all they'd been through so far—for the first time in a long time, they had some semblance of stability. As he'd professed at the start of their voyage, Captain Bwanbale was a man who kept a steady routine. The fare Ano had secured for them guaranteed that they ate three times a day at least, had a place to clean themselves and their clothes, and had a safe place to sleep each night. On the other hand, the free time aboard the ferry gave Koffi entirely too much time to think, to worry. They had twelve days—less than two weeks—left to find Atuno and Itaashe. Now they had to find a bracelet too.

She'd already tried, in the days following their encounter with the water goddess, to use her affinity to find the pearl bracelet, to feel for it the same way she'd tried to find the gods. The problem was, *unlike* with the gods, she'd come up with nothing. It was an unsettling feeling, and Koffi couldn't shake it no matter how hard she tried. She resolved to focus on what she could feel: a pull toward Atuno. He, at least, seemed to be in roughly the direction they were heading, for now.

By the morning of the third day, when Bwanbale announced that the ship would be stopping at a port for the day, Koffi was more than ready to leave the ship. She watched as their destination came into view. From what she could see, the town was smaller than Lkossa or Bandari, but there was an antiquity about it that suggested it predated both.

"What is this place?" she asked as Njeri and Makena joined her.

"According to Bwanbale, the town's called Sokidogo," said Njeri.

"Why are we stopping here?" Koffi asked.

"Bwanbale says it's a scheduled stop for him," Njeri continued. "Sokidogo is a major port for fishing and trade. Honestly . . ." She cast her eyes back toward Sokidogo's docks. "I don't think it's a bad idea for us to take advantage of it and buy more supplies so that we're ready when we need to get off the *Nzinga* permanently."

The group disembarked together, with promises to Bwanbale that they'd return in time for departure the next morning. As soon as they'd left the docks, Zain veered away from them, toward a different part of town.

"Be back later!" he said cheerfully.

"Hold it," said Njeri. "Where are *you* going?"

Zain looked wounded. "Can't a spirited young man go for a wholesome jaunt around town?"

"Sure," said Njeri curtly. "Except that nothing about *you* is wholesome."

Zain sighed dramatically. "If you *must* know, one of Bwanbale's crewmen said there's an entertainment district on the west side of the city. Apparently, it's a haunt for several self-professed 'mind readers.'" He grinned. "*I'm* going to pay them a visit."

"Hm. That seems ill-advised." It was Safiyah who spoke up. She was shouldering a bag and looking at Zain with unmistakable interest.

Zain's brows rose. "You could join me? I wouldn't mind the company."

Safiyah shook her head ruefully, but she did fall into step with him as they made their way into the city.

"We're going into town too," said Njeri. "Sokidogo is supposed to have some of the south's finest textile shops. Makena wants to see them so she can criticize them."

"I do *not*!" Makena said defensively. "I just want to see if they're of quality."

"Great!" Koffi turned to them. "I'll join you."

Makena and Njeri exchanged looks.

"What?"

"Actually, Koffi . . ." Makena now looked distinctly uncomfortable. "Njeri and I . . . well, no offense, but we . . . well, we were hoping to . . ."

"We want some time together," said Njeri. She gave Koffi a significant look. "*Alone.*"

"Oh. *Oh.*" A new understanding dawned on her. "Sorry! I didn't realize you were—"

"We were going to tell you!" said Makena quickly. "It's just . . . there's been so much going on and it's all been happening so fast, so we . . ."

Njeri took one of Makena's hands in hers and squeezed. "We are taking things *slow*."

"Congratulations," said Koffi. "Really. I'm happy for you."

"Thank you," said Makena. She hesitated. "Look, if you want to come with us—"

"Nah." Koffi shook her head quickly. "You all go ahead."

"We'll meet back here for lunch," said Njeri. With that, she steered Makena toward the city too, albeit in a different direction. Koffi watched them go and tried to grapple with a complicated new array of emotions. She was happy for Makena and Njeri—if any two people deserved happiness, it was certainly them—but she couldn't ignore a pang of sadness too. If they were together now, maybe Makena and Njeri wouldn't need or want her around anymore. It wouldn't be intentional, but she imagined that they would just grow apart. The idea of that, of losing two friends at once, hurt more than she expected. She blinked back tears.

"You okay?"

Koffi turned, surprised, and realized too late that she had been left alone with Ekon. For several seconds, they looked everywhere but at each other.

"So . . ." She finally made herself break the awkward silence. "Are you going into town too?"

"Have to," said Ekon. "I've been doing some inventory on the boat and we're low on supplies." He paused. "Do you want to come with me?"

Koffi raised a brow. "Are you inviting me to go shopping with you?"

"I might be," said Ekon carefully. "But also . . . I was thinking we might be able to look for a map."

"A map?" Koffi repeated.

Ekon nodded. "Amakoya said that Atuno would be where the earth touches the sky. I have a rough idea of Eshōza's geography, but . . ." He looked around. "That doesn't help me much in this situation. I figure a map might help us plan our next move. So, want to come?"

It was a question more loaded than it had any right to be. Koffi pushed against all her emotions. It was too easy to recall the way she'd felt when she'd seen Ekon holding Safiyah's hand a few days ago, but . . . it was also just as easy to remember another time when she and Ekon had trekked into a city to collect supplies for an adventure. She nodded before she could overthink it any further.

"Sure," she said. "I'm assuming you already made a grocery list?"

Ekon solemnly held up a scrap of papyrus. "I'll have you know it's enumerated and alphabetized."

Njeri had mentioned that Sokidogo's name translated to "little market," but the longer Koffi and Ekon walked through its maze of winding streets, the more the name left Koffi baffled. They'd only ventured into the city proper an hour ago, and already Koffi had lost track of how many markets, vendors, and street peddlers she'd seen. She remembered her first time exploring Lkossa's markets and thinking they were big; that seemed laughable now.

"Gods," she said as they turned a corner and stepped onto another street packed with carts. "Does it ever end?"

"Not really," said Ekon. He was holding up a different folded piece of colored papyrus and doing a rather impressive job of reading it while walking. "This says that there are over one thousand permanent stalls in the city. Technically, they're all smaller, separate markets, but they overlap so much that people rarely distinguish one from another. That's how the city got its name; it's just a collection of little markets." He looked down at his papyrus again. "Ooh, it looks like the street vendors have organized their own labor union, how nice!"

Koffi frowned. "Ekon, what are you reading?"

"Nothing!" Ekon hid the papyrus behind his back. "It's nothing."

"Is that a *tourist brochure?*"

His expression turned sheepish. "It was free!" he said defensively. "And I'll have you know it's full of useful information." He held it up again and kept reading while effortlessly sidestepping a harried-looking man selling cabbages. "For example, it says right here that a few decades ago, Sokidogo was completely buried."

"Buried?" Koffi repeated. She was careful to swipe an apple from one of the carts only when Ekon's eyes were on the papyrus. "What do you mean?"

"Just what I said." Without looking up, Ekon took the apple from Koffi's hand and tossed it back to the vendor's cart. "Apparently, the Ndefu flooded really badly, and . . . well, you see how close this place is to it."

"It's basically on top of the river."

"Right," said Ekon. "The water created a mudslide, which compromised the structure of a lot of the older buildings." He paused. "After a few years, they came back and just built a new city right on top of the old one." He looked down at his feet and cringed.

"Well," said Koffi, "*that's* extremely creepy."

"Just a bit." Ekon pointed. "Let's turn down here, I think this might be a wider selection of fruits and vegetables."

The street they moved onto was still busy, but smaller and quieter than most of what they'd seen so far. It seemed Ekon's guess had also been right; where before most of the stalls had been stacked high with trinkets and jewelry, the vendors here were almost exclusively selling fresh fruits and vegetables. Koffi took in the scene and felt a moment's homesickness.

"Ooh!" Ekon's eyes landed on something a few feet away and he picked up his pace. "Come on!" He led them over to a cart staffed only by one old man. He gave them a wave, and Koffi's eyes dropped to what he was selling. Piled within the stall was a bright fuchsia-colored fruit. They glittered in the late-morning sunlight.

"What are those?" she asked.

"Sugar apples!" said Ekon standing straighter. "They're my favorite!"

"Tuh," said Koffi. "I've never had one."

Ekon gave her a sidelong glance. "It's not too late?"

Koffi considered, eyeing the fruit. "I'll try."

Ekon slipped the woman two silver coins before offering one of the sugar apples to Koffi. She took a generous bite from the fruit and tried to ignore the intense way Ekon was watching her.

"Well?"

"Eh. It's . . . okay."

He looked as though he'd been slapped. "Okay?"

"If you like that sort of thing."

He shook his head. "It is mathematically impossible not to like sugar apples." His expression changed slightly. "But thanks for trying it." The words were sincere.

"I lied," she said quietly. "The sugar apple was . . . pretty good."

"Aha," said Ekon with a grin. "I'm always right."

Koffi rolled her eyes. "Don't go getting a big head."

"Ah, Koffi." Ekon took her arm in his. "It's far, *far* too late for that."

Koffi had had real reservations about their ability to find a map in a place as jam-packed and crowded as Sokidogo, which was why she was surprised when Ekon abruptly pointed out a shop and said, "There!" Koffi followed his gaze. From the outside, the place appeared to primarily house scrolls and journals, but once inside, they found that there were any number of maps too. After a quick chat with a shop associate, Ekon beckoned Koffi to a back corner where several maps were stacked high. He pulled one carefully out of the pile, then laid it flat across a small table.

"All right, so we're here." He put a finger on a spot on the map and dragged his finger to the left. "The next large city from here is Kugawanya, right where the Ndefu splits into two rivers."

Koffi nodded. "I've never heard of Kugawanya," she said. "But it's in the direction I've been feeling a pull toward."

"Makes sense," said Ekon. "It's a big city, and if I recall, there are some shrines and temples to the Six located there. We may not know exactly where Atuno or Itaashe are, but maybe we can find clues at one of their places of worship, like we did for Amakoya."

It wasn't much to go on, but Koffi was relieved they had something. "Good," she said. "We can get back to the *Nzinga*, rest up, and head out tomorrow. With any luck, we'll be to Kugawanya in a day's time."

❧

They made their way back to the docks an hour later, opting to avoid most of the city's traffic by taking a longer detour around its border instead. From that vantage point, Koffi admired the many boats moored at Sokidogo's docks, all bobbing up and down in harmony as though dancing to an unheard song. She sighed and Ekon looked up.

"What?"

"All my life, all I ever wanted to do was leave home," said Koffi as she continued watching the boats. "I used to dream of traveling with my mama and Jabir, and I thought if I ever got the chance to leave Lkossa, I'd never return." Her gaze lifted to Ekon. "Now all I think about is returning. Ridiculous, right?"

Ekon's expression grew serious. "I don't think that's ridiculous at all." His steps slowed, and Koffi changed her own pace to match his. Ekon seemed to be deep in thought. "There are always going to be beautiful things to see out there in the world," he said, looking at her, "but there's no place quite like home."

They were simple words, but they snuck past all of Koffi's defenses. She worried the end of one of her braids. "I just hope home is what I remember, if I ever get back to it."

Ekon put a hand on her shoulder. *"When,"* he said gently, *"when* we get back."

At last, they reached the part of the docks where the group had agreed to meet. Koffi didn't know if she was more surprised or relieved to see everyone there. Ekon nodded toward them.

"We've got good people on our side," he observed.

Before she could stop herself, Koffi shot him a look. "Even Zain?"

Ekon took a deep breath in and out. "Even Zain. He's . . . a talented daraja. And he looks out for people."

It wasn't lost on Koffi how much effort it had taken Ekon to say something kind about Zain. She swallowed her own pride and said, "Safiyah seems really nice too."

Ekon seemed careful not to let his face betray anything. "She is nice," he said lightly. He hesitated. "Look, Koffi, about the other day . . ."

Koffi's face warmed. "We don't have to talk about it."

Ekon's fingers began to tap at his side. "No, I want to. The thing is, Safiyah and I—"

"There you are!" They'd drawn close enough for Makena to notice and wave them over. Njeri, Safiyah, and Zain looked up too, and the six of them walked around the docks until they found some benches to sit on while Ekon passed out some food.

"Did you get what you needed from town?" Njeri asked between bites of bread.

Ekon nodded. "I tried to buy nonperishable food," said Ekon, "that should last us for the next few days . . ."

Koffi continued surveying the docks while the rest of them ate. At this hour of the day, they were full of people—fishermen, dockhands, peddlers, beggars—all going about their normal business, and yet something set her on edge. She combed through her mind, trying to put her finger on it, but the realization came to her slowly. It wasn't the people around her that had made her suddenly uneasy, it was something more subtle than that. It was the air itself. It had imperceptibly cooled and stilled. When she looked to the sky, the sun was still there, but it was now clear of the gulls that had circled only an hour ago looking for food. She frowned.

"What is it?" Ekon was the first to notice the look on her face as Koffi rose.

"I don't know exactly," said Koffi, looking around, "but something doesn't feel—"

A scream tore through the air, and her blood ran cold.

The world seemed to slow as Koffi turned east and saw the people running toward her. They were locals, that much was clear, and every single one of them had the exact same look of panic on their face. Koffi recognized that specific brand of panic, but that did nothing to prepare her for what she saw just behind the running people.

Gray faces.

A violent shiver ran through her body as she processed the cluster of Untethered making their way toward the docks, toward *them*. They'd been unsettling enough in the fog of the southern marshlands; Koffi found them so much worse to look at in broad daylight. They weren't moving fast, there was still plenty of time to get away, but something about the slow way they ambled forward made them appear even more menacing. At once, all six of them were on their feet.

"What do we do?" asked Zain.

"Run," said Koffi, her mouth dry. *"Run!"* She turned on her heel and led the way as she headed in the same direction of the city itself. It seemed that word of the creatures was spreading; already the vendors and peddlers nearest to their docks were either scrambling to pack up their wares or abandoning them entirely to make a run for it. Koffi whirled around. "Down there!" She pointed to a less-populated street, and glanced over her shoulder to make sure the rest were still following. They headed toward it, then stopped again.

A second swarm of the Untethered was coming up from the other end of the alley, this time holding weapons. She watched with horror as the one leading the group swung an ax at an elderly seamstress.

"They're everywhere!" Zain shouted. "How?"

It was a question digging into Koffi's mind, but what Njeri said next distracted her.

"They have archers." Koffi didn't miss the ill-disguised fear in Njeri's voice as she said it.

"If they do what they did back on the marshlands, they'll take out hundreds at once," said Ekon. "We need to move everyone out of here."

Koffi looked between the people still running down the road and the Untethered, getting closer. "I have an idea." Her gaze met Ekon's. He shook his head.

"Koffi, *no*." He grabbed her shoulders. "You can't do what you did on the marshlands again. It knocked you unconscious."

"I'll be fine," said Koffi. "I know my limits. And we don't have many other choices here."

The Untethered were picking up their pace now, drawing closer by the second. Ekon looked from them to Koffi.

"Thirty seconds," he said quietly, "no more."

Koffi nodded. "No more."

Ekon's fingers were tapping a frantic rhythm against his side, then he nodded. "Okay," he said, "I trust you."

Koffi felt a stab of guilt, but she ignored it as she faced the Untethered again. They were only a few yards away from her now. She focused on the glint of their arrows and knives as they charged forward.

Please let this work, she prayed. She took a deep breath in and let it out, tried to clear her mind, then summoned the splendor, letting it rise from her feet and legs. Her arms spread out instinctively as she prepared to direct it, even as the Untethered closed in. If she could create the same type of dome she'd summoned before, it would buy the rest of them time to flee. Her arms rose higher, and she relished the familiar heat coursing through her veins.

Then she felt it.

It was subtle at first, the sharp prickle in her right arm, but then the pain became excruciating. A cry escaped her as she fell, cradling her arm, and seconds later she had a chilling revelation: Her entire body was numb. When she tried to stand, the muscles refused to cooperate. Her breath went shallow in panic.

"Koffi!"

Two sets of arms grabbed Koffi's middle and brought her back to her feet. When she nearly toppled again, they held on to her. She looked up to find Ekon and Safiyah on either side of her.

"Can't move," said Koffi. She caught a flash of movement as Zain and Njeri ran past her. Zain put his hand out, and several of the Untethered at the front shuddered, grasping at their heads. Njeri wielded her staff, swinging it threateningly as they got closer.

"Go!" Njeri shouted over her shoulder. "We'll hold them off for as long as we can!"

It was futile; the two of them weren't enough to keep that many Untethered at bay. Koffi tried to say as much, but even her lips wouldn't move anymore. Her entire body had shut down.

"Come on!" Makena guided one of Koffi's arms over her neck while Ekon did the same with the other. "They may not be able to hold them off for long, but they're giving us a head start."

That was what I wanted to do, Koffi thought. The world was growing hazier by the second. In her periphery, she saw Ekon looking around. Most of the streets were empty now, but she could guess at what he was thinking: They had no idea where any of these roads led.

"Hey!" Safiyah yelled. "Over here! I see a way out!"

"Go!" Ekon shouted. "We'll follow!"

Koffi felt herself being half dragged, half carried down a small side street. They ducked into the passage at the same time Zain and Njeri fell in behind them.

"We created some distance," said Njeri, "but we need to move."

"I think this might let out ahead," said Makena. "I can see light!"

Sure enough, when Koffi squinted, she made out a patch of sunlight. She didn't know what they would do to keep the Untethered back once they reached it, but even seeing the light gave her some hope.

"We're almost there!" said Ekon.

She tried to speak, but the exhaustion made it too difficult. Her knees gave out, and she felt pain as she landed on them.

"Koffi!"

Her name was the last thing she heard before she fell into darkness.

CHAPTER 15

KUGAWANYA

KOFFI

Koffi woke with a start. It took her a moment to reorient herself and get a sense of her bearings. Slowly, she pieced together that she was sitting near a campfire and that Ekon, Zain, Njeri, Makena, and Safiyah were all talking. She heard snatches of their conversation.

"Someone needs to tell her—"

"Tell me what?" she asked.

The others jumped.

"Koffi . . ." Makena sounded oddly cautious. "You're awake."

"Where are we?" Koffi said. "I don't remember anything." She was tired of not remembering.

"In a thicket, outside Sokidogo," said Njeri. "You passed out as we were leaving. We barely made it."

"Made it?" Koffi sat up. "What are you talking about?"

Silence fell, and no one seemed eager to speak first. Koffi looked around at each one of them until her eyes stopped on Ekon.

"Tell me."

"The Untethered invaded the city," said Ekon. "They . . . they killed almost everyone in town."

It took Koffi a moment to register the shock, her whole body went numb as she processed the words. *Everyone.* The Untethered had killed everyone. She looked up, shaking her head.

"What about Bwanbale?" she asked. "What about his crew?"

"We're not sure," said Zain. He looked uncharacteristically sober. "But, Koffi, there's more . . ." He nodded, and Koffi realized he was indicating toward her arm. She looked down and started.

The silver pocks had moved all the way along her arm, past her elbow, and looked less like pocks now and more like an angry silver rash. There was nothing mystifying or beautiful about them anymore.

"They're getting worse." Njeri said what no one else seemed willing to. "Koffi, I think you should seriously consider how much you use the splendor from here on out."

"That's not an option," Koffi snapped. The response came out harsher than she intended, but once she'd said it, there was no taking it back. "We still have to find Atuno and Itaashe and Amakoya's bracelet, and we only have . . . ?"

"Eleven days," said Ekon.

"It's not going to matter how many days we have left for anything if you kill yourself!" said Njeri. The skin between her eyebrows pinched. "Koffi, I'm serious. You can't keep putting everything on your shoulders, you have to let us help you."

Koffi opened her mouth and closed it. She was eerily reminded of something Badwa had said to her.

You are strong, but even you *aren't strong enough to bear the* *world's weight alone. Eventually you will break.*

"All right." Ekon raised his hands. "Here's an idea. We may not have transportation anymore, but we do at least have some supplies, and a new destination."

"We do?" asked Makena.

"We do." Ekon nodded. "Kugawanya is the next major city from here. Koffi and I saw it on a map before we left Sokidogo. We'll head there to see what we can find, and we'll try to do it without Koffi having to use any more splendor for the time being. All right?"

"We should sleep," Njeri suggested. "Then, in the morning, we keep heading west."

With their slower pace, it took longer than she would have liked, but Koffi breathed relief when—after two days' travel—the city of Kugawanya came into view at the end of the thicket.

In her opinion, it wasn't as pretty as Bandari, but it had its own sense of industriousness that she could appreciate after days spent in more rural towns and villages along the river. From a distance, she could see why the city had earned its name; it meant "divide," and there was a visible split in the Ndefu that sent it in two different directions. From the map Ekon had purchased, she knew that one branch of it continued northwest into the Furaha Lake while the other split off into a smaller southwestern river called the Southern Ndefu River. She breathed relief as they passed through the port city's gates and entered the city at large.

"We're going to find an apothecary to treat these wounds," said Zain, gesturing to himself, Njeri, and Makena. "Meet back here in a bit?"

Koffi nodded. "Sounds like a plan."

"We still need food," said Safiyah. She regarded the open markets in the distance. "I'll take of that."

When she'd gone, Koffi realized that she and Ekon were on their own.

"What about you?" Ekon asked. "What are you going to do?"

Koffi paused, thoughtful. "I have an idea," she said. "Follow me."

❧

There was one good thing about Kugawanya at least. It was crowded.

Parts of Lkossa certainly had their dense areas, but it was nothing like this. Here there were so many people moving that Koffi found the crowd itself almost carried her if she stood still for too long; she had to constantly keep moving and looking around, which prevented her from having to think too hard about any particular thing. She picked up her pace as the crowd shifted like a natural current, guiding her into a bend in the narrow road they were on.

"Hey!" Ekon was behind her, but just barely. "Wait for me!"

"Walk faster," said Koffi. "We need to keep moving."

"Where are we going?"

"You'll see," said Koffi, looking ahead. Farther down, she rose on tiptoes as the crowd pushed them forward. Several feet ahead, the side street they were on opened up to a much larger road. To the right, a line of open stalls was filled with fresh produce, and peddlers called out prices much the way they did back home; to the left, a group of canvas tents was pushed together.

"That's it!" said Koffi. It took some careful maneuvering to get to the right side of the crowd, and even then, it reminded Koffi of jumping out of a river with a strong current. But once they were standing before the tents, things seemed to calm. The tents closest to them were connected by an arch that was made of different textiles, which gave the illusion of a tunnel.

"After you," Ekon offered.

Koffi braced herself, then ducked between the two tents. Almost at once, her senses went into overload.

There were merchants in Lkossa, certainly, but she'd never seen so many packed into such a small place at once. Many of the merchants were men, but several women stood in front of and behind tables with their heads bowed toward customers. There were a thousand different conversations happening, but in Koffi's ears it all sounded like one low collective buzz, a chorus of bees hard at work. She noted tables overflowing with brooches, necklaces, and other beautiful accessories. She studied each display, hopeful.

"What are you trying to find?" Ekon asked.

Koffi's eyes roamed. "There! Let's talk to him." She nodded, and they made a beeline for a man who looked slightly less busy than the others. His head was shaved clean, but a short woolly black beard covered the entire bottom of his face. As they got closer, Koffi could see that most of his display table was covered in chunky gold jewelry that wasn't quite as shiny as some they'd already passed.

"Good afternoon," he said in an accented voice. "What can I help the two of you with today?" Koffi didn't miss the way he looked over both of them as he asked, with not a small amount of reluctance.

"Good afternoon." She kept her greeting genial. "My *husband* and I were just doing some shopping, and he mentioned an interest in a very particular piece of jewelry. I'm wondering if you might be able to help?"

She ignored the choked look Ekon gave her as the merchant gestured toward the table before him. "I specialize in basic gold pieces, common diamonds . . . I might have some opals . . ."

"What we're looking for is very specific," said Koffi. "A bracelet, actually, made from real black pearls."

The merchant stared for a moment in what looked like real surprise; then he started to laugh. It was a belly-deep sound, which might have been endearing if not for the expression that came with it. The merchant was looking between Koffi and Ekon with unmistakable pity. He used a thumb to wipe the tears from his eyes.

"You'd have better luck asking for textile made from yumbo hair," he said. "A real black pearl bracelet? Do you have any idea how much such an item would be worth?"

"Hundreds of silvers, no doubt?" Ekon asked.

The merchant shook his head. "Try *thousands*. The only place to get black pearls is the Machungu Sea, which is teeming with sharks and the like. Divers charge a fortune just to make the trip."

"Question," Koffi interjected. "If that kind of bracelet isn't sold in the merchants' district, how would it get sold or traded?"

The merchant paused. "High-value items like that are usually made for highborn families and temples. When they want to acquire or sell something in their inventory, the deal is typically done privately, within the buyer's home."

Koffi's heart sank. If Amakoya's bracelet had been lost to the heirloom collection of some wealthy family, it could be anywhere.

"Thank you." Ekon was still cordial, but his voice lost some of its enthusiasm. "We'll be on our way."

Koffi was exhausted by the time they'd finished their interviews with the rest of the merchants, and not sorry to leave the trading district behind. She'd expected, by now, for the streets to be thinning out as late afternoon moved into dusk, but to her confusion, they seemed to be getting busier and busier the farther they ventured into Greater Kugawanya. Eventually Ekon used his height to find the rest of the group.

"Any luck?" asked Njeri as they reconvened and moved off to the side.

"Most of the merchants repeated the same thing," said Koffi. "None of them have seen or even heard of Amakoya's bracelet. It's like it vanished into thin air."

Njeri sucked her teeth, but Koffi noticed that Makena was now looking at her with a curious expression. Her head was cocked and the skin between her eyebrows was pinched.

"What?"

"I know what we said before . . ." Makena's words came slowly. "But maybe Koffi should try the splendor again, now that we're actually in the city."

A jolt went through Koffi's entire body.

"That's *brilliant*, Makena!"

"Hold on." Ekon raised both hands. "Koffi, no offense, but . . . are you strong enough for this?"

Koffi tried to suppress a reactionary annoyance. She knew Ekon was being thoughtful, as always, but she still didn't want to think about not being strong enough to do something. Badwa's words came back to her, her warning. She wasn't supposed to be using the splendor anymore, but . . .

"It'll be more difficult than before," said Zain. "This city's huge, and what you're looking for is small. You'll have to use a lot of energy, and you'll have to do it in an extremely controlled way to be successful—and that's *if* the bracelet is truly even here."

"I'm going to try." Koffi was resolute now, and Zain nodded. The rest of the group looked apprehensive.

"Do you need space?" Makena asked.

Koffi paused. She realized that no one else, with the exception of Zain, had really seen her use the splendor to find something. Their only reference to what she was like when she channeled the splendor was what she'd been like when she'd been fighting Fedu. "No," she said. "I just need to focus. I've never seen the bracelet myself and I'm only going off of Amakoya's description. I'm not sure how that'll affect my ability to find it."

"There's a bench over there," Njeri pointed out. "Maybe you should sit. The last time you summoned, it took a lot out of you."

Koffi moved to sit, and tried to ignore the eyes on her.

"Focus, Koffi." Zain seemed to be reading her thoughts. "Forget everything else, just try to focus."

Koffi took a deep breath and closed her eyes. She tried to imagine Amakoya's bracelet, a small string of iridescent black pearls, hued with the same greens and blues of the sea from which they came.

Focus, she told herself.

She tried to summon the splendor slowly, but it came in its usual rush, and she drew in a sharp breath as she felt it surge through her body, rising from her feet and moving all the way to her fingertips. She gasped.

"Koffi!" Someone was speaking, but they sounded far away. "Are you okay?"

She couldn't answer. Her eyes were still screwed shut, and she was still trying to picture that bracelet. It was floating in a great darkness now. Slowly she unclenched one of her fists.

Show me, she willed the energy. *Show me where it is. Find it.*

She opened her eyes and blinked once, twice . . . In the daylight, the particles of light around her hands were fainter, but still distinct as they formed and grew and then broke apart. The rest of the group moved out of the way as the particles began to form a chain. Koffi stood.

Show me where it is.

Without warning, the particles of splendor surged forward, leading a winding path down one of the streets. People gasped and moved away.

"Follow it!" Koffi started to walk.

"Koffi, wait!" someone shouted.

But Koffi was running as fast as her feet could carry her down the street where the splendor was guiding her. Every time the light flickered or disappeared, she panicked; then relief flooded her when she saw it again. More than one person stopped to stare at her as she ran, several glared, but she paid them no mind as she wove through Kugawanya's contorted streets, hoping Ekon, Safiyah, Zain, Makena, and Njeri would be able to follow.

Closer. I'm getting closer.

She felt it like an instinct, something in her core intensifying as the lights grew brighter, as more of them appeared. The crowds were thickening as she made her way toward the city's center, and distantly she could hear cheering and a sort of jingling, but she took no notice of it. Up ahead, people were gathered near a main road; there were mules and camels crossing before them in a long procession. The chain of splendor arched above the crowd and—

"KOFFI!"

She jolted as someone caught her arm, for a moment pulled out of the trance the splendor had put her in. She looked up and met Ekon's gaze; he was still holding on to her arm. At first, she was angry with him, until she realized where they were. She was standing right on the curb, one foot already on the busy street. She blinked.

"You were nearly trampled by that camel," Ekon said, anxious.

Koffi shook her head and blinked several more times before she processed his words. She looked around. Now that she was at the front of the crowd, she could see that the procession was actually a parade. Dancers wrapped in gauzy veils pirouetted past with tiny bells tied to their ankles; young boys in crisp white tunics were throwing rice and copper coins left and right, which people were eagerly scrambling to collect. She frowned.

"What . . . is this?"

Njeri, Zain, Makena, and Safiyah finally caught up. They were out of breath and shared Ekon's look of concern.

"Koffi, are you okay?" Makena asked.

"I'm fine," said Koffi. "It was better this time, I didn't feel like I was going to pass out." She pointed to the parade again. "What's going on here?"

"It's the Bonding," said Njeri. "The southerners are beginning to celebrate."

Koffi started. "The Bonding isn't happening for another week."

"Maybe so," said Ekon, "but it looks like the festivities in the south start far earlier. People seem to love an excuse for festivity here. It gives the highborns a chance to flaunt their wealth."

Koffi watched, bewildered, as a family dressed in matching green outfits passed them on a team of camels. "I don't understand," she said eventually. "This is where the splendor led me, which means Amakoya's bracelet has to be here." Unless her affinity was wrong. She didn't want to consider that possibility.

Ekon surveyed the crowd. "There are at least two hundred people standing on this part of the street alone," he said. "The splendor didn't point you in any specific direction from here?"

Koffi stared again at the last place she'd seen any hint of the splendor. It had glinted at her from the middle of the road, but that made no sense.

"It was a good try, Koffi, really." Makena's words were sympathetic; somehow that made Koffi feel worse.

"But—"

"If there's nothing else Kugawanya can offer us," Safiyah cut in, "I suggest we continue toward the Kusonga Plains and hope that we are able to find Atuno and Itaashe. As it is, the journey from here is still quite long—"

She kept speaking, but her words faded as the ground began to shake. People around them gasped and shifted, and some cried out in surprise. A single word came to Koffi's mind.

Earthquake.

She thought of Lkossa's Rupture, of the stories Mama had told her when she was small about what had happened. There had been an earthquake then too. Several people—including her—were now looking around in confusion, and then her eyes settled on something coming up the road.

It wasn't an earthquake at all.

For a few seconds, she didn't realize what she was looking at as the four hulking shapes lumbered forward. They were huge creatures, with cracked gray skin and massive trunks as thick as young saplings. Koffi blinked, surprised.

Elephants—they were *elephants*.

Except that there was something different about these beasts. They were not the size of normal elephants, but far larger. The crowd hushed slightly as the animals marched toward them, though a buzzing persisted as people gawked and admired them. The four elephants were carrying elaborate saddles on their backs, covered in silk and bejeweled with rubies and sapphires that dazzled in the sunlight. Handlers sat near the elephants' necks, with short crops, guiding them forward as they followed the procession, but Koffi's eyes drifted back to the saddles. Sitting atop each was a person dressed in finery from head to toe. She noted a man and woman first, followed by a younger man who looked a few years older than her, and then a girl who seemed a few years younger.

"Excuse me." She tapped a man standing next to her. "Sorry, who are those people?"

The man looked at her as though she'd grown a second head. "That's the magistrate and his family."

Koffi frowned. "The magistrate?"

"The head of the city," said the man, again with an air of impatience. "They always ride through the streets on their war elephants and give back to the citizens." When a copper coin arced through the air and landed a few feet from him, the man stopped their conversation to dive for it. Koffi looked to the magistrate's family. Indeed, now that she was looking more closely, she could see that the man in front was tall and had a certain regality about him; a red sash was tied across his torso, denoting his position. His wife was wearing similar colors, and her waves to the crowd were polite but reserved. Koffi's eyes went back to the two children. They were well-dressed; both wore shades of red as well. Suddenly she went still.

"Are you seeing what I'm seeing?" She wasn't sure who she was talking to, but when she pointed, it was Ekon who moved up to stand beside her.

"What? What is it?"

"That girl, the magistrate's daughter." The breath left Koffi's body as she continued to stare in disbelief. She knew the moment

Ekon saw what she had because he clapped a hand over his mouth, transfixed. The others were slightly slower to understand.

"What are you two seeing?" asked Safiyah.

"That girl's arm," said Ekon in a hollow voice. "Look at her *arm*."

Koffi was still staring in awe, but she heard the sounds of recognition one by one; there were gasps, and sighs, and even a groan.

The magistrate's daughter was wearing a bracelet on her wrist, one made of a curious string of black pearls.

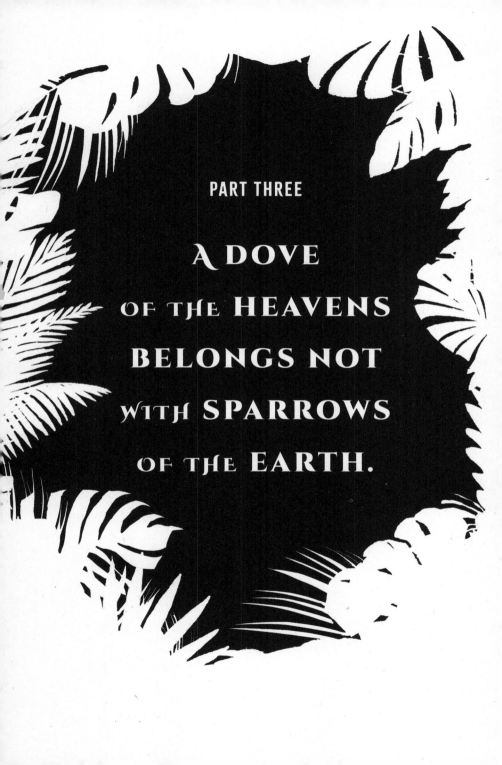

PART THREE

A DOVE
of the HEAVENS
BELONGS NOT
with SPARROWS
of the EARTH.

IMPUNDULUS

AKANDE

Year 893

The moon lights our path as we make our way through the river-bank's underbrush.

With every passing second, I feel it, a growing anticipation. This far into the dry season, the air is crisp, slightly charred from the smell of burnt harvest leaves. The night is quiet and serene. When I pull back the reeds and bramble of the bank and find our raft is where I left it, I grin.

"See?" I whisper. "*Told* you no one would move it."

Behind me, Izachar is making his way down the bank. Every so often, he glances over his shoulder.

"Yeah, yeah," he says under his breath. "So the raft's there. We still have to get it downriver—without being caught."

"Relax, we're not going to get caught, everyone's asleep." I stoop low and push more of the grass aside, trying to get the raft out of its hiding place. "Now, if you don't mind, I could use some help."

Izachar kneels beside me, and together we push until the raft is close enough to the river for the waves to pick it up. I place one of my feet on it and gesture.

"And now, my friend, adventure awaits."

Izachar awkwardly hops on to the raft, trips, then nearly plummets right into the river headfirst. I barely suppress a chuckle as he regains his balance, then settles at its center.

"Ready?"

"As ready as I'll ever be." Izachar eyes the water warily. "Let's go."

I push the raft off from the bank, letting it catch in the river's current. In seconds, we're gliding west at a pleasant pace.

"This had *better* be worth it, Kan," Izachar grumbles as we float. "My apprenticeship starts tomorrow morning and I've got to be up at dawn."

"It *will* be worth it!" I say. "Impundulus only come through the south once a year."

"Yeah, yeah." Izachar tries but fails to maintain his guise of disinterest as he looks around. The lights of Kugawanya are already fading, turning to small pinprick dots in the night. On either side, the riverbank grows darker and wilder. "You're sure you know where we're going?"

"Definitely." I nod, looking ahead. "I've taken this trip every year since I was little. Babu and I—" Unexpectedly, something catches in my throat, choking off the rest of the words. An old but familiar pain presses down on my chest and makes it hard to breathe for a few seconds. He tries to hide it, but I see Izachar's worried look.

"Sorry, Akande," he says softly. "I know it's still hard."

"Don't worry about it." I make myself shrug and look ahead. "It's okay."

He doesn't say anything else, which makes the moment worse. In the silence, there's nothing to stop the wave of sadness that washes over me without warning.

I knew my babu was dying. I'd had plenty of time to prepare for it. That didn't make it any easier when he actually did. I'd expected grief to come in one wave, to pass over me once. But that's the thing about grief; it's illogical, a many-headed monster. It's also cruel. If the gods had been just, maybe they'd have let those last memories of my grandfather be the best ones, memories where he got to be strong, and healthy, and fierce. But the gods hadn't been kind. My final memories of Babu are the memories of a stranger, a withered and bedridden old man who, at the end, I only recognized by voice. Nothing about that seems fair.

"Hey." Izachar's craning his neck and pointing. "What's that over there?"

My heart leaps, and for a moment, my grief is replaced by real excitement. To an inexperienced eye, there's nothing particularly remarkable about the few streaks of lightning dancing over the plains to the left of us, it just looks like a normal passing storm. I know, though, that it's no storm. I grin.

"That's them," I say. "We can stop here."

We bank the raft on the opposite shore, and together disembark. By now, the forks of lightning are getting bigger, illuminating the sky every few seconds, but they're still distant.

"How are we going to find them?" Izachar asks.

"Got that covered." I wiggle my fingers for dramatic effect. "Watch and learn."

I close my eyes and summon the splendor slowly, the way I've been practicing for years now. No matter what, no matter how many times I do it, nothing ever truly prepares me for the warm rush I feel when it rises from the earth and fills my body for a few seconds, coursing through my veins, muscles, and bones. I let myself enjoy that familiar sensation briefly, then commit myself to focus and control, thinking purposefully about what I want to do. Slowly, particles of the splendor leave my hands, bobbing along in the air to form a long sparkling chain that leads onto the open plains. Against the night's darkness, they look like fallen stars. Izachar whistles low.

"What are those?"

"One of the last things my babu taught me before he got really sick," I say with some pride. "I can use splendor to find things, as long as I have a rough idea of what I'm looking for. The splendor will make a path and lead us right to it."

"You mean that this path will just take us to the impundulus?" Izachar asks.

"That's the plan."

He turns to me. "What are we waiting for? Let's go!"

The plains are different at night.

In the darkness, it's harder to see anything, as those miles of golden-yellow grass are replaced by an endless black sea only occasionally interrupted by trees. Not tonight, though; tonight, the splendor I've summoned creates a path in the dark, and I feel a special kind of joy as Izachar and I run after it. Izachar whoops loudly, jumping in the air, and the sound echoes all around us. I run faster.

In these moments, grief and sadness can't catch me.

Gradually, the splendor begins to fade, and when we reach a certain part of the plains, it disappears almost entirely. Only a few tiny fragments hover around us. Izachar turns to me, confused.

"Where'd they go?"

"That's it," I say, looking around. "If the path stops, that means the impundulus must be nearby."

He looks at the sky again, hopeful. "There was lightning before," he notes. "Could they have moved on?"

"Nah." I'm still looking around. My excitement builds. "They're here somewhere. We just have to—"

My words are interrupted be a pealing screech, jarring and sharp against the quiet of the night. We both jump in alarm, looking all around us, but then Izachar points skyward again, smiling.

"Look!"

Impundulus are indigenous to the west; some legends say the god Atuno himself was the one who created them as a gift to a mortal he loved. I don't know how much of that is based in truth, but what I *do* know is that there are no words to describe the feeling that rises within me as we watch the first pair of impundulus sail past us on the wind. Their bodies are sleek, plumed in long black and white feathers, and sparkling as they beat their wings and form ribbon upon ribbon of lightning so bright that my eyes water. The lightning under their wings barely has time to fade before another one flies through the sky, flapping massive wings that remind me of a heron, and leaving in its wake tangled bolts of lightning that have the faintest touch of a purple hue. Another one of their shrieks sounds in the night, but this time it doesn't scare me.

"Okay." Izachar's still gazing up at the sky. "I admit, *this* is pretty cool."

If grief is a many-headed monster, I think the worst of those heads is the loneliness. I feel my grandfather's absence all the time, in the moments I least expect it. But tonight, I don't feel as alone. Izachar and I fall into silence as we continue watching the impundulus, soaring and gliding across the sky like they're performing the dance of their ancestors. They make me think of something my grandfather said once, about these plains.

Our family has been coming to these plains for generations. Many centuries ago, our ancestors formed a special connection with it. It's in our blood, our soul.

I didn't understand him back then, but now I think do. Before, I felt sadness, but in its place now there's a calm. It grounds me and takes away some of the pain I thought would never leave. It occurs to me that, if I didn't have to, I'd never leave this place. If I could feel this way forever, I would.

That moment of peace evaporates almost instantly when I hear a crunch in the grass to my left. It's a soft sound, so faint compared to the impundulus' birdsong that I'm not sure at first that it's real. When I hear it again, though, I freeze.

"What was that?"

Beside me, Izachar tears his eyes from the sky, confused. "What?"

"That sound." I turn, surveying the plains around us. They look empty, but I can't shake the feeling. Something isn't right. My ears prick as I listen for that sound again.

"I didn't hear anything," says Izachar. "Are you sure you—"

"LOOK OUT!"

I grab Izachar, and we duck as an arrow snakes past us in an upward trajectory. It's fast, but I watch with slow terror as it cuts through the air. I can see what's about to happen, but there's nothing I can do to prevent it. The arrow catches one of the impundulus in its breast, and with a keening screech, the lightning in the sky around it fizzles out. It seems to take forever for the creature to fall, plummeting through the air. I wince when its body hits the ground with a thud. The other impundulus scatter at once. Silence follows.

Neither of us speaks. Beside me, I can feel Izachar's body trembling against mine as he holds himself up by his elbows and tries to keep still. Centuries seem to pass before I hear it again, a crunching sound in the dry grass. It's the sound of footsteps. Carefully, Izachar raises a finger to his lips, and uses another to point. I follow it until I see what he does.

I know at once that the two approaching men are not from here. Their clothes aren't right, too heavy for the south's temperate weather. Their skin is a dark brown like ours, and they each have a quiver of arrows. Izachar and I crouch lower in the grass as they draw near, but they don't seem to see us, and pass without even looking in our direction. They stop a few feet away, but in the quiet, I can hear them perfectly.

"You're sure you got it?" asks the first man. His accent is as thick as his cropped hair and mustache, but I can't place it— *definitely* not a southerner.

"I'm sure." The second man has the same kind of accent, but he's clean-shaven and completely bald. His head is bent as he searches in the grass. "It fell around— Ah, there it is." He stoops down, and my stomach turns when he holds up the impundulu's dead body by its neck. The creature is limp in his grasp. He smiles, and the starlight catches the white of his teeth. "Told you they'd be out here," he says, examining the impundulu with some admiration. "This one's old, too—look how long its feathers are."

Mustache whistles low. "Nice. You sure you won't get in trouble?"

"Nah." The bald man waves a dismissive hand. "You've seen what the southern merchants are like. They'll trade anything, for the right price."

My hands ball into fists as the first waves of anger lap at me. The bald man is lying. Southern merchants, even the lowest of them, would never trade for the feathers of an impundulu. They're rare creatures, sacred. The longer I stare at it, the sicker I feel, and it takes me a moment to understand why. My gaze fixes on the dead impundulu, on its now-empty black eyes. The emptiness brings back a memory I don't want to relive. I try to temper it, but it returns with a fierceness. Babu. I see my grandfather's body being lowered into the ground back home, round gold coins placed in both his hands. He's too still, too thin, so unlike the man I knew. That's what death does: It turns everyone into strangers. My teeth grind as I watch the man still holding the dead impundulu, examining the various parts of its body.

"You know, I bet if I carved it up, I could sell it in parts," he muses, "the wings for one sum, the beak for another, the feet—"

My body seems to move of its own accord. I only catch a glimpse of Izachar's shock as I stand.

"Hey!"

The men both jump, startled for a moment, but when they find me in the dark, they relax. The bald man, still holding the impundulu, offers an easy smile.

"Hey, kid." He looks me over, visibly amused. "Isn't it past your bedtime?"

"You shouldn't be hunting here." I can barely hear my own voice over the blood pounding in my ears. "Impundulus are endangered."

Mustache laughs uncomfortably, but the bald man still looks unfazed.

"Endangered, you said?" He shakes the dead impundulu in his grasp, feigning new interest. "Sounds like I'll be raising my asking price, then."

"You *can't* trade it."

"Can't?"

I'm not alone anymore. The grass rustles behind me, and now Izachar is standing next to me. The men regard us with apprehension.

"Hey, back off, both of you," the bald man says with new edge. "You just get back to wherever you're from, and there won't be any trouble for anyone."

"Akande." Izachar's voice is barely a whisper in my ear. "We should go."

"Listen to your little friend," the bald man says.

My anger builds as he smirks. When I take a step forward, I don't miss the way his free hand moves deftly to his belt. Beside me, Izachar stiffens.

"Akande . . ."

"Go home, boys." Mustache looks ill at ease. "We don't want any trouble."

"What are *they* going to do?" asks the bald man. There's a

challenge in his expression, a haughtiness. "If they want the bird so badly, I'd like to see them come and take it."

It happens without warning. Babu always told me that the key to being a good daraja is a balance of focus and control, but both slip from me as my toes curl in the dirt and I summon splendor from the earth. It comes without hesitation, in an onslaught of heat, and I direct it to my hands so that when the energy leaves me, it takes the form of white flames. They scorch the grass between us and the men, and I feel a sense of satisfaction when their faces change. The first man, the one who already looked uncomfortable, steps back with his mouth ajar. The second man drops the impundulu and stares at me in horror.

"You're . . . you're one of them," he says in a hollow voice.

"Sell it in *parts*." My voice sounds far away. "Isn't that what you said you wanted to do?" I take another step forward. "How would *you* like it, being cut up and sold for *parts*?"

"I'm sorry!" The man raises his hands. He looks terrified now. "I'm sorry, I didn't know!"

A small voice, maybe the voice of reason, tells me the battle's already won, but it's drowned out as more and more adrenaline courses through me. More splendor is building within me. I hold on to it, relishing the way it makes me feel bigger, more powerful.

"You didn't care." The words echo in my head. "That bird was innocent, but you didn't care. You killed it because you were bigger, just because you *could*."

I open my hands and more splendor leaves them. Focus and control, that's what my babu always told me was important, and that's what I use as I will those flames to form a circle around the men, trapping them. The flames dance higher, pushing them into its center, and I listen as the grass around them crackles and burns.

"Akande!" I can hear Izachar's voice, but I ignore it and focus on the men.

"How does it feel *now*?" I call to them over the flames' roar. "How does it feel to be the small one? The helpless one? I don't think your arrows will do you much good anymore."

The men begin to scream as the flames close in. "Please!" one of them calls. "Please, we don't want to die!"

I'm mesmerized by the flames, by the power of the splendor as it flows through me. The world feels more and more distant, detached . . .

"AKANDE!"

A voice brings me back to the present, and when I turn, Izachar is staring at me. He looks wary, but I see another emotion in them, one that looks almost familiar.

"This isn't you," he says quietly, pointing at the flames, "and this isn't what he'd want either."

He doesn't say his name, but my babu's face grows vivid in my mind. The same expression I see on Izachar's face is the one I envision on his, and I recognize it for what it is: disappointment. At once, the flames of splendor stutter. I hear my grandfather's voice. I imagine what he'd say if he saw me right now.

You lost focus. You lost control, boy. I thought I taught you better.

"Stop this," Izachar whispers. *"Please."*

It's done. I pull the splendor back to me and it burns as it rushes through my body and into the earth. As soon as the flames are gone, the two men take off at a run, only looking over their shoulders at us every few strides. I watch as they disappear into the darkness, but guilt still lingers in their wake. Izachar's the one who moves first. Carefully, he combs through the grass, and eventually he bends down. When he straightens again, the dead impundulu is cradled in his arms.

"We should bury it," he says.

Tears prick at my eyes and I hate myself for it. Another head from that many-headed monster. All I can do is nod stiffly, but Izachar takes the hint and stoops down to begin digging with his hands, plowing up the dry dirt without a word. I take a deep breath and kneel beside him to help. It takes time, but eventually our hole is big enough. Izachar lays the dead bird inside it, and bows his head.

"I don't know if animals get to go to the godlands," he admits, "but if they do, I hope this one does."

I don't want to cry, but this time, I can't stop the tears as they slick my cheeks. That's another thing about grief. Sometimes it's a monster you can recognize and fight. Other times it's like rain; it finds ways to seep into the cracks of whatever shelter you've built and drown you in the sorrow. I sniffle hard and drag my arm across my face.

"Sorry."

Izachar puts a hand on my shoulder. Slowly he shakes his head. "Don't be sorry for missing him."

My throat tightens again. There are lots of words I want to say, but none of them will come now. Izachar sits with me anyway. In that moment, I get the feeling he'd sit with me forever, if I needed it.

I don't know how much time passes before I can breathe again, and I don't know how Izachar knows, without me saying it, that I'm okay.

We turn back and head home.

CHAPTER 16

The RIVER DANCERS

EKON

Ekon felt the pounding of the elephants' feet as they thundered past, making the ground tremble. He looked at the elephant with the girl sitting atop it, then at her wrist. There was no doubt about what she was wearing there; the black pearl bracelet was unmistakable. Then he turned his gaze to everyone else in their group—Koffi, Safiyah, Njeri, Makena, and Zain. They all had the same look of foreboding on their faces. In the end, it was Njeri who spoke first.

"We should move."

They wove through the crowd, but Ekon focused on the parade of elephants and the girl. They were headed toward a massive manor, partially obscured behind towering white stone walls. He watched until the procession had completely disappeared, then turned to face everyone else.

"Well," said Zain. "This isn't good at all."

"It's not ideal," Njeri agreed.

"That's got to be the bracelet," said Zain. "The splendor led Koffi to that exact spot, and I don't think there are many black pearl bracelets in this city."

Safiyah shook her head. She looked deep in thought. "How would the magistrate's daughter have even come by such an item? Amakoya said it was stolen and that she'd never been able to find it."

Finally, Ekon spoke. "I don't think it matters. What does matter is how we're going to get it. I'm sure the magistrate's got plenty of security in and around his home. Breaking into it will be next to impossible."

"We need that bracelet," said Koffi. "You heard what Amakoya said. She won't join our side without it."

"Then what we really need is a plan," said Zain. "A way to get into the magistrate's home."

Ekon tapped his fingers at his side. Plans were supposed to be his forte, one of the things he was good at, but at the moment, he couldn't come up with anything. They were distracted suddenly as a commotion filled the air directly to their right. Ekon looked up, at first expecting to see another procession making its way through the streets. Instead, he saw a group of people dressed in bright colors. Their faces were painted in elaborate whorls of orange and yellow and white; ribbons of sparkling fabric swayed around the sleeves of their tunics and at the waist. They were dancing and clapping as they passed. Ekon noticed two of them holding a long banner between them: THE KUGAWANYAN RIVER DANCERS. When he looked back at the group, they were still frowning except for Makena.

"What?"

"I think I've just figured out how we're going to get into the magistrate's home."

"Really?" Zain pursed his lips. "How?"

"Easy." There was a mischievous touch to Makena's smile. "We're going to walk right through the front doors."

The frequency with which Ekon found himself committing crimes these days was only a little bit troubling.

In the hours since they'd watched the procession, the sun had fallen beneath Kugawanya's skyline and the city's air had taken on a distinct chill. Ekon shivered against it and looked ahead to the magistrate's home looming several yards away. It had seemed regal from a distance, but this close, with golden light throwing its windows and stonework into sharp relief, it was more foreboding, even menacing. He watched as trickles of well-dressed people formed a line outside its gate and gradually began to file in.

"Psst. Ekon!"

Ekon looked up, then made his way deeper into the shadows of one of the city's outermost buildings to stand with the rest of the group. Makena was standing in the midst of them with her hands on her hips. She gave him a cursory once-over.

"We're just about ready to go," she announced, nodding with approval. "Looks like my measurements were right, the outfits really came together."

Zain snickered, and Ekon felt his cheeks warm. "Why is mine so tight?"

Makena rolled her eyes. "Don't be silly, Ekon. It's formfitting."

"Zain's costume isn't *formfitting.*"

"There wasn't enough material!" said Makena, exasperated. "Besides, that cut is very fashionable in the south."

"Yeah, Ekon." Zain elbowed him in the ribs. "Relax, you're *fashionable.*"

Ekon opened his mouth to say something else, but Makena interrupted. "It's almost time," she said, looking past them at the magistrate's manor. "Are there any final non-clothes-related questions?"

"Are my marks covered?" asked Koffi. She lifted her arm.

"Yes," said Makena. "Now, to confirm: Njeri will be at the back of the magistrate's house with a mule and wagon in exactly ninety minutes. Whether or not we find the bracelet, that's when we leave. Is everyone clear on that?"

Each of them nodded, and Zain raised his hand. He was giving Njeri a shrewd look.

"How are you going to procure a wagon and mule?"

Njeri raised her staff. "I can be persuasive."

"We'll know if we're going with Plan A or Plan B once we're inside the manor and have a better lay of the land," Makena continued, "so for the time being just follow my lead, and remember to stay in character." She took a deep breath. "Let's go."

No one spoke as they waved goodbye to Njeri, then fell into a single-file line behind Makena. They hadn't coordinated it, but their steps naturally fell in sync as they made their way toward the magistrate's manor, and Ekon let his fingers tap against the side of his thigh with the cadence.

One-two-three. One-two-three. One-two-three.

It's going to work, he told himself as they walked. *It has to.*

To Makena's credit, her plan had proven to be a good one. She hadn't had much money at all, but she still managed to take a few bits of bargain fabric haggled from the city's markets and use them to accessorize and add to the clothes they were already wearing so that they appeared to be in uniforms not unlike the ones they'd seen the troupe from earlier dressed in. When Zain had disappeared and returned with face paints—no one cared to ask how he'd procured them—Makena had been able to complete the look by adding designs and streaks of color to their faces, arms, and necks. To a stranger, at least, they'd look convincing.

Ekon just prayed that was enough.

By the time they reached the front of the magistrate's home, they were standing directly under its light. Ekon felt the eyes first, then the murmurs as they moved up in line, closer and closer to the main doors. He tried to make his fingers still, but they seemed to only move faster and faster the more nervous he became.

"Hey." Safiyah was standing behind him in their line, but she reached out and grabbed his hand, holding it until his fingers stopped. Her voice was soft when she spoke. "It's okay to be nervous," she whispered, "but don't let them see it. Smile, it's all just a performance."

Ekon didn't turn around, but he did nod, and eventually Safiyah let go of his hand again. He tried to think back to his training with the Sons of the Six, how anything the brothers had imparted to him could be of help now. He forced himself to turn his lips upward into something of a smile, and at once, one of the older women standing near him and observing him smiled back. He relaxed just slightly.

It's a performance, he repeated in his mind. *Just a performance. You can do this.* His fingers had stopped their tapping when he looked ahead and stopped short.

"Who are they?"

There were two armored men standing at the entrance. For one panicked moment Ekon thought of the Sons of the Six, but just as quickly he realized that was impossible. These men were warriors, that was certain, but their uniforms were different. They didn't wear the blue and gold of the Sons; their attire was deep bronze and accented in black.

"I've heard of them," said Zain. He was standing in front of Ekon. "I think those are members of the Southern Guard."

"The what?"

Zain glanced back at him with a wry expression. "Relax, I don't think they're like your Sons of the Six exactly. They're not religiously affiliated. They're sell-spears, warriors who can be hired to serve whoever pays the best. The only thing they're loyal to is coin."

Despite everything, Ekon had to temper a confusing sense of revulsion as they neared the Southern Guards; his performance smile became harder to maintain.

"We didn't plan for this." He said the words through his teeth, but loud enough for the rest of the group to hear. "We didn't account for armed warriors."

"It'll be fine," said Zain. "Just stick to the plan."

It seemed to take forever, but gradually they reached the front of the line, and one of the guards stepped forward. His dark eyes softened just slightly as he eyed Makena, who had to be almost two feet shorter than him, but his hand still stayed on the short spear at his hip.

"State your business here, woman."

"Good evening," said Makena. She offered a practiced curtsy as she smiled and looked up at the guard. "We are the Kugawanyan River Dancers," she said theatrically, "the southern capital's latest and greatest entertaining troupe. Perhaps you've heard of us?"

"I'm afraid I haven't." The guard's expression was unmoved as he held up a long scroll with his other hand and scanned it briefly before looking back at Makena. "And your troupe is not on the list of expected guests."

Makena didn't miss a beat. She swatted the air good-naturedly. "Of course we're not," she said affably. "We're not guests of the magistrate; we're a surprise feature, requested by the magistrate's wife herself as a gift to her husband."

The guard's brows knitted together.

"You're free to find the Lady Magistrate and confirm," Makena offered, "though I would imagine she's probably with the magistrate now. I would hate to be the one to ruin the surprise . . . especially given how much she paid for our performance . . ."

Ekon could practically hear the guard thinking the words through, and to some degree he even felt a level of sympathy for the man. He was caught between two choices: allowing unconfirmed guests in, or incurring the magistrate's wrath by disturbing them while they were entertaining guests. His lips pressed together in a tight line.

"Entertainment is to use the servants' entrance," he finally said in a gruff voice, nodding to a pair of doors several feet away and conspicuously out of the main light. "See that you don't speak to any guests unless you are spoken to directly. You're also not permitted to partake in any of the refreshments. There's a well at the back of the house for water."

Makena offered a second, lower curtsy. "Of course, sir," she said sweetly. "We are consummate professionals." She then led the way toward the side door the guard had indicated. No one was guarding that door, so Makena held it open as the rest of them filed inside quickly. The corridor they found themselves in was tight and cramped, and only illuminated by a small sconce overhead. Makena pushed her way in too, closed the door, and then she spoke.

"We have about eighty minutes." She looked up at Ekon. "Do I have that time right?"

Ekon nodded.

"We'll enter the main hall, then split up," she went on. "Me and Koffi will be in one group, Safiyah is on her own, then Ekon and Zain can go together."

Great. Ekon didn't hide his deepening frown as Zain blew a kiss his way.

"Don't forget the signal." Makena smoothed the front of her tunic a final time. "Let's go."

Ekon listened as they continued down the tight corridor toward the bright light at its end. Already, he could hear music and the buzz of several conversations happening at once. He braced himself.

It's a mission, said a voice in his head. *Just like any other mission. Find the target and execute the plan.*

Makena led them around a corner and Ekon blinked at the sudden onslaught of light. They were on a terrace, and below them a party was in full swing. A long banquet hall stretched before them, completely tiled in cream marble and packed with well-dressed people. At once a few people noticed them and pointed, clapping.

"Game faces," said Makena. She was already smiling to the crowd as she began to pirouette and wave a ribbon in her hands. Ekon followed suit, waving his own ribbon, albeit with less enthusiasm, as they made their way down the steps. When they were level with the crowd, most of the guests turned back to their conversations.

"Okojo!" Zain jerked his head. He was already heading left. "This way."

Ekon huffed but had no choice but to follow as Zain marched directly into the crowd. He looked over his shoulder and caught one final glimpse of Koffi before she and Safiyah were gone, and then he was forced to look ahead again. People moved out of the way as they walked, but they also stared. Ekon's fingers began to tap again.

"Look," Zain said under his breath. "Straight ahead."

Ekon hadn't noticed before, perhaps because the room was so packed, but at the front of the banquet hall, a long table draped in white linen was arranged, and sitting behind it was the magistrate. Up close, Ekon saw that he was a severe-looking man, tall and regal with a precise fade cut and several golden chains about his neck. The young man to his right, a boy of twelve or so, had to be his son. On the magistrate's other side sat his wife, and then the person they were looking for, his daughter. She was younger than Ekon had thought initially, a girl of no more than eight. Her black twists were arranged in an elaborate sort of updo, and at present she was leaning against her mother, looking supremely bored while the magistrate's wife murmured something into her ear.

"Is she wearing the bracelet?"

"I don't know," said Ekon. "Her arm's down, I can't tell from here."

Zain blew out a breath, but together they moved closer. They'd only taken a few steps when they heard it. Three sharp whistles to their left. Ekon tensed. That was the signal, or at least one of them. He wasn't sure who had given it. Several of the guests looked up for a moment, confused, before returning to their conversations.

"She's not wearing it," said Zain, shaking his head. "So it's Plan B, then."

Ekon silently cursed. If they were enacting Plan B, it meant that someone in their group had already gotten a good enough view of the magistrate's daughter to see that she wasn't wearing the bracelet anymore. That meant they'd have to search the house for it.

"Fall back," Zain muttered, and Ekon felt the slightest hint of annoyance at the unnecessary command. Slowly, they both moved away from the magistrate's table to stand within the crowd.

"I'm going to try to go through there." Zain nodded subtly toward an arched entryway. "You want to take the one facing south?"

"Sure," said Ekon through his teeth. "I'd love that."

If Zain heard the sarcasm, he didn't catch it. Without another word, he turned on his heel, making a point to do a neat pirouette with his ribbon and leaving Ekon alone. He felt the eyes of guests on him again as he continued to stand there.

Move. Go.

He headed toward the other entryway, taking care to do an awkward spin or turn every few feet to keep up appearances. Relief flooded him as he ducked into the dark, but it was only brief. Before him stretched a dark corridor with any number of doors and smaller passages. Voices sounded behind him, and he made himself keep walking, looking as deliberate as he could. He passed one hallway, then another, then stopped at the third and turned into it. This new space had slightly more light, but it was longer.

Think, think, he told himself. *If that girl's not wearing the brace-let, then it's somewhere here, likely a bedroom. The manor is only one story high, which means it's down one of these halls, in one of these rooms...*

"Hey!"

Ekon jumped. Someone had appeared at the other end of the hallway and was walking toward him fast. His pulse quickened as he tried to think what to do. If he ran, the person—whoever they were—would definitely know he was guilty. If he stayed... He started to turn, but the voice sounded again.

"Hey, stop!"

Ekon relaxed as the hall's sconce light finally illuminated the face of the person: a young woman. She was dressed in a modest tunic and headwrap and looked a few years his junior; if Ekon had to guess, she was one of the magistrate's kitchen girls. She was holding a tray of neatly arranged breads and cheeses in her hands, and when she finally stopped before Ekon, she glared.

"What are you doing here?" she asked. "You're an entertainer."

"Uh . . . ," Ekon stammered, realizing too late that he hadn't remembered to think of an alibi. "I, uh . . . I was sent back here to help. Something about being shorthanded—"

"The kitchens are that way," the girl said impatiently, jerking her head over her shoulder. "If you're going to help, grab a tray, and be quick about it! Cook's in a foul mood!"

"I—"

But the kitchen girl didn't even give him the chance to respond. With a harried look, she stepped around him and continued down the hall in the direction he'd come, leaving Ekon alone again. Slowly, he calmed.

The kitchen, right. Head there.

He felt a tiny bit of hope as he kept walking. If the servants believed that he was there to help serve food, they might be more willing to speak with him. He could figure out a way to ask one of them where the magistrate's daughter's rooms were, and then . . .

He stopped, having reached the end of the hallway and a new problem. He was now staring at a blank wall, and two paths that veered in opposite directions. The kitchen girl had indicated that the kitchens were back the way she'd come, but . . . Ekon hadn't seen which hallway she'd come down initially. He groaned, and his fingers began to tap against his side in earnest.

One-two-three. One-two-three. One-two-three.

It's simple probability, he reasoned. *There's a 50 percent chance the kitchens are down one of these hallways. You just have to pick.*

But the longer he looked between the two, the less sure he became. He looked for light, listened for sound, tried to discern anything that would make the right choice obvious. But it was no use, each hall was equally dark and quiet.

Come on, Ekon. Choose . . .

He took a deep breath, charged down the tunnel to his right, and began to count. *One-two-three. One-two-three. One-two-three.*

The new tunnel was dimmer than the first, but he quickened his steps to be in time with his counting. *One-two-three.* There were two possibilities that would come of this. One, he would find the kitchens and continue with his plan, or two, he'd turn around and find them anyway. He thought about what Safiyah had said. This was all a performance. As far as anyone in these halls knew, he was a hired entertainer, and as long as he continued to act like that, he'd be okay. He exhaled when he finally saw a hint of light at the end of the hall and heard voices, then picked up speed.

One-two-three. One-two-three. Yellow light flooded the hall now, and he made out an open door. He was feet from it when he stopped. The voices he heard did not sound like the voices of other kitchen girls. They were men's voices.

"How long until this is over?" one grumbled.

"A few more hours at least."

Ekon inched forward just enough to peek around the corner.

The room he'd been about to walk into was small, certainly not the kitchen. It was bare, windowless, and devoid of anything except for a few rickety wooden chairs and a table with some cheap-looking cups and a battered teapot. Two men were sitting near the table, both wearing uniforms of the Southern Guard. For several seconds, the warriors said nothing as they sipped their tea. Then one drained his cup and set it down.

"That correspondence," he said. "The one that arrived at the barracks yesterday. Did the captain ever say who it was from?"

"It was a missive from the Sons of the Six out east," said the other warrior. "They're looking for a fugitive. Okojo something."

Ekon went still.

"Their reports identified him in Bandari, and then again on the Ndefu heading west. They think he might pass through Kugawanya at some point."

"What do they want him for?"

The second warrior shrugged. "He abandoned post or something." He leaned in. "They're offering a nice reward for him, though, a thousand dhabus."

The first warrior whistled low. "That's a pretty sum. They didn't mention whether or not he had to be taken alive, did they?"

"Interestingly enough they did not."

It took Ekon several seconds to make himself move, retreating in careful steps as he sank into the shadows. He'd taken one, two, three, four steps before he felt it: the sharp prick of a knife at his back. His skin cooled as a rough voice sounded in his ear.

"And who might you be, boy?"

CHAPTER 17

POWER

KOFFI

They were running out of time.

Koffi tried not to think about it as she wove among the guests of the magistrate's party. Ekon loved numbers; he seemed to have a constant clock going in his head that kept a perfectly accurate count of everything and helped him find reason in the world around him.

He loved numbers, but Koffi hated them.

Five. There were five of them here and still one bracelet to find. She'd heard the whistle as clearly as the rest of them and knew what it meant. The magistrate's manor had an infinite amount of rooms and corridors, and they had . . . She didn't even know how much time she had left. When Makena suddenly appeared beside her, she started.

"Sorry."

"It's okay. Have you seen any of the others?"

Makena nodded. "Safiyah got caught up with some woman

who wanted to talk about her costume. I saw Zain and Ekon both head into corridors about ten minutes ago."

Koffi swallowed. "Do we have much time?"

"A little over an hour, but Njeri will be on her way here soon."

Koffi searched the room, desperate.

She went still, and beside her, a small gasp escaped Makena.

Two of the Southern Guards were frog-marching Ekon forward. They stopped before the magistrate.

"Apologies, sir," one of them said in a gruff voice. "But the matter was urgent and needed to be brought to your attention immediately."

The magistrate looked between the guards and Ekon several times, visibly confused. "What is it?"

"This young man was found sneaking through the halls of your home, sir. We have some reason to believe he may be a fugitive."

"A *fugitive*?" The magistrate looked incredulous now. A moment's surprise passed over his face before it was replaced with anger. "How is that even possible? How did he get in? The entrances to my home are supposed to be guarded by *your* men, Captain."

For the first time, Koffi saw that warrior who'd first addressed the magistrate look uncomfortable. "They were, sir, and rest assured they still are. But we believe the fugitive got in using a disguise, and possibly with help from the inside." He cast an accusing look around the room.

The magistrate's frown deepened. "I will have the truth," he said imperiously. He addressed Ekon for the first time. "What is your name, boy?"

Koffi held her breath as all heads turned toward Ekon. He

looked around the room, and it occurred to her then how young he looked, despite his height. He looked distinctly lost. "I—I—"

"He is thin." The magistrate's wife, sitting next to him, assessing. "Perhaps the boy was just hungry, sneaking into the kitchens for food?"

The magistrate stroked his chin. "Perhaps," he mused. "But if that is the case, then let the boy tell us himself. Speak plainly, boy, about your business here. Were you trying to steal from me? If you are honest, I may grant you clemency."

Ekon continued to stammer. "I—I was—"

Koffi knew, even now, what was going through Ekon's mind. He was stalled, disoriented. None of this had been part of either scenario they'd planned for, and Ekon thrived on plans. She watched as his eyes grew wide with panic, and willed him to see her, but he kept looking around the room. When the magistrate spoke again, his tone was decidedly less kind.

"If you will not speak," he said, "perhaps one of your co-conspirators will." He snapped his fingers abruptly and pointed. "Seize that one."

Koffi tensed as the warriors parted the crowd and moved in the direction the magistrate had indicated. She braced herself, waiting to see which person from their group they'd grab. She heard a sharp cry, and then her heart sank. The guards came forward with a young man, a *real* performer, dressed in costume. He looked to be about their age, perhaps a bit older, and though his costume was different, the resemblance was close enough. He trembled as the guards brought him to stand next to Ekon, and the magistrate looked him over too.

"What is *your* name, boy?"

"Jolo," the performer said immediately. "It's Jolo . . . sir."

"And where are you from, Jolo?" asked the magistrate.

"Here, sir," said Jolo. "I was born and raised in Kugawanya."

The magistrate nodded slowly. "What's *his* name?" he asked, pointing to Ekon.

"I—I don't know, sir. I've never seen him before."

The magistrate tsked. "You disappoint me, Jolo. I was hoping you'd be the honest one."

Jolo shifted his weight from foot to foot. "Sir, I'm not lying, I'm not! That man isn't from our troupe. He didn't even come in with us, I swear it!"

"Husband." The magistrate's wife leaned in again, touching his elbow lightly. "Is it possible that this one's telling the truth? The boy might be merely dressed like a performer. I can see his costume is slightly different."

"It is possible," the magistrate agreed. "Which means that we don't know if there are others in the room who are impersonators."

Koffi tensed.

The magistrate turned his gaze on Ekon again. "You are sure you don't want to tell me your name or where you're from, boy?"

Ekon was silent.

"Very well, then. I see only one way forward." He nodded at Jolo. "Cut out that one's tongue."

"What?" Jolo stepped back, but the two Southern Guards grabbed both of his arms. Several people in the crowd began to mutter among themselves. "Sir, please, I did nothing! Please!"

"Husband." This time the magistrate's wife's tone was sharper. "This is not appropriate. Your children are here, and our guests—"

"Silence, woman. I'll have no more of your hissing in my ear."

He raised his hand, and his wife leaned back quickly. "Someday, gods willing, my son will inherit my title as magistrate of this city," he said mildly. "Tonight, I intend to teach him a valuable lesson on how I rule it. Lying is the worst of all sins. A man who will lie will just as easily steal. A man who steals will just as easily kill. I will not abide lying in my city, and I will certainly not abide lying in my own home."

Koffi looked from Ekon to Jolo to the magistrate. Around him, guests were beginning to look visibly uneasy, but if anything, the magistrate appeared to be enjoying himself. It took her a moment to recognize why the look on his face, the one of quiet triumph, looked familiar. Then it came to her. She remembered Fedu; he'd looked the same way as he'd dangled that young daraja girl by her hair back at Thornkeep. Like Jolo, that girl had done nothing wrong, but the god hadn't cared because, for him, it had everything to do with power.

One of the guards withdrew a long dagger from his hip, and Koffi watched as the silver metal glinted in the room's dim orange light. Jolo began to scream in earnest, and though Koffi had thought initially that he looked older than them, in that moment he sounded childlike, no different from that daraja girl as she'd kicked at the air in vain.

All fell silent, and Koffi felt a new panic set in as one of the warriors grabbed Jolo's shoulders to keep him from moving. The other warrior closed in, dagger raised.

No. Koffi couldn't watch this, she didn't want to, but she couldn't turn away from it either. Nausea rose within her as the warrior used the hilt of the dagger to hit Jolo hard in his stomach. The young man wheezed and slumped forward in pain. At once, the warrior grabbed him by the jaw and pried his mouth open. Jolo groaned, and the magistrate sneered.

No. A stronger voice was suddenly in Koffi's head now. She barely noticed the hum of energy as it released within her, coursing through her veins and setting her skin ablaze.

Stop this. When the chorus of voices filled her head, she did not flinch away from them. She'd heard them once before, at the boundary of Thornkeep. This time she was not afraid of them. *You have the power to stop this. Stop this. Stop this. Stop—*

"STOP IT!" Koffi yelled the words aloud, and they reverberated around the hall like a thunderclap. The people standing nearest to her whirled around, startled, and one by one she felt the eyes of everyone else in the room as they fell on her. Finally, even Ekon found her in the crowd, but she didn't look at him long. Her gaze fell on the magistrate, who was rising from his seat slowly, looking puzzled.

"What's this?" he said. "Who is she? Another one of the impostors? Another fugitive?"

"Let him go." Koffi said the words firmly in the room's quiet, but in her mind she heard the chorus saying them. Her vision began to tunnel and darken.

"You presume to give me commands, girl? In my city, in my own house?" The bemusement left the magistrate's voice as his expression hardened. "Seize her too."

Koffi watched it happen slowly. In her periphery, she saw two more of the Southern Guards in their bronze armor making their way toward her from across the room. Makena was still standing next to her, and she felt more than saw her friend shift imperceptibly closer to her, as though to shield her.

And then she erupted.

The world grew small around her as the splendor left her in a rush, emitting from her hands and exploding from her with a sound that shattered every one of the hall's windows. She raised her arms as screams filled the room, as people began to run from her. Her own lips parted in awe.

Stop this, the chorus chanted with new fervor. *Stop them, stop them all.*

Her hands were still raised, and the splendor was still whirling around her, but in that haze she searched. It was harder now, through the tunneled vision, to make out any one distinct person, but her gaze caught one: the magistrate. It was his golden chains that had given him away, glinting in the sconces' light. The man had gathered up the hems of his fine robes and was running with the rest of the party's guests toward the doors, pushing his wife and children ahead of him and looking back at her nervously.

Stop them, said the chorus. *Stop him.*

Koffi closed her right hand into a fist so that the splendor ceased to flow from it, and instead directed all the energy into her left hand. She felt the effect of that shift instantly, the way the splendor shuddered through her as it was redistributed. It made the entire left side of her body feel heavier. Her teeth clenched as the magistrate continued pushing, getting closer and closer to the way out.

No. Stop him. There was an eagerness, a hunger in the chorus's collective voice now.

She wasn't conscious of making the decision, but she relished the feeling as the splendor reshaped itself to form a sparkling spear as long as her own body. Even holding the weapon made her feel powerful, and in that moment, she decided that was what mattered: power. She stretched her arm back in a slow arc.

"Koffi!" Some different voice was calling to her, one that she knew, but it was distant. "Koffi, wait—"

She screamed again as she flung the spear at the magistrate with all her might and felt its energy crackle through the air. The crowd's screams rose in pitch as the splendor spear soared through the air. It missed the magistrate by several feet, but hit the wall with a terrible crash. One of the long tapestries hanging from it caught flame, and the entire manor shuddered. Koffi watched as several pieces of plaster and stone fell from the ceiling; she watched, with satisfaction, as one hit the magistrate and he went down with a groan.

Good, the chorus of voices praised her. *Now finish him.*

Koffi's steps were slow as she crossed the banquet hall. It was mostly empty now, but it still seemed to take an unnaturally long time for her to close in on the magistrate. With every step toward him, the splendor around her seemed to grow, sparkling with new energy.

Finish him. Finish him.

The magistrate was on his stomach, a small pool of blood forming near his head. Either he hadn't noticed her approach, or he didn't have the strength to face her. Smoke from the tapestry on fire was filling the room, and he was already coughing hard. Each time he tried to rise, his arms trembled, then gave out beneath him.

Weakling, said the chorus. *See how weak he is now? He is not like you, he never had any true power . . . you can show him what real power is.*

Koffi was deliberate as she raised her left hand for a second time. A thrum of pleasure coursed through her as another splendor spear formed in her palm. The blade's tip looked like ice as it glinted against the fire's light. She threw her arm back again, poised, ready—

"Baba!"

Koffi stopped, startled by the sudden interruption of a new, strange sound. That voice, the one she'd just heard, hadn't belonged to the chorus in her head; she'd never heard that one before. She looked around the hall, confused, and then she found the person the voice belonged to.

It was a girl, no older than eight.

She was wearing a beautiful red dress, elaborately decorated with golden beads. Her thick black hair had been arranged in two buns atop her head, but one of them had come undone and was now sticking straight up. She was standing at the doorway that everyone else had already fled through. Tears tracked down her cheeks.

"Baba!" she wailed. "Baba, come on!"

"Get *back*, Hasina!"

Koffi's gaze returned to the magistrate. He was still struggling to rise, but he'd lifted his head. There was a large cut above his eyebrow that blood was streaming from, but he was paying the wound no attention. He was watching the girl, desperate. "*Go. Find your mother!*"

"No, Baba!" The girl was trembling, afraid, but she wouldn't move.

Finish him, the chorus urged. *You have the power now, he does not. Finish it.*

Koffi was still holding the splendor spear, her arm still arched back. One part of her, the part that felt most alive in this moment, wanted to throw that spear as hard as she could, to do what the chorus said and finish it. She looked back at the girl, the one the magistrate had called Hasina. She was still standing at the door, but she'd doubled over and begun to cough. The smoke in the room was thickening, and the smell brought back a memory.

Suddenly she was at the Night Zoo.

Glass was cutting her elbows and palms. She and Mama were crawling together out of the Hema as it collapsed in a fiery heap. She smelled the acrid stench of smoke, heard the screams of beast-keepers and animals alike as they ran, and she saw her mother's face. It had been filled with fear, the same fear that shone bright in this girl's eyes as the flames danced higher and higher in them.

Finish him. The chorus's command held a savage bite, but it sounded farther away. *Finish him. Do not be weak, finish—*

"Koffi!"

Koffi winced and felt a jolt of pain as someone rammed into her, knocking the splendor spear from her grasp. She felt it leave her, watched as it fell to the ground and splintered into a thousand tiny pieces, and then she fell too. Her head hit the beautiful marble and she saw stars tangling with the flames. She blinked once, twice, then looked up. Someone was standing over her.

"Koffi!" Ekon's expression was inscrutable. "Come on, get up! Hurry!"

She felt his arms lifting her back to her feet, holding her when the room tilted slightly before it steadied.

"Can you stand?"

She couldn't speak, but she nodded.

"I'm going to pick up the magistrate," said Ekon. "Grab the girl, tell her to follow us!"

"What?"

Ekon was already running toward the magistrate. The fire from the tapestry had worked its way down the wall, and more debris was falling from the ceiling. Slowly, carefully, he helped the man to his feet. When he saw Koffi watching them, he glared.

"The girl!"

Koffi started, looking left. Hasina, the magistrate's daughter, was in the room now, crouched in a ball. Her head was tucked into her arms, and she was coughing hard between sobs. Koffi's head was still pounding, but she made herself focus as she approached the girl carefully and stooped low.

"Hey!" She tapped the girl's shoulder. "Come with me, we need to get you out of here!"

The girl lifted her head and screamed as she saw Koffi, scrabbling away from her.

"No! No, get away! Don't hurt me!"

"I won't!" Koffi tried to yell, but the fire's roar was too loud now. Hasina was still shaking her head.

"Koffi!" Ekon had the magistrate over his shoulder now. "Come on!"

Koffi didn't stop to think, she lunged, snatching the girl's arm and hauling her to her feet. Hasina pulled back for an instant, but when another stifling wave of smoke blew toward them, they both ducked down low. Koffi could barely see Ekon's legs. He was heading toward one of the broken windows.

"Come on!" She didn't wait for the girl to answer, but followed Ekon. She watched as he braced himself and leaped, knocking out pieces of glass before he disappeared into the night. She and Hasina reached the window, but the girl hesitated. The splendor had shattered most of the windows, but the frames were still edged with long shards. Koffi braced herself.

"We have to jump through, there's no other way," she shouted. "We'll do it on three. One, two—"

In the end, she bore the worst of the shards. A cry tore from her as she felt them slice her clothes, scratching her arms and bare legs, but most of the glass broke as she charged through, which meant it didn't scratch Hasina. Something caught on her ankle, and together they tumbled into a set of bushes. For several seconds, she just lay there, gasping and taking in cool breaths of fresh air. Slowly, she turned to Hasina. Her chest was rising and falling fast as she met Koffi's gaze.

"Are you hurt?"

The girl shook her head.

"Did you leave anything behind that you needed?"

Slowly the girl shook her ahead again, reaching into her dress's pocket. Koffi caught a glint of something black—

"Koffi!"

She sat up at the same time Hasina did. Ekon was crashing toward them. A few feet behind him, the magistrate was standing, albeit unsteadily. Ekon didn't look at Koffi, but knelt in front of Hasina.

"Your baba is badly hurt," he said gently. "But he's going to be all right. Stay with him until you see another adult, okay?"

Hasina nodded.

"Good." He stood again, and when he looked at Koffi, all the gentleness was gone from his face. "We need to get out of here before—"

"Koffi! Ekon!"

Koffi looked right at the same time Ekon did. It was still difficult to see much in the darkness outside the fire's light, but she could hear something: the creak of wheels, galloping hooves. She tensed, bracing herself to run, but relief crashed through her when Njeri's wagon came around the corner. Safiyah and Makena were leaning out from either side of it.

"Hurry, get in!"

Njeri did not slow the wagon, so Koffi and Ekon were both forced to take running leaps and grab the side of the wagon before crawling into its back. As soon as they were both in, Njeri drove the mule harder so that they picked up speed. Koffi glanced back a final time as they sped into the night. She saw now that at least half of the magistrate's manor was on fire; swirling walls of red and gold flame contrasting brilliantly with the sky. In their light, she caught a glimpse of the magistrate and his daughter, watching them go in silence.

CHAPTER 18

The CHEMOSIT

EKON

Ekon tried to count the sounds of the mule's hooves pounding into the dirt as they left Kugawanya behind.

One-two—One-two—three.

No matter how hard he tried, the three count came to him disjointed and broken; too many other thoughts were crowding his mind now, all vying for attention. Some of the things he was picturing were horrid, frightening images burned into his memory. Other things felt less tangible, more like the stuff of nightmares. In a way, a part of him hoped that some of what he'd seen in the magistrate's manor hadn't been real. He was pulled from his thoughts when their wagon slowed to a stop.

"The mule won't go any farther," said Njeri. Her voice was taut, shaky. "I stole it from a farmer in town, and I'm betting it isn't used to traveling on uneven terrain. We'll have to leave it here and continue on foot."

"Will it be all right?" asked Makena, regarding the mule.

Njeri nodded. "We're not so far from town that it won't be able to wander back if I unhitch it."

Everyone filed out of the wagon while Njeri worked quickly to untie the harness from the mule. It took a moment for Ekon's eyes to adjust to the darkness, but slowly, under the starlight, he was able to take in their surroundings.

Behind them, Kugawanya was little more than a distant ball of yellow-orange light, though Ekon thought he could still make out a thin plume of smoke where the magistrate's manor continued to burn. He turned to take in the landscape before them. Njeri had been right. Ahead, for as far as he could see, there was uneven grassland. The ground beneath his feet was soft and wet.

"We're back in the southern marshlands," Makena explained, "albeit much farther west now. The end of the Ndefu overflows here because the earth is so low. The trek north will be muddy, but if we keep going, eventually we'll end up on the edge of the Kusonga Plains."

"Will any of those warriors be able to follow us?" asked Njeri.

"I don't think so," said Makena. "I made enough diversions as we rode to keep the warriors off our trail for at least the night. They might find some of our tracks in the morning, but they'll mostly disappear in the marshlands, that's the advantage of this route. Besides, I doubt they expect us to head north, there's not much in the way of real civilization from here." She looked around at the group and sighed. "I know we've all have had a very long night, and things haven't gone according to plan, but the more ground we cover tonight, the safer it'll be to rest."

"We should keep moving," Njeri agreed. "Makena, do you want to lead?"

They started into the marshlands. Ekon had taken several paces before he realized that Koffi was the only one among them who hadn't moved. She was turned away, and still staring at Kugawanya. She hadn't moved.

"Koffi? You okay?"

"I . . ." She looked over her shoulder, confused. "Wait, we're . . . we're not going back?"

"*Back?*" Ekon didn't manage to keep the shock from his voice.

Njeri stopped, frowning. "What are you talking about, Koffi?"

"The bracelet!" said Koffi impatiently. "It's there, at the magistrate's manor. I saw it myself, I almost got it. His daughter had it in her pocket the whole time. If we could just sneak into the city again, form a new plan, and—"

"Hold on." Zain was shaking his head. For the first time since Ekon had met him, he looked genuinely at a loss for words. "Koffi, you can't be serious."

Koffi stared. "What do you mean?"

"I don't know what you *think* just happened back there, but . . . we barely made it out of Kugawanya. That place is crawling with warriors by now."

"We don't even have the advantage of disguises anymore," Makena pointed out. "The magistrate, the warriors, and everyone else at that party will be on high alert, checking for anyone suspicious who enters the city now. It's not safe."

Koffi shook her head, as though she couldn't believe what she was hearing.

"You all knew when we started this that it was going to be dangerous. What changed?"

"You almost got everyone *killed!*" He hadn't meant to yell, he hadn't meant to lose control, but when he spoke, the words escaped Ekon in an angry rush. "You set fire to a building and put everyone in it at risk. You almost killed someone."

"I would never have done that," Koffi spat. "You know I wouldn't have."

Ekon shook his head. "I don't, Koffi. That's why I had to stop you."

He watched her face as the meaning behind his words registered. Confusion turned to anger. *"You,"* she whispered. "You were the one who knocked me to the ground."

Ekon flushed. "I had to, Koffi. Someone had to intervene."

Koffi grimaced. "I was fine, I had everything under—"

"You were *not* in control." Something warned Ekon to stop talking, but he couldn't hold the words back now. "You were reckless and you didn't think about the consequences of your actions. You put everyone here in danger, and it's selfish that you'd do it again so willingly."

Koffi reeled as though he'd slapped her. He saw the hurt on her face for an instant, and then it was gone. In its place, Ekon saw venom.

"At least I did *something,*" she said. *"You* were too much of a coward."

He had yelled, she had whispered, but in the end it was her words that left the deeper wound. Ekon winced against their sting and hated himself for the sudden tightness in his throat. *Coward. Coward. You were a coward.* He felt those words carving themselves into his brain.

One-two-three. Coward. One-two-three. Coward. One-two-three. Coward.

No one spoke.

"In the Enterprise, when we disagreed on something, we put the matter to a vote," Safiyah murmured. "Maybe we do the same now, to figure out what to do next."

"Sounds fair to me," said Zain.

"All in favor of going back to Kugawanya to try to get Amakoya's bracelet, raise your hand."

Koffi's hand shot up, but it was alone. Something in Ekon seized as he watched her look around at them one by one. Slowly, her face fell.

"Makena?" Her voice was small.

"I'm sorry, Koffi." Makena looked down.

"Zain?"

Finally, Koffi looked to Ekon. She didn't say his name, and her expression was flat as she waited for his answer.

"It's too dangerous."

"All in favor of continuing on to the Kusonga Plains, raise your hand," said Safiyah.

One by one, each hand except for Koffi's rose. Ekon watched as emotion clouded her face. He saw the hurt, the betrayal, then lastly the anger.

"It's decided," said Safiyah. "We keep going."

Night turned to dawn, then dawn turned to day.

At first, Ekon felt fine; enough adrenaline was still pumping through his veins to keep him alert as they followed Makena and trekked north through the barren marshlands. But by late morning, fatigue began to creep in, and when it was clear the others were past the point of exhaustion, Zain offered to keep watch while they took intermittent naps before continuing on. The rest was brief, and by late afternoon, they were on the move again. As they walked, Makena laid out the next part of their journey.

"The Ndefu can't be far from here," she said, "and it won't be nearly as difficult to cross because this section's not as wide."

Her prediction, unfortunately, proved inaccurate.

Ekon heard the river before he heard it, a low and constant rush of water. By the time the group reached it, he saw that the plan they'd come up with was going to have to change drastically.

The Ndefu River in this region might have once been the modest stream Makena had described, but now it was a full river, flowing west in a strong current. Njeri sucked her teeth.

"The rains must've been heavier than usual this year," she posited aloud.

"We're not going to be able to get across it on foot, the current's too strong," said Zain. "Personally, I think we should make camp here for tonight and brainstorm a new plan in the morning."

No one seemed to have the energy to suggest otherwise, so they found a patch of mostly dry land and settled on it for the night. Njeri had secured some food at the market in Kugawanya while they'd been preparing to infiltrate the magistrate's home; now she carefully rationed it so that everyone had just enough dried fruit, nuts, and dried meat to fill their stomachs at least partially. Even then, as Ekon tried to lie down and go to sleep, he found it a struggle. He was still thinking of everything he'd seen back at the manor—the guards, Jolo, the fire, Koffi... It was the second time he'd seen her like that, and she'd been entirely unrecognizable. He played everything out in his head with a distinct sense of discomfort, remembering the moment he'd seen her holding that splendor spear. There hadn't been time to think; he'd done the only thing he'd known to do in that moment. He couldn't hit her, he'd never hit her, but he'd had to stop her. He cringed as he remembered knocking into her, hearing her gasp, and watching her as she'd fallen to the floor. He couldn't do that again, but ... he didn't know what he'd do if that kind of thing happened again, if something more drastic would be required to stop her from hurting someone else.

It was your fault, said an imaginary voice in his head. *If you hadn't gone the wrong way, if you hadn't been caught by those guards...*

He tried to shake the voice from his mind, but it was no use, and the longer it lingered, the more clearly another thought came to him.

The missive.

He had tamped down the memory of the conversation he'd heard between the two Southern Guards, but now it was coming back to him.

From the Sons of the Six out east. They're looking for a fugitive. Okojo something...

He felt a chill as the words found new purchase, as he slowly realized what they meant. The Sons of the Six were still after him, even after all this time and distance. The shock was undeniable, but he knew he shouldn't have been truly surprised. He'd undergone the same training that every other initiated Son of the Six had undergone; he knew their principles and beliefs. The Sons of the Six valued courage, fortitude, loyalty, and, perhaps above all, resilience. He'd managed to thwart them twice now; they would not allow it to happen a third time. Ekon thought of his older brother. Kamau was one of the best warriors of their generation. *He* would turn Eshōza upside down to find him. All this time, Ekon had been focused on the plans for the immediate future—most of which revolved around getting Koffi to the Kusonga Plains and stopping Fedu. He realized now, though, that he hadn't given nearly enough thought to what would happen in the after, if they were successful. They might be able to save the world at large, but . . . *his* world was still broken.

Ekon rose before dawn and tried not to think about the internal clock in his head. They had seven days, a week left, before the Bonding.

He listened as the others woke up to see the same thing he did: The Ndefu River's surge had not lessened overnight; if anything, it had gotten worse. Together, they stared down at it in silent dismay.

"I just don't see how we can cross it," said Makena. "Not without getting swept away."

"I think I have an idea." Zain was looking from the river to the opposite bank. "We can't cross the river individually, but we might be able to do it together."

"Together?" Njeri's brow furrowed. "What do you mean?"

Zain massaged his chin. "Before Fedu kidnapped me, when I was little, my friends and I would play a game at our river. We'd hold hands and make a chain so that we could get to the deeper parts of the river without getting swept away. There were fewer of us, and the river back then was less deep, of course, but I think it's the same principle." He looked up. "We hold hands, and one at a time, we step into the river. Each time a new person steps in, the people already in line step to the left, until gradually we're all the way across. By the time the last person in the line is stepping in—"

"The first person will be stepping out," said Njeri. "That could work."

"The only thing is, we'll have to do it slowly," Zain warned. "One misstep, and we'll all get pulled into the current."

"I think it's our best bet at this point," said Makena.

Njeri nodded. "Then let's try."

Zain led the way as they scrambled down the Ndefu's muddy banks and reached its edge. Closer to the water, Ekon saw how strong the river's current truly was. Gingerly, Zain put one foot in the water, then another before extending his hand. Ekon tried not to resent the fact that Koffi took Zain's hand next, and as the two of them waded farther in, they were followed by Njeri, then Safiyah, then Makena. The river deepened as they slowly made their way across, and Ekon watched as the river rose to Zain's middle.

"This is the deepest part," Zain said, indicating. "Makena, you'll need to be especially careful here. We'll all have to move really slowly."

276

"Maybe we should count?" Makena had taken another step into the river. The water was at her knees.

"Good idea," said Ekon quickly. "I'll start it."

"It makes more sense for me to," said Zain. "I'm already in the water, Ekon."

Ekon glowered. "You're up to your middle in water. I've got the better view from here on the banks." *And I'm a better counter* . . .

"Just let him do it, Ekon," said Koffi coolly. "It's not a big deal."

Ekon opened his mouth, then thought better of it.

"Each time I get to three, everyone takes a step to the left," Zain called out. "One-two-three."

In sync everyone, including Ekon, stepped. The river's water chilled him instantly, but he kept his expression impassive. If no one else had betrayed their discomfort, he certainly wouldn't be the first.

"One-two-*three*."

Once again everyone stepped, but this time Makena was off; she stumbled slightly in the water, and both Njeri and Ekon lost their footing as they moved to catch her.

"Sorry."

"It's not *your* fault." Ekon didn't bother keeping the accusatory tone out of his voice as he glared down the line. "Make sure you're actually stepping when you're *supposed* to!"

At the front of the line, Zain and Koffi both looked up, frowning.

"Our steps are *fine*, Ekon," said Koffi.

Ekon shook his head. "They're not, Makena almost fell."

"Ekon . . ." Makena looked uneasy. "It's fine, I'm okay, I—"

Ekon watched in horror as Makena slipped again, and this

time she lost her grip completely and fell into the water with a loud splash. The movement had a chain reaction; Safiyah lost her footing too, and when Ekon reached to grab her, he fell forward. His head ducked below the water, and when he reemerged, he was being carried down the river.

"No!"

Ekon kicked, trying to find the river's bottom, but it was no use. Every time he gained some sort of footing, the current pushed him so that he toppled, falling beneath the surface again. The next time his head bobbed up, he was gasping for air.

"Makena! Ekon!" He heard someone calling, but as the water continued sweeping him away, he had no sense of the direction it was coming from. He managed to turn his head and caught a glimpse of Makena's head before it went beneath the water. Instinct took over then. If he couldn't beat the river's current, he'd have to swim with it. He dived down and propelled himself toward Makena. The next time he dived, he saw her body and swam toward her, pushing her up so that her head was above the water with his. She was coughing hard.

"Hang on," he said. "Just try to keep your head up!"

Makena only coughed in response, and Ekon looked around, frantic. He blinked several times and saw that up ahead there was a fallen log. They were a few feet to the left of it, but if he could move slightly, it would catch them. They only had seconds. He made himself calm. He couldn't tap his fingers as he tried to hold Makena and paddle at the same time, but he still counted.

One-two-three. One-two-three. One-two-three.

He threw his weight as hard as he could and pulled Makena so that the current caught them and dragged both of them toward the log. Pain ricocheted through one of his ribs as he caught the impact of it, but it did the trick and stopped them both from going any farther downriver. Here the water was slightly calmer, and Makena was able to grab hold of the log.

"Are you okay?" he asked.

When Makena nodded, he helped guide her to the bank. They'd barely gotten to shore when the rest of the group came downriver after them. Ekon watched as each of them did the same thing he and Makena had, grabbing the log and using it to slow them down so that they could move to the bank. He helped each of them up, and once they were all on land again, he took account of their new location. It seemed the river had taken them at least a quarter of a mile west. He was grateful they weren't still on their way to the Furaha Lake.

"Saved us a little bit of time, I suppose," said Njeri. "We're slightly closer to the Kusonga Plains, though we'll still have to walk north."

"How much ground do you think we can cover today?" Zain asked. He was already wringing out his tunic.

"On foot, we could cover a few miles, but we'll have to look for more rations. Most of our food was lost in the river."

"Then we'd better get going." Zain started to walk, but Njeri shook her head.

"I think we need to stop again," she said. "Everyone's clothes are soaked, and it's colder here." Even as she said it, Ekon shivered. In answer, Zain frowned.

"We can't keep stopping like this." For the first time, there was real annoyance in his voice. "We're not going to cover any decent ground."

"And we *definitely* won't cover any ground if one of us gets pneumonia." Makena jumped in now. "We don't have to stop for long, just long enough to build a fire and dry off a little bit. We can still make good time today."

Zain looked unhappy, but it was clear he was outvoted. Without waiting for his answer, Makena and Safiyah began to look around for things they could use in the fire, leaving Njeri, Ekon, Koffi, and Zain standing by the river.

"Whatever's going on between the two of you"—Njeri pointed at Ekon and Zain—"you need to sort it out, now."

"I'm not the one with a problem." Zain shrugged, but it looked forced. "Ekon's the one that thinks he knows everything."

"I do *not*." Even to his own ears, Ekon's voice sounded whiny, and he hated it. "You're the one who refuses to listen to anyone—"

"Hold on." Koffi had said nothing so far, but now, standing between them, her eyes shot toward the marshlands. "What's that sound?"

Ekon stiffened. "What sound?"

Zain shook his head. "I don't hear anything."

"Neither do I," said Njeri.

But Koffi was now walking toward the marshlands, her head slightly inclined. "It . . . sounds like music," she said. "I think I recognize the tune, but I don't know where . . ." She continued farther into the high grass of the marsh, and instinctively Ekon stepped after her.

"Koffi, wait." Then he started. He'd only moved a few steps forward, but it had made a difference; now he heard the same sound too. It *did* sound like music, though not any music he'd ever heard before. The tune was keening, long, and it echoed through the air. When he looked back, Njeri and Zain wore matching expression of bemusement.

"Could someone be out there?" Zain asked.

"I don't know." Ekon felt an immediate sense of unease. "But I don't like it."

"Safiyah and Makena just went to look for kindling," Koffi noted. "But I don't see them anymore."

Ekon whirled around and felt a plummeting sensation. A mist had descended on the marshlands, sudden and opaque. That small sense of unease turned into outright panic.

"We need to find them, right now!" He was already running in the direction he'd last see them. "Safiyah! Makena!"

"Makena!" He heard Koffi's voice fading as she ran in another direction. *"Makena!"*

Ekon's breath shortened as the panic intensified. The last time he'd seen a mist like this, the Untethered hadn't been far behind. Was it possible that they'd found them again, followed them all this way? He fought a violent shiver down his spine as he kept running.

"Safiyah! Makena!"

There was no answer, only the echo of his own voice. Ekon heard the dry snap of a branch and whirled to see someone near him in the mist. He reached for the dagger at his belt, bracing himself.

"Who's there?" he called out. "Show yourself!"

"Ekon!"

He started. It was Makena's voice. She sounded frightened.

"Ekon, help me!"

"Where are you?" Ekon looked all around, moving in a slow circle as he tried to discern anything in the mist. Makena sounded close, but he couldn't see her. "Makena! Keep talking!"

"Ekon, I'm afraid!" He heard a tremble in Makena's voice now, she sounded on the verge of tears. "Please, help me!"

"I'm coming!" Ekon called out. "Just tell me where you are. Keep talking, and I'll find you!"

"Ekon!"

He started again as another voice—Safiyah's—sounded.

"Ekon, where are you?"

"Safiyah! Are you with Makena?" Ekon actually raised his hands, trying to feel his way through the opacity. "I can hear you, but I can't see you!"

"We're together!" she called out. "But we can't see anything either."

"Just keep talking!" he repeated. "I'll follow your voices, or you can follow mine!"

"Ekon!" If Safiyah had heard him, she gave no indication of it. "Please, we can't see anything."

Ekon turned, looking for something, anything that could help him get his bearings. His eye suddenly caught a faint red light moving in the darkness.

"Safiyah! Makena!" he called out. "Listen to me, there's a reddish light, do you see it?"

There was a long pause because Makena sniffled. "Yes."

"Head toward it," Ekon instructed. "I'm going to walk toward it too. We'll meet up there and figure out how to find the others. They can't have gone far in this."

"Okay, Ekon."

He was already charging toward the light. Somewhere near him, he heard footsteps, but he continued walking. That little red light was the only point of reference he had now; if he lost it, he'd lose Makena and Safiyah again. In the quiet, he could hear his own ragged breath, the crunch of his own feet in the underbrush.

"Safiyah, Makena, can you still see the light?"

Safiyah was the one who answered this time. "I think so . . . yes."

Ekon picked up the pace. The light was getting closer, or at least he thought it was a light. It had been reddish before but now it seemed to be changing. It faded to orange, and it appeared to be flickering. He started to run toward it, hoping and praying that Makena and Safiyah would too. He breathed relief as the mist around him lifted as suddenly as it had descended, but then he stopped short, confused.

"Makena? Safiyah?"

The two girls were crouched around a small fire, holding their hands out as they warmed themselves. They looked up at Ekon, confused.

"Ekon?" Safiyah was frowning. "Where were you? Where's everyone else?"

"I . . ." Ekon looked over his shoulder. There was still a mist in the air, but it appeared to be thinning now. "I . . . We went looking for you." He shook his head and pointed over his shoulder. "I thought you were in that mist, lost."

Makena shook her head. "We just went to get kindling. We've been back for about ten minutes."

Ekon looked between them now. "But I heard you. I heard your voices. You were asking for help."

"Help with what?" Safiyah asked. "We've been here this whole time. We came right back."

"But—"

"Ekon!"

From the opposite side of the fire, Koffi suddenly stepped out of the mist with Zain and Njeri. All of them were breathing hard.

"Oh gods, thank goodness you're all right." Koffi's eyes were fixed on Ekon. "You're not hurt?"

"Hurt?" Ekon stepped back. "Why would I be hurt?"

"We heard you screaming." Koffi's expression was drawn. "But we couldn't figure out where you were."

Now Makena stood. "We've been here, and we didn't hear anyone screaming. We haven't heard a sound."

Ekon felt it like a creeping instinct. Everyone was staring at each other now, confused.

"Something's not right," he said. "*I* heard you two, but you've been here. *They* heard me, but you all didn't . . ." He massaged his brow. "That doesn't make any—"

"LOOK OUT!"

Ekon ducked just in time. There was a rustling sound, a screech, and then a massive shadow passed over him. When he looked up, he felt the blood drain from his face.

He'd read about any number of Eshōzan creatures, beasts of lore and myth alike, but he'd never read about an animal like the one hovering over them now.

At first glance, he thought to call the thing a bird, but that word fell grossly short. Certainly, the beast had massive black wings—each time it flapped, Ekon felt a rush of cold air on his face—and a shiny black beak that ended in a long, lethal point, but there any resemblance to a bird stopped. Its actual body was gray, wrinkled, and horrifically . . . human. Its eyes shone a lurid, bloody red, and Ekon realized now with a chill what he'd really seen through the haze of the mist. The creature dived again, and this time its feet—long and clawed—barely missed Njeri's head. She somersaulted out of its range and sent sparks of the splendor at it, her teeth bared. Zain and Makena wasted no time jumping in, following Njeri's example and shooting splendor of their own at the creature. It was to no avail; the beast simply flew higher and higher, out of reach, then out of sight in the fog and mist. Zain swore.

"Wait until it comes back down," he shouted. "When it's low enough, we'll—"

His words were cut off by another shriek, this one far worse than the one before. Ekon jerked forward, then fell to his knees, and he wasn't the only one. He watched as, beside him, Safiyah dropped the dagger she'd been holding and curled into a ball. Koffi, Njeri, Makena, and Zain were still standing, but there were tears slicking their cheeks as they strained to stay upright.

"We . . . have . . . to . . . cover our . . . ears," Koffi said through her teeth. Her voice barely carried over the screech.

"That's what it wants us to do," Zain replied. He was trembling from head to foot. "If we stop shooting at it, it'll be able to come down and pick us off one by one."

Of course. Ekon was on the ground, rendered almost entirely immobile, but he still understood the truth of it then. *That's how it kills its prey,* he realized. *It drives them mad, waits until they're weakened and vulnerable, then makes its kill.*

He watched, helpless, as Makena fell first, curling into a ball like Safiyah had and rocking back and forth.

"I can't!" she cried. "I can't take it!"

"Keep at it!" Njeri ordered. "It'll have to tire eventually!"

But now Zain was beginning to sway, his lips loosely parted. When the creature raised the frequency of its shrieks, Ekon watched as Zain collapsed too and did not move again. Only Koffi was left standing, and she looked fatigued. When the winged creature swooped low, she tried to direct her splendor at it but missed. Ekon saw the hint of a spear form in her hand, then fall away.

Ekon strained, trying to rise, but it was no use. Each time the birdlike creature shrieked, it sent fresh new waves of pain down his spine, like a knife stabbing at his skin. He looked up and saw Koffi's arms were still raised, but she'd fallen to her knees. The creature swooped the lowest it had dared to yet, only a few feet above them, and Koffi only just managed to fend it off. Ekon braced himself for the inevitable.

And then the screeching sound abruptly stopped.

He wasn't sure, at first, what he was seeing. The sky above was still pale, but now there were creatures flying through it. He thought it was more of those creatures, but no, now he saw that they were birds, herons. Some were entirely white, others had blue and black crests about their faces, but all were huge, far larger than any heron he'd ever seen before. One screeched, and it seemed to signal to the others as they swooped in unison. He watched as they began to beat their wings and peck at the monster. The gray creature screamed, hissed, and tried to swipe at the birds, but to no avail. The herons were quicker, nimbler, and always managed to fly just out of reach before swooping down again to peck at the creature with unnatural grace. In minutes, the battle was won. As quickly as it had appeared, Ekon watched as the creature covered its head with its tattered black wings and began to retreat, disappearing into the fog and the marshes.

Only when it was gone did the herons stop circling and land, some perching on one foot while others marched through the grass on stilt-like legs, looking for food. On the ground, their size was even more pronounced. Ekon braced himself, waiting for the herons to turn their beaks on them, but to his surprise, the massive birds weren't even looking in their direction anymore; their long necks were turned east, toward the sun. Ekon followed their gazes, and started.

The morning sun had finally crested over the horizon, bathing the plains around them in warm red-gold light. Amid them, Ekon noticed the silhouette of someone walking steadfastly in their direction. It was impossible to see any distinct details on their face as they approached, but Ekon gathered that they were tall and broad-shouldered. The person was carrying a staff and seemed unhurried as they approached, but Ekon's heart began to pound in earnest. He couldn't explain why, but there was an intangible sense of power radiating from the stranger as they drew closer. Beside him, he felt Safiyah shift so that their shoulders brushed.

"Who is that?" she whispered.

Ekon opened his mouth, but the words never left it. The stranger was close enough that the details of his face were discernible. His skin was a warm shade of brown, and deep laugh lines carved into the corners of his eyes and around his mouth. Thick black dreadlocks fell around his shoulders, haphazardly tied back as though only on second thought. He wore a plain white tunic.

"Ah," he said, "and who might you all be?"

Ekon could find no words to say in answer as he met the gaze of Atuno, the god of the skies.

CHAPTER 19

THE PALACE IN THE SKY

KOFFI

In her life thus far, Koffi had met three gods.

Each one of them had been, in their own way, a being of immense power; she'd thought, up to that point, that she could no longer be awed by any one of the Six.

She was proven wrong as she stared at Atuno.

He was, at first glance, unformidable and unassuming. Initially, one might think him a common shepherd, a middle-aged man with thick black dreadlocks and a modest white tunic, slightly frayed at its edges.

"You . . . you helped us."

"I did." The god of the sky twinkled with some amusement. "As it happens, you might say that I'm partial to mortals, having loved a few in my existence." His gaze lifted. "The chemosit is a dangerous being to have as an adversary," he said. "You all should not linger here long."

"Atuno . . ." Koffi hesitated. "The truth is, part of the reason we're here is because we've been looking for *you*."

"For me?" The god's expression was bewildered. "For what cause?"

Koffi took a deep breath. She'd thought that, as time passed, it would be easier to explain everything that had happened in a succinct way, but the truth was, it seemed to get harder each time.

"We've been looking for you because we need your help," she said. "Your brother Fedu is trying to destroy this world, and we need the help of the other gods to stop him."

Atuno frowned, but it wasn't with anger. "My brother?"

"You might want to sit down." Ekon stepped forward. "It's sort of a long story."

Atuno did sit down, and slowly, carefully, Koffi explained to the god what had happened. When she got tired, Ekon jumped in, and sometimes Njeri, Zain, or Makena added commentary too. Safiyah stayed quiet. When they were finished, Atuno sat for a long time without saying anything. He steepled his fingers and took several deep breaths in and out. At first, when he looked up, Koffi couldn't name the expression on the god's face. It took her a moment to realize it was sadness.

"I must take some responsibility in this," he said. "I am the eldest of my siblings, and I had a responsibility to oversee the actions of my brothers and sisters to ensure they were each doing what we've been tasked with for millennia." He shook his head. "Fedu resented that his lot left him with the realm of death, and I always suspected he wished for more power than he was given. I never thought it would come to this." He looked off into the plains for a few more seconds before seeming to remember himself. "You said you had visited my other siblings?"

"Just one, Amakoya," said Koffi. "Badwa was already on our side, and she's gone to speak with your brother Tyembu."

"Wise," said Atuno, nodding. "Tyembu is a powerful god and a formidable ally, but stubborn, and slow to make decisions."

"Amakoya agreed to help us," Ekon added. "Uh, sort of. If you and Itaashe did, that might be enough to stop Fedu."

"Then let there be no doubt, on my account," said Atuno. "I will stand with the rest of my siblings, and against my brother. He must be punished." He frowned, and though Koffi couldn't be certain, she thought she saw a golden glint in them, like lightning.

"Thank you, Atuno," she said in earnest. "Truly." She shifted her weight. "Um, speaking of your siblings . . . we still need to find Itaashe and ask her too. You wouldn't happen to know where she is, would you?"

"Mm." Atuno scratched his chin, pensive. "In that regard, I'm afraid I can be of no help to you," he said. "Of my brothers and sisters, my youngest sister is perhaps the most elusive. She commands the winds, and as such takes after their nature, never staying in one place for very long."

"Even if you could tell us a general idea of where she might be," said Ekon, "it would be a huge help to us."

Atuno looked thoughtful. "Itaashe considers the Ngazi Ranges and the Kusonga Plains part of her realm," he said. "She often moves between them. At this particular time of the year, she is more than likely somewhere on the Kusonga Plains, though where, even I could not say."

Koffi and Ekon looked at each other.

"That's where we're headed," said Ekon. "If we just keep going to the plains as planned, maybe we'll run into her."

"There's a chance," said Koffi slowly.

"The plains are vast," said Atuno. "With luck, you may find my sister, but it will take some time for you to cover the plains in full."

Ekon's shoulders slumped. "I was afraid you'd say that."

Atuno looked thoughtful. "I cannot help you find my sister, but I can better equip you for your journey."

Koffi looked up. "You can? How?"

Atuno smiled. "I can provide you with supplies for your journey—fresh clothes at the very least."

Koffi looked around, and she noticed she wasn't the only one. Njeri, Makena, Zain, and Safiyah appeared just as confused. It was Ekon who said what everyone else was likely thinking.

"Uh, that's a generous offer and all," he said tentatively. "But . . . where is all this stuff coming from?"

Atuno blinked. "My palace, of course."

Ekon looked around. "Your . . . ?"

"Ah, of course." Atuno seemed to remember something. He looked to the herons. They hadn't moved since he'd arrived, but under his gaze, it was as though they thawed, ruffling their white feathers and stretching their stilt-like legs. He nodded to them.

"If you please."

Koffi was just about to ask who he was talking to when the herons abruptly took off. They soared higher and higher, heading straight for the clouds. At first Koffi thought they'd gone entirely, but then she noticed something. The clouds directly above their group were changing shape, lowering. It took her a moment to understand what she was seeing. The herons Atuno had sent away had reappeared, but they were moving in a deliberate way now, spiraling, using their massive wings and long beaks to cut through those clouds and contour them into something else entirely. She watched them carve out one dome, then another, then parapets and towers. Her jaw dropped as the herons carved out windows and archways, and, last, a set of stairs. Koffi stared. It was a palace made entirely from clouds. When they were finished, the herons rose to circle its highest towers. Atuno gestured.

"After you."

"Wait." Ekon's brows rose. "You want us to . . . just walk onto those? Those *clouds*?"

"Yes." Atuno looked amused. "Is that a problem?"

"It's just . . . clouds may *look* solid, but they're actually formed by larger clusters of water drops and ice crystals that, when filled with enough water—"

"Step out on *faith*, boy." Without hesitation, Atuno ascended the first stair. "And you might find the world looks different." He started up them. "By the way, if you *are* planning on coming up, I'd hurry," he said over his shoulder. "The roast won't be as good cold." He reached the top and opened a rounded door made from the same white clouds. Then he disappeared inside, leaving the rest of them below.

"Well?" Makena looked around at all of them. "What do we do?"

"I don't know if I trust it." Njeri was eyeing the cloud stairs warily.

"Uh, neither do I," said Zain, "but . . . he did just mention a roast."

"Zain." Njeri rolled her eyes. "You can't make potentially life-altering decisions based on your appetite."

"*Can't* I?" Zain said mildly. He took a deep breath, then jumped onto the first step. Koffi held her breath, unsure of what she'd see, but Zain landed on it with a soft thud. He stared at his feet, then looked up, grinning. *"All right."* He turned and headed up the stairs, leaving the rest of them behind.

"What do we do *now*?" asked Ekon.

Koffi looked from the rest of the group to Zain, then made her decision. Her pulse quickened as she raised her foot and let it fall on the first stair as Atuno and Zain had, but then she felt it find something solid and soft. She took another step, then another.

"It's okay!" She looked over her shoulder. "We can trust it."

The others gave each other uncertain looks before they followed. The air chilled and thinned the higher they climbed, and there seemed to be more stairs than Koffi had thought initially, but eventually she reached the same door Atuno had gone through. Wisps of cloud blew past her as she ducked under an arched entryway. She stopped.

The exterior of Atuno's palace was cool and white, a whimsical tribute to the clouds from which it'd been made. Inside was a different matter. Koffi found herself in a room filled with rich and vibrant colors. The walls were covered in massive mahogany bookshelves, each of them filled with any number of assorted items—harps, and koras, and other instruments she'd never seen before. She gazed up at the ceiling and noticed that it had been rendered into a huge mural, a painting of beautiful white herons to match the ones she'd seen outside. Most impressive, though, were the books. Never in her life had she seen so many. There were some wedged between knickknacks on the bookshelves but just as many stacked on the ground in piles taller than her. Some looked old, some looked new, some had strange items placed between the pages to serve as makeshift bookmarks.

"I've died."

She turned in time to see the rest of the group stepping through the door, led by Ekon. His mouth had formed a perfect O. "There can be no other explanation," he said numbly. "I have died and ascended to paradise."

"I take it that means you find my accommodations suitable?" They all turned as Atuno stuck his head around another large pile of books. Behind him, Zain was already holding a plate, smiling as he chewed. "Come, we can eat in the sky parlor. I'm afraid the dining room's been taken over by a volume of encyclopedias at present."

They followed him out of the foyer and through a hallway into a smaller room. There were still plenty of book piles there, but the walls and domed ceiling were made entirely of glass, which allowed a great amount of sunlight into the room. Several chairs were set up in the middle of the room around a long table, which was already laden with food. Koffi's stomach growled.

"Sit, sit." Atuno gestured. "There's more than enough for everyone."

Koffi looked to Makena for only a moment before throwing

caution to the wind and sitting down. The rest followed, until only Safiyah was left standing. She hesitated.

"You're not hungry?" Atuno asked, easing into a chair at the head of the table.

"It's not that, it's . . ." Safiyah frowned. "How come you're being so kind to us?"

Atuno's brows rose. "Did you expect me to be *un*kind?"

Safiyah pursed her lips. "Your sister wasn't exactly welcoming when we visited her realm."

Atuno laughed, and it was warm, jovial sound. "That sounds about right," he admitted. "Don't take it personally. She's a strong ally when she's on your side, but Amakoya has always been . . . shall we say, thorny, particularly with mortals. As you can see"— he indicated the room at large—"I've chosen to spend my immortality in pursuit of other things." He looked back at Safiyah. "Rest assured, child. No harm will come to you in my home. I have little interest in violence and, more importantly, it would be poor etiquette."

Safiyah paused a second longer before settling down in a seat. Koffi turned her attentions to the food before them. For all this time, since leaving Thornkeep, she'd been subsisting on whatever food they could store and carry with them. Seeing real food now almost felt like something out a dream. There were wide bowls full of different soups, seasoned rice, steaming meats, and various types of sliced bread. Her mouth watered, and she found herself unable to choose at first. While she filled up her plate with a little of everything, Zain spoke up.

"So," he asked. "What's with all this . . . stuff?"

For the first time, Atuno looked slightly embarrassed. "As an immortal, I have a lot of time on my hands," he said. "Generally, I have a habit of collecting anything that fascinates me—books, instruments, most things related to the arts. You mortals have a way of continuing to be inventive."

"There's something I don't understand, though," said Ekon around a mouthful of rice. "In the Greater Jungle, when we met her for the first time, Badwa said that Fedu was able to do what he's done because, for years, you and your siblings were sleeping."

Koffi looked up. She knew where Ekon was going with his question and tried to meet his eye, but Atuno caught it and shook his head.

"It's all right," he said gently. "Let him ask."

"It's just . . ." Ekon hesitated. "If you weren't really sleeping, if you've just been here in your palace for all these years, how come you haven't stopped Fedu sooner?"

Everyone at the table got quiet as all heads turned to Atuno. For several seconds, the god simply sat with his elbows propped on the table and his fingers steepled. Koffi found it strange, but he almost looked like his youngest brother in that moment. He sighed.

"My sister was not wrong about me," he said. "I may not have been 'sleeping' in the way that you think of, as mortals, but it's true that I've been willfully ignorant to the world around me for many centuries. It was not a coincidence or an accident. It was a conscious choice that I made, long ago."

"Why?" The question escaped Koffi before she could stop it.

He met her gaze, sorrowful. "My siblings and I were never

given any choice in our purposes as gods," he said. "We were brought to this world with a single directive, to protect and to defend the realms of this earth, forever.

"At first, I was delighted by the idea of that, the idea of being the lord and ruler of something, and for many centuries, I served in the role without question or complaint." She watched as his expression turned bitter. "It took some time for me to see the cruelties of it all. I am an all-powerful being, but I do not have the power to free myself from this place. I am a prisoner here and may not enter any other realm unless one of my siblings allows it. I rule the sky, the air, the stars, and the sun itself, but I cannot control the one thing I've always wanted to."

"What's that?" Ekon asked.

"Time," said Atuno. "I cannot control time. I cannot stop the friends I've made from getting old; I've never been able to stop the lovers I've taken from turning to dust. As it turns out, being a god, an immortal, is a lonely duty. I suppose I grew resentful of it, and so I shut myself in here and chose not to pay attention to the world around me. For that I am sorry."

No one dared speak. Abruptly, Atuno stood.

"There is nothing I can do about the decisions I've made; I cannot change what is done," he said, "but perhaps I can change what will be." Without warning, he turned on his heel, leaving the room. Koffi listened, and everyone sat perfectly still while the god's footsteps could be heard moving across the giant abode. When he returned, his arms were full with an assortment of items.

"Gifts," he explained, "to help you in your endeavor."

"Ooh, presents!" Zain rubbed his hands together.

Atuno pushed the plates and bowls from their meal aside and laid each item on the table. He looked at Zain first.

"For you." He held up a helmet. It was sleek and gilded. "You mentioned before that you were a daraja of the Akili order. That means your power is your mind. This will help you protect it."

"Nice." Zain took the helmet from him and admired it a moment before sliding it over his head. "And a perfect fit!"

"For you, girl." Atuno addressed Njeri, holding a long polished staff. "You have not told me what you are, but you do not have to. I know a fighter when I see one. Take this, I have no doubt that you will need it, and use it, in time."

Unlike Zain, Njeri said nothing as she moved around the table to collect the staff, though Koffi thought the girl's eyes looked slightly wet before she blinked hard. Atuno moved on to Makena.

"There are battles won with swords," he said, "but there are others won with mere needle and thread." He held up a tiny needle and thread, both colored a glittering silver-white. "Use them well."

Makena took them carefully in her hand and bowed. "Thank you," she whispered before sitting again.

"*You* have learned to be discerning of the world around you. You are quiet, thoughtful." Atuno was looking at Safiyah now. He offered her a quiver of arrows and a white bow. "For when you'd rather let these do the talking."

Safiyah took the bow and arrows and sat down. Koffi became keenly aware that she and Ekon were now the only ones Atuno had not addressed. The table before him was empty, except for a small sack. The god looked back and forth between them before settling on Ekon.

"Come."

Ekon stood, and it seemed to take forever for him to approach the god. Atuno regarded him for a long time before he spoke.

"You are a warrior, no?" he asked. "But I see that you lack a proper weapon."

Ekon dropped his gaze and mumbled something Koffi couldn't hear.

"Speak up." There was a ringing command in Atuno's voice. "What did you say?"

It seemed to take great effort for Ekon to repeat himself. He looked pained. "I said, no, sir, I'm not a warrior, not anymore."

Atuno stared at him hard, and in that moment more than any other, he looked like the immortal being that he was. "Lift your head and stand up straight."

Ekon obeyed, and at the same time, Atuno stuck his hand into the sack. When he withdrew it, he was holding a dagger. There was a collective gasp at the sight of it, and Ekon started. Koffi had never seen anything like it. The dagger's hilt was gilded, like Zain's helmet, and the blade was iridescent. It reminded her of something, but she had trouble thinking of what.

"It is called a nyota blade," Atuno explained. "One of the only ones of its kind, the blade was fashioned from the core of a star; its metal is celestial and incredibly powerful." He offered it to Ekon, but Ekon only stared at it.

"Sir, I can't take that," he murmured. "I'm . . . I'm not a warrior anymore."

"You've already said that."

"I ran away." Ekon hung his head. "I abandoned the brotherhood I swore oaths to. I am not worthy of that weapon. It should go to someone braver, someone more honorable."

Atuno stared at Ekon a long time before he pressed the blade's hilt into Ekon's hands and closed his fingers around it. "Sometimes the most honorable thing a man can do is stand up for what is right, even if that means standing alone. I have made my decision. The blade is yours, and I *command* you to take it."

Ekon nodded, then sat back down. Finally, Koffi felt the god's gaze turn on her.

"And you?" he asked. "Do you want your gift?"

Koffi hesitated. The truth was, she wasn't sure, but she stood anyway and moved to stand beside Atuno. His hand was already in the sack. She held her breath as his hand slowly started to withdraw. She was surprised to see, once he'd pulled his hand out, that he was holding only a long white feather, by its stem, pinched between two of his massive fingers. He held it up for her.

"For you."

Reluctantly, Koffi plucked the feather from his hand. She examined it, then looked up. "What is this?"

"A feather taken from one of my own herons," he said.

"Oh. I see."

Atuno smiled. "Should you ever feel that all hope is lost, hold it in your hand and speak my name. You'll find that help will come."

"Thank you." Koffi tried to make it sound genuine and not disappointed.

"There are sacks for you near the door," said Atuno. "They are filled with the provisions you will need for the rest of your journey. If you intend to find my youngest sister before the Bonding,

I'm afraid you cannot stay here. You will need to keep moving."

"Figured as much," said Zain.

"Zain." Njeri frowned. "There's no need to wear the helmet *inside.*"

"It's my helmet," said Zain defensively. He'd moved to stand in front of the room's glass walls, trying to catch his reflection in the panes. "And I'll wear it whenever I want to. It's stylish."

Just as Atuno had indicated, six knapsacks were placed by the door, and one by one, he handed them out. Koffi took hers last, and tucked her heron feather into it.

"Thank you, for everything."

Atuno nodded. "We will meet again," he said. "But until then, I wish you good luck and good fortune on your journeys. In general, I think you'll find the plainlands to be kinder than the marshlands."

"Here's hoping," said Ekon as he shouldered his bag.

"The Kusonga Plains are not far from here if you keep east," Atuno noted. "A word of caution, though: Mind that you avoid any swallowers if you see them."

"Swallowers?" Koffi asked. Even she had never heard of such creatures.

Atuno nodded. "They do not look it, but they are among the plains' most dangerous carnivores, perhaps because they are frequently underestimated."

"Got it." Zain stepped forward, still wearing his helmet. Njeri was now glaring openly at him. "Walk east, avoid danger, save the world. A solid plan if I've ever heard one."

They descended the steps of the sky palace together, and Koffi found that the journey down seemed to take far less time than the journey up. All too soon, they were back on the plains again.

"Until we meet again," said Atuno. He waved his hand and the herons flew into the clouds. Koffi watched as Atuno waved a final time, then began to climb the stairs. With each step he took, the stair behind him grew wispy, until Koffi found herself looking to the sky and staring at nothing but fluffy white clouds once more.

THE BRIDE PRICE

AKANDE

Year 894

My favorite sound is Danya's laugh.

In a way, it reminds me of the Ndefu, the way it rises and falls depending on the weather. Sometimes when Danya's trying not to laugh, she snorts, which she finds embarrassing. I think it's cute.

Other times—like right now, when no one else is around—I get to hear her real laugh. It's a sound that comes from deep within her, and it reminds me of a song.

I think I'd do almost anything to hear that sound.

"Okay, hear me out." This afternoon, we're stretched out side by side on a blanket, soaking up a rare bit of sunshine in the midst of harvest season. The sky is vivid blue and full of puffy white clouds. I point to one. "That one is definitely a war elephant."

Danya follows the path of my finger, then frowns. "A war elephant?"

"The ears are right there, and then the trunk's kind of over there . . ."

She rolls over so that she's propped on one elbow, and raises a brow.

"That . . . is a very weird-looking elephant."

"Not if you squint."

She scrunches her face up and looks back at the sky. "Mm . . . still weird."

"You just lack vision."

There. Like that, she's laughing once more, and my heart skips. A ray of sunlight breaches the clouds overhead at precisely the moment she turns to me, and it casts her entire face in warm gold light. I watch her, trying to memorize all the little details. Danya's arms, legs, and face are long, but they suit her. She wears her black hair in braids, but when the sunlight hits them—the way it's hitting them right now, actually—I can see tiny flecks of light brown around their edges, as though she's managed to steal some of that sunlight, just for her.

"What?"

I start. "Huh?"

"Is something on my face?" Some of that light leaves Danya's eyes as she looks down, embarrassed. She moves her hand to cover one of her cheeks. "It's the pimple, right? My mama bought me an ointment to hide it, but—"

"You're beautiful."

Danya's head snaps up. "What?"

I make myself repeat the words. "I think . . . you're beautiful, just the way you are."

We've been sitting side by side on this blanket for an hour, but only now am I realizing how close we actually are. I watch as different emotions pass over Danya's face—there's confusion, and then a shy smile.

"You do?"

"Yeah." I swallow hard. "I *do*."

In the end, after all the daydreams, the wondering, she's the one who bows her head toward mine. I freeze as our lips meet, but it only takes a second for me to recover as my hand finds her cheek and pulls her in. I've wondered what those lips might taste like; as it turns out, they taste like honey and sugarcoated strawberries from the market stalls, and . . . if sunshine had a taste, I'm thinking she'd probably taste like that too. I'd never thought there could be a feeling better than the rush that comes when I summon splendor, but now I know better. I could summon all the splendor in the world, and it wouldn't come close to feeling as good as this.

The moment's over as quickly as it began, when she pulls away and abruptly sits up.

"I'm sorry." She looks down at her hands. "I'm *really* sorry, Akande. I shouldn't have done that."

My brows shoot up. "You *definitely* should have done that. In fact, if you wanted to do it again . . ." When her expression doesn't change, I sit up too. "Wait, did I misunderstand?"

"No." Danya hugs her knees. She looks even sadder now. "You didn't misunderstand anything. I like you, Akande. A lot."

My brows still haven't lowered. "Sorry, I'm confused."

"We can't do that again," she murmurs. "It's . . . It would be improper."

"Improper?"

"I'm of marrying age," she clarifies, "and we're not officially courting. You haven't spoken with my parents." Her gaze meets mine. "My aunties say I shouldn't even be alone with you anymore without a chaperone, because of what people might think."

"What would they think we're— *Oh.*" My cheeks warm at both the implication *and* because . . . well, I'm seventeen. Some thoughts are better left private. After a pause, I take one of her hands in mine. I'm not sure if it's the right thing to do, but it's the only thing I can think of in this moment. I squeeze it gently.

"Danya," I say quietly, "if you want, I'll go to your father right now and ask him if I can formally court you. I'll ask for your hand in marriage."

She looks up at me, surprised. "What?"

"I love you." The words leave me in a hurried, jumbled mess. They scare me, but I feel a sense of relief saying them aloud too. They don't feel forced. "I've loved you, Danya, from the first time I saw you. I'd do anything to make you happy, to make you laugh."

"Akande . . ." A single tear rolls down Danya's cheek. I let go of her hand to brush it away.

"I don't have a lot of money," I continue, afraid that if I stop, I'll lose my nerve. "But I can get a job and start saving. Izachar can get me an apprenticeship like his. I can *save.* I'll build us a house, buy you nice clothes. You'd never work a day in your life." I pause for a beat, thoughtful. "Unless you *wanted* to work, which I'd also fully support."

"Akande, listen to me." Danya's voice has raised in pitch. "I *can't* marry you."

There aren't words to describe the sudden blast of cold that shudders through me, a combination of shock, sadness, disappointment, and—worst—humiliation. I drop her hand and look away.

"It's not because I don't care about you!"

"Right," I mumble. "I'm sure there's a perfectly reasonable explanation here."

"There is." When I look back at Danya, her bottom lip is trembling. "It's my father. He won't let me marry unless my bride price is paid. He's traditional, and considers it nonnegotiable."

"How much?" I ask. "How much is your bride price?"

Danya looks away from me, sheepish. "Technically, you're not supposed to ask me."

"Oh." Heat fills my cheeks. "I'm so sorry, I—"

"But I'll tell you," she says. "It's five hundred udasi."

I'm not expecting that number. For a moment, just thinking about that amount of money numbs me. "How much time do I have?" I ask. "How much time do I have to come up with the money?"

"Not long," says Danya sadly. "There is already someone who's expressed interest, an older gentleman . . ."

My fists clench at the very idea of Danya with some lecherous old man. I jump to my feet as the anger and disbelief finally explode from me. "Can't you just say no?"

Danya shakes her head. "It's what my parents want. They like him and believe he'll be a good husband."

"What does that even mean?" I fight to keep the desperation from my voice.

"It means they think he'll be able to provide for me," says Danya.

"We're only seventeen!" I throw my hands up. "Who gets married at seventeen, anyway?"

Through her tears, Danya smiled just a little. "You just said *you* wanted to marry me."

I drop my hands. "Yeah, well . . . that's different." When Danya shakes her head again, I sit back down and tilt her chin until her eyes meet mine.

"You don't have to marry him," I press. "You don't have to be with him if you don't love him."

She sighs. "If the suitor makes a good enough offer, my parents will expect me to marry him. There's nothing else I can do. Traditions don't care about love."

I lean in, pressing our foreheads together. "So *break tradition*. Break with convention, and break every rule that doesn't let you live a life that makes you happy."

When Danya looks up at me then, it's the saddest I've ever seen her. "If only it were that simple, Akande." She stands. "I should go."

"Danya—"

"I'm sorry."

She says nothing else as she turns and walks as fast as she can toward the city. I watch her go until I can't see her anymore.

And the sun seems to shine a little less bright.

CHAPTER 20

THE SWALLOWERS

EKON

The three days after their encounter with Atuno were uneventful. For that, Ekon was grateful at first.

The god of the sky had been right about one thing, and the more time that passed, the more clearly he saw it: The plains *were* nicer than the marshlands. Farther south, the earth had been damp, and a constant chill in the air had seeped into his bones and made his teeth chatter. The marshlands had been vast, always dark, and shrouded in a veil of mist that gave him the ever-present and ever-unsettling feeling that something was watching him. Not so in these plainlands. For as far as he could see, the waist-high grass was pale yellow, and at this time of the year, there was sunlight, but it was not harsh or overbright or overbearing. The air was temperate and mild, and for the first time, Ekon found he could relax. They weren't in the Kusonga Plains yet, but they would be soon. There was, in all honesty, only one downside to this place.

310

It was *dull.*

He panned the space around him, searching for something new to count. In the last hour since they'd finished their lunch break, they had passed exactly one tree—one and a half if the old stump they'd seen was to be counted. He'd tried, for a time, to count his footsteps, but after step *three thousand fifty-four,* even he'd lost interest in the numbers. On the one hand, he felt foolish, silly for almost wishing that something would happen, anything to shake up the monotony of their walking, but on the other hand . . . he felt the dagger at his side. In three days, he hadn't gotten used to its new weight on his hip; the weapon was heavier than his old dagger, the one he'd once inherited from Baba. Every so often he stared at it, thinking of what Atuno had said as he'd given it to him.

Sometimes the most honorable thing a man can do is stand up for what is right, even if that means standing alone.

He wanted to believe those words, wanted to believe that maybe there was still a chance that he could be honorable, but he still couldn't. Not, at least, until he got Koffi back to the Kusonga Plains.

"I'm bored!" Not for the first time, Zain—who was bringing up the rear of the group—raised his voice to interrupt the quiet with the kind of whine that set Ekon's teeth on edge. "Are we *there* yet?"

"You already asked that ten minutes ago." Njeri didn't bother looking back as she continued on. "For the last time, we will get there when we get there. Now hurry up, you're slowing down our pace."

"We've been walking for *hours,*" said Zain. "Can't we stop for a break? I'm *starving*. You heard what Atuno said. My brain is my *weapon*, and it needs sustenance, in the form of a snack."

"We just had lunch and I already gave you a snack." Now it was Makena who cut in. She glanced over her shoulder. "The crackers, remember?"

Zain pouted. "I want another!"

"*No*. No more snacks."

Ekon kept walking too, but out of the corner of his eye, he saw Zain come to a stop. He tensed.

"*Fine,*" he said curtly. "You all won't listen to reason, so now I'm forced to take more drastic measures." He cleared his throat. "I'd now like to enact . . . the potty break policy."

At this, there was a collective groan from the group. Ekon turned and glared.

"*Zain.*" He tried to keep his voice calm, measured. "We have a schedule in place. The potty break policy is only to be used for emergencies—"

"This *is* an emergency." One of Zain's brows rose. "I have to go. And look." He craned his neck and pointed. "I spy with my little eye a water hole. It's practically a divine sign. We can all take a little break and refresh our drinking gourds."

Ekon opened his mouth to argue, but Koffi stepped in, massaging the bridge of her nose.

"Fine, Zain," she said with resignation. "We can take a break, but it needs to be a quick one. We've still got a lot more ground to cover before sundown."

Zain perked up. "Finally, a fellow voice of reason!" He didn't wait for anyone else to speak as he made his way across the field. Ekon's fingers tapped at his side for a moment, but he made himself maintain his calm. If he was going to prove to himself—and to Atuno—that he was even potentially a warrior worthy of the weapon he'd just been given, then he'd consider this his very first test in self-restraint. The rest of them followed Zain, who'd already found a spot by the water's edge. He'd folded his hands behind his head, as though enjoying an afternoon catnap.

"Nice of you to join me."

"Remember, this is a quick break," said Koffi. "Just enough to refill drinking gourds . . . and take care of whatever other business you need to." She turned to Ekon. "Six minutes. Ekon, can you time us?"

"Done."

"Hey!" Zain sat up, frowning. "That's not enough time."

"Nine minutes, final offer," said Koffi flatly. She nodded in Ekon's direction. "Then we keep going."

Zain didn't answer, but he did move over to the water's edge to start filling his own gourd. Ekon knelt at it too and cupped enough of the water to douse his face. He would never admit it aloud, but he was, in a way, glad that they had stopped. Despite it being in the direct sunlight, the water was cool to the touch, refreshing as he splashed his face. He let his muscles relax, just for a second. Atuno had said the Kusonga Plains weren't far. Unlike a city, there was no real or official marker that would indicate when they were there, but they had to be close.

Njeri and Makena sat down near the water hole and massaged their feet. Safiyah was examining the arrows Atuno had given her, delicately testing their points with the tip of her finger. Zain, meanwhile, had stood.

"I'll be back."

"There was literally no reason for you to announce that," said Njeri.

Zain grinned impishly before heading into the grass, and everyone else made a point of looking in another direction. Ekon stayed by the water's edge while Koffi sat down beside him. At first she didn't speak, but when Ekon felt her eyes on him, he looked up.

"Can I . . . talk to you?"

Ekon's fingers began to tap in earnest, but he made them calm. "Sure. About what?"

"Back in Kugawanya." She looked away, gnawing at her lip. "What you said after we got out of there, after the fire . . ."

Guilt panged in Ekon's stomach. "Koffi, I'm sorry. I shouldn't have said those things."

"Yes, you should have," she said with a stern expression. "A good friend will call you out when you deserve it, and what you said made me think." She sighed. "Having so much of the splendor's changed me, and not just physically. I didn't recognize that, and I've been pushing myself without acknowledging the splendor's effect on me. Badwa taught me to stay in touch with myself, especially emotionally, and I haven't been doing that." She looked up at him again. "So thanks for reminding me. I know now it's because you care."

Ekon swallowed. "I do care, Koffi. I care a lot."

She nodded and tried to smile, but it wouldn't hold.

"What's wrong?" he asked.

"I was just thinking of Adiah, and something she once asked me to do," said Koffi. "She said if Fedu ever gets to her again that I should kill her to stop him. At the time, I thought it was a horrible thing to ask, but now I get it. I don't want Fedu to win, even if that means I don't make it."

Ekon felt a growing unease. "Koffi, don't think like that—"

"So now I'm asking you the same," said Koffi. "If, by some chance, Fedu gets to me, then . . ." She met Ekon's gaze. "Then promise me you'll do anything you can to stop him from taking the splendor from me, Ekon." Her expression grew fierce. "Anything."

Ekon froze. He knew what she was asking, but he couldn't make himself face it. She was still staring at him expectantly, and all he could hear were his mother's words.

You will kill the one you love most.

"Ekon," Koffi said in a quieter voice. "Promise me."

"I—"

"Hey!"

Everyone looked up. Zain was making his way back to the water hole. "Look what I found!" He held up a small tan rock, no larger than a cantaloupe. Ekon squinted to get a better look in the sunlight. At a glance, there was nothing exceptional about it except for its relative roundness, but then Zain rotated it, and Ekon saw that there were tiny veins of colors covering the rock's entire surface. They shone iridescent in the light, then disappeared based on the angle he held it. "Isn't it cool?"

"Zain." Njeri sounded tired now. "Put it down."

"Why?"

"What did we say about touching things that aren't ours? You can't just go picking up everything you find. Our storage room in our backpacks is finite, and we still have a ways to go."

Zain's expression turned sullen. "Fine. Whatever." He tossed

315

the rock over his shoulder. "You know, you people have really managed to make what could have been a very epic adventure boring as—"

His words were cut off by a long bellow, deep and menacing as it echoed around the plain. Zain swiveled around at the same time as the rest of them jumped to their feet. Ekon felt it, a tremble in the earth beneath them; with it came a distinct sense of unease.

"Zain," he said as quietly as he could, "that *rock* that you just picked up—where exactly did you find it?"

"It was right over there." Zain pointed a few feet away. "There in that bit of grass, next to the other rocks that looked just like . . . oh."

Ekon barely had time to process Zain's words before there was another shudder in the ground beneath them, this one so violent that the water from the pond splashed high into the air and Makena stumbled.

"I don't have a good feeling about this," she said, looking back at them.

"Neither do I," said Koffi. "Let's get out of here."

"For once, we find ourselves in perfect agreement," said Zain, moving quickly. They started back toward the place where they'd been walking before, Safiyah and Njeri following, but Ekon stayed still. The tremors in the earth had stopped, but he still couldn't temper that uneasy feeling. His fingers tapped, counting out a rhythm he was still trying to learn.

One-two-three. One-two-three. One-two-three.

He looked around the plainlands again, tense. Except for that strange bit of trembling, the land was as quiet and empty as it'd been all morning, but something still seemed off. It took him a moment to discern what: that quiet. In the last three days, the plains had never gotten particularly loud, but there'd always been some kind of ambient noise—birdsong, the distant howl of a jackal, or the chatter of a far-off hyena. Not now. Now there was an eerie silence, as though all of the plainlands were waiting for something. He shifted his feet just slightly, trying to listen, then he felt it. Not a tremor, but a subtle movement right beneath him. Had he been walking, he wouldn't have noticed it, but he was standing still—still enough to notice the way the grass shifted slightly, as though something had passed through the earth, heading in the same direction they were. He realized a second too late what was about to happen.

"HEY, LOOK OUT—"

There was a boom, an explosion of dirt, a scream. In the chaos of it, Ekon looked away for a moment, shielding his face as the sun was momentarily blotted out. Slowly he lowered his arm, and the horror that found him turned his skin cool.

The creature before them was massive and round, colored the same tan as the dirt, as the "rock" that Zain had so carelessly thrown. Its limbs were small, tiny things, but compensated for by the beast's massive mouth, which at the moment was open wide. Ekon had never read about this particular kind of creature, but more of Atuno's words came back to him then. He remembered a warning the god had given them.

Mind that you avoid any swallowers if you see them. They do not look it, but they are among the plains' most dangerous carnivores, perhaps because they are frequently underestimated.

The swallower advanced, and each step it took, even on those little legs, made the earth shake. Ekon wanted to think of a

317

strategy, some clever way they might thwart it. He only had one idea at the moment, though.

"RUN!"

They scattered in different directions, and the swallower roared again, a deep guttural sound that Ekon felt hum in his bones. He looked over his shoulder and stopped. The swallower had decided to follow Koffi. She was running, but it was gaining on her fast. He gritted his teeth and doubled back.

He watched Koffi raise her hands as the swallower bore down on her. A spark of splendor left her hands, visible in the sunlight, but when the beast bellowed again and reared back, he knew it had found its mark. Koffi backed away slowly, arms still raised, but the swallower continued to advance.

"Hey!" Ekon shouted, trying to get the creature's attention. It turned, saw him, and headed for him instead. Instinct took over as he withdrew the nyota blade and continued to run, slicing through the air. The swallower might have been large, but its small legs in proportion to its massive body made it unwieldy and awkward unless it was running in a straight line.

Great, thought Ekon. *I can take advantage of that.* A plan came to mind. If he could keep running in circles, he could make the swallower dizzy, then strike once it was sufficiently disoriented. He'd just picked up his running speed when he heard a sound that made his heart sink.

A tremor, and then another loud boom.

The second swallower was slightly smaller than the first, but faster. Ekon watched with horror as this one headed for Safiyah.

"Safiyah! Look out!"

Safiyah glanced over her shoulder midstride, but not quickly enough. The swallower was upon her in an instant. She tried to pull an arrow from the quiver at her back, to nock the bow as she continued to run. It was no use, and when the second swallower bellowed again, making the ground tremble, she tripped. Ekon's pulse quickened.

"Ekon!"

Koffi was closer to him and backing away as the swallower bore down on her. "Help!"

Ekon's stomach clenched. He looked at Koffi, and then back at Safiyah. She was still on the ground, crawling backward frantically on her hands and knees as the swallower howled its rage. He made a split-second decision.

"Hang on, I'll be right back!" He took off before he had time to think or second-guess the question. His nyota blade was already drawn, and he came around the side of the second swallower and used his blade to cut along the beast's back, not a deep wound, but enough to distract it from Safiyah. It turned toward him, and Safiyah took advantage of the moment, nocking her own arrow and shooting. The shot landed near the beast's eye, and it roared in pain.

"One second!" Ekon was already running back to Koffi and the other swallower. She shot a spark of splendor at it, but it no longer seemed to care. It opened its mouth wide, and Ekon heard a terrible whooshing sound. A chill went up his spine as he saw Koffi's body begin to move toward the swallower against her will, as though she was being sucked in by an invisible force. Now he understood why these creatures were called swallowers.

"Ekon, help!"

Ekon had just taken a step forward when he heard a third boom and then a fourth. The breath left his body as two more swallowers exploded from the ground, roaring and enraged. A few feet away, Safiyah was nocking another arrow; in another direction, Njeri had her staff in hand. But Zain only had his helmet, and Makena had no weapon at all. They were outnumbered, and as more swallowers came—which now seemed likely—they'd be completely overwhelmed. Panic set in as Ekon looked around. He tried to manipulate the numbers in his mind, but no matter how he configured and reconfigured, the truth stared him in the face. They couldn't take them all.

Think. Think.

His fingers tapped as he tried to make sense of this, to divine some sort of plan. But the plainlands were empty; they offered no escape, no way to retreat without being seen and followed. One of the swallowers bellowed again, and Ekon's vision begin to tunnel.

No.

He tried not to think about the way his lungs felt tight, the way it was getting harder and harder to breathe, but that just intensified his panic. He tried to focus on the numbers, on the counting.

One-two-three. One-two-three. One-two-three.

"Ekon!"

Koffi's voice sounded far away now, or was that Safiyah's? Ekon couldn't tell anymore. He turned in a slow circle, looking for an escape and finding none. He heard a distant clanging in his ears; his vision grew blurrier still.

One-two-three. One-two-three. One-two-three.

The clanging grew louder, and Ekon shook himself, blinking hard to try to refocus. He'd thought, at first, that the sound was in his head, but the longer he listened, the clearer it became. The clanging was real, and though it had started off as a distant sound, it was growing louder. He even thought he was beginning to hear more than one bell.

He turned again and started.

A group of people were running toward them, people Ekon had not seen before. At first, he wondered how he'd missed them—there had to be at least ten approaching. But then he understood; the tunics they wore were a distinct golden brown, the exact color of the plains around them. The people were shouting, and in their hands they held huge cattle bells, the ones he heard. He tensed, but they seemed to have no interest in him or anyone else in their group. Instead, they directed their attention to the swallowers. The beasts had stopped their roaring and bellowing as the clanging had gotten louder, but now, to Ekon's surprise, they were backing away, visibly agitated by the sound. The people did not hesitate; they advanced toward the swallowers. They did not touch the creatures, but they yelled and shrieked and rattled their cowbells as hard as they could. It did the trick. Ekon didn't understand it, but the swallowers continued to retreat, some running out onto the plains and others burrowing back into the earth. Only when the last of the swallowers was gone did the people lower them.

"Thank you." It was all Ekon could think to say. He was still out of breath, but there was undeniable relief and gratitude in his voice. "For a second there, I thought we—"

His words were cut off as a middle-aged man stepped forward, looking stern.

"I think it would be best if you came with us."

CHAPTER 21

MJOMBA WISE

KOFFI

"I don't feel good about this."

Koffi kept her eyes ahead as she, Ekon, and the rest of the group continued walking with the mysterious people that had saved them from the swallowers. She felt Zain's gaze on her, waiting for an answer, and when she did reply, she kept her voice low.

"Just keep calm," she murmured. "They haven't given us any reason to worry, and they're not armed with anything but those cowbells. So for now, let's just assume the best intentions."

The plains had been empty for most of the day, but up ahead she was beginning to see new shapes on the open grassland. There were domed huts that looked to be fashioned from the same grass that surrounded them, and she saw more than one long line of smoke rising from somewhere within what appeared to be the people's camp. The closer they got, the more she was able to take in. There were people moving about the camp, and already some of them had stopped to stare as they approached. She noted that toward the entrance to the camp two large men were posted, both carrying longspears.

"What were you saying?" Zain quipped under his breath. "Something about them not being armed?"

Koffi didn't have time to answer. They were being herded forward, and she suspected that, even if they'd wanted to turn back now, it wouldn't be permitted. The two men—the *guards*—eyed them suspiciously as they passed, but didn't speak a word as they entered the camp. For a moment, Koffi was taken aback.

The campsite here made the one they'd once set up back in the marshlands look rudimentary and crude. Upon closer inspection, she saw that the domed tents were decorated with tiny symbols in shades of red, blue, yellow, and green. Bowls of food were stacked high in one area, while livestock was sequestered toward the camp's outer edge. It was more like a village.

One of the people, the bearded man with a shaved head who'd spoken to them first, indicated toward a set of logs that had been arranged into a sitting area. Without a word, they sat down.

"Who is the leader among you?" he asked.

Koffi looked up, making eye contact with each person in their group. When no one else volunteered, she raised her hand. "Me."

The man nodded. "Very well. Mjomba Wise will see you momentarily."

"I want to go with her," said Ekon. He hesitated. "Uh, please."

The man blinked, unfazed. "So be it. He will summon you when he is ready." He left them without a word.

"Have any of *you* all ever heard of someone called 'Mjomba Wise'?" Njeri whispered. "Because I haven't."

"Atuno didn't mention him before," Zain pointed out. All

joking and laughter was gone from his voice now, and he looked thoughtful. "Which *could* mean that he's not a threat . . ."

"Or that Atuno hasn't been paying attention," Makena added. "You heard what he said, he's been in that sky palace for centuries. And since we're in the plains, this technically isn't part of his realm, it's Itaashe's."

"We could ask these people if they know where we might find her," Safiyah suggested. "Maybe she has a temple or place of worship, like the House of Wise Waters."

Zain shook his head. "Atuno definitely would have mentioned another temple if there was one; that would be the most obvious place to look for Itaashe."

They were interrupted when the bearded man returned. "He will see you now." When they all stood, he raised a hand and shook his head. "Only you two," he said, pointing to Koffi and Ekon.

Koffi tried to catch Ekon's eye, but he was already looking ahead, braced like a warrior being called to battle as he nodded. Safiyah, Njeri, Makena, and Zain did not speak, but they each looked solemn.

"Caw-caw if there's trouble," Zain whispered. "We'll jump in if needed."

"Do *not* caw-caw." Njeri glared at Zain. "We'll be close by, Koffi. Don't worry."

The bearded man had started to walk; now he was looking over his shoulder impatiently. Koffi stood too and fell into step beside Ekon as they followed him away from the seating area and toward a domed hut larger than the rest. He indicated for them to stop while he went inside first, and when Koffi strained, she thought she heard another voice. Seconds later, the bearded man emerged from the hut, frowning.

"Enter," he instructed.

Koffi took a deep breath; then together she and Ekon ducked into the hut. The change was almost instant.

The inside of the hut was warm and dark, the air slightly stale. It took her a moment to adjust, but gradually, she was able to take in more of the interior's details. The floor was heavily layered with animal pelts, and a small bed pallet was arranged in the corner. Something shifted in the darkness, and she realized suddenly that there was someone sitting directly next to it, almost statue-still. She opened her mouth to speak, unsure of what she would say, but the figure in the corner beat her to it.

"Who are you?" It was a male voice, raspy and dry.

"My name is Koffi," she said carefully. Ekon was still beside her, and she thought at first to introduce him too, but the stranger hadn't asked for his name. Silence stretched between the three of them; in the dimness, she couldn't discern any real features on the speaker's face. Eventually, she spoke again.

"Are you the ruler of this place?"

Again, the figure shifted. "This land knows no ruler," he said, "it has never known one."

That was some progress. Koffi decided to take her chances with her next question. "Then who are you?"

Every muscle in her body tensed as she heard a scraping sound and saw a sudden flicker of light. She relaxed when she realized what it was—a flint rock. She watched gnarled brown hands fumble to light a waxy candle that looked to have seen better days. Her breath caught when the owner of those hands finally brought the candle close enough to him to illuminate his face. The man staring back at her was frowning.

"Bold of you," he growled, "to be asking *me* questions."

Beside her, Ekon shifted his weight. "I'm sorry?"

The old man swung the candle just slightly so that they were both cast in its faint light.

"I'm told there are more of you," he said. "You come into the Kusonga Plains with no respect, antagonizing the swallowers and stirring up all sorts up trouble—"

"We didn't antagonize them!" Koffi had been planning to maintain a level of measured calm, but the words escaped her before she could stop them. "They attacked *us!*"

The old man's eyes narrowed. "A likely story, but that still doesn't explain why—"

All three of them turned around as the tent's flap opened without warning. In the sudden glare of light, Koffi had trouble seeing who'd entered the tent at first; then she made out a young woman. She looked to be only a few years older than her. She gave Koffi and Ekon a kind smile before directing her attention at the old man.

"Mjomba Wise," she said gently, "I'm sorry to interrupt, but it's past midday. You forgot your prune juice."

Koffi looked back at the old man in time to see him put the candle down beside him and cross his arms. "Don't want it," he said grumpily. "I *hate* prunes."

The young woman gave him a stern, if not slightly affectionate look. "Mjomba," she said patiently, "the healers were clear in their instructions: at least one cup a day, every day."

The old man—Mjomba Wise—mumbled something unintelligible as the young woman knelt to place the cup before him, then kissed his forehead.

"It's *good* for you," she said. "If you really can't stand the taste, just hold your nose, but promise me you'll drink it. I'll be very sad if you don't."

The old man didn't meet her gaze. "Yes, yes. Of course."

She rose and offered him a small bow before leaving the tent as quickly and quietly as she'd entered it. Not a second later, the old man lifted one of the back flaps of the tent and poured the entire cup of juice into the grass outside before scrunching his face. When he turned back and found Koffi and Ekon still there, he jumped.

"You will tell *no one* what I just did."

Koffi smiled, inspired by an idea. "How about a barter?" she asked. "You tell us your real name, and in exchange, we'll keep our silence."

Mjomba Wise's brows knitted together. "My real name?"

"Well, it's not 'Uncle Wise,'" said Ekon.

The old man frowned. "I have been called many names in my hundred and sixteen years. Most of the people around here just call me 'uncle' as a sign of respect." He sighed. "Many years ago, my parents gave me a different name."

Without consciously realizing it, Koffi held her breath.

"Akande," said the old man as he looked up at them. "My name . . . is Akande."

Koffi nearly choked. Beside her, she thought Ekon might be having a similar reaction. "Wait," she said, "you're him. Akande."

Akande's brows knit deeper. "What do you mean?"

"I've read about you!" Koffi stepped forward, and when Akande's expression changed to one of outright alarm, she continued quickly. "What I mean is, I was in this library and I found your name . . . in a book!"

Akande's lips pursed. "That does not sound promising."

Koffi stilled. "You're from the Order of Vivuli," she said, "the Order of Shadows."

This earned her a very different reaction. Akande stiffened.

"How did you know that?" he asked in a low voice.

"Because . . ." Koffi took a deep breath. "I'm one too." She paused, considering. "Which means . . . you might be able to help me."

"Tuh." Akande's expression shifted yet again. This time, he looked wry. "I am over a century old, girl, and it's been years since I even attempted to channel the splendor," he said. "I very seriously doubt that *I* could be of any help to you."

"Aren't you at least curious, though?" asked Ekon. His fingers were tapping at his side, the way Koffi knew they did when he was nervous or agitated, but his voice was remarkably calm. "How often do you meet other darajas in the same order as you?"

The question seemed to strike a chord. Akande looked between them and sat back, steepling his fingers.

"A while ago, I met another daraja," Koffi began. "She'd taken in a substantial amount of the splendor nearly a hundred years ago, at the last—"

"At the last Bonding," said Akande. He was frowning. "I remember it."

"She kept it in her body for ninety-nine years," said Koffi, "and when someone tried to take it from her, she gave it to me."

Akande's reaction was visceral. "It was transferred?" he asked. He looked bewildered. "From that daraja to you?"

Koffi nodded. "It's affected my affinity. I can do things that . . . I don't think I would have been able to do before."

"Like what?" Akande asked.

"I can find things. I've even found a god," said Koffi. "I can also make weapons. A short while ago, I made a spear entirely of splendor."

Akande shuddered.

"I want to understand this power," Koffi said. "I want to know how to use it. This is bigger than me, or you, or any one person now. The entire fate of Eshōza might depend on my ability to control this." She stared at her hands. "If I could use this power—"

"I won't help you."

Koffi looked up. "What?"

"I won't." Akande had only shuddered before; now he was looking at Koffi with an expression of sheer terror that she didn't understand. His lips trembled as he formed the words.

"Get out."

"Akande." Koffi took a half step forward, and the old man moved away from her. She tried to keep the desperation from her voice. "Akande, please. We've come all this way—"

"GET OUT!" There was no softness in the old man's voice as he got to his feet. "Get out, get out, GET OUT!"

"Koffi." Gently, Ekon tugged at Koffi's arm. "We should go."

Koffi was left with no choice but to follow Ekon out of the tent and into the afternoon light. Akande's screams followed her as she did.

CHAPTER 22

DESTINY

EKON

In the last two and a half hours, Ekon had watched Koffi try to appeal to Akande four times.

The first and second times, Ekon had heard the result of those attempts in the form of Akande's yelling. The third time, he'd heard Koffi yell back. The fourth and final time, Ekon had looked up in time to see Koffi being escorted back to the logs where he and the rest of the group were sitting, by the same young woman they'd seen before. She looked decidedly worn.

"I'm sorry." Her apology sounded genuine as she gestured for Koffi to sit down. "But I'm going to have to ask you not to bother him again. Mjomba Wise is very old, and the healers already tell us his blood pressure is too high. This kind of agitation just isn't good for him at his age."

Koffi grimaced as she dropped down onto one of the logs and crossed her arms. She looked over at her shoulder and shouted at the young woman's back, "He didn't drink his prune juice, by the way!" Then she turned around and crossed her arms. "It's no use." She blew out a breath. "He won't change his mind, no matter what I say! I've never met anyone so stubborn."

"I have," said Ekon mildly.

Koffi glared, but it didn't last. After a moment, she sighed in resignation.

"Look, Koffi." Ekon threaded his fingers together, opting for a different tactic. "I'm not going to pretend that Akande being unwilling to help you isn't a disappointment, it is. But look at it this way." He gestured toward the sky. "We have our answer from him in no uncertain terms, and it didn't even take us that long to get it. The sun is still high enough that we can cover a good amount of ground if we head out soon."

Koffi looked up at him, frowning. "What are you talking about?"

It was Ekon's turn to frown. "We're leaving, aren't we? The Bonding is in four days. We may not be able to get Akande to help us, but if we can get to the Kusonga Plains, there's still a chance to find Itaashe, and maybe the other gods can get the splendor out of you safely."

Koffi was staring at him with an expression he couldn't read at first. "Ekon . . . ," she said slowly. "We can't leave. Not yet."

Ekon sat up straighter. "What are you talking about, Koffi? We have to." He looked to Njeri, Safiyah, Zain, and Makena. All of them looked stricken, but none of them spoke. He turned back to Koffi. "We've had a plan, the same plan from the very start. You have to get rid of the splendor before the Bonding. If Fedu finds you—"

"We still haven't found the other gods," said Koffi. "And now that we've found Akande, another daraja with the same affinity that I have . . ." She looked wistful. "I just need a little more time."

"Of course." Ekon shook his head. There was more anger in his voice than he'd expected. "Of *course* you're doing this."

"Doing what?" Koffi's voice had gone sharp.

"*This!*" Ekon stood and threw up his hands, gesturing at the scene around him. His voice was rising, but he didn't care. "We have trekked all over Eshōza for weeks now with a mission. We are literally days away from seeing it through, and now you want to change the plan!"

Koffi stood too. "Ekon, this may come as a shock to you, but life doesn't always go according to your plans."

"*Our* plan," said Ekon. "It was supposed to be *our* plan, at least until you . . ." He bit his tongue, but it was too late. Koffi's eyes flashed.

"Until I what?" she asked.

"Koffi." Makena had gotten to her feet, Njeri too. "Look, we're all tired. Maybe we should just get something to eat and rest."

Koffi shook her head. "Until I *what*?" Her voice was dangerously low. There was a challenge in the question, and something in Ekon finally snapped.

"Until you changed." He didn't yell, but the words still carried a sharpness. "The splendor in your body, that kind of power, it's changed you, Koffi. If no one else is going to say it, I will. You haven't thought of anyone else, of anyone's needs, or of what everyone else is sacrificing to help you." He raked his hands through his hair. "I just don't understand why you always have to make everything so difficult."

He regretted the words as soon as he said them, but it was too late. Koffi physically winced as though she'd been struck. There was a finite moment in which he saw real vulnerability on her face, real hurt, before her expression hardened. Ekon watched as her frown deepened, and she regarded him with a new, flat expression.

"If you think I'm so difficult," she said coolly, "then don't let me hold you back."

It was Ekon's turn to wince. The floodgates opened in his mind and a thousand different emotions came through. There was anger and certainly fatigue, but beneath it, when he was honest, there was pain. At that moment he wanted to go back six minutes and redo the entire conversation, but he couldn't. The words his mother said returned to him.

We can remove the stone from the pond, but we cannot remove the ripples it leaves behind.

He jutted out his chin as he matched Koffi's gaze, then shrugged. "Fine," he said in the most offhand voice he could muster. "This was a waste of time anyway."

He didn't want to see Koffi's reaction to the words, he just turned on his heel and stalked away.

Ekon walked until the campsite was out of view.

There'd been no storm before; now it descended in a rush. In the distance, he heard the rumble of impending thunder. The winds picked up, roaring around him until he could hear nothing but their howls. Forks of lightning wove across the sky, and he stared up at them as the rain came down. He still didn't turn around. He couldn't.

"What's the point?" There was no one around, but he yelled the words anyway. "What's the point of even trying? I can't control fate or destiny, no matter how hard I try, no matter what I do, so why bother?"

The wind gave him no answer, and he dropped his head, staring at his own hands.

"I *tried*," he said quietly. "And it didn't matter. I give up."

"Do you really believe that?" asked a small voice.

Ekon started and looked around. He'd been alone—he *knew* he'd been alone—but suddenly he wasn't. The plains were bare, except for a slight woman standing a few yards from him. Her dress was white and black braids danced around her head, though Ekon felt no wind. He stood.

"Who . . . who are you?"

The woman gave no answer, and Ekon suddenly noticed something else. There were four pairs of glowing yellow eyes amid the waist-high grass. He knew at his core that they were lions. He reached for the dagger at his hip.

"Be still, son of Okojo," said the woman, whose expression had not changed. "And do not think to use the weapon my brother gave you to harm those who have not harmed *you*."

It took a moment for her words to register. When they did, Ekon jolted.

"Your brother," he repeated. "Then that means . . . you're Itaashe. We've been looking for you."

In answer, the goddess blinked.

"We need your help," said Ekon quickly, "please. Your brother Fedu is planning to do something terrible during the upcoming

334

Bonding. We've tried to stop him, but we're not powerful enough on our own. Badwa, Amakoya, and Atuno have already agreed to help us, but we need you too. Please."

Itaashe still seemed unfazed. "You have not answered my question."

Ekon stopped short. "Your question?" he repeated.

"About destiny and fate," she said. "Do you really believe that you can't control it?"

Ekon paused, then said, "I don't know. Maybe."

"And that means, then, that you shouldn't try at all," Itaashe parroted back to him. "It means there is no point."

"Wait, no," said Ekon. He shook his head. "I *don't* believe that, not really." When Itaashe said nothing, he went on. "Growing up, I *thought* my destiny was set. I thought being an Okojo made my destiny certain. I was supposed to be a warrior, like my brother and my father and all the other men in my family." He sighed. "But I made choices, and those choices changed my destiny.

"Plenty of bad things have happened because of that choice," he went on, "but good things have happened too. I probably never would have left home, but I did. I wouldn't have made new friends, people I can really be myself around." He swallowed hard. "I would have never found my mother."

"So what *do* you believe?" Itaashe's face was expressionless, though the lions had begun to circle her. Ekon watched as the breeze rippled through their golden-brown fur, and felt an imperceptible shift in the air.

"The truth?" Ekon sighed. "I believe all of our destinies probably are shaped from the moment we're born, and the more we try to control it, the more likely we are to play right into its hands." He stood up straighter. "But I don't think that means we shouldn't try to take ownership of whatever destiny is in store for us. If anything, I think that means we should try even harder to do the right thing, to work toward the best outcome possible." He paused. "I don't think I have to kill the person I love most."

A beat passed in which the goddess said nothing. Ekon felt her eyes on him, the cool assessment in her dark brown gaze. He was surprised when a small smile touched the corner of her lips.

"Very good, son of Okojo." She nodded, and the four lionesses that'd been circling leaped. Ekon felt the breath leave his lungs for a moment, but instead of rushing at him, they darted away, disappearing into the grasslands. Itaashe cocked her head.

"I've known about my brother's misconduct for some time," she said. There were traces of sadness in her voice. "I never thought that it would come to this." She sighed. "But if this is what it will take to stop him, I *will* help you. You have my word."

Ekon stared at her. "You will?"

"I will."

"Then . . ." He looked over his shoulder. In the new darkness, the campsite's light was visible, but only just. "Then I have to go back, I have to tell the others."

Itaashe nodded. "I will find you again, when the time comes."

Ekon needed no further encouragement. He looked back at the goddess again, just to make sure it was all real, before turning on his heel and racing back toward the campsite as fast as he could. The clouds were still heavy and dark, and thunder rumbled in the distance; he pressed on, ignoring the strain in his lungs. He pictured Koffi's face with each stride, determined.

Maybe there's a chance now, he thought. *With all five of them on our side, just maybe we can actually do this.* That thought gave him new fuel and he pumped his legs harder. Up ahead, the campsite was still distant, but he could begin to make out details: the flickering light of the torches at its entrance, the lines of smoke rising from the domed tents. He focused on those details, counted his footsteps as he ran.

One-two-three. One-two-three. One-two-three.

Almost there.

One-two-three. One-two-three. One-two-three.

Almost. Almost there.

He was so focused on his counting that at first he didn't even notice the small prick in his arm.

It was tiny, nearly negligible; there was even less pain than from a bee's sting. Ekon moved to brush his arm, but then his fingers grazed against something. He stopped, confused, and looked down at his upper arm. Near the biceps, there was an object protruding from the skin, small and white.

Dart. The word came to him at the same time as the dart's effects took hold. He lost his count as the world around him blurred and a buzzing filled his ears. He dropped heavily to one knee and felt the pain of it, but there was nothing he could do to keep himself upright. He collapsed on his side and the world upended. His lips were numb; he couldn't form words. He wasn't even sure he could make any sounds.

One . . . one . . .

It seemed to take forever for the shadow to fall over him. Perhaps if he'd been in his right mind, Ekon would have known at once who it was. Instead, he stared up at the blurred figure standing over him for several seconds, confused. Only when he heard the voice did terror take over.

"Hello, Ekkie."

He stared up at Kamau for a half second and watched his older brother raise the wooden blow dart to his lips. There was a second tiny prick of pain in his arm, and then everything around Ekon went black.

CHAPTER 23

THE RAGE

KOFFI

Koffi was still fuming as she stalked through the campsite.

Makena, Njeri, Safiyah, and Zain had each tried to stop her, to reason with her. It hadn't mattered. She couldn't explain to any of them how she felt, and the more she tried, the more frustrated she became. The more quickly she walked, the faster Ekon's words seemed to nip at her heels, following behind.

I just don't understand why you always have to make everything so difficult.

The words crept past all her defenses to deal their blow, and the tears that stung her eyes made her even angrier. Had he actually meant that? She wanted to believe he hadn't, but . . .

The edge of the campsite was marked by a small pond, and Koffi was grateful to find it vacant. She settled at its edge and stared into the water's flat surface. Something stabbed between her ribs as she studied herself. She barely recognized the girl in her reflection, the one who looked haggard, gaunt, a shadow of her normal self. She'd gone through all of this, traveled all these miles and made all this effort—and for what?

I tried, Badwa, she said to her reflection. *I tried.*

Footsteps to her left drew her gaze over her shoulder. Standing a few feet away, Akande was holding a water jug. His mouth twisted at the sight of her.

"Gods above," he groaned. "Can't I get a moment's peace without you following me?"

Koffi turned and stood. "I wasn't following you," she said. "I was here first!"

Akande's brow arched. "A likely story."

Perhaps the wise thing to do would have been for Koffi to turn and leave, to not respond to the old man's gibe. Instead, she matched his glare with one of her own.

"You want me to be a disturbance?" she asked. "Fine, I'll be a disturbance."

Akande's frown deepened. "What are you talking about?"

"I'm not going to leave it alone," said Koffi. "And I'm not going to stop asking you for answers. My friends and I have been all over Eshōza, we've risked our lives to get here. And now you won't even help us. So, you leave me no choice." She extended her left arm, rotated it so that it was palm up, then took a deep breath and summoned the splendor. Her skin prickled as it came to her, and she watched the tiny silver marks on her begin to illuminate, bright even in the midday sun.

"STOP!" Akande was staring at her, horrified. "What are you doing, girl?"

Koffi took another deep breath, keeping calm. "If you're not going to listen to what I have to say, then maybe you will after I've shown you what I can do with my power."

"Stop it," he hissed, "you'll kill yourself."

"Then help me," said Koffi. She could feel the splendor building in her core, hot, but she kept summoning it. "Teach me how to control this power, or at least tell me why you can't."

She thought for a moment he might call her bluff. The daraja looked to the splendor on her arms. Then, without warning, he raised his hands.

"Stop!" he shouted. "I mean it!"

Koffi lowered her own hand, and breathed relief as the splendor receded into her body. Her brow was covered in a sheen of sweat, and she was breathing hard, but she jutted out her chin.

"So you'll use your power to stop me?" Koffi said through labored breath. "But not to do something that actually matters?"

Akande was shaking his head. She hadn't seen him this angry yet. "You're arrogant," he said, "and a fool."

"You have no idea what I've been through," said Koffi. Her fingers dug into her palm. "You have no idea how it feels to—"

"To be filled with rage?" Akande's brows rose. "To be consumed by it all the time, even when you're at rest?" He shook his head. "Sit down, girl."

Koffi started to protest. "I—"

"Please." Something in the old man's voice had changed. There was a pleading beneath its current. He gestured, and they both settled on the ground.

"You want to know why I won't help you?" he said. He was gazing into the pond. "It is not because I wish to see you fail."

He hesitated. "It is because I have not channeled the splendor in decades."

"You . . . ?" Koffi stared, unsure of what to say. Whatever she'd expected from the old man, it hadn't been this. "I don't understand."

Akande stared at the water's surface for so long that Koffi began to wonder if he'd heard her. When he looked up again, his expression had a distant quality. She saw pain in it.

"It was so many years ago," he said faintly. "But it feels like yesterday."

Something told Koffi not to say anything else. She waited for Akande to go on; eventually, he did.

"I didn't always live on these plains," he said. "When I was young, I lived in a river town called Kugawanya. I was the descendant of a long line of powerful southern darajas, the last before me being my grandfather." Akande hung his head. "He was a better teacher than I ever deserved."

"What happened?"

His laugh was harsh. "The same thing that has destroyed any number of young people." He looked suddenly sad. "I fell in love. Her name was Danya. At the time, I thought the feelings were mutual, that she wanted to be with me as much as I wanted to be with her. Then, one day, Danya told me she was to be married. She told me the only way her father would call it off was if I was able to pay her bride price, a sum far above what I or my family could afford."

"What did you do?" asked Koffi quietly.

Akande looked at her. "The only thing my seventeen-year-old mind could contrive," he said. "I entered into a prizefight in the

342

hopes that I could win and get the money I needed." He shook his head. "I was so foolish. My grandfather taught me many things, but above all, one lesson was more important than any other: to keep focus and control. Not doing so, he warned, could have dangerous effects. He told me that when a daraja meddled with that kind of power, there was always a price to be paid." He met Koffi's gaze. "I did not listen to him, but I was not the one who ultimately paid the price for it."

Goose bumps rose on Koffi's skin, and she swallowed hard.

"We met by the riverside and I brought my best friend, Izachar, with me," said Akande. "In the end, we never did properly finish the fight—my younger sister, Namina, saw to that—but as we were leaving the riverside, something happened." He covered his face. "My opponent, Jumo, said something crude about Danya, and I broke the most important rule my grandfather had taught me. I lost focus, and I lost control. I summoned the splendor like I had so many times before, but this time, when it came, it was different, taking the form of a dagger."

Koffi found that she was able to picture the weapon, sparkling silver and white, not unlike the spears she'd used on Fedu.

"I thought I'd managed to scare him with it," Akande went on. "I thought that I was the one in control. But I was careless, and when I felt someone behind me try to pull me back, I cut my dagger through the air and didn't think twice about it."

Koffi stiffened.

He shook his head. "I wasn't counting on Izachar being so close to me. He was too close. By the time I realized what I'd done, it was too late."

A chill shuddered the length of Koffi's body. "He died?"

"I thought so at first." The look on Akande's face was horrid, full of grief and anguish. "I *wish* the gods had been so kind as that." For a long time, he stared out into the plains, into the nothingness. "I fled from the city the night it happened, but I kept an ear to the ground, and eventually I heard the whole of it. The wound from the splendor's cut was fatal, it damaged nearly every nerve and organ in his body, but it didn't kill him instantly. The healers wanted to give him something, herbs, to end his suffering humanely, but Izachar was his family's only child, and they couldn't let him go. It took his body nearly a week to finally expire." He blinked, and the tears finally fell. "I used to tell myself that because his mind was probably gone long before that, he wasn't in any pain at the end, but . . ." He hung his head. "He suffered. I *know* he suffered. You say I don't know what it is to feel rage, girl? I live with it, every single day.

"The worst part is, I so wanted love. I was too thick-skulled to see what was obvious: I already had love. I had it in my mother and father, in my sister, in Izachar."

Koffi froze. "Izachar?"

"My best friend," said Akande. "That was his name."

"He . . ." Koffi stilled. A thought had just occurred to her, one that rooted her to the ground and shallowed her breath. "He had curly hair, didn't he?"

Akande looked up sharply. "How could you know that?"

Koffi swallowed. The words on her tongue were unsteady; she was almost afraid to speak them.

"Some time ago," she said slowly, "I started having dreams about a boy." She blinked hard, and tears fell. "He wanted me to come here. He led me to these plains."

Akande shook his head. "That's impossible."

"Is it?" Koffi asked. "I am a daraja of the Order of Shadows. My affinity doesn't just allow me to find the things I'm looking for; in the past, it's allowed me to act as a bridge between life and death. Is it so hard to believe that he'd find me, that he'd lead me to you?"

The old man wrapped his arms around himself. "I didn't mean to do it." He shuddered. "Do you understand now, girl?" He sounded pained. "Do you understand why I won't use the splendor? They teach us darajas that our ability to channel the splendor is a *gift*." He spat the word. "In actuality, it is a curse, a cruel sort of blight. It makes us a hazard to everyone around us, it makes us dangerous."

Koffi didn't hesitate. "Sometimes dangerous things are just misunderstood things," she said quietly.

The old man's eyes stayed trained on her.

"Akande, I am sorry for what happened to you, and to Izachar. But I know he wouldn't have wanted you to carry this with you for the rest of your life."

"You think because you might have seen some whisper of him that you know my friend?" Akande snapped, but he sounded more wounded than angry. "You know nothing."

"I know that he was a good friend," said Koffi. "That he was willing to stand at your side on the most important night of your life, and that at the end the last thing he did was to try to help you, because he didn't want you to destroy yourself."

"He bet on me," Akande whispered. His eyes had that faraway quality again. "He bet all he had . . . on *me*."

Koffi moved close enough to rest a hand on his shoulder. He

cringed at her touch and his face crumpled, but he didn't move away.

"If he could it do all again, I think he would do the same thing," she said. "Because that's what real love is."

Akande stared out at the savanna. "I ran from Kugawanya after," he murmured. "I was still so blinded by what I thought was love that I thought I could win Danya over. I had no money, so I went east. I was desperate for something of high value to sell for food, and I figured the temple might have tithe gold for me to take. I used my splendor to find the most expensive item in it; it led me to this instead." He reached into his pocket and withdrew something. Koffi started.

"Amakoya's bracelet," she said. "It was you! *You* were the thief!"

The old daraja stared down at it, almost as though he hadn't heard her. "By the time I returned to Kugawanya, I learned that Danya had already married, and half the city's young men had been duped into showering her and her family with gifts. We'd all been had." He hung his head and sat still for several seconds.

"But I don't understand," said Koffi. "I looked for that bracelet and my affinity led me to Kugawanya, to the magistrate's daughter. She had a replica."

Akande looked up at her. "Our affinities are one and the same," he said. "If you'd never laid eyes on the bracelet, if you didn't truly know what you were looking for, it would have been very easy to be led to the wrong bracelet. You can have this one if you want, it proved useless in the end." He tossed it to her and Koffi caught it; then she watched his shoulders slump. It occurred to Koffi that, in all her life, she'd never seen someone in so much pain.

"Akande," she tried carefully, "we have the same affinity, and you know what I can do with it, because you've done it yourself."

He flinched.

"I'm not asking you to help me with my affinity for myself," said Koffi. "I'm asking because I want to protect my friends too. The truth is, Fedu—the god of death—is planning to re-create this world, and to do that he's going to kill every person who isn't a daraja. People like Izachar wouldn't be spared. Millions of innocents are going to die if I don't stop him."

For the first time since their conversation had started, Akande's brow rose, and he looked more like himself. "And you're so sure you're the one who's destined to save us all?" he asked wryly.

Koffi jutted her jaw. "If no one else is volunteering."

Akande laughed softly. "You're so much like her."

"Who?"

"My sister, Namina," he said. "She wasn't a daraja, but she was fierce too." He looked sad again. "She wasn't a daraja, so she died decades ago, but she was by far the strongest person I've ever known."

"Akande." Koffi still had her hand on the old man's shoulder. She squeezed. "Will you help us?"

A beat passed before something in his expression changed. He straightened his shoulders and shifted his stance. Then he nodded. "I will."

Koffi didn't stop to think about it. She threw her arms around the old man, hugging him tight. Akande stiffened, then hugged her back.

"KOFFI!"

They both turned around in time to see Makena running toward them. One look at the girl's face told Koffi something was wrong. Makena's lips were set in a thin line. Njeri and Zain weren't far behind her. They were wearing similar expressions.

"What is it?" Koffi asked. "What's wrong?"

"Koffi, I'm sorry." It was Zain who stepped forward. Uncharacteristically, he looked genuinely apologetic. "I promise, we tried to stop them."

A distinct feeling of unease was forming in the pit of Koffi's stomach. "Stop who?"

"It happened really fast." Makena picked up where Zain had left off. "We didn't even know he'd been following us."

Now the feeling burgeoning in Koffi's chest was becoming more acute. She imagined a name, a face, and she tensed.

"What happened?"

In the end, it was Njeri who stepped forward. Njeri, who was always direct and never sugarcoated anything. Even she looked hesitant to speak.

"Njeri." Koffi met her gaze. "Tell me."

Njeri took a deep breath. "One of the other members of Akande's camp saw Ekon heading out in the plains. They kept an eye on him, just in case, but he never came back. Some of the other scouts are saying they saw someone putting him on a wagon. The person doing it looked like a warrior." She gave Koffi a meaningful look. "They said the person looked just like Ekon."

"Kamau." The name tasted like ash on Koffi's tongue. "His older brother."

"They were last seen heading east," said Njeri.

Koffi shook her head. "Of course they were. He's taking Ekon back to Lkossa. He was a Son of the Six and he deserted. They'll punish him."

Makena tensed. "What will they do to him when he gets back?"

"I don't know," said Koffi quickly. It wasn't the truth; she *did* know. She just didn't want to say it aloud. She couldn't. The others seemed to understand.

"We've got to help him," said Safiyah. Her voice was tight and strained.

"I agree," said Zain, "but how? Ekon's brother had him on some sort of small wagon. We would never catch up on foot."

"In that specific regard," Akande interjected, "I think I may be able to help. Follow me."

CHAPTER 24

THE KUSONGA MAIDENS

KOFFI

Koffi and the others followed as Akande led them deeper into the plains.

She felt the brush of the high grass against her legs, against the backs of her hands. The sky was darkening, and with its change in color came a new sense of dread.

Ekon. Kamau.

It was all too easy to remember the first time she'd met Ekon's older brother in the Greater Jungle. He was almost a perfect copy of Ekon. She pictured him taking Ekon unaware, capturing him. A shiver ran down the length of her body. If Kamau had found Ekon, it meant he'd been tracking them this whole time without them having any idea of it, and if he'd been that desperate to take Ekon back to Lkossa, she knew there was only one possible outcome. She looked up at Akande and tried to keep the desperation from her voice.

"Akande!" she shouted over the wind. "How much farther? We really need to get going!"

"Trust me," said Akande, "it's worth the wait."

Koffi gnawed her bottom lip and looked over her shoulder. Behind her, Safiyah, Zain, Njeri, and Makena had looks of the same frustration and confusion. She slowed down enough for Makena to catch up to her. Makena took her hand and squeezed.

"We'll get him back, Koffi," she whispered. "I promise."

"The last things I said to him." Koffi couldn't keep the tremor out of her voice. "They were terrible, I didn't mean them. I didn't get to tell him—"

"He knows you didn't mean them," said Makena gently, "and he didn't mean what he said either. You have to know that."

Koffi wished that reassurance was enough, but it wasn't. She blinked hard, surprised and angry to find tears on both of her cheeks. She gritted her teeth. Now wasn't the time to *cry*, that was the last thing she needed. She pressed down that emotion and felt a stab of pain in her ribs sharp enough to make her bend over and gasp.

"Koffi!"

In an instant, Makena, Safiyah, Njeri, and Zain were surrounding her. They were trying to help, but Koffi didn't know how to tell them that the crowding made it worse.

"Koffi?" She heard Zain's voice and felt his hands on her back. "I've got you, okay? I'm going to lower you to the ground, you need to sit down."

Koffi felt more hands, and then she was sitting on the dirt. In the dirt, the wind was slightly less strong, but there was still pain.

She massaged her temples, trying to ignore the words she knew were coming.

You have to face your emotions, Koffi. Badwa's voice echoed loudly in her head. *There will be consequences if you don't.*

It was true, she *knew* it was, but she didn't have time to face whatever complicated array of emotions was churning in her at this moment. Instead, she stood.

"I'm fine." She forced out the words and looked straight ahead, then blinked. "Wait, where did Akande go?"

All five of them turned around, confused. Akande had been there, only a few strides ahead of them; now there was no sight of him as far as the eye could see.

"I don't like this," said Zain, tense.

"Neither do I," Makena added.

Koffi searched the plains. It didn't make sense. Akande was an exceedingly old man; he couldn't have run off. *But he could have fallen.* She took a step forward and called out.

"Akande! Akan—"

A single sound cut her off at once: a low, guttural roar.

The hairs on the back of her neck stood on end at the same time as she heard someone yelp. In the corner of her eye, she thought she saw Njeri's hand move to the staff at her hip. It was much darker now, but not so dark that she couldn't make out the shapes appearing in the fields behind them. She imagined what Ekon would do if he was here and began to count. *Four.* There were four dark shapes making their way toward her, parting the grass as they padded silently through. Her breath shallowed so that it was hard to focus on anything else. She reached for the splendor and relished the warmth as it started in her feet.

Closer, she willed the silent shapes, *just a little closer . . .*

"Girl! *What are you doing?*"

Koffi started and felt the splendor recede. Akande's voice carried over the wind, and when she squinted harder, she saw that he was sitting on top of one of the four shapes making his way toward her. He was frowning.

"Akande?" She tried and failed to keep the incredulity out of her voice. She didn't know how she'd missed it before, but there was no doubt it was him. "Where . . . where were you?"

"You young people." Akande shook his head as he kicked a leg over and slid off one of the lionesses. "You never *listen.*"

Koffi opened her mouth to ask another question, then closed it. The dark shapes that had been making their way over to Koffi were now discernible even in darkness. Lionesses, four of them. They were larger than normal, but that wasn't what frightened her about them. There was something in their golden eyes, a kind of restrained power, an inexplicable knowing as they surveyed her. They were looking at her as though they saw all of her all at once. She felt Makena, Njeri, Zain, and Safiyah press closer to her.

"Akande." Even Zain's voice was shaking. "What are you playing at?"

The old man's brows rose. "You said you needed a way to get to Lkossa quickly. These lionesses will take you, *if* you ask politely."

"He's joking." Njeri sounded hoarse. "He has to be."

In every encounter with a beast up to this point, it'd been Koffi who'd been unafraid to approach first. She was supposed to be trained for this, trained not to be afraid. Not this time. The lionesses circled them, and the closer they came, the more firmly she felt anchored to the ground, unable to move. She was surprised when, to her left, it was Makena who moved first.

"Kena!" Njeri yelled. "What are you doing?"

"Akande says they're safe," said Makena calmly. "I trust him."

Koffi tried to voice a warning, to say something as Makena broke from their huddle and approached one of the lionesses. A low growl rumbled through the grass. Makena kept walking forward. When she was within a few feet of the lioness, she stopped and curtsied, completely lowering her head. It was a quick gesture, not even particularly graceful, but Koffi felt a shift in the wind. The lioness eyed Makena a moment and cocked its massive head. Then, inconceivably, it purred. Makena started, and Akande laughed.

"Well done, girl!"

Makena turned back to the rest of the group. "I think it's okay!"

Koffi hesitated, but one by one, Njeri, Safiyah, and Zain approached the other lionesses. In turn, they each bowed, and in turn the lionesses nodded their head in acknowledgment. Koffi had never seen anything like it.

"This one likes me!" Zain said, grinning as one lioness nuzzled his head.

"There are five of you," said Akande, "so two of you will have to ride together."

"Makena and I will," Njeri volunteered. Makena nodded in agreement.

"They're fast," Akande continued. "If you leave soon, you'll get to Lkossa in a day's time, probably shortly after Ekon does."

"Koffi?" Safiyah turned around. "What do you think?"

Slowly, Koffi approached the last lioness. It looked to be the biggest of the four, and she watched herself in the reflection of its golden-brown gaze. It took no small effort to keep the tears from falling. It took her a few more seconds to realize what had caused that reaction: The lioness reminded her of the Shetani, of Adiah. She held the creature's gaze a second longer before offering it a low bow. She was almost certain the lioness returned the gesture. Without warning, the wind suddenly picked up, bending the waist-high grass for miles around. Akande's brows furrowed.

"You need to get going," he said more firmly, "now."

"What about supplies?" Zain asked as he hoisted himself onto one of the lionesses. Beside him, Njeri, Makena, and Safiyah had already mounted theirs.

"You won't need much for such a short journey," said Akande, "but the lionesses know this land. They'll stop at the right places for food and water. You just have to trust them."

"And you're sure they know where we're going?" Makena said. Her arms were wrapped securely around Njeri's waist.

Akande nodded. "Of that, I am certain." He looked to Koffi. "Time to go, girl."

Koffi took a deep breath, then moved to the side of the lioness she'd bowed to. She didn't let herself think about it as the lion lowered itself to the ground and she hoisted herself onto its back and swung a leg over. Against her skin, its fur was coarse and warm, but not uncomfortable. The beast rose, and Koffi swallowed hard. She looked back at Akande, still on the ground.

"And what about you?" she asked. "What will you do?"

"What I've spent most of my life doing," he said wryly. "What I want. I'll find my way to you." He jerked his head. "Now go, while the winds are favorable, it'll make you faster."

Koffi nodded, ignoring the hard lump that was rising in her throat. She hadn't known Akande long at all, she had no right to be sad that she was leaving him. She still was. The wind picked up and any words she might have said to the old man were lost in it. He held a hand to his forehead and squinted as his robes billowed around him.

"I wish you all a safe journey!" he shouted over the howls.

That was the end of it. Zain leaned in first, seemingly a natural, and he and his lioness took off into the dark. Safiyah followed suit seconds later, and then Makena and Njeri. Koffi looked over her shoulder one more time before she leaned forward too. It was all the lioness seemed to need, because at once it leaped forward, bounding away into the dark.

Home, Koffi thought as the wind tore through her hair. *Finally, we're going home.*

PART FOUR

The EARTH DOES NOT CHANGE ITS COLORS to MATCH the CHAMELEON.

The DAILY SPECIAL

AKANDE
Year 894

I smell the river before I see it.

But today, there is no time to stop by the Ndefu. I only give it a cursory glance as Izachar and I walk along its edge, eyes set forward with purpose as we head toward our destination.

"Akande?" I don't turn to look at Izachar's face, but I can hear the nervousness in his voice. "I don't feel good about this."

The truth is, I don't either, but I don't say that as we pass one of the river's docks. "It'll be fine, Iz. Trust me."

Most of Kugawanya was built with the Ndefu in mind, but in some places the water seeps where it shouldn't. In time, the neat borders of the city proper give way to rougher parts of town where the buildings are elevated on stilts and the river water is not blue green but a silty brown.

"You know where you're going?" asks Izachar.

I nod, jerking my head. "This way."

From the river we head into Kugawanya's slums, a part of the city that admittedly I've never spent much time in. Babu always forbade me from wandering here when I was small, and now I understand why. The people here—even the small children—have a worn, haggard look about them. I try not to make eye contact with the beggars as I pass, but I still feel them watching us as we weave through its narrow, grime-coated streets. When twenty minutes pass, Izachar speaks up again.

"I think we're lost."

"Not lost," I say quickly, "just a little turned around. Here!" I nod to a gentleman sitting against a wall. "We'll ask him for directions."

Without waiting to hear Izachar's thoughts, I head straight for the young man and stoop down so that we're level. Up close I can see he's probably closer to my age, but something about him is aged.

"Excuse me," I say, "I was wondering if you could tell me where—"

I'm not prepared for him to grab the front of my tunic in tight fists, pulling me close so that our noses are inches apart.

"Just a little more," the young man says quietly. "Please, man, I'll pay you back."

I try to retreat, but his grip tightens. My pulse shoots up in alarm. "Pay you . . . back?"

"Just a taste." The young man doesn't seem to have heard me. "Just a little bit of sumu powder, my friend, that's all I need—"

"You!"

All three of us look up as someone else appears behind us, and my heart lurches so hard it hurts. It takes a moment for me to realize that the old man I'm now looking at isn't Babu, but some-one else. His expression pinches as he regards the addict.

"Leave him alone and get lost," he says quietly, "before I report you."

The young man tenses, assessing, before he lets me go and slinks down the street and into a different alley. I breathe out in relief once he's gone.

"Thank you."

"It's not safe for young people to be around this area," the old man says gruffly.

He's so much like Babu. My stomach knots at the thought. "Sorry," I say, "we were just looking for someone."

The old man's brows rise. "Here?"

I nod. "He's called Yakow. He's a—"

"I know what he is." The old man's voice becomes even gruffer. "Stay clear of him, if you ask me. The bookmaker is nothing but trouble."

Beside me, I can practically feel Izachar's eyes boring into me. "Please," I say in earnest. "It's really, really important we find him today."

The man's studies us as though he's trying to read our very souls before he decides his answer. Finally, he says, "There's a bakery two blocks down on the corner." He gestures in the gen-eral direction. "Go inside and ask for the daily special. That's how you'll find Yakow."

I nod. "Thank you."

"Be careful, boy," the old man says sadly. Without another word, he continues down the street.

The old man's instructions are dead-on. Two blocks from where we were, I spot an old-looking mudbrick shop squeezed on a street corner between two buildings. I swallow hard as Izachar and I duck under the door, flinching at the sharp peal of a silver bell overhead, and make our way to the shop's front counter. Notably, the girl working behind it looks half my age.

"We're closed today," she says before I can open my mouth.

I pause. "But we haven't told you what we want."

Her expression doesn't change. "We're out of everything. Come back another time."

"C'mon, Akande," says Izachar. "We have our answer, let's just—"

"Wait!" I remember what the old man said. The girl stills as I lean in slightly and lower my voice. "I'd like the daily special."

The girl nods. "Right this way," she says in a different voice, leading Izachar and me to a back door I hadn't noticed before. She opens it, gestures, and we enter a significantly darker room with low ceilings and a smokiness in the air that is nothing like the way a bakery should be. I recognize the sour stench of tobacco, old banana wine, and something that reminds me disturbingly of blood. It's only when my eyes settle that I notice the room's not empty. In its back corner there's a large table with several different stacks of coin purses on it, and behind them stands a wrinkly man with gray hair. In the room's darkness, his yellow smile is bright.

"Well, well . . . ," he says in a creaky old voice. "How can I help you boys?"

"Sir." I try to keep the tremble from my voice, but it's a struggle. "My name is Akande. This is my friend Izachar."

The old man says nothing in reply.

"We're here because we—well, I—wanted to place a bet."

The old man purses his lips, for the first time looking thoughtful. "You're not from the slums," he says. It's not a question. "You traveled across town to find me."

"Yes, sir," I say.

Yakow nods. "I'm touched by your efforts, but I'm afraid I cannot help you," he says. "I don't have anything to bet on at this time."

My heart starts beating faster, and I recognize the distinct cadence of rising panic. "You don't have anything?" I repeat.

Yakow shakes his head. "The racing season is done. There's nothing for you to bet on."

Panic sets in. All I can think about is what will happen if I can't get the money I need to buy Danya a gift valuable enough for her bride price. I think of what she said, of her other suitors, and my lungs constrict.

Come on, come on, think of something, anything.

"I do wish I could help you," Yakow is going on. "You know, I like to run bets on just about anything, but—"

An idea comes to me so suddenly that I jolt. "Wait!"

The old man's eyebrows rise in surprise, as do Izachar's.

"What if . . ." I shift my weight from foot to foot. "What if I could give you something else to bet on, something good?"

"Then I'd find myself intrigued," said Yakow. He inclined his head. "What did you have in mind, boy?"

"A prizefight," I say quickly.

Izachar sucks in a breath at the same time Yakow sits back. Several beats pass before he speaks again in a lower voice.

"I'm no saint when it comes to matters of the law," he says, "but you do know that prizefights are illegal in Kugawanya, boy?"

I nod. "All the more reason to do it. People will be eager to see one, to place bets."

"True." A slow smile is creeping across the bookmaker's face now. "And who did you have in mind for this prizefight?"

"Myself."

"Akande!" For the first time, Izachar speaks up. "Akande, you can't."

"Have you ever been in a prizefight before, boy?" I look over my shoulder at Yakow. There's no mistaking the intrigue in his expression; I just have to close the deal.

"I haven't." I sidestep Izachar, ignoring the look he's giving me, and continue to address the old man. "But I'm strong and I'm trained. My grandfather . . ." The words are harder to say than I expect. "My grandfather was a daraja."

If Yakow looked intrigued before, he looks near feverish now. "Interesting," he says, stroking the wisps of hair on his chin. "That is very interesting." For a moment, he looks away from us, thoughtful. "Of course, I'd need some time to plan, to get the word out to the right people."

My heart is pounding again, but this time it's not with fear but excitement. "Will you do it, then?"

"I'll need a few days," says Yakow again. "I have a mind to put you against one of my better fighters, just to make things interesting. He's called Jumo."

"I'll fight anyone," I say quickly. "Just name the time and place."

Yakow nods. "Three days' time," he says. "Meet down by the river in three days, after midnight." His expression turns sharp. "You tell anyone about this, and the deal is off. I will control who is and isn't invited to watch, understand?"

"And the winner of the fight takes the prize money?" I ask.

Yakow gives me a wry look. "That is, by definition, how a prizefight works." He waves us away. "Off with you now, I have work to do. I'll see you in three days' time."

I'm so excited about what I've accomplished that I don't notice Izachar's face as we leave the bakery and head back into the slums. In fact, I don't notice anything at all until we're halfway home— walking along the Ndefu—and I notice Izachar has stopped completely at the water's edge.

"Iz?" I ask. "What's wrong?"

My friend shakes his head. "I don't feel good about this, Akande," he murmurs, "I really don't. I can't explain it, but I have a bad feeling about it."

"It's going to be all right, Iz." I throw an arm around my friend's neck. "I'll win the money I need, buy Danya something for her bride price, and then I can marry her. Simple."

Izachar makes a face. "You barely know her."

I bristle. "That's not true. I love her."

When Izachar says nothing, I move so that I'm standing in front of him, so that he has to look at me.

"Come on, Izachar," I try in a different voice. "Haven't *you* ever cared about someone so much you'd do anything for them?"

My friend looks sad, but nods. "I have."

"Then you understand how I feel."

"I do."

"It's just a onetime thing," I say, putting my hand on my friend's shoulder. "One time to get the money I need, and then we'll laugh about it someday. Deal?"

Izachar nods. "Deal."

I'm done. I'm leaving my fate to chance or to the whims of the gods. Three days from now, I'm taking destiny into my own hands, once and for all.

CHAPTER 25

TERRIBLE THINGS

EKON

Ekon awoke to a pain in his skull and the smell of firewood in his lungs.

He knew at once that something was wrong, and it wasn't just because he wasn't sitting upright. He was lying on his side, but where, he didn't know. Slowly, carefully, he rolled onto his back and stifled a groan. His brain still felt foggy, but he deduced that he was on something hard and wooden. His wrists were bound in front of him with rough wool, and when he tried to move his fingers, they felt numb and tingly. He'd been tied up awhile. He braced himself, counted in his head, then made himself sit up. The sudden movement blacked out his vision again, and now there was no stopping the long groan as the blood rushed from his head. He heard a voice and jolted.

"About time."

Ekon blinked hard. All around him, it was dark, but he forced his vision to focus. He could just make out a tiny interruption amid the black before him. When he blinked again, he realized that it was a tiny fire a few feet away, and crouched beside it was a single figure. Ekon blinked again and then felt his heart thud hard. His mouth went dry as he regarded the young man staring back at him.

"Kamau."

In answer, his older brother nodded, but said nothing else. Ekon swallowed hard. He couldn't be sure if it was the dimness of the night around them, but even from here he thought his older brother looked different. It took Ekon a moment to realize why. There'd always been a sharpness to him, a quiet sense of command. Now his older brother looked haggard. He was still wearing the blue-and-gold uniform of a Son of the Six, but his clothes were torn, and his arms and legs and face were latticed with scrapes and cuts. His hair was unkempt. Ekon paused before he spoke again.

"How did you find me?"

Kamau let out a harsh sound. Perhaps he'd intended it as a laugh, but it was much cooler. The hairs on the back of Ekon's neck stood on end, and Kamau shook his head.

"It was easy for you to forget." He spoke so quietly, Ekon had to lean in to hear him. He looked up at Ekon and jolted, as though he'd been startled. "How could you forget, Ekkie? You're bookish. Brother Ugo always said you were a quicker study, but *me* . . ." He looked past Ekon and his expression grew distant for a moment. "I was the better tracker and hunter, the better *warrior*. You weren't even close."

He said the words gently, but they still smarted when Ekon

heard them. Kamau stared out at the plains beyond them. Ekon waited another beat before speaking again.

"You tracked me down."

"Of course I did," Kamau snapped, grimacing at him. "It was easy, once I found your caravan. There were a few times you separated from them, a few times I was worried. But I always found you again. I'm the best, Ekon. Me, *only me*."

Something about those words prompted another question in Ekon's mind. "Where are the other Sons?" He knew the gesture was unnecessary, but he still glanced over his shoulder. They were certainly alone. "Don't tell me Father Olufemi let you leave Lkossa on your own?"

He hadn't expected Kamau's reaction. At the mention of Father Olufemi, his brother visibly tensed.

"He'll understand," said Kamau. He seemed to be talking more to himself than to Ekon. "He's angry now, and I may have to do penances for my sins when I return, but I will be forgiven. *I am a true kapteni*. I never gave up on my mission. I found you. I will bring you back. I will be forgiven."

Ekon read between the lines. "You defected, like me."

"Not like *you*!" said Kamau. Ekon sat back. His brother's voice was rising in pitch. He spat into the fire. "I'm not like you. I went on a *holy mission*. The gods themselves ordained it. I was sent to find you and return you to face justice. I knew I wouldn't fail . . ." He swayed, and Ekon noticed his eyes were no longer just distant but unfocused.

"Kamau," said Ekon. "Kamau, are you okay?"

His brother did not answer. He was seated on the ground, but as the wind picked up, Kamau continued to sway. He rocked back and forth, then abruptly collapsed inches from the fire.

"Kamau!" Ekon stood in the bed of the wagon. His arms were tied in front of him, which made movement difficult, but he jumped down and looked around. It seemed Kamau hadn't brought much with him; there was little on the wagon besides a small knapsack. Ekon stared at the mule still hitched to the wagon, then at his brother lying on the ground. For one fractional moment, he thought of making a run for it, but . . . no, something overrode the thought and forced him to keep looking around. He noted a small water gourd, and he stooped down, praying it wasn't empty. He carefully picked it up, waddled over to Kamau, and tipped the contents of the jar over Kamau's face. The minute the water splashed him, he sat up, gasping, then jumped to his feet. He looked straight at Ekon, then roared, knocking the gourd out of Ekon's hand.

"HEY!"

Kamau had always been stronger, and there was no exception now, especially not when Ekon was restrained. He tried to brace for it, but no amount of bracing could prepare him for the pain that rocked through him as his brother slammed him onto his back. In an instant they were children again, fighting in the bowels of the temple over some game gone wrong. Ekon's arms were bound, but his legs were still free. He waited until his brother shifted slightly, then kneed him in the gut as hard as he could. Kamau let out a gasp, then rolled off him. Not a particularly dangerous blow, but enough to knock the wind out of him. Kamau landed on his back and stared up at the sky.

"How . . . did you do . . . that?" he asked between breaths.

"I learned it from you," said Ekon, "when we were little."

Kamau stared at him for a second. "I didn't think you were paying attention."

"I was always paying attention, Kam." He hadn't expected his throat to get tight, and he coughed to cover the sound. Kamau's expression was curious now, assessing, and Ekon changed the subject quickly.

"Look, I'm still tied up." He held up his bound wrists to emphasize the point. "And I don't even know where you've taken me, so I'm not going to run, okay?"

Kamau waited a beat before answering. "Fine."

"You've been following me," said Ekon, "but I'm guessing you've never risked getting close enough to find out what I'm doing? Why I left?"

Kamau's silence was an answer in itself, and Ekon took advantage of it to keep going.

"You remember what I tried to tell you, way back?" he asked. "About the Shetani and Brother Ugo not being what we thought?" He leaned in. "I wasn't lying, Kamau. I know how it sounds, I know from the outside what it looks like, but hear me: This is even bigger than I thought, bigger than you and me, bigger than the Sons of the Six, or even Lkossa. Something really bad is going to happen soon if I don't find Koffi and help—"

"You're worse off than I thought." Kamau was shaking his head again. If he'd looked mildly curious before, he now looked repulsed. "Those spice merchants you left with radicalized you, turned you into a criminal." He grimaced. "I'm glad Baba never saw this."

Ekon tensed. Those words were almost identical to the ones Shomari had once said to him. In that moment, he wanted to get up and punch Kamau, yell at him, do something to make him hurt as much as he'd hurt him. Instead, he took a deep breath and went on.

"There's something else," he said in a barely audible voice. Kamau's gaze returned to Ekon, alert. "It's about our mother," Ekon whispered. "I found out that she's alive. She's been alive this whole time."

Ekon watched the impact of the words register on Kamau's face. There was initial shock, sadness, relief; the anger came last. Kamau glowered.

"Liar."

"She changed her name," Ekon went on, "and completely changed her identity. She's been operating as an underground herbs and spices merchant." He paused. "If you've been following the caravan I was on, you saw her too. You didn't even know it."

"No," said Kamau, though he sounded much less sure now. "I would have recognized her."

"Would you?" asked Ekon gently. "We were young when she left, and she looks different now. She's older."

He watched the calculations on Kamau's face, watched as his brother replayed his entire mission in his mind. Ekon saw the moment it clicked, the moment he realized it was true. His face hardened.

"Even if that woman *is* Ayesha Okojo," he said, "that woman abandoned our family years ago. She's no mother of mine. She's dead to me. The brothers and sons of the Temple of Lkossa are my family. After Baba, they're the only family I've ever known."

Ekon clenched and unclenched his fists. "I felt the same way," he said. "Sometimes I still feel that way. But, Kamau ..." He leaned in as close as he dared. "She had her reasons for doing what she did. I won't take away her right to tell you, but . . . I talked to her, and I believe her. She's sorry and she loves us both. I know she wants to make it right."

"She can't, she left us," said Kamau. He was staring into the fire a little too intently. "She didn't say goodbye."

Ekon nodded. "People make mistakes. That doesn't mean they don't deserve our forgiveness."

Kamau shook his head. "Some things are unforgivable."

"Not with family," said Ekon. "You taught me that too." He stared down at his hands for several seconds. When he looked up, Kamau had turned his back. He was facing the fire, outlined in red-orange light. He spoke again, and his voice was much softer.

"I've done horrific things, Ekon," he whispered, "terrible things."

"That wasn't you, Kam," said Ekon. He kept his voice just as soft. "That wasn't who you really are."

Kamau scoffed. "Wasn't it?"

"You were drugged," said Ekon. He wanted to stay calm, but it was impossible to keep the defensiveness from his voice. He didn't even know why he felt the need to defend his brother from himself, but he leaned forward. "You were a kid—we both were—and we were groomed from adolescence by the brothers of the Temple of Lkossa to be totally allegiant, to never question *anything*, to just . . . obey." He shook his head. "Those people who died—"

"The people we murdered," Kamau said harshly.

Ekon stopped short. He still remembered the boy from the Night Zoo, the way his body had been mangled like an actual monster had found him. He swallowed hard before continuing. "What happened to them was terrible," he said more quietly, "and I know you're going to have to live with that for the rest of your life. I can't imagine what that's like. But you should know, they're not the only victims. You're one too—you and any other person Father Olufemi and Brother Ugo drugged."

Kamau had been turned away from Ekon; now he looked over his shoulder at him. His face was contorted in anguish.

"I tried to stop taking it," he said, "when I started to understand what was happening, I tried . . ." He shook his head. "I couldn't do it, I needed it. I felt terrible without it, like I was going to die."

"You were *addicted*," said Ekon. "You were sick."

Kamau sighed. It was a quiet sound, soft, but Ekon heard old pain in it; he recognized it.

"All our lives, we were told the world was split into good and evil," Kamau said as he stared into the flames again. "They told us everyone fit on one side or the other." He looked up at Ekon. "Where do people like me go?"

"With everyone else." Ekon spoke without hesitation. "Because the truth is, they lied to us. No one is entirely good or evil. We all fit somewhere in between. And it doesn't matter how many times we mess up, if we're still trying to do the right thing. There's always hope for that."

Kamau chuckled lightly. "I thought I was supposed to be the optimist. Not you."

"Kamau." Ekon tried to stay calm. He had one chance, one shot. "It's not too late for you either. What's happened . . . you may not be able to take it back, but you can do things to try to redeem yourself for it. You can help me, and Koffi, and Mama—"

He knew instantly that it had been a mistake; Kamau stiffened, then stood and shook his head.

"Almost," he said, "you almost got me. That's clever, Ekkie. You've gotten more cunning in your time away."

"Kamau." Ekon stood too. He couldn't even count to settle his nerves. "Kamau, please."

"You tried to poison my mind." There was an eerie pitch in Kamau's voice, and Ekon couldn't ignore a sinking feeling. "You tried, but my faith protected me. I won't let you do that again."

Ekon opened his mouth to speak, but this time a cloth was stuffed into his mouth. He gagged, taking a sharp breath in through his nose, and Kamau moved behind him and bent the crook of his arm around his neck. He began to squeeze. Ekon knew the maneuver: It was a chokehold. His hands were still bound, but he tried to tap his fingers into the air, counting the seconds as the world around him grew dark again.

One-two-three. One-two-three. One-two—

"We're going back to Lkossa," he heard his brother say. "We're going home tonight."

Ekon tried to breathe but found he could not. The world around him was getting smaller; the only thing he could discern was the light of the fire, no larger than a candle's flame.

One-two-three.

And then he was lost again.

CHAPTER 26

HOMECOMING

KOFFI

In the day it took to travel from the plains to Lkossa, Koffi had tried to prepare herself for what it would feel like to see Lkossa again. Still, her breath caught as she saw its lights, as they came to a stop when the city's gates came into view. They dismounted the lionesses quickly.

"Thank you," Koffi said to the one she'd ridden. "I don't know if you can understand me, but *thank you*. And please thank Akande for me, if you can."

The lioness inclined her head, almost a nod, before bounding away into the wider plains and out of sight. The other three followed, leaving the group alone.

"Now what?" asked Zain.

"Ekon's brother would have taken him to the Temple of Lkossa," said Koffi. From there, she could just barely make out the temple's white dome. "It's one of the most fortified areas of the city, and they may even be expecting us, so I don't think we should go there without a plan."

"I agree," said Njeri, "but then, where can we go?"

Koffi had known the question was coming, but she still didn't want to answer it. "I only know of one place," she said. "The Night Zoo."

By the time they'd reached the city's gate, the sky was dark. Koffi had anticipated possibly seeing Sons of the Six at the city gates, but to her relief, none were there. She considered it. Perhaps with the threat of the Shetani gone, the city had relaxed just slightly. That thought gave her some hope. She led Makena, Zain, Safiyah, and Njeri through the city's winding streets as best she could. At several points, she had to double back—she'd only ever been on these streets twice before—eventually, though, she found the familiar road that led up the hill to the Night Zoo. She swallowed hard as they started up the incline. The walled-in perimeter loomed higher and higher. When they were within a few feet of it, Koffi gestured as they veered to the right, to an even darker side of the compound.

"Ah, Koffi?" said Zain. He was staring up at the massive walls. "Not to point out the obvious, but . . . unless you've been holding on to a key to the gates that you didn't tell us about, I don't see us getting in here."

Koffi nodded. "I've only ever left the Night Zoo," she said. "I've never tried to break in, but . . ." She steepled her fingers, thinking. "I heard a story once, more of a rumor really. Some of the beast-keepers said there was a part of the wall where the bricks were uneven, thick enough to step on and climb. They always talked about it as a means of escape, but . . ."

"We could use those bricks to get in," said Njeri, reading her thoughts.

Koffi touched her fingertips to the brick wall. "Right."

"Any idea where those special bricks might be?" asked Safiyah.

Koffi crouched down. "To be honest, I'm not sure."

"We'll all look, then," said Njeri. "Between the five of us, we can find it."

"Wait!" Zain had already dropped to his knees, his nose inches from the wall. "Here, I think this is it." He ran his palm up and down a section of the wall. "It's a lot subtler than I expected, but the bricks here jut out just slightly." His expression was grim when he looked up at them. "It's not going to be easy for all of us to climb, and it's a long way down if one of us falls."

"Maybe we don't have to all climb up it that way," said Makena. "If even one of us can get to the top, that person can drop something down to help hoist the others up."

"Like what?" asked Njeri.

Without a word, Makena reached into the sack slung on her shoulder and held up a rope. "I snagged it from Akande's camp before we left."

Njeri blinked. "*You* stole?"

Makena stared at her feet, looking sheepish. "I'm not proud," she said, "but we needed it."

Njeri blinked. "I think I love you."

A smile spread across Makena's face.

"This is all very sweet," said Zain, still kneeling, "but we're running out of time. What are we doing?"

"I'll go first." Koffi watched Safiyah step forward, looking resolute. "I'm a good climber."

"We'll stand below you and try to spot," said Zain.

Safiyah said nothing else. Makena handed her the rope as she walked right up to the wall and looked it over. Koffi thought she was about to say something else, but without warning, she leaped. Her feet scrabbled against the brick for a half second, and Zain ran to stand under her, but then she found her footing and began to scale the wall in earnest.

"I've definitely done more enjoyable things," she called over her shoulder, "but it isn't so bad." Once she reached the top of the wall, she dropped the rope down, and Njeri went next, followed by Zain.

"Do you want to go next?" asked Makena.

"Nah," Koffi said with a casualness she didn't feel. "You go ahead."

Makena nodded, then reshouldered her bag. She only had to climb halfway up before Njeri and Zain pulled her the rest of the way. From where they stood, Koffi could only see four black silhouettes, outlined in moonlight.

"Your turn, Koffi," said Zain.

Koffi took a deep breath, then, before she could overthink it, grabbed the rope and began to climb. The irony of it wasn't lost on her; for most of her life, she'd dreamed of leaving the Night Zoo, of running away from it and never returning. She'd been all over the continent of Eshōza, and in the end, she was right back where she'd started. She didn't have any more time to reflect on that as she felt two sets of hands grab the back of her tunic and pull her the rest of the way up. Then she was sitting on the ledge of the Night Zoo's wall. She'd been here before, perched right here between worlds. This time it felt so different.

"Where are we going from here?" asked Safiyah.

Koffi made herself turn and actually look into the Night Zoo. There was still evidence of what had happened there—the Hema, the massive tent where Baaz had once hosted performances, was gone, and a much smaller and shabbier tent had been erected to replace it. She listened and heard the familiar sounds of the Night Zoo's residents, the low growls, hisses, and trumpets. Most of the grounds were dark; it seemed Baaz wasn't hosting a show tonight. Her gaze roamed until she found what she was looking for.

"There." She pointed. "The beastkeepers' huts are there. That's where my mother would be."

"And you're sure it's safe to go there?" asked Njeri. "You're sure none of the other beastkeepers would raise the alarm?"

Koffi paused. The truth was, she wasn't sure. "It's our only option."

"Well," said Zain, "that makes it easy, then."

Jumping down from the wall was easier than climbing it, and as soon as they were all on the ground, Koffi made a run for it. This place was familiar; she knew it like the back of her hand. She led them past the wells she'd gone to so many times as a little girl to fetch water for Mama, past the paddocks where she'd mucked hay for the zebras that lived there. Tears fell as the memories came flooding back, but she pushed them down as they kept running. Finally, they reached the beastkeepers' huts. She held a finger to her lips and gestured for them to follow.

It was just as she remembered it: tiny, dilapidated brown huts clustered in an uneven line like broken teeth. Hay littered the ground, the result of roofs constantly being destroyed by the weather. She'd lived at Thornkeep for a time, in more finery than she could fathom. It was humbling to return to this, to remember what life had once been.

"Are they going to hear us?" Njeri asked softly.

"No," said Koffi, and she knew it was true. Baaz worked the beastkeepers hard; sleep was a luxury that wasn't wasted. "They'll all be trying to get as much sleep as they can. Work begins at dawn."

Njeri nodded, and they went on, but then Koffi stopped short. At first, she wasn't sure if it was in her imagination, but . . . She went perfectly still. Now she was sure she'd heard it: approaching footsteps.

"Koffi?" Zain whispered. "What's—"

"Get down!"

There was a scuffle, and they ran behind one of the huts just in time. Koffi's heart leaped to her throat as the light of a torch touched the place where they'd just been, and the long shadow of a person approached. She felt Makena's hand gripped around her wrist, holding tight; she heard Njeri and Zain trying to keep their breath shallow as they sat crouched together.

Please, Koffi prayed, *please turn around.*

The light was getting closer to them, and now Koffi understood the truth of it. They were caught. If they stayed where they were, they'd be found; if they made a run for it, they'd be captured too. She braced herself as the light inched closer to their hiding spot, and at the last minute she screwed her eyes shut. The back of her eyelids turned red as light touched them, and she heard the footsteps stop right before her.

"Koffi?"

Koffi opened her eyes with a start. There was a boy standing before her holding a torch. A boy she knew.

"Jabir!"

She didn't stop to think about it. In an instant, she'd run to him. She heard a soft cry as Jabir's arms wrapped around her and he hugged her tight.

"Koffi." Her friend's voice quivered. "How did you do it? How did you come back?"

A laugh escaped Koffi. "How much time do you have?"

Jabir was still holding on to her. "When we heard that the Shetani had been captured by a girl, we thought we might see you," he said. "Then we heard the Shetani was dead, and there was no more talk of the girl who'd captured it. Your mama and I thought . . ."

Mama. "Jabir, where's my mother?"

"She's safe," he said. "She's recovered from things really well, all things considered."

Koffi chose not to dwell on the last part of that statement. "Can you take us to her?"

"Us?" Jabir looked over her shoulder and seemed to notice the others for the first time.

"Like I said : . ." Koffi followed his gaze, then shrugged. "How much time do you have?"

"I'm going to guess not much," he said. "Come on, I'll take you to your mom."

They moved quickly down the path until Jabir pointed out

a hut notably dirtier than the others, and Koffi's heart fell. She'd been the one to help Mama keep their tiny home neat. Jabir stopped before the door and rapped his knuckles near its entrance.

"Jabir?" said a small voice. Koffi braced herself.

"Go on," he said to Koffi, nodding.

Koffi tried to move but suddenly found her feet wouldn't move. "I can't," she whispered. It didn't make sense. She'd been thinking about returning to Mama from the moment she'd left; now something was stopping her and she didn't understand what. She jumped when Makena moved to stand beside her. She took her hand and squeezed it.

"She's your mother, Koffi," said Makena softly. "It'll be okay."

Koffi squeezed Makena's hand back. She took a deep breath, then ducked into the hut. At first, she struggled to discern anything in the dark, then:

"Jabir." The tone of the voice coming from the back of the hut was severe. "If I've told you once, I've told you twice about running around after lights-out. If Baaz catches you, he'll—" Koffi's mother laid eyes on her and froze. Her mouth hung open.

"Mama." Koffi's voice cracked. "I'm home. *I came home.*"

. She'd wanted the words to be prepared, more eloquent, somehow encompassing every emotion she'd felt since she'd last seen her mother. But those words were the only ones she had. Her mother continued to stare at her, her expression blank.

"Koffi."

"I'm sorry, Mama." Koffi stared at her feet. "I know it's the middle of the night and I didn't come back when I said I would and you and Jabir had to take the blame for me, and—"

Her mother placed her hands on either side of Koffi's face. Her eyes were wet. "My ponya seed."

There was no logical reason that those should have been the words that finally did it, but they did. A beat passed, and then Koffi began to cry in earnest. Her mother pulled her into her arms, and she cried harder.

"Mama," she said between sobs, "Mama, I'm so sorry."

"Shh." Koffi felt her mother's hands running over her hair, pulling her close. Her voice was gentle but firm. "You don't say sorry for anything. *I'm* sorry. Koffi, I kept so much from you that I shouldn't have. My mother . . . I didn't tell you anything about her . . . I kept her from you."

"She found me again," said Koffi, "in her own kind of way."

Her mother gave her a curious look, then chuckled. It was a sadder sound than it should have been. "I'm sure she did." Abruptly, she looked up. "How did you get here? Are you alone?"

Koffi pulled back. "Actually, no. Mama, so much has happened, I don't even know where to start."

"You don't have to tell me everything all at once," said Mama. "As long as you're here. We have all the time in the world."

A lump rose in Koffi's throat. She tried to hide her reaction, but it was no use. Her mother saw it instantly.

"What is it?"

"Mama . . ." Koffi took a deep breath. "I thought I'd never see you again, and I'm so glad to see you now, but . . ." She made herself say the words. "But I have to go again. There's something I need to do. One of my friends is in trouble, and I have to help him."

She'd expected her mother to be angry, possibly to cry. Instead, Koffi's mom surprised her by nodding.

"How can I help?"

"Koffi!"

They both looked up. Jabir had stuck his head into the hut's entryway. "Sorry to interrupt, but we need to talk."

Koffi looked back at her mother, hesitant, but she was gesturing.

"Come inside."

One by one, the rest of the group squeezed within the confines of the hut. Zain was the first to speak.

"Ah, and you must be Koffi's sister!" he said. Njeri elbowed him hard in the ribs, and he amended. "I mean, mother. It's nice to meet you, Auntie."

Koffi's mother gave him an amused look. "And you too, young man."

"Jabir," said Koffi, "what is it?"

"Your friends were filling me in on what's going on," said Jabir. "They said you need to get into the Temple of Lkossa?"

Koffi nodded. "As soon as possible, can you help us?"

Jabir pursed his lips. "I can try, but . . ." He hesitated.

"What?"

"Just before lights-out, Baaz gave all the beastkeepers a message," said Jabir. "He received the notice earlier tonight. The city's going to be observing the Bonding, and security is going to be tightened everywhere."

Koffi swallowed.

"There's more," Mama added. "There's some sort of event

happening at the temple tomorrow, some sort of punishment being carried out, so traffic in that area will be unusually thick."

Koffi exchanged a look with Safiyah.

"That could be for Ekon," said Njeri, reading their minds.

"Then it's settled," said Koffi. "We need to get into the temple grounds and stop whatever they're planning to do there tomorrow."

"The temple is in the Takatifu District," Jabir pointed out, "and that's not an area of Lkossa open to the public." He gave Koffi a meaningful look. "I don't think bringing a high-quality goat is going to get us through this time."

"No." Koffi frowned. It seemed like the harder she tried to think of an idea, the more difficult it was to grasp one. "What we need is a distraction, something that will catch the Kuhani and the Sons of the Six totally off guard, a spectacle or a commotion. *Something.*"

"Wait a minute." Everyone in the hut turned to stare at Jabir. He was sitting up straighter, and Koffi recognized the look on his face. She'd seen it so many times before. Jabir only looked like that when he got an idea. He searched the hut, then pointed to Zain. "*You're* wearing blue."

No one spoke for a beat.

"Of course I am." Zain looked down at himself, confused. "I'm a member of the Order of Akili. I always wear blue."

"It's kind of his thing," Njeri added, rubbing her eyelids.

"But you're wearing a very specific *shade* of blue," said Jabir. His nodded at Koffi. "Are you seeing what I'm seeing?"

Koffi raised a brow. "Sorry, no?"

Jabir smirked. "*You* all see a young man named Zain," he said, walking around Zain slowly. "But with a little creativity . . . I see someone very different. *I see a messenger from the Temple of Lkossa, a messenger who reports directly from the Kuhani, and one with a very special request for one Baaz Mtombé.*"

Koffi stared at Jabir, incredulous. "You're not thinking . . ."

"Oh *yes*. Yes, I am," said Jabir. "It's time for a brand-new show at the Night Zoo."

CHAPTER 27

MERCY

EKON

The following day was a blur, and Ekon found himself able to count little of it.

The first time he'd woken up, he'd been almost sure it was morning; the sky above him was pale blue, cloudless. He'd barely had time to raise his head before he felt another prick in his arm and lost consciousness. The second time, he'd been more careful, waiting to open his eyes until he was sure that Kamau was otherwise occupied driving the cart. It didn't matter. Even if he hadn't been bound, even if he wasn't so thirsty his throat burned, the effects of whatever his brother had put in the darts had taken its toll on his body; everything was hazy and slowed. His own fingers felt too heavy to lift, let alone tap against his side. As quickly as he'd risen, his head lolled and he was asleep again, only distantly conscious of the feeling of the wagon rolling beneath him. The next time he came to, Kamau was standing over him, his frame outlined in silvery moonlight. "We're here," he said quietly. "Get up."

Here. Ekon knew what that had to mean, but he still wasn't prepared as Kamau hauled him to his feet and helped him get down from the wagon. The world tilted slightly at the sudden movement, and he swayed on his feet. Kamau threw him a sidelong glance before tipping what remained of the water gourd into Ekon's mouth. Ekon drank gratefully.

"Thank you."

"Don't thank me," said Kamau gruffly. "I can't have you passing out. We've got a bit of a walk to the temple."

For the first time since they'd stopped, Ekon looked around. He started. It had taken him a moment, but now he saw it. A long wall of trees rose up on his left; to his right, he could see the distant lights of northern Lkossa.

"We're on the border of the Greater Jungle," he said aloud.

"People still don't like to come near here," Kamau said in answer. He grabbed a cloak from the wagon's bed and draped it over Ekon's shoulders. In the humid heat, the fabric was heavy and thick. Ekon shifted uncomfortably.

"Keep that on," Kamau warned. "I don't want anyone to see you until we've made it to the temple." He gave Ekon a foreboding look. "And if I were you, I wouldn't want to be seen either. You're not exactly a favorite here anymore."

I never was. Ekon thought the words but didn't say anything aloud, nor did he protest as Kamau grabbed him by the arm and steered him toward the city. It was pitch black, but neither of them needed to see much; they'd walked this path on patrol any number of times. It had been weeks since Ekon had last been on it, but muscle memory kicked in, and even through all the fatigue, his footsteps found their old cadence again. Instinctively, he began to count.

One-two-three. One-two-three. One-two-three.

The sounds of Lkossa reached him first; shortly after came all the smells. Ekon hadn't been sure if he'd ever see his home again, let alone how he would feel if he did. But whatever he might have expected, it wasn't how he felt now. As they crossed the city's official border, Kamau quickened their pace, trying to keep them moving fast with their heads bowed. That didn't entirely stop Ekon from taking it all in. It was nightfall, so most of the traders had packed up their wares for the night, but there were still children playing oware on the streets. Women were still pulling laundry from lines strung between the windows of the mudbrick buildings, and every so often a waft of street food lingered under his nose and made his mouth water. *Home.* He felt a dull pain in his chest. He'd missed this place, missed Lkossa. He saw the city differently now. Kamau didn't lead him through the paved streets they'd used to walk without care or fear; he directed them toward the slums and alleyways, the places they'd once only gone when they had to. A distant memory cropped up in Ekon's mind; he remembered the time he and Kamau had chased a young girl here. It'd been the first time he'd met Themba. That felt like another lifetime ago. He swallowed hard.

They reached the golden pillars marking the Takatifu District sooner than Ekon expected or wanted. In his old life, they would have stridden right through without issue, but tonight, when Ekon squinted, he made out a figure standing at the gates. Kamau was still holding on to his arm, frog-marching him forward, but even he faltered slightly as they neared the warrior.

"Not a word," said Kamau under his breath.

Ekon kept silent. They'd taken only a few more steps before the warrior unsheathed the golden hanjari dagger on his belt. Ekon winced against the familiar sound of the metal scraping free. It only occurred to him now that he still had his own dagger, hidden in the folds of his tunic. It was tiny, possibly too tiny for Kamau to have realized it was there. It didn't matter now; the Son of the Six raised the torch he was holding so that he and Kamau were illuminated in glaring red-gold light. Ekon couldn't see, but he heard a scoff.

"Unbelievable."

Ekon blinked hard and looked away for a moment. When he turned his head again, he found that he was staring at a familiar young man. Fumbe. He was one of Kamau's co-candidates. He wasn't even looking at Ekon; his eyes were fixed on Kamau.

"I wasn't surprised when your brother deserted," Fumbe said in a low voice. "He was always weaker. But not you, Kamau. I never thought I'd see the day."

"I didn't defect." Kamau's voice was surprisingly calm. "I went on a mission. I brought a traitor home to answer for his sins."

Fumbe's eyes flicked to Ekon for the first time. If his brother's friend had ever had any love for him, it was gone now. A half beat passed before Fumbe placed one hand on Ekon's chest and shoved hard.

"*You,*" he said through clenched teeth. "You dare show your face here?"

Kamau moved between the two of them. "He is not to be harmed," he said curtly. "I order it."

The sneer on Fumbe's face twisted further still. "And who do you think you are, giving orders?" he asked in a cool voice.

"I *think*," said Kamau, "that I made a lifelong oath, and that the brothers of this temple made me the youngest kapteni in its history for a reason." He jutted his chin in a gesture so familiar to Old Kamau than Ekon cringed. "You may not choose to let me in, but if I am absolved, I will be a kapteni again, and I will remember who mistreated me."

Ekon glanced between them. He knew his brother well enough not to be fooled by the neutral and unbothered expression on his face. The tell was in his eyes; Kamau's were flicking back and forth, waiting for an answer. He could tell Fumbe was weighing his options too. A beat passed before the warrior relaxed slightly and stepped back. He was still frowning.

"State your business here, Kapteni."

"I want an audience with the Kuhani, now," said Kamau. "Tell him I have the traitor Ekon Okojo."

Fumbe looked as though he might refuse him again, but then he took a deep breath and turned on his heel. "Come with me," he said.

None of them spoke as Fumbe led them up the winding hill and toward the Temple of Lkossa. Kamau was staring straight ahead, and though he still had a viselike grip on Ekon's arm, he seemed much more distracted now. Ekon took advantage of that to look from his hooded cloak. It felt so strange to see the Temple of Lkossa still exactly where he'd left it, looking the same as it had all his life. The gleaming white alabaster, the golden flicker of candlelight in so many of the windows—it was home, until recently the only home he'd ever known. But there were changes that he couldn't deny. As they neared it, Ekon felt a distinct chill in the air around the temple, a sense of foreboding he couldn't shake.

All too soon they'd reached the temple's massive front doors, and Fumbe ushered them inside. They'd barely crossed the threshold when Ekon heard the pounding of footsteps. He didn't have time to so much as turn before someone punched him in the face. His vision exploded in a shower of stars, and he reeled back. He heard the scuffling of several feet, raised voices.

"Brother!" someone shouted. "Stop!"

"Let me go!" Ekon knew that voice. "He deserves it!"

Ekon blinked hard. When his vision refocused, he found that Kamau had yanked him backward while several Sons of the Six held on to Shomari. In all his life, Ekon had never seen his former co-candidate so angry. Spittle was gathering in the corners of Shomari's mouth.

"He got that old daraja witch to use her magic on me!" he screamed. "He's one of them, filth! Traitor!"

"Enough."

The room quieted at once, and Ekon looked up at the sound of a voice he knew well. He shouldn't have been surprised to see Father Olufemi making his way toward them, and yet he was. So much had happened, but the old man appeared exactly the same—immaculately dressed and eerily calm. If he was surprised to see Ekon or Kamau, he gave no show of it. Instead, his eyes cut to Shomari.

"What is the meaning of this, Mensah?"

"Father?" The astonishment on Shomari's face was plain. "They . . . the traitors have returned. They dared to come back. They ought to be punished—"

Father Olufemi raised a hand and silenced him. For the first time, his eyes fell on Ekon. His expression was inscrutable.

"These young men are sworn Sons of the Six who have returned to their home," he said calmly, "and they will be treated as such."

Ekon felt the shock reverberate around the room. A small sound—maybe a gasp—escaped Kamau's lips, and more than one of the Sons of the Six raised their eyebrows. Shomari sputtered.

"But, Father—"

"Question my word again, Mensah, and *you* will be the one to face punishment," said Father Olufemi sharply.

In a different life, in different circumstances, the threat would have been funny. But Ekon couldn't temper the growing sense of unease unfurling in his rib cage as Father Olufemi looked between him and his brother. He spoke to Kamau first.

"Release him," he commanded.

At once, Kamau let go of Ekon's arm.

"Come with me," the clergyman said. "We will speak in my office."

They moved through the temple's main halls and then up the winding stairs that led to the Kuhani's office. Ekon grew tenser with each step. The last time he had been here, in this hall, had been when he'd overheard Kamau getting hasira leaf from the Kuhani. He still remembered the desperate expression on his brother's face, the way his heart seized when he'd finally understood what was going on. Ekon hadn't realized how much memory a single place could store within its walls. They walked down the short hallway, and Father Olufemi entered his office first. Once they were inside, he closed the door.

"Sit."

Kamau obeyed instantly, but Ekon hesitated.

"I prefer to stand," he said.

He'd expected resistance, but Father Olufemi nodded obligingly, then took a seat behind his desk. For several seconds, he said nothing as his eyes moved between the two of them, as though doing some sort of unspoken assessment.

"It's still hard to believe the two of you are grown men," he said softly. "I remember when you came to the temple as small boys. You've both grown into admirable warriors."

I'm not a warrior, thought Ekon, *not your kind of warrior.* Father Olufemi's eyes glinted, as though he could read his mind.

"It's also hard to believe how much has happened in these last few weeks." He shook his head with what looked like genuine remorse. "So much pain, deceit, dishonesty . . ."

Ekon bristled.

"But I was once young too." Father Olufemi steepled his fingers and went on. "My faith has become more grounded as I've gotten older, but years ago, when I first pledged my service to the Six, I'm not proud to admit there were moments of doubt, even moments when I strayed from my faith." He looked up at Ekon. "Just as the two of you have strayed."

"Father." Kamau rose from his chair, and Ekon hated the expression on his brother's face. Once again, there was that pleading, desperate look, a yearning. "Please forgive me. I left the Temple without official leave and without your permission, but I brought back my brother."

"I know, Kapteni Okojo," said Father Olufemi. "Your disobedience was well-intentioned." He sighed. "I don't need to tell the two of you how far back the Okojo family's history with the Sons of the Six stretches. It is a long and esteemed legacy, certainly something the two of you should be proud of."

Ekon was still standing farther away from Father Olufemi, braced for anything, but now he was confused. This wasn't what he'd expected.

"We teach obedience, strength, and honor within these walls," said Father Olufemi. "Perhaps what we do not talk about nearly enough is the strength found in showing mercy. Which is why I'd now like to make the two of you an offer."

Ekon held his breath.

"I will absolve you both of any crimes levied against you," he said, "and I will do it tonight."

Ekon stiffened. "I don't think warriors like Shomari will be okay with that."

Father Olufemi nodded. "They may not like it, but ultimately, it isn't their decision. Sometimes we must lead by example, by showing mercy to others the way the gods show mercy to us."

Ekon thought of the way Fedu had looked back at Thornkeep, the way he'd been willing to sacrifice so many lives for the sake of his own ambitions. He hadn't shown mercy at all. He grimaced.

"I don't think I want that kind of mercy," he said.

"Ekon!" Kamau whirled on him. "Shut up!"

"Tell me," said Ekon, stepping forward, "what are the conditions of this 'mercy'? What do you expect of us in return?"

The smile that touched the Kuhani's face was slow, chilling. "Only two things," he said. "First, the two of you must admit to your wrongdoings, both here and also in public for all the city to witness. Second . . ." He leaned in. "You will tell me the current whereabouts of the Shetani."

Ekon laughed. He hadn't meant to, but the sound bubbled up from his throat and escaped him before he could stop it. Kamau gawked at him, and the Kuhani's eyes narrowed.

"I can't tell you where the Shetani is," said Ekon, "because she's dead and gone. She died here, in the sky garden."

"Then you can tell me the whereabouts of the daraja who freed the Shetani," said Father Olufemi. "She is, perhaps, even more dangerous than the beast."

"I can't do that either," he said.

"Because she is dead?" asked Father Olufemi.

"No," said Ekon, "because she is my friend, and I wouldn't betray her."

"Father." Kamau moved to grip the edge of the Kuhani's desk. "I, Kamau Okojo, admit to you now that I have sinned. I ask for clemency and for the forgiveness of you, the brothers, and the warriors of this temple. I will make the same admission before the entire city if I have to." He looked over his shoulder. "Ekon?"

In answer, Ekon said nothing.

"The deal is only valid if both of you admit to wrongdoing," said Father Olufemi, "and if Ekon gives me the information I need."

Ekon raised himself to his full height. "Then you already know my answer."

The Kuhani seemed to stare at him for a century. Ekon wanted to tap his fingers against his side to count the seconds as they

397

ticked by, but he resisted. Eventually the old man leaned back in his chair. He looked resigned.

"Then there is no more I can offer," said Father Olufemi. He rapped his knuckles against the wood twice. There was barely time to react. The doors to the office burst open, and Ekon felt a blade at his back. His heart seized as Kamau spun around, eyes wide.

"Wait, please!"

"Take them to the dungeons," said Father Olufemi as the Sons of the Six filed in. "And prepare the courtyard for executions at dawn."

CHAPTER 28

JAIL

EKON

When Ekon was a small boy, few places unsettled him as much as the Temple of Lkossa's dungeons.

He made a point of avoiding the place, and not just because it was dark and damp. There was a chill there no matter the season, and he always had the inexplicable feeling that someone was watching him there, even when he was all alone. As a warrior-in-training, he had vowed that, as soon as he was initiated, he would never set foot in the dungeons again.

Now he sat in the dungeons chained.

One-two-three.

He'd quickly run out of things to count. There were fifty-eight links on each of the chains fastened around his wrists, sixty-two links on the two chains that tethered his ankles to the wall. The walls of the cell he and his brother had been shoved into by the Sons of the Six were too grimy to count the bricks, and he'd already counted eleven rods of steel to make up the bars locking them in. He resorted to tapping his fingers against his thigh, using the count to keep him calm. It helped, but only a little. He breathed in and out and tried to find that familiar rhythm.

One-two-three. One-two-three. One-two-three.

"Will you stop?"

His looked up, surprised. On the wall opposite him, Kamau was glaring, and watching his hands.

Ekon frowned. "What?"

"That ridiculous tapping," Kamau spat. "I can't believe you still do that."

"I've always done it," said Ekon. He didn't know where his calm was coming from, only that the angrier Kamau seemed to get, the easier it came to him. "It helps me when I'm feeling stressed."

"I'll bet you are feeling stressed," said Kamau bitterly. "We're in here because of you."

"We're in here," said Ekon, "because you brought us back to Lkossa, because you actually thought Olufemi would forgive you."

"HE DID FORGIVE ME!" Kamau roared. He tried to stand, but the chains fastened to his arms and legs held him back. He looked murderous, and momentarily, Ekon was glad they were both chained. "And he forgave you too! All you had to do was admit you were wrong, it was simple!"

"That wasn't all he wanted me to do," said Ekon quietly. "He wanted me to betray someone, my friend."

"Your *friend*," Kamau mocked. "What? That Gede girl? The daraja? You barely know her."

"I know she's put her life on the line for me plenty of times," said Ekon. "More times than I deserve."

Kamau shook his head. "I never thought I'd see it." He no longer sounded angry, but somehow that made Ekon feel worse. "I never thought I'd live to see the day when my own brother would become a stranger, a man without honor."

The words were quiet, but they still hurt, more than Ekon had expected them to. He swallowed. "You may never believe me," he murmured, "where I've been, what I've seen, or what I've done. But I'm telling the truth, Kamau."

Kamau turned away as much as the chains allowed. It was a small thing, but it was also childish, and it hit a nerve. Ekon's fingers stopped tapping. He sat up straighter.

"You want to know what I've been through?" he said, his voice rising. "Fine. I joined a gang of illegal spice and herb traders that our *mother* runs."

Kamau said nothing.

"You know I went all the way down south, to Bandari, because you followed me," Ekon went on. "But I'll bet there was a period of time after that when you couldn't follow me, no matter how hard you tried to track me." He was staring at Kamau, so he didn't miss the tiny shift in his brother's expression.

"You couldn't find me because I went into the *Realm of the Dead*, into the god Fedu's realm. It wasn't the first time I'd seen him or fought him."

A muscle in Kamau's jaw twitched, and Ekon went on.

"After that, I took a ferry up the Ndefu. I met Amakoya, the real Amakoya. Again, not my first time running into her. After that, I met Atuno."

Now Kamau was facing him. His expression was inscrutable.

"And most recently," said Ekon, "right before you *kidnapped* me, I met Itaashe on the plains." He tried to throw up his hands, and the chains clinked around him. "You said the gods sent you on a mission, you say your faith leads you in everything. Olufemi talked about 'faith.' I'm telling you now not just what I believe, but what I've seen." He leaned forward as much as the chains would allow. "You helped raise me, Kamau. You know, more than anyone else in the entire world, how badly I wanted to be a Son of the Six, how badly I wanted to be like Baba."

At the mention of their father, Kamau flinched.

"Do you really think I'd throw that all away," he asked, "abandon over a decade of training for nothing?"

"I don't know," Kamau finally said. He was grimacing, but the tone of his voice didn't match it. "I don't know what you'd do, because I don't think I know who you are anymore."

"Then I'll tell you," said Ekon. He began to tap his fingers in earnest. *One-two-three. One-two-three. One-two-three.* "I'm not your kid brother anymore, and I'm not a warrior-in-training." He scoffed. "I'm not even a warrior anymore, and I don't think I ever really wanted to be.

"I don't like fighting. I like numbers. I'm *good* at numbers, and puzzles. I tap my fingers." He nodded down at his own hands. "Because when I get nervous, or stressed, it calms me down, and I'm not ashamed of it." Ekon dropped his gaze. "I want to be brave—I try really hard to be—but sometimes I get scared. But I try anyway, because someone once told me that being brave isn't about never being afraid, it's about trying anyway." He stared up at the dungeon's grimy ceiling and took a deep breath.

"I know what's probably going to happen tomorrow," he said more quietly. "And you do too. Father Olufemi is going to sentence us to die unless we do what he wants. You probably think I'm an idiot for not agreeing to his deal. The thing is, Kam . . ." Ekon's fingers stopped. "Given the choice, I'd rather die tomorrow. I'd rather die than betray the people I care about, and I'd rather die with the honor in *that* than keep living without it."

Time seemed to slow as Kamau looked up again. Ekon found he couldn't read his brother's expression. He saw anger, but other things too—regret, confusion, sadness. His throat bobbed as he swallowed hard, and when he did speak again, his voice was little more than a whisper.

"You're right."

That was the last thing Ekon had expected. "What?"

"What you said about honor," said Kamau. "You're right. That's what we're taught as Sons of the Six, that honor is the most important thing." There were tears in his eyes. "So why did they make us do it, Ekon? Why did they drug us? Why did they force us to kill those innocent people?"

It was hard for Ekon to find the right words. "Sometimes people use good things for bad reasons."

A single tear trailed down Kamau's face. "I thought he'd understand," he whispered. "I really, really thought he'd understand. I thought if you just came back, if I could put things back to the way they were before . . ."

"That everything else would go back to the way it was," Ekon finished.

Kamau let his head fall back against the wall. "But that can't happen, can it?" He seemed to be asking himself the question as much as he was asking Ekon.

"No," said Ekon, "it can't."

Kamau nodded. "Everyone always said I was the stronger one between the two of us, the better warrior."

Ekon flinched.

"But that was never really true," said Kamau. "You've always been the stronger one, the better man." He lowered his voice. "I'm sorry I didn't see that until now."

"It's never too late to start over," said Ekon. The words felt hollow, and Kamau offered a sad smile.

"I think in this case, it might be," he said.

"For what it's worth," said Ekon, "if I could choose, I'd always choose you to be my brother, Kamau."

Kamau smiled. "I'd always choose you, Ekkie."

Neither of them spoke again. Instead, Ekon sat back and let his fingers tap against his leg. A few times he dozed off. One of the times he woke up, he thought he saw Kamau across the cell, tapping his own fingers against his leg. He couldn't be entirely sure that it was a dream.

CHAPTER 29

The EXECUTION

EKON

One-two-three.

Ekon heard the footsteps coming and sat up. He counted them. Seconds later, a pair of Sons of the Six appeared at the cell's door.

"Sons of Okojo." It was too dark to identify the warrior who was speaking. "I have a message from the Kuhani. He is offering you both a final opportunity to accept his generous proposal, to admit to wrongdoing and provide the whereabouts of the daraja he is looking for."

"I'll answer for us both," said Kamau. "We don't want the Kuhani's deal."

There was a long silence before the warrior spoke. "Then in the name of the Six, of the Kuhani who presides over his city, and the brotherhood you pledged your life to, I sentence both of you to die."

Ekon's fingers began to tap frantically, and his blood pumped so fast and hard he could barely hear anything. He was only faintly aware of the two warriors entering the cell, detaching him and Kamau from their chains and leading them out of the cell and up the temple's stairs. He counted their steps.

Forty-five. Forty-six. Forty-seven.

Eventually, they reached the top, and the warriors led them out one of the side doors. The sudden glare of dawn's light made Ekon wince. Distantly he heard the sounds of cheering, and he saw that more than one ribbon was streaming from the temple's window. A realization hit him.

Bonding Day. *Today* was Bonding Day.

"Wait!" A new rush of desperation filled Ekon. He tried to free himself from the Sons' grasp, but they only tightened their grip on him. One of them took Kamau and dragged him around the corner of temple and out of sight.

"Ekon!"

"Kamau!" Ekon lunged, trying to turn in the same direction. One of the warriors hit him below the ribs with something blunt, and the breath left Ekon's body. He doubled over in pain and stared at the grass. A shadow fell over him.

"Gag him." It was Father Olufemi's voice.

Ekon clenched his jaw as the warrior pulled him to his feet again. He pinched Ekon's nose until he was forced to open his mouth, and at once a cloth was stuffed between his teeth. Another warrior appeared at his other side and grabbed his free arm. They turned him around to face Father Olufemi. The old man was smiling.

"A waste," he said coldly, "a perfect waste. Take him to the ritual platform."

Ekon's body stiffened, but he could say nothing as the warriors walked him around the temple in the opposite direction they'd taken Kamau. He knew when they were getting closer to the ritual platform even before he saw it; the din of people was growing louder. When he finally saw it, his legs gave out for a moment, but the Sons of the Six propped him up and half marched, half dragged him toward it. Ekon started to count.

One-two-three. One-two-three. One-two-three.

Fifteen. He took fifteen steps to get to the platform, then an additional five as he marched up the small set of stairs. The platform wasn't large, just a crudely assembled wooden block a few feet wide. The Sons of the Six had had to make it quickly. As he stepped onto the platform, he heard the roar of a crowd, and for the first time he actually surveyed the people who'd come. The Takatifu District was usually closed to the public, but that rule seemed to have been relaxed today; there were hundreds of people gathered. They hissed and booed as Ekon was led forward to face them; more than one person threw rotten fruit at his feet. Ekon hung his head.

They'll never know the truth. That was, for him, the saddest part. *They'll never know what really happened.*

He searched until he found Kamau. The Sons of the Six were holding him, forcing him to stand at the very front. He wasn't gagged, but the crowd was too raucous to hear anything he said. Ekon sighed.

I love you, brother. He hoped Kamau would understand. He continued surveying the crowd, going back as far as he could. It was to no avail. Not a single familiar face. Something in him finally surrendered.

I'm sorry, Koffi. He hoped she would understand too. *I love you.*

In the corner of his eye, he caught a movement, and then Father Olufemi stepped forward. He raised both hands in the air, and the crowd silenced almost instantly. The old man paused for a beat before speaking.

"My children!" he said. "I wish you a blessed and prosperous Bonding Day! This day, above all others, is a day to celebrate the holy bond we have with the gods who oversee us and watch over us. It is a sacred day, one usually filled only with celebrations and joy.

"But just as the gods show us love when we do things to honor them, the gods show their wrath when we do things to dishonor them. Such is the case today. I am sad to share that these two men stand convicted of sedition."

The crowd began to boo, but Father Olufemi raised his hands again.

"Life is sacred, and not to be taken without consideration," he went on. "Let it be said here and now that I spent all night in solitude and prayer, reflecting and asking the Six for guidance on how best to act in their name." He bowed his head and almost—almost—looked contrite. "Their answer is woefully clear. These men must be made an example of, they must die here today, before you all."

I used to believe him. Ekon shook his head. *I actually used to believe him.*

"It grieves me to do this," said Father Olufemi, "even if I do it in the name of the gods I faithfully serve. And so I give this sinner one final opportunity to repent." For the first time, he turned. Ekon felt the Kuhani's eyes boring into the side of his face, but he refused to look at him.

"Ekon, Son of Okojo," he said, "you are sentenced to die, unless you agree here and now to repent your sins in full. What do you choose?"

Ekon did not answer. Instead, he counted the names of all the people he loved. *One-two-three.* Koffi. Safiyah. Kamau. His mother. His father. The man he'd once thought Brother Ugo was. He thought of the friends he'd made, the people he'd grown to care about. Makena. Njeri. Even Zain.

One-two-three.

"Your answer of silence will suffice," said Father Olufemi. "With haste, son of Okojo, I sentence you to death."

The crowd cheered, and even though Ekon wanted to be brave, his knees buckled as the words echoed in his mind. He tapped his fingers. Somewhere behind him, he heard the scrape of metal, not the short scrape of a hanjari dagger, but of a much longer blade. The crowd's cheering reached a new pitch, and he closed his eyes.

One-two-three. One-two-three. One-two-three.

And then he heard the trumpets.

CHAPTER 30

The DAY ZOO

KOFFI

"Are you sure this is going to work?" Koffi muttered.

"Not at all," said Jabir cheerfully. "But it's going to be entertaining, that's for sure."

Koffi was standing just outside the Night Zoo's walls, waiting. Above, dawn had almost broken across Lkossa's cracked sky; streaks of light blue interrupted the black. It should have been a peaceful morning, but she was on edge.

"Koffi," said Jabir in a lower voice. "You've got to relax, part of this working depends on how convincing you can be."

Koffi threw her friend a withering look. "Easy for *you* to say," she hissed. "You're not the one wearing a dress." She sighed. It hadn't seemed like much time had passed since she'd left Lkossa, but already she'd forgotten how humid it was in the east. She lifted the hem of her heavy dress to let a slight breeze touch her ankles. Makena had made the dress with some spare blankets found near the paddock and a little bit of creativity, and Koffi was grateful for her friend's fast thinking, she just wished she'd had more breathable material to work with. Jabir gave her a sympathetic look.

"Hopefully you won't have to wear it for long." He looked over his shoulder. "Here they come!"

Koffi stiffened. She wanted to look over her shoulder but kept her gaze fixed ahead and raised her chin slightly.

"Look *snobbier*," Jabir whispered.

She did her best, trying to mimic the many rich women she'd seen come into the Night Zoo all her life. She held her head high and tried to talk in an unbothered, unhurried way. Over the pounding in her chest, she could make out voices growing louder and louder. Seconds later, she slowly turned.

Baaz Mtombé hadn't changed much in the weeks since she'd last seen him. Her former master still wore luxurious robes—today's was a faded orange—and jewelry that shone a bit too brightly in the morning light to be real. His black-and-blond dreadlocks were tousled, and he was yawning as he approached. He wasn't alone.

"Your master won't be disappointed," he said in the grand voice he reserved only for his shows. "As you may have already heard, my Night Zoo boasts an impressive array of creatures, the largest in all the eastern region."

"Yes, yes." Zain—or rather, the person he was *pretending* to be—waved his hand dismissively. He was wearing his blue tunic, but thanks to some tailoring courtesy of Makena, he passed for a messenger from the Temple of Lkossa. "As long as we can leave now. The Kuhani was very clear in his instructions. He wants it to arrive in time for this morning's earliest activities."

Behind him, Koffi met Njeri's gaze. She, Makena, and Safiyah were standing behind Zain, all dressed in the same kind of modest tunics beastkeepers wore.

Please, Koffi prayed, *please let this work.*

"It's curious timing," said Baaz as they stopped before Koffi. "I'd heard there was going to be an execution this morning, some Son of the Six who defected."

Koffi's breath caught.

"Are you questioning the Kuhani's decision-making?" Zain asked, letting one brow rise.

"Not at all!" Baaz replied quickly. Finally looked Koffi. She froze for a moment, waiting for the inevitable reaction. Instead her former master offered her a courteous smile.

"Good morning, young lady," he said with a sweeping bow. "My name is Baaz Mtombé, it's a pleasure to make your acquaintance."

Koffi breathed relief and shot a glance toward Zain. He was now staring at Baaz very hard.

He doesn't really see you, she had to remind herself as she curtsied. *He sees a young woman, but not one he's met before. That* was thanks to a little help from Zain.

They'd come up with most of the plan last night, and then gone over it again and again well into the early hours. Koffi was still nervous. After a beat, she forced herself to smile back.

"It is a pleasure, Uncle," she said. "My name is Keshia."

"A beautiful name," he said pleasantly. "The Kuhani's messenger says you are the Kuhani's niece?"

"Yes." Koffi bowed her head.

"Then I cannot possibly allow you to walk all the way to the Temple of Lkossa from here. Jabir!" He snapped his fingers. "Get one of the zebras!"

"Sir!" Jabir bowed his head and went sprinting back into the Night Zoo's grounds. He returned with one of the older male zebras in tow.

"Bolo's gentle," Baaz assured her. "You'll be safe on him."

As long as I keep my fingers away from his mouth, Koffi thought. She knew Bolo well. She let Jabir help her onto the zebra's back as Baaz turned to direct the rest of the animals coming out of the Night Zoo, led by beastkeepers. It was quite an assortment. There were three gorillas, at least one collared cheetah, an impundulu, and of course the cackling hyena. To Koffi's relief it was muzzled.

"Will this appease your master?" Baaz asked Zain.

"It will," said Zain. "We should get going."

"Just one more thing." Baaz raised a finger. "The matter of payment . . . ?"

Zain smiled. "Of course. You may collect payment at the temple. My master is, understandably, quite busy today."

"Of course," said Baaz. He looked slightly annoyed but kept his voice light. "I imagine the Bonding is a busy day for many people."

Koffi exchanged a glance with Zain and swallowed a sense of unease. She'd lost track of time out on the plains, and Ekon's capture had thrown any remaining plans they'd had off course. The Bonding had come and she still had the splendor in her body.

Fedu hasn't arrived yet, she told herself. *All you have to do is get through the day. He won't be able to do anything after today.*

There was a bit more shuffling as Baaz arranged the beasts and their keepers, and then they were off, making their way into Greater Lkossa.

Koffi had expected it to take some time to make their way from the Night Zoo to the Temple of Lkossa; they were practically on opposite sides of the city. What she hadn't anticipated—or, more accurately, under-anticipated—was the effect Bonding Day celebrations would have on their plan. The normally busy streets of Lkossa were packed to capacity, making their march especially slow. People stopped and stared at the procession as they made their way through, and Koffi hoped that they'd have the same reception at the temple. She glanced up at the sky. It was well past dawn by now. Even as some people watched the animals of Baaz's Night Zoo, others were more eagerly making their way toward the Takatifu District. She swallowed and tried to urge her zebra to move faster.

Please, she begged the sky, *please don't let us be too late.*

She wasn't sure what to feel as they finally reached the double columns that marked the start of the Takatifu District. She'd only seen those columns once before, when she'd been bound and arrested by the Sons of the Six as a prisoner. She lowered her head. Zain might be able to use the splendor to cast an illusion over Baaz, but she knew he wouldn't have the strength to do the same to every Son of the Six, and more than enough of them knew her face. From behind her, she heard Baaz begin to shout.

"Make way! Make way!" he said, nudging people out of the way. "We have strict orders, and we're late!"

People moved, but begrudgingly. Koffi peered ahead, looking for any sign of Ekon or the Sons of the Six. She noted that the lawns in front of the Temple of Lkossa were crowded, but there was no one in uniform.

"Around the back!" she shouted over the din. "They must be there."

From his spot a few paces behind her, Zain nodded and whispered something to Baaz. In turn, he began to steer the Night Zoo's procession slightly to the right. Koffi had the luxury of being in front, so she was the first to see the platform. She started when she realized who was on it.

No.

He was far enough away to look tiny from here, but the two figures standing on the platform were unmistakable. She recognized the man on the left. He was shorter and wore a fine blue robe. That was Father Olufemi, the Kuhani and leader of all Lkossa. The figure standing next to him was slighter and taller. He wore a shabby brown tunic, and his head was bowed.

Ekon.

She couldn't hear what Father Olufemi was saying from where she was, the crowd's boos and cheers were too loud. She turned around to tell Zain and Jabir, but they were already staring ahead.

"We have to do something!" she shouted. She turned back around and watched in horror as a third warrior ascended the platform. He was dressed in a Son of the Six's blue-and-gold uniform and was carrying a long silver knife.

"Zain!"

"Baaz!" Zain turned to the man quickly. "Please signal for the trumpeters to begin!"

Baaz startled. "Now? You're sure you don't want to wait until we're closer—"

"NOW!"

Baaz nodded quickly and made an elaborate signal. At once the brassy ring of trumpets filled the air, and people began to turn in their direction, looking away from the platform. That was their cue. Koffi guided the zebra forward. People were throwing her dirty looks, but she didn't care. She needed them to hear those trumpets, to stop what they were about to do.

"LOUDER!" she called over her shoulder, and a second later, the trumpets' volume increased. Now people closer to the platform were beginning to turn in her direction, puzzled at the sudden commotion. It was now or never. Koffi turned and found Njeri several paces behind her. She nodded.

Now.

Njeri let go of the harness holding the gorillas; seconds later, Makena released the cheetah. Screams filled the crowd as the animals were released in all directions. Koffi jumped down from the zebra before it could buck her. She landed near Zain.

"Get to Ekon!" he shouted over the noise. "Go!"

Koffi turned on her heel and began to run. Most people were running in the opposite direction, trying desperately to get away. Good. The fewer people, the better. On the platform ahead, she could see the Kuhani looking around, as confused as everyone else. An idea came to Koffi. She summoned the tiniest amount of splendor she could and directed it inches from the old man's head. Tiny sparks whizzed past him, and he yelped, running down the platform's stairs quickly. Only Ekon remained standing on it now.

"Ekon!"

He searched for a moment, then found hers. He jumped down from the platform and ran toward her.

"Koffi?" Tears streaked Ekon's cheeks. "How did you . . . how'd you find me? How'd you get here?"

"It's a very long and complicated story and I'm almost sure we don't have the time for me to tell it to you now," said Koffi. "Come on, this way!" She took Ekon by the hand and started to run. Something large, black, and hairy passed her.

"Was that a *gorilla*?"

"Long and complicated story, remember?" Koffi looked back and forth, trying to find the nearest way to escape. If she could just *get Ekon out of here* . . .

"I see Makena!" Ekon shouted. "Over there!"

Koffi couldn't see over the heads of the people still running through the lawns of the temple, but she changed course and headed in the direction he'd indicated, her heart pounding.

Almost, she willed, *almost. We've got Ekon, now we just have to get out of here.*

There was a break in the crowd, and Koffi exhaled as Makena and Njeri sprinted toward them. Njeri didn't even break her stride.

"That way," she shouted. "I saw a way out back there. Zain, Safiyah, and Jabir were headed that way."

It was within reach, Koffi felt it. She set her sights on the Takatifu District's gate and ran harder, tightening her grip on Ekon's hand.

Almost, almost. It was a chant in her head now. She ignored the ache in her legs and the burning in her lungs; instead, she focused on the words.

Almost, almost. We're almost out of here.

She was so focused on those words that at first she didn't

notice the way Lkossa's cracked sky suddenly darkened. Had she been paying more attention, she might have sensed a new chill in the air, the smell of something rotted and fetid. As it was, she only realized something was wrong when Makena screamed.

"Koffi, look out!"

Koffi whirled around and stared into the eyes of the god of death.

CHAPTER 31

BROTHERS AND SISTERS

KOFFI

"Hello, Koffi."

Koffi tried to find words, any words to say as Fedu approached her. Those nearest to him shrank away, some of them screamed, others simply averted their gazes. He paid them no attention.

"What a momentous day for us to . . . reunite," he said.

"Get away from me," said Koffi. One of her hands was still holding on to Ekon. Next to her, she felt him stiffen. She started to reach for the splendor in her body, then stopped.

"Oh, no need to repress your power, Little Knife," he said. "You've done that quite enough." He spread his arms wide. "Our time is now. You and I, we're going to re-create this world, just the way I promised you we would."

"She's not helping you." Ekon stepped in front of her. "She never will."

Fedu didn't even look at Ekon. His eyes stayed trained on Koffi.

He chuckled softly. "You think she has a choice, that's amusing." He gathered his robes about him and gave her a sympathetic look. "We both know the truth, Koffi. You can't outrun me anymore. You are caught."

"And if I fought you again?" said Koffi. She jutted her chin. "You didn't fare so well last time."

A flicker of emotion passed over Fedu's features, so brief she wasn't entirely sure it had been real. She thought she saw fear there. But just as quickly, the god's smile returned. "I won't deny that you are powerful," he ceded. "In fact, you might be the most powerful daraja to walk this earth. Without doubt, you could summon the splendor right now and injure me as gravely as you did before. But that requires control, precision. You are more worn down than you were when we last battled, and you now possess neither." He gestured to Ekon, still standing in front of her. "Would you take that chance? Would you risk hurting your loved ones?"

"Don't listen to him, Koffi," said Ekon through his teeth. "He's trying to manipulate you."

"You might manage to spare Ekon," Fedu went on. His tone was neutral, as though they were talking about something as mundane as the color of the sky. "But do you have enough control to stop yourself from hurting others?"

Koffi sucked in a breath and looked around. Everyone was looking at either her or Fedu, and the fear in their expressions was shared. They were afraid of Fedu, but they were afraid of her too.

"Or perhaps you don't care," Fedu mused. "Perhaps you believe that a few dead mortals is worth the cost of disabling me long enough to make your escape." Fedu smiled. "But then you wouldn't really be any different from me, would you?"

"I'm nothing like you," said Koffi in a low voice.

"No?" Fedu's brow rose. "Then you have sealed your own fate. If you will not defend yourself, there is nothing else stopping me from taking the splendor in your body and using it for myself."

"We won't let you take her!"

Koffi started as Zain emerged from the crowd to her right, trailed by Safiyah.

"Neither will we!" Makena and Njeri entered the opening from the opposite side. Fedu offered them a mirthless smile.

"Will you have your friends die for you, Koffi?" he asked softly. "You may be powerful enough to face me, but they are not. I could kill them all right here and now—"

"No!" Koffi held up her hands. "Stand back, all of you." She pried her hand free from Ekon's. "You too."

"Koffi." Zain was glaring at Fedu. "We're not letting him take you."

"And I'm not watching any of you die," she said through her teeth. "Move back."

"Finally, a bit of sense." Fedu clapped his hands in applause as the others moved away from her. "Now that the heroics are out of the way—*come here*, Koffi."

Koffi swallowed, then forced her feet to move one after the other. She stopped in front of him, and he opened his arms, as though to embrace her.

"Summon the splendor," he ordered.

"No," said Koffi flatly.

Fedu grinned. "Do you really think you are powerful enough to defy me, to stop me? You, a mere mortal girl?"

"No," said Koffi. She reached into her pocket and held up a feather.

Fedu's brow furrowed for a moment as he eyed the feather. "You think a feather will stop me? Your mind is more broken than I thought."

"I don't think a feather can stop you," said Koffi, "but I know someone else who can. Atuno."

Without warning, a bolt of lightning cracked across the sky, followed by a thunderclap. The force of it shook the earth, and brought Koffi to her knees. The slate-gray sky grew darker and clouds gathered directly above them. Koffi knew what was coming, but still nothing prepared her for the moment those clouds parted and a figure larger than life emerged from them, dropping down from the heavens. Her gaze shot to Fedu, and she saw the horror on the god's face.

"Atuno."

"Brother." Gone was the pleasant voice of the god Koffi had once visited in the south. In many ways, Atuno looked as he had before, but now something about him had changed. Koffi realized what it was: He was dressed in armor the color of lightning, and that same color shone in his eyes. His teeth were bared, and he did not even look at Koffi.

"You have defiled the very purpose of our existence," he said in a cold, terrible voice. "You have betrayed your brothers and your sisters alike. It is an unforgivable sin, and you will desist, now."

Koffi looked back at Fedu. The horror wasn't quite gone from the god's face, but he looked decidedly less afraid. "So you've decided to fraternize with mortals again, brother?" he asked coolly. "After all this time, watching so many mortal friends die and come to my realm, I'd have thought you'd learned how foolish that is."

Koffi could see the momentary effect of the words on Atuno, but he shook his head. "This supersedes the mortals," he said. "You seek to destroy the world we were given to protect. I will not allow it."

"Will you war with me, brother?" Fedu rose to his full height. "You, who have been in hiding in your sky palace all this time with your books and your nonsense? I'm not sure you alone would beat me."

To Koffi's surprise, the god of the sky smiled. "Who says that I am alone?"

Another crack of lightning split the sky. This time, Koffi covered herself as a terrible wind picked up. She bowed her head, and when she looked up again, she saw a lone figure moving through the wind, her hair flying around her face. Her face was angular and sharp, and something about her almost seemed birdlike. Like Atuno, she too was dressed in armor. Koffi knew who she had to be.

"Itaashe," she whispered.

The goddess glanced at her, then over her shoulder. Two more figures were making their way forward on the wind: a man and a woman. Koffi was still on her knees, and she stared up at both of them in awe. She recognized Badwa, but the man standing next to her was enormous. He was a compilation of broad, massive shoulders, a barrel chest, and a surly expression. Heat seemed to singe the air when he moved. Koffi knew who he was too. Tyembu, god of the desert.

"Ah." Fedu's voice remained light. "It seems, after so many years, almost all of my siblings wish to see me at once. I'm touched." He looked to Atuno. "It seems you didn't manage to convince Ama—"

His words were cut off as rain clouds suddenly gathered above. Koffi watched as a woman appeared in the midst of them, wearing silver-blue armor. Koffi recognized her. Unlike the rest of the gods, Amakoya did look at Koffi. There was a silent question in her arched black brows. Koffi reached into the pocket of her tunic and withdrew what she knew the water goddess was looking for. Without a word, she tossed the pearl bracelet into the air. The sea goddess caught it in one hand and nodded, then faced Fedu.

"Behold, the Six," Fedu murmured. "After all this time, together at last."

"Brother." Amakoya's voice was like a thousand voices, a chorus full of rage. "You will stop this now, or you will die."

Fedu feigned shock. "The five of you mean to kill me, your own brother?"

"You are no brother of mine!" Tyembu roared, and his voice was low and terrible. Another wave of heat scorched the air and several surrounding people whimpered. "You are a corruption, an abomination! And you will be stopped, one way or another." He turned his palms upward and Koffi watched as a warhammer appeared, made entirely from what looked like real flames. He bared his teeth.

"Must it all end in violence?" Fedu's voice was still calm, but

Koffi heard the tremor in it. She realized she'd never seen the god of death sound truly afraid before, but now the other gods were looming closer. She held her breath.

"Koffi!" Ekon shouted. "Look out!"

Too late, Koffi's head snapped to the right. She felt the wind knocked from her body as someone grabbed her and hauled her forward so that she was pressed against someone's chest. The edge of a blade grazed her jugular. She heard Fedu's chuckle.

"If even one of you moves against me," he whispered to his siblings, "I will kill her, here and now. Then I will rip the splendor from her corpse."

"No!"

Koffi's eyes darted left, in time to see Zain running toward her with a small blade in his hand. Fedu flicked a second knife through the air so that it knicked Zain's arm as it sailed through the air. Zain fell to the ground with a moan.

"Leave, all of you." Fedu's voice had become more menacing now. "Or she will die."

Koffi looked up at each of the five gods. Their faces were impassive, stoic. She wondered, at that moment, if perhaps they would let her die. Who was she, after all, to them? She thought she saw the truth in their faces. Amakoya's fist clenched, and Tyembu swung his hammer. Badwa tensed but didn't move. Even Atuno looked defeated. Koffi looked to Itaashe last. She was arguably the only one of them who still looked unperturbed. She met Koffi's eye then, and Koffi thought she saw two tiny movements: a wink, and the twirling of one of the goddess's fingers. In the next moment, a western wind howled, tearing through the lawns. Koffi's hair blew back from her face with the force of it. She closed her eyes and tried to raise an arm to shield herself from the worst of it. When she opened them, her mouth went dry.

There, in the middle of the lawns, stood an old man she knew.

"Akande!"

The daraja looked up at her with an expression that came very close to impatience. "I told you I would come," he said, as though that comment explained everything. He assessed her, then refocused on Fedu. "You've managed to get yourself into even more trouble than I anticipated, which is admittedly impressive."

"Another mortal." Fedu was still standing behind Koffi with his knife to her neck, so she couldn't see his facial expression as he assessed Akande. "You can't possibly think you're stronger than me."

"Not stronger," said Akande. His tone was light. "But strong enough."

Fedu didn't have time to ask what he meant, and Koffi didn't have time to prepare herself for what the old man did next. The world slowed as he raised both arms and opened his palms so that they were facing her, and then she felt it. The splendor in her body was beginning to move, to answer a summons that wasn't hers. She understood with terrible slowness.

Akande, don't. She opened her mouth to speak, but no words would leave it; she could do nothing but watch in silent horror as Akande took the splendor from her body. She watched as more of it rose from the ground, as silver marks appeared on his skin and his veins turned white. He screamed in agony but didn't lower his hands.

"NO!"

Koffi thought she heard Fedu shouting over the roar of the splendor as it moved from one daraja to another. "NO! STOP!"

Akande did not stop. His frail knees wobbled violently, his brown skin began to glow, but he kept his arms raised. She watched what little hair remained on his head turn brittle and blow away like dust. She understood suddenly what was about to happen.

"Akande!" She tried to summon some of the splendor, to stop Akande from doing what she thought he was. "Stop, it'll kill you!"

Akande's entire being was illuminated in white-gold light now. The splendor he'd taken from Koffi filled every pore in his body. He did not show any pain. He only smiled as his eyes turned glassy.

"Babu," he whispered. "It's been so long."

There was a blaze of light, so bright and glaring that Koffi turned away. She heard more than one person cry out, and the ground quivered with the impact of it. Slowly she lowered her arm and stared at the place where Akande had been standing. There was nothing there but a few small fragments of the splendor, floating and twirling through the air. She went cold.

"NO!"

Fedu had released her momentarily, but at once he grabbed her again and spun her around to face him. He looked truly deranged now.

"You threw it away," he seethed. "All of it! You fool, I'll kill you my—" He jolted, and a gasp escaped his lips. Koffi felt his grip on her loosen. He stared past her for several seconds before collapsing to the ground. When he fell, she found he had a familiar-looking blade in his back. Ekon was standing behind him.

"The nyota blade," said Koffi in awe.

"The nyota blade." Ekon nodded.

"He has been incapacitated!" said Tyembu, stepping forward. "Now is the time to obliterate him!"

"I agree," said Amakoya, her expression flinty.

Koffi looked from Fedu to the other gods. The former was on the ground, panting hard as he tried to crawl away. She moved without thinking. "Wait!" she said, raising her hands. "Wait, you can't kill him!"

"Koffi?" Ekon was staring at her with nothing but incredulity. "What do you mean? This was the whole point of asking for their help. They're powerful enough to end him, once and for all."

Badwa stepped forward. "Koffi, my brother has done terrible things," she murmured. "He deserves to die."

"Then so do I," said Koffi. She could barely believe the words coming out of her mouth, but once she'd started, she found it hard to stop. "And frankly, so does almost every single person on the earth. We all do terrible things. We just make ourselves feel better by telling ourselves that there's some grand reason for it. No one is ever the villain in their own story. That includes Fedu." She turned in time to see Fedu shudder.

"And so what would you have us do?" Tyembu said with a growl. "Would you have us simply leave him to his own devices, so that he can do this again in another hundred years?"

Koffi shook her head. "No. I don't think Fedu should be killed, but I don't think he should be free either."

"What do you propose, then?" This time, it was Itaashe who spoke.

Koffi paused for a beat, thoughtful. "A prison," she finally said, "a place where he is confined and can't ever hurt anyone else ever again. A place where he doesn't get to use death to escape the consequences of his actions." Koffi took a deep breath in and out. "There's already been too much of it."

There was a long pause as the five remaining gods looked at each other, considering. Then Badwa turned and pointed a hand toward an open stretch of the Temple of Lkossa's lawn. A cracking sound filled the air as a mound of dirt rose up from the ground, growing larger and larger. Amakoya pointed too, adding water until the mound had turned to mud. Tyembu pointed next, and a ring of fire formed at the base of the mound, burning its edges black. Itaashe pointed too, sending gusts of wind around the mound. Koffi watched as a mountain formed before her. Atuno stooped down to take hold of his brother, then launched himself into the sky. He flew without wings and without effort, carrying Fedu's limp body in his arms. When he reached the very top of the mound, he dropped Fedu into it and pointed directly up at the sky. A bolt of lightning streaked across it, ribboning between the clouds until it struck at the mound and calcified it. Atuno stared at the new mountain that had formed, then nodded in satisfaction. He descended back to the ground.

"It is done," said Itaashe. "Fedu will be imprisoned within this mountain forever."

Koffi felt the very subtlest hint of relief for only a moment, then:

"Abominations!"

Koffi looked up in time to see Father Olufemi pointing at the gods, trembling. Several Sons of the Six were watching him warily, and she noted that none of them seemed particularly interested in joining him. Amakoya sneered.

"Be silent, mortal," she snapped. Father Olufemi seemed not to have heard her. He began to point at them.

"I am the mouthpiece of the gods!" he said, his pitch rising. "These are clearly illusions, conjured with daraja witch magic." He turned to the closest Sons of the Six. "I command you to destroy them, to—"

The rest of his words were cut off as a ribbon of fire shot across the sky and struck him. There was no time for him to scream, and as quickly as he was there suddenly he was no more than a pile of ash on the ground. Tyembu chuckled darkly, brandishing his fiery warhammer, and only looked contrite when Badwa gave him an exasperated look. Koffi looked from the pile of ash that had once been the Kuhani to the Sons of the Six still in the crowd. The emotions on their face varied, but Koffi thought she saw relief in more than a few of them.

"Koffi!"

There was something frightening about the tone of Ekon's voice. Koffi turned around, and a cold fear lanced through her body. Zain was lying on the ground a few feet away, his eyes glassy. Koffi closed the distance between them in a few bounds. She fell to her knees before Zain and took inventory of him. His lips were pale, bloodless.

"I don't understand," she said. Her hands were shaking too

hard to be of any use. "The knife Fedu threw barely touched him."

"The blade was poisoned," said Amakoya. She actually sounded sad.

"Help him!" Koffi screamed. "Please, one of you, help us!"

"We can restore his life to him if he wishes it," said Badwa, "but we'll have to act quickly. He doesn't have much time left on this earth in his current state."

Koffi looked up at the gods and goddesses, incredulous. "What do you mean, if he wishes it? Of course he wishes it." She looked to Zain again. "Tell them."

Of all the things she'd expected Zain to do in that moment, the last thing she'd expected was for him to smile.

"There is another option," Badwa added quietly. "My brother is gone. He has allowed countless souls to exist untethered in his realm for an innumerable amount of years." She bent her head. "They will need someone to look after them, to help them."

"No." Koffi shook her head. "That's not an option."

"Koffi." Zain's voice was soft, a whisper. "Maybe . . . maybe now I can do something that matters. I can start a new life, one where I can help others."

Koffi's eyes stung as she blinked them. "I'm not ready for you to say goodbye to this life yet."

She watched as Zain's breaths grew less and less frequent, as his chest stopped rising and falling. Eventually, it stopped altogether, but Koffi still wasn't ready for the moment when Itaashe took his body in her arms.

"He will be in the realm of the dead," she said calmly. Without another word, she rose into the air and disappeared. One by one, the other gods and goddesses saluted Koffi and vanished as well. Atuno was the last of them.

"We owe you a great debt," said the sky god. "Do not hesitate to ask, should you need anything at all."

Koffi exchanged a glance with Ekon. "Actually, there is something we could use some help with . . ."

EPILOGUE

EKON

Six Months Later

One-two-three.

Ekon tapped his fingers against his desk, frowning. A square of parchment was spread before him, and he'd been staring at it for the better part of—he thought back—twelve minutes. He'd been staring at the scroll for twelve minutes, trying to configure the charts and graphs covering it, yet they still didn't make sense. His frown deepened.

"Tuh. You look cheerful."

He looked up and found that Koffi was standing in the doorway to his office. Her expression was tentative, and when her gaze dropped to the scroll, she made a face.

"Do I even *want* to know what you're doing?"

"I'm trying to do inventory!" Ekon threw his hands up. "In the last month, we bought eighteen pounds of carrots, five hundred bales of hay, and forty bags of oats."

Koffi nodded. "That sounds right."

"But the numbers aren't adding up." Ekon glared at the scroll again. "There are at least two and a half bags of oats missing, and several unaccounted-for bags of carrots." He steepled his fingers and looked up at Koffi, solemn. "I think we're being robbed. I may have to contact the authorities and file a formal report."

Koffi flinched. "Maybe hold off on that."

Ekon blinked. "Koffi?"

"They were hungry!" Koffi said defensively, crossing her arms. "What do you expect me to do, let the baboons starve?" She gave Ekon a knowing look. "You know how they get irritable when they're hungry. Remember that time when they raided your office and put poo in your—?"

"No need to bring up the past," said Ekon quickly. He leaned back in his chair and pushed the parchment away. Koffi moved to sit on the edge of his desk. He sighed.

"I suppose there's no point in explaining to you the values and benefits of keeping a proper and accurate inventory at a nonprofit animal sanctuary?"

"None," said Koffi with a smile.

"Well, then, I think my work is done," said Ekon.

"And just in time!" Koffi jumped off the desk. "I need you to come with me!"

Ekon raised a brow. "That sounds ominous."

"Come on!" She took his hand in hers and pulled him to his feet so that they were suddenly very close. It wasn't the first time she'd done it, or even the second. Ekon's stomach still swooped.

"You know," he said in a lower voice, "you can't keep doing that to get your way."

Koffi smirked. "Watch me."

The sun was setting as they made their way out of the main building and onto the reserve's grounds. It was the same view Ekon saw every evening, but months later he still hadn't quite gotten used to the sprawling lawns and paddocks as far as the eye could see. Koffi nodded, and he fell into step with her as they walked their usual path around the perimeter.

"We're probably going to need to build a new aviary soon," she said abruptly. "The impundulus we acquired need more space."

"I see," said Ekon in his best professional voice. "Dare I ask how much this expansion is going to cost us?"

"You might," said Koffi. She counted off on her fingers. "I'd say it'll be about . . . three thousand fedhas."

Ekon pursed his lips. "That seems high."

"It's not like we're going to run out of money," Koffi said as they walked. "Thanks to Atuno's *extreme* generosity."

"That doesn't mean we shouldn't budget responsibly," Ekon muttered.

"Which is why you're our accountant and I'm responsible for outreach, rescue, and development," said Koffi. "Besides, I originally calculated two hundred and seventy-four. But since I knew it would bother you, I just rounded up to the next closest number. You know, math!"

"Koffi, that's *not* how math works—"

"Hey! You guys!"

They both looked up in time to see Makena running toward them. She was holding up what looked to be a large and very

435

lumpy blanket. "What do you think?" she asked, holding up the lump.

Ekon cocked his head. "It's . . . well, it's . . ."

"What are we looking at, Makena?" Koffi asked.

Makena raised the lumpy blanket higher, nonplussed. "They're giant blankets," she announced, "for Yusufu and Chacha!"

Ekon blinked. "You made blankets . . . for the elephants?"

Makena beamed. "I was thinking it's going to be getting cooler soon, they'll need protection from the elements."

Koffi opened her mouth to speak, but Ekon was faster. "I think that's a great idea, Makena," he said in earnest. "Thank you."

"I still have to make tunics for the macaques," said Makena thoughtfully. "So far, I've got about three done, but they never sit still enough for me to get accurate measurements."

"They like fruit," Koffi pointed out. "You could incentivize them with pieces of mango?"

"Brilliant!" Makena clapped. "I'll be back!" She raced off in the opposite direction before Koffi or Ekon could say another word. Ekon gave Koffi a sidelong glance.

"Will that actually work?"

Koffi grinned. "It might."

Ekon shook his head and started to walk again, then stopped. Makena's brief visit had distracted him, and he hadn't realized where they now were. Most of the landscaping was bright and colorful—Makena had insisted on decorating everywhere with flowers. But this was the one part of the grounds that had been kept modest. A black stone marker had been erected, surrounded by white lilies. The name ZAIN was carved into the stone.

"I still miss him," Koffi said without preamble.

"I do too," said Ekon, "and believe me, that's not something I *ever* thought I'd say."

Koffi smiled. "He'd be happy to hear it." She looked up at him. "And I think he'd like what we did with the Night Zoo."

"I think most people do," said Ekon. "Well, except maybe Baaz."

Koffi's brow furrowed. "You're sure he won't renege on our agreement?"

"He hasn't so far," said Ekon with a shrug. "And I have a feeling Itaashe's lionesses probably helped to . . . persuade him."

"You're probably right," said Koffi. "And anyway, the Akande Animal Sanctuary has a nice ring to it."

"It does." Ekon paused. "I got another letter from my brother today."

Koffi kept her tone light. "Oh?"

He nodded. "He finally found my mother in Bandari a few weeks ago. They're on the move, but he's going to stay with her for a while and help her set up a new Enterprise, one that's legitimate this time. Safiyah's going to help too."

"Did he say anything about the Sons of the Six?" asked Koffi.

Ekon shrugged. "They're still disbanded, and a lot of them went missing after the Bonding. Kamau did say he and my mother are working on developing herbal treatments to help curtail the symptoms of hasira leaf addiction. He's hoping he can find and help some of them. I think maybe they've both found new purpose, together."

Koffi offered him a smile. "I'm really glad to hear that, Ekon."

"Me too."

"By the way, do you think your mother might be willing to

send some Asalian pepper spice blend with Kamau's next letter? I've really wanted to try some."

Ekon grinned. "I'll ask." He watched as Koffi looked out onto the reserve and sighed. In the dying light, the beastkeepers still out on the grounds were little more than silhouettes, but when her gaze fixed on two in particular, he knew who they were.

"I'm glad *your* family is safe too, Koffi," said Ekon.

Koffi blinked hard. He thought he saw a tear, but it was too quick for him to be sure. When she looked up at him again, there was a mischievous look in her eyes. "Well, now that the day's business is taken care of—"

"Who said it was taken care—?"

"We can move on to some fun." Koffi lifted her gaze to the red-orange sky. "We're just in time."

Ekon's brow rose. "Time for what?"

"For the surprise!" said Koffi. Ekon's pulse quickened as she effortlessly slipped her hand into his and tugged them toward the reserve's exit. "Come on, it's this way!"

"I don't like this." Ekon's eyes shifted left and right as he and Koffi made their way deeper and deeper into the slum district of Lkossa. "Generally, I don't like being in this part of town after dark."

"Relax." Koffi was still walking with purpose, though to what, Ekon couldn't say. "We're almost— Aha! Here we are!"

The frown on Ekon's face immediately deepened. They'd reached the end of one of the alleys. Propped against its wall was an old wooden ladder that looked to be of questionable sturdiness. Koffi rested a hand on it, turned, and beamed.

"Up we go!"

"Koffi." Ekon began to tap his fingers. He didn't want to feel anxious, but he couldn't help it. "This seems like an exceptionally bad idea."

Koffi turned again, and Ekon was immediately wary of the innocent look on her face. "You don't have to come up, if it's going to make you uncomfortable . . ." Ekon's breath caught sharply as she closed the gap between them in a single step so their lips were inches apart. His heart thudded hard. "But *I'm* going up."

She turned before he could say another word, ascending the ladder with maddening grace. Ekon groaned, massaged the bridge of his nose, then followed. He kept his eyes on Koffi until she disappeared onto the building's roof, and after that his eyes stayed trained on the night sky while he counted each rung of the ladder.

Ten-eleven-twelve . . .

"This had better be good!" he called up as he reached the last few rungs. "You know how I feel about spontaneous—" He reached the top of the ladder and stopped. "Oh."

The entire roof of the building had been decorated, streamers and ribbons of green, gold, and blue were festooned about, and several blankets and pillows were strategically placed to create a seating area. Standing beside a large plate of neatly diced fruit, Koffi was grinning and holding up a bottle of wine. She smirked.

"Weren't expecting *that*, were you?" she asked.

For a moment, Ekon was at a loss for words. "You . . . planned," he said quietly. "You . . . minced."

"I did!" Koffi looked distinctly smug as she settled on the blankets and patted a spot beside her.

Ekon's eyes narrowed. "Wait, where'd you get that wine?"

"Shh! Hurry, you'll miss it!"

"Miss—?" Ekon was interrupted by a loud and long squealing sound. He tensed for a half second, then to his right he saw it. Rising high in the night sky was a firework, blue as sapphires and sparkling just as bright. It exploded with a boom, and Koffi looked back at him, her eyes alight.

"Come on!"

Ekon sat beside her and they watched the fireworks together. When the last one fizzled out, Koffi raised a brow.

"You *see*?" she teased. "See what happens when you trust me a little, when you don't plan every—" Her breath caught as Ekon pulled her against him, and it was his turn to smirk.

"I don't plan *everything*," he murmured. "Not with you." Their lips met, and Ekon's stomach swooped. He wondered if he'd ever manage to get used to that feeling. When they pulled apart, he was surprised to see that Koffi looked distinctly guilty.

"All right." She tapped her fingers. "I have a confession."

Ekon wasn't entirely ready to move on from the previous subject, but he sat back and braced himself. "Oh?"

"This outing idea may or may not have had two motives," she said with a guilty smile. "I have to tell you something."

Ekon pursed his lips. "Go on."

"I'm going away," Koffi blurted, "tomorrow."

"What?" Ekon stiffened. "Where? Why?"

"Not for long," Koffi added quickly. "Njeri and I are going on another rescue expedition, this time to save a baby rhino," she said, for the first time looking thoughtful. "Some villagers a few days west of here have sighted it several times on its own. We believe it's probably orphaned. Poachers are already circling."

"They haven't gotten it yet?" Ekon asked.

"Nope."

"Well, then—" Ekon stopped short. "We have to help it."

"We do," Koffi agreed. "Apparently, it's got a temper."

"You two should get along well," Ekon said mildly. "Have you picked out a name?"

Koffi smiled. "Actually, I've picked out two."

"Of course you have."

"If it's a boy," said Koffi, "I am going to call him Apollo. If it's a girl, I think I'll name her Adiah."

"Both of those names have three syllables each," Ekon noted, "so they're good to me."

Abruptly, Koffi's expression changed. She looked more tentative.

"You're going to be okay, right?" she asked softly. "While I'm gone?"

Ekon took her hand in his and rubbed the pad of his thumb against her skin. He waited a beat before answering.

"Well, I would recommend utilizing the wilderness first-aid pamphlet I made for you," he said lightly, "but . . . you're not going to read that."

Koffi grinned. "True."

"I would also ask you to be careful, and not to do anything too dangerous or brave." His smile turned wry. "But I know you won't do that either."

"Also true."

He smiled. They were, in almost every way, opposites. He wouldn't have had it any other way. "You know I'm always okay with you doing the things that make you happy, Koffi. And you know I'll be here waiting for you when you get back?"

"I know you will," she said quietly. "And you know I *will* always come back, right?"

He did know, but instead of saying as much, he took her hand in his and kissed her, counting each time their lips met.

One-two-three.

AUTHOR'S NOTE

The river vessel our heroes briefly travel on in this book is called the *Nzinga*, which is named after Nzinga Ana de Sousa Mbande (1583–1663), the former queen of what is now modern-day Angola. In addition to her military and political shrewdness, Queen Nzinga is notably remembered for her staunch opposition to Portuguese conquest in Central-West Africa.

The **ilomba** (ee-LOM-bah) mentioned in this story comes from the traditional stories of the Bovale people, who are based in Zambia and Angola. In their mythos, malomba (plural form) are commonly said to take the form of sea snakes. For practical purposes, I took the creative liberty of making the ilomba featured in *Beasts of War* a river snake instead, but much of its physical description is otherwise aligned with its lore.

The **chemosit** (CHEM-oh-seet) comes from the traditions of the Nandi people of Kenya. Sometimes called the "Nandi bear," depictions of the chemosit vary widely. Naturally, the descriptors used in this book favor the most unsettling ones I could find.

The **swallowers** found in this book were inspired by a creature called a **khodumodumo** (koh-DOOM-oh-DOOM-oh); its lore comes from the Sotho people of southern Africa.

I first cursorily referenced the **impundulu** (im-pun-DOO-loo) in *Beasts of Prey*'s first chapter, as Koffi and her mother are moving through the Night Zoo. I remained intrigued by them, and ultimately decided to bring them back for *Beasts of War*. The impundulu comes from the mythos of the Xhosa people of South Africa. In oral and written tradition, the bird uses its wings and talons to summon thunder and lightning.

While **mermaids** are conventionally linked to Western European folklore, references to them appear in many different parts of the world, including the African continent. In West Africa, many merpeople are affiliated with the deity (or collective pantheon of deities) called **Mami Wata**. Mami Wata is also sometimes conflated with the Yoruba water deity Yemọja.

ACKNOWLEDGMENTS

Although the Beasts of Prey trilogy was published between 2021 and 2024, it reflects nearly a decade's work.

To Puddin', master of three elements, thank you for being exactly as you are and for never complaining when I go into Bat Mode™. Dolly and I love you, even when you call her a "foul little beast."

Thank you to my entire family—especially Mom, Dad, Corey, and Ashley—for your love, support, and encouragement.

I've gotten by with the help of many friends near and far. Thanks to the ones who were there when I needed it most.

My thanks to my literary agent, Pete Knapp, and the great people at Park & Fine Literary and Media—especially Stuti Telidevara, Andrea Mai, and Emily Sweet—for their consummate professionalism and advocacy.

A sincere thanks to my editor, Stacey Barney, for her invaluable guidance, encouragement, and mentorship. (Also, thanks for greenlighting the topless mermaids.) Thank you to the teams at Penguin Young Readers and G. P. Putnam's Sons for their support throughout this trilogy: James Akinaka, Kara Brammer, Trevor Bundy, Venessa Carson, Theresa Evangelista, Alex Garber,

Jacqueline Hornberger, Cindy Howle, Carmela Iaria, Todd Jones, Jen Klonsky, Misha Kydd, Jen Loja, Lathea Mondesir, Shanta Newlin, Summer Ogata, Sierra Pregosin, Colleen Conway Ramos, Emily Romero, Olivia Russo, Kim Ryan, Shannon Spann, Marikka Tamura, Caitlin Tutterow, Felicity Vallence, and Chandra Wohleber. Thanks also to the artists responsible for this trilogy's covers and maps: Elena Masci and Virginia Allyn.

Abby: Your razor-sharp (but always kind) insight made this book stronger and helped me cross the last finish line. You have my gratitude, and my appreciation.

Thank you to the readers from all walks of life who've stuck with me until the end of this series. (Especially B!) You've all brought me so much collective joy. My additional thanks to the many educators who've supported this series, especially the wonderful team at the Arkansas State Library—Karen O'Connell, Jennifer Chilcoat, and Jennifer Wann—who have been incredible advocates within my adopted home state.

Finally, to Koffi and Ekon: It feels strange to say goodbye. Nevertheless, thanks for letting me tell your stories. It was all in my head, but the two of you will never stop feeling real to me.

ESHŌZA

THE BARAFU SEA

THE BARIDI REGION

Jasiri River

THE MOTO SEA

The Ngazi Ranges

JUU

The Katili Desert

ASALI

Furaha Lake

THE DHAHABU REGION

Southern
Ndefu River

Kinywa Bay

THE
NYINGI ISLES

CHINI